The Fifth Woman

Other Kurt Wallander mysteries by Henning Mankell

Faceless Killers

The White Lioness

Sidetracked

The Fifth Woman

Henning Mankell   A KURT WALLANDER MYSTERY

Translated from the Swedish by STEVEN T. MURRAY

THE NEW PRESS NEW YORK

LIBRARY OF CONGRESS CATALOGING-IN-PUBLICATION DATA
Mankell, Henning, 1948–
    [Femte kvinnan. English]
    The fifth woman / Henning Mankell ; translated from the Swedish by Steven T. Murray.
        p.   cm.
    "A Kurt Wallander mystery."
    ISBN 1-56584-547-1 (hc.)
    I. Murray, Steven T.   II. Title.
PT9876.23.A49 F4613 2000
839.73'74—dc21   00–021873

Originally published as *Den Femte Kvinnan* in Sweden by Ordfront Förlag, Stockholm.
Published in the United States by The New Press, New York, 2000
Distributed by W.W. Norton & Company, Inc., New York

The New Press was established in 1990 as a not-for-profit alternative to the large,
commercial publishing houses currently dominating the book industry.
The New Press operates in the public interest rather than for private gain,
and is committed to publishing, in innovative ways, works of educational, cultural,
and community value that are often deemed insufficiently profitable.

The New Press, 450 West 41st Street, 6th floor, New York, NY 10036

www.thenewpress.com

Printed in the United States of America

9 8 7 6 5 4 3 2 1

The Fifth Woman

"With love and care the spiderweb
weaves its spider."
—UNKNOWN AFRICAN ORIGIN

Africa—Sweden

May—August 1993

was in this capacity that she had learned of the events that took place one night in May in a remote desert town.

Outwardly the facts of the case were clear, easy to grasp, and utterly terrifying. Four nuns, French citizens, had been slaughtered by unknown assailants. The women's throats had been cut. The perpetrators had left no traces, only blood; thick, congealed blood everywhere.

But there had also been a fifth woman, a Swedish tourist, who had renewed her residence permit in the country several times and happened to be visiting the nuns on the night the assailants appeared with their knives. Her passport, found in a handbag, revealed that her name was Anna Ander, sixty-six years old, in the country on a legal tourist visa. There was also an open-return plane ticket. Since it was bad enough that four nuns had been murdered, and since Anna Ander seemed to have been traveling alone, the detectives on the case, in response to political pressure, decided not to mention the fifth woman. She was simply not there on that fateful night. Her bed was empty. Instead, they reported her death in a traffic accident and then buried her, nameless and unknown, in an unmarked grave. All her belongings were discarded, all traces of her erased. And it was here that Françoise Bertrand entered the picture. *Early one morning I was called in by my boss,* she wrote in the long letter, *and ordered to drive out to the scene at once.* By this time the woman was already buried. Françoise Bertrand's job was to get rid of any last traces of her and then destroy her passport and other effects.

Anna Ander had supposedly never arrived or spent any time in the country. She had ceased to exist, obliterated from all official records. But Françoise Bertrand discovered a travel bag that the sloppy homicide investigators had overlooked. It was lying behind a wardrobe. Or maybe it had been on top and then fallen off, she couldn't tell. But there were letters in it that Anna Ander had begun to write, and they were addressed to her daughter in a town called Ystad in faraway Sweden. Françoise Bertrand apologized for reading these private papers. She had asked for help from a drunken Swedish artist she knew in the capital, and he had translated the letters for her without knowing anything about the case. Françoise wrote down the translations as he read, and a picture gradually began to take shape.

Even then she already had serious pangs of conscience about what had happened to this fifth woman. Not only about the fact that she was murdered so ruthlessly in the country that Françoise loved so much but which was so torn by internal strife. In the letter, she tried to explain what was happening in her country, and she also told something about herself. Her father was born in France but came to Africa as a child with his parents. There he grew up, and later married

Prologue

The letter arrived in Ystad on August 19th, 1993.

Since it had an African stamp and must be from her mother, she waited to open it. She wanted to have peace and quiet when she read it. From the thickness of the envelope she could tell there were many pages. She hadn't heard a word from her mother in over three months; surely she must have plenty of news by now. She left the letter lying on the coffee table and decided to wait until evening. But she felt vaguely uneasy. Why had her mother typed her name and address this time? No doubt the answer would be in the letter. It was close to midnight by the time she opened the door to the balcony and sat down in her easy chair, which was squeezed in among all her flowerpots. It was a lovely, warm August evening. Maybe one of the last of the year. Autumn was already at hand, hovering unseen. She opened the letter and started to read.

Only afterwards, when she had read the letter to the end and put it aside, did she start to cry.

By that time, she also knew that the letter was written by a woman. The style of the handwriting was not her first clue. There was also something about the choice of words, how the unknown woman tentatively and cautiously approached the task of describing as mercifully as possible all the gruesome events that had occurred.

But there was no mercy involved. There was only the act itself. That was all.

The letter was signed by Françoise Bertrand, a police officer. Her position was not entirely clear, but apparently she was employed as a criminal investigator for the country's central homicide commission. It a local woman. Françoise, the oldest of their children, had always had the feeling of having one foot in France and the other in Africa. But now she no longer had any doubt. She was an African. And that was why she was so tormented by the antagonisms tearing her country apart. That was also why she didn't want to contribute to the wrongs against herself and her country by erasing this woman, by drowning the truth in a fabricated car crash, refusing even to take the responsibility for Anna Ander's presence. Françoise Bertrand had begun to suffer from insomnia, she wrote. Finally she decided to write to the dead woman's daughter and tell her the truth. She forced herself to act in spite of the loyalty she felt to the police force. But she asked that her name be kept secret. *I'm writing you the truth,* she concluded her long letter. *Maybe I'm making a mistake by telling you what happened. But how could I do otherwise? I found a bag containing letters that a woman wrote to her daughter. Now I'm telling you how they came into my possession and forwarding them to you.*

Françoise Bertrand had enclosed the unfinished letters in the envelope.

Along with Anna Ander's passport.

Her daughter didn't read the letters. She put them on the floor of the balcony and wept for a long time. Not until dawn did she get up and go into the kitchen. She sat motionless at the kitchen table for quite a while. Her head was completely empty. But then she started to think, and suddenly everything seemed simple to her. She realized that she had done nothing but wait all these years. She hadn't understood that before: the fact that she had been waiting, or why. Now she knew. She had a mission, and she didn't need to wait any longer to carry it out. It was time. Her mother was gone. A door had been thrown wide open.

She stood up and went to get her box with the slips of paper she had cut up, and the big ledger she kept in a drawer under her bed. She spread the folded slips of paper on the table in front of her. She knew there were exactly forty-three of them. One of them had a black cross. Then she started unfolding the slips, one by one.

The cross was on the twenty-seventh one. She opened the ledger and ran her finger down the column of names until she reached the twenty-seventh row. She stared at the name she had written there and slowly saw a face materialize in her mind.

Then she closed the book and put the slips of paper back in the box.

Her mother was dead.

She no longer had any doubt. And now there was no turning back. She would give herself a year to work out the grief, to make all her preparations.

Once more she went out on the balcony. She smoked a cigarette and gazed out over the waking city. A rainstorm was moving in from the sea.

Just after seven she went to bed.

It was the morning of August 20th, 1993.

Skåne

21 September—11 October 1994

Chapter One

J ust after 10:00, he finally finished the poem.

The last stanzas had been difficult to write; they took him a long time. He had wanted to achieve a melancholy yet beautiful expression. He broke off several attempts by tossing them in the wastebasket. Twice he was close to giving up altogether. But now the poem lay before him on the table—his lament over the middle spotted woodpecker, which had almost disappeared from Sweden; it hadn't been seen in the country since the early 1980s. One more bird about to be eradicated by humankind.

He got up from his desk and stretched. With every passing year, it was harder and harder for him to sit bent over his writings for hours on end.

An old man like me shouldn't be writing poems anymore, he thought. When you're seventy-eight years old, your thoughts are of little use to anyone but yourself.

At the same time he knew that he was wrong. It was only in the Western world that old people were viewed with indulgence or contemptuous sympathy. In other cultures, age was respected as a time of enlightened wisdom. He would keep writing poems as long as he lived, as long as he could manage to lift a pen and his mind was as clear as it was now. He was not capable of much else. Not anymore. Once, a long time ago, he had been an expert car dealer, the most successful in the region. He was known as a tough negotiator in business deals. And he had certainly sold a lot of cars. During the good years he had owned branches in both Tomelilla and Sjöbo. He had amassed a fortune large enough to let him live in style.

But it was his poetry that really mattered to him. All the rest was ephemeral necessity. The verses lying on the table gave him a satisfaction he seldom felt.

He drew the curtains so they covered the picture windows that faced the fields rolling gently down toward the sea, somewhere beyond the horizon. He went over to his bookshelf. In his lifetime he had published nine collections of poetry. There they stood, side by side. None of them had sold more than a small printing. Three hundred copies, sometimes a few more. The unsold copies were in cartons in the basement. But they had not been banished there. They were still his pride and joy, although long ago he had decided to burn them one day. He would carry the cartons out to the courtyard and put a match to them. The day he received his death sentence, either from a doctor or from a premonition that his life would soon be over, he would get rid of the thin volumes that no one wanted to buy. No one would be allowed to throw them onto a trash heap.

He looked at the books standing on the shelf. He had been reading poems his whole life, and he had memorized a lot of them. He had no illusions; his poems were not the best ever written. But they weren't the worst, either. In each of his poetry collections, which had been published about every five years since the late 1940s, there were individual stanzas that could measure up to anyone's standard. But he had been a car dealer by profession, not a poet. His poems were not reviewed on the cultural pages. He hadn't received any literary awards. And his books had been printed at his own expense. The first poetry collection he put together he had sent around to the big publishing houses in Stockholm. They were always returned with brusque refusals in preprinted form letters. One editor, however, had taken the trouble to make a personal comment. He said nobody would want to read poems that were about nothing but birds. *The spiritual life of the white wagtail is of no interest,* the editor had written.

After that, he stopped turning to publishers. He paid for publication himself. Simple covers, black text on white paper. Nothing expensive. The words between the covers were what mattered. In spite of everything, many people had read his poems over the years. And many of them had expressed their appreciation.

Now he had written a new one, about the middle spotted woodpecker, a lovely bird no longer seen in Sweden.

The bird poet, he thought.

Almost everything I've written is about birds. About the flapping of wings, the rushing in the night, a lone mating call somewhere in the distance. In the world of birds I have found an intimation of the innermost secrets of life.

He returned to his desk and picked up the sheet of paper. The last stanza had finally worked. He placed the paper back on the desk. He felt a sharp pain in his back as he crossed the large room again. Was he getting sick? Every day he listened for signs that his body had started to betray him. He had stayed in good shape throughout his life. He had never smoked, always eating and drinking in moderation. This regime had endowed him with good health. But soon he would be eighty years old. The end of his allotted time was fast approaching. He went out to the kitchen and poured a cup of coffee from the coffee maker, which was always on. The poem he had finished writing filled him with both sadness and joy.

The autumn of my years, he thought. An apt name. Everything I write could be the last. And it's September. It's autumn. Both on the calendar and in my life.

He carried his coffee cup back to the living room. He sat down carefully in one of the brown leather armchairs that had kept him company for more than forty years. He had bought them to celebrate his triumph when he was awarded the Volkswagen franchise for southern Sweden. On a little table next to his armrest stood the photo of Werner, the German shepherd that he missed more than all the other dogs that had accompanied him through life. To grow old was to grow lonely. The people who filled your life died off. Finally even your dogs vanished into the shadows. Soon he would be the only one left. At a certain point in life, everyone was alone in the world. Recently he had tried to write a poem about that idea, but he could never seem to finish it. Maybe he ought to try again, now that he was done with his lament for the middle spotted woodpecker. But birds were what he knew how to write about. Not people. Birds he could understand. People were usually incomprehensible. Had he ever once understood himself? Writing poems about something he didn't understand would be like trespassing in a forbidden area.

He closed his eyes and suddenly remembered *The 10,000 Kronor Question* during the late fifties, or maybe it was the early sixties. The TV screen was still black-and-white back then. A cross-eyed young man with slicked-back hair had chosen the topic "Birds." He answered all the questions and received his check for the incredible sum, in those days, of 10,000 kronor.

He had not been sitting in the television studio, in the isolation booth with headphones over his ears. He had been sitting in this very same leather armchair. But he too had known all the answers. Not once did he even need extra time to think. But he didn't win any 10,000 kronor. Nobody knew about his vast knowledge of birds. He just kept writing his poems instead.

He awoke with a start from his daydreams. A sound had caught his attention. He listened in the darkened room. Was there someone moving outside in the courtyard?

He pushed away the thought. It was just his imagination. Part of getting old meant suffering from anxiety. He had good locks on his doors. He kept a shotgun in his bedroom upstairs, and he had a pistol close at hand in a kitchen drawer. If any intruders came to this isolated farmhouse just north of Ystad, he could defend himself. And he wouldn't hesitate to do so.

He got up from his chair. There was another sharp twinge in his back. The pain came and went in waves. He set his coffee cup on the drainboard and looked at his watch. Almost 11:00. It was time to go outside. He squinted at the thermometer outside the kitchen window and saw it was 7° Celsius. The barometer was rising. A slight breeze from the southwest was passing over Skåne. The conditions were ideal, he thought. Tonight the flight would be to the south. The long-range migratory birds would pass over his head by the thousands on invisible wings. Although he wouldn't be able to see them, he could feel them out there in the dark, high above his head. For more than fifty years he had spent countless autumn nights out in the fields, just to experience the feeling of the night birds passing somewhere up above him.

The whole sky is moving, he often thought.

Entire symphony orchestras of silent songbirds would be leaving before the approaching winter, heading for warmer climes. The urge to leave lay deep in their genes. And their unsurpassed ability to navigate by the stars and the earth's magnetic field always steered them right. They sought out the favorable winds, they had built up their layer of fat, and they could stay aloft for hour after hour.

A whole sky, vibrating with wings, was beginning its annual pilgrimage. The flight of birds toward Mecca.

What is a person compared to a night flyer? A lonely, earthbound old man. While up there, high above, a whole sky sets off on its journey.

He had often thought it was like performing a sacred act. His own autumnal high mass, standing there in the dark, sensing the departure of the migratory birds. And then, when spring came, he was there to welcome them back.

The night migration was his religion.

He went out to the entryway and stood with one hand on the coat hanger. Then he went back to the living room and pulled on the sweater lying on a stool by the desk.

Along with all the other vexations, getting old meant that you got cold more quickly.

Once more he looked at the poem lying there finished on the desk. The lament for the middle spotted woodpecker. It had turned out the way he wanted at last. Maybe he would live long enough to put together enough poems for a tenth and final collection. He had already decided on the title:

High Mass in the Night.

He went back to the entryway, put on his jacket, and pulled a cap over his forehead. He opened the front door. The fall air was filled with smells from the wet clay. He closed the door behind him and let his eyes grow accustomed to the dark. The garden was desolate. In the distance he could see the glow of the lights in Ystad. Otherwise, he lived so far from his other neighbors that only darkness surrounded him. The starry sky was almost completely clear. A few clouds were visible on the horizon.

On a night like this, the migration was bound to pass above his head.

He started walking. The farmhouse he lived in was old, with three wings. The fourth had burned down sometime early in the century. He had kept the cobblestones in the courtyard. He spent a lot of money on a thorough renovation of his farmhouse, which was still not completed. In his will he would give it all to the Cultural Association in Lund. He had never been married, never had any children. He sold cars and got rich. He had had dogs. And then the birds had appeared over his head.

I have no regrets, he thought, as he followed the path that led down to the tower he had built himself, where he usually stood to watch for the night birds. I regret nothing, since it is meaningless to regret.

It was a beautiful September night.

Still, something was making him uneasy.

He stopped on the path and listened, but all he could hear was the soft sighing of the wind. He kept walking. Could it be the pain that was worrying him, those sudden sharp pains in his back? The worry was prompted by something inside him.

He stopped again and turned around. Nothing there. He was alone. The path sloped downward, leading to a little hill. Just before the hill there was a broad ditch over which he had placed a footbridge. At the top of the hill stood his tower. From his front door it was exactly 247 meters. He wondered how many times he had walked along this path. He knew every turn, every hollow. And yet he walked slowly and cautiously. He didn't want to risk falling and breaking his leg. Old people's bones grew brittle, he knew that. If he wound up in the hospital with a broken hip he would die, since he couldn't endure lying idle in a hospital bed. He would start worrying about his life. And then nothing could save him.

He stopped suddenly. An owl hooted. Somewhere close by, a twig snapped. The sound had come from the grove just past the hill where his tower stood. He stood motionless, all his senses alert. The owl hooted again. Then all was silent once more. He muttered peevishly to himself as he continued.

Old and scared, he thought. Afraid of ghosts and afraid of the dark.

Now he could see the tower. A black silhouette against the night sky.

In twenty meters he would be at the bridge crossing the deep ditch. He kept walking. The owl was gone. A tawny owl, he thought.

No doubt about it, it was a tawny owl.

Suddenly he came to a halt. He had reached the bridge that led over the ditch.

There was something about the tower on the hill. Something was different. He squinted, trying to see details in the dark. He couldn't make out what it was. But something had changed.

I'm imagining things, he thought. Everything's the same as always. The tower I built ten years ago hasn't changed. It's just my eyesight getting blurry, that's all. He took another step, out onto the bridge, and felt the planks beneath his feet. He kept staring at the tower.

There's something wrong, he thought. If I didn't know better, I'd swear it was a meter higher than it was last night. Or else it's all a dream, and I'm looking at myself standing up there in the tower.

The moment the thought occurred to him, he knew it was true. There *was* someone up in the tower. A silhouette, motionless. A sudden twinge of fear passed through him, like a lone gust of wind. Then he got mad. Somebody was trespassing on his property, climbing his tower without asking him for permission. It was probably a poacher hunting the deer that usually grazed around the grove on the other side of the hill. He had a hard time believing it could be another birdwatcher.

He called out to the figure in the tower. No reply, no movement. Again he grew uncertain. His eyes must be deceiving him; they were so blurry.

He called out once more but got no answer. He started to walk across the bridge.

When the planks gave way he fell headlong. The ditch was more than two meters deep. He pitched forward and didn't even have time to stretch out his arms to break his fall.

He felt a hideous pain. It came out of nowhere and cut right through him, like red-hot irons piercing his body. The pain was so intense he couldn't even scream. Just before he died he realized that he had never reached the bottom of the ditch. He remained suspended in his own pain.

His last thought was of the night birds migrating somewhere far above him.

The sky moving toward the south.

One last time he tried to tear himself away from the pain.

Then it was all over.

The time was twenty past eleven on the night of September 21, 1994. That night, huge flocks of song thrushes and red-winged blackbirds were flying south.

They came out of the north and set a southwest course over Falsterbo Point, heading for the warmth that awaited them, far away.

When all was quiet, she walked carefully down the tower steps. She shone her flashlight into the ditch. The man named Holger Eriksson was dead.

She switched off the flashlight and stood still in the darkness.

Then she walked quickly away.

Chapter Two

Just after five o'clock on Monday morning, the 26th of September, Kurt Wallander woke up in bed in his apartment on Mariagatan in central Ystad.

The first thing he did when he opened his eyes was look at his hands. They were tanned. He leaned back on his pillow again and listened to the autumn rain drumming on the window of his bedroom. A feeling of satisfaction came over him at the memory of the trip that had ended two days earlier at Kastrup Airport in Copenhagen. He had spent an entire week with his father in Rome. It had been hot there, and he got a tan. In the afternoons, when the heat was most intense, they had sought out a bench in the Villa Borghese where his father could sit in the shade, while Kurt took off his shirt and turned his face to the sun. That had been the only conflict between them the entire trip. His father simply couldn't understand how he could be vain enough to spend time getting a tan. But it had been a trivial conflict, and its only purpose seemed to be to give them some sense of perspective on their trip.

That happy vacation, thought Wallander as he lay in bed. We took a trip to Rome, my father and I, and it went well. It went better than I could have ever imagined or hoped.

He looked at the clock on the nightstand. He had to go back on duty today. But he was in no hurry. He could stay in bed for a while yet. He leaned over the stack of newspapers he had glanced through the night before, and started reading about the results of the parliamentary election. Because he had been in Rome on election day, he had sent in an absentee ballot. Now he could see that the Social Democrats had taken a good forty-five percent of the vote. But what did that actually mean? Would there be any changes?

He dropped the newspaper to the floor. In his thoughts he returned to Rome one more time.

They had stayed at an inexpensive hotel near the Campo dei Fiori. From a roof terrace right above their two rooms they had an expansive, beautiful view over the whole city. There they drank their morning coffee and planned what they were going to do each day. Wallander's father always knew what he wanted to see. Wallander sometimes worried that his father wanted to do too much, that he wouldn't have the strength. He was always looking for signs that his father was confused or absentminded. The illness was lurking there, and they both knew it. The illness with the strange name, Alzheimer's disease. But that entire week, the week of the happy vacation, his father had been in a glorious mood. Wallander felt a lump in his throat at the thought that the whole trip now belonged to the past and now remained only as a memory. They would never return to Rome; it was the one and only time they would ever make the trip, he and his almost eighty-year-old father.

There had been moments of great closeness between them. For the first time in nearly forty years.

Wallander pondered the discovery he had made, that they were a lot like each other, much more than he had ever wanted to admit before. Especially the fact that they were both definitely morning people. When Wallander told his father that the hotel didn't serve breakfast before seven in the morning, he protested at once. He dragged Wallander down to the front desk and in a mixture of Skåne dialect, a few English words, and some German phrases, as well as a number of random Italian words, he managed to explain that he wanted to have *breakfast presto*. Not *tardi*. Absolutely not *tardi*. For some reason he also said *passaggio a livello* several times as he was urging the hotel to start its breakfast service at least an hour earlier, at six o'clock, at which time they would either get their coffee or seriously consider looking for another hotel. *Passaggio a livello,* said his father, and the desk clerk had looked at him in shock but also with respect.

Naturally, they got their breakfast at six o'clock. Wallander later looked in his Italian dictionary and found that *passaggio a livello* meant railroad crossing. He assumed that his father had mixed it up with some other phrase. But he didn't know what, and he was wise enough not to ask.

Wallander listened to the rain. The trip to Rome, one brief week, seemed in his memory an endless and bewildering experience. What time he wanted to have his morning coffee was not the only thing his father had fixed ideas about. He had also matter-of-factly and self-confidently guided his son through the city; he knew what he wanted to see. Nothing had been haphazard. Wallander could tell that his father had been planning this trip his whole life. It was a pilgrimage, which Wallander had been allowed to take part in. He was a component in his father's journey, an invisible but ever-present servant. There was a secret significance to the journey that he had never been able to grasp. His father had traveled to Rome to see something he already seemed to have experienced within himself.

The third day they had visited the Sistine Chapel. For almost an hour Wallander's father stood staring at the ceiling that Michelangelo had painted. It was like watching an old man send a wordless prayer directly to heaven. Wallander himself soon got a crick in his neck and had to give up. He understood that he was looking at something very beautiful. But he knew his father saw infinitely more. For an instant he wondered facetiously if his father might be searching for a grouse or a sunset in the huge ceiling fresco. But he regretted his thought. There was no doubt that his father, commercial painter that he was, stood gazing at a master's work with reverence and insight.

Wallander opened his eyes. The rain was drumming on the window.

It was on the same evening, their third in Rome, when he suddenly had a feeling that his father was preparing something he wanted to keep as his own secret. Where this feeling came from Wallander had no idea. They had eaten dinner on Via Veneto, way too expensive in Wallander's view, but his father insisted that they could afford it. They were on their first and last trip together to Rome, so they ought to be able to afford a decent dinner. Then they strolled slowly through the city. The evening was warm, they were surrounded by people everywhere, and Wallander's father had talked about the ceiling fresco in the Sistine Chapel. Twice they lost their way before they finally found their hotel. Wallander's father was greeted with great respect after his breakfast outburst, and they picked up their keys, received a polite bow from the desk clerk, and went up the stairs. In the corridor they said good night and then closed their doors. Wallander lay down and listened to the sounds from the street. Maybe he thought about Baiba, maybe he was just falling asleep.

All of a sudden he was wide awake again. Something made him uneasy. After a while he put on his robe and went down to the lobby. Everything was quiet. The night clerk was sitting watching TV on low in the room behind the front desk. Wallander bought a bottle of mineral water. The clerk was a young man working nights to finance his theological studies. That's what he had told Wallander the first time he came downstairs to buy some water. He had dark, wavy hair and was born in Padua. His name was Mario and he spoke excellent English. Wallander stood there holding his water bottle and suddenly heard himself asking the young night clerk to come upstairs and wake him if his father showed up in the lobby during the night, or happened to leave the hotel. The desk clerk looked at him; maybe he was surprised, or maybe he had worked there long enough that no nighttime requests from hotel guests could surprise him anymore. He nodded and said, certainly, if the senior *signor* Wallander went out during the night, he would knock on the door of room 32 at once.

It was on the sixth night that it happened. That day they had strolled around the Forum Romanum and also paid a visit to Galleria Doria Pamphili. In the evening they went through the dark underground passages that led to the Spanish Steps from the Villa Borghese, and ate dinner in a restaurant; Wallander was shocked when the bill arrived. It was their last night, and this vacation, which could never be described as anything but happy, was coming to an end. Wallander's father showed the same boundless energy and curiosity that he had on the whole trip. They walked through the city and stopped at a café for a cup of coffee and toasted each other with a glass of *grappa*. At the hotel they picked up their keys—the evening had been just as warm as all the other evenings that week in September—and Wallander fell asleep as soon as he fell into bed.

It was half past one when the knock on the door came.

At first he didn't know where he was. But when he jumped up, half awake, and opened the door, the night clerk was standing there, and in his excellent English he explained that *signor* Wallander's father had just left the hotel. Wallander threw on his clothes. When he reached the street he saw his father walking with purposeful steps along the opposite sidewalk. Wallander followed him at a distance; he thought that for the first time he was tailing his own father, and he knew that his premonitions had been right. At first he was unsure where they were heading. Then, when the streets began to narrow, he realized they were on their way to the Spanish Steps. He still kept his distance. And then, in the warm Roman night, he watched his father climb all the way up the Spanish Steps to the church with two towers. There his father sat down; he looked like a black dot way up there, and Wallander kept himself hidden in the shadows. His father stayed there for almost an hour. Then he stood up and came back down the steps. Wallander continued to tail him; it was the most mysterious assignment he had ever carried out, and soon they were at the Fontana di Trevi. His father did not toss a coin over his shoulder, but just watched the water spraying out of the huge fountain. His face was lit enough by a streetlight for Wallander to catch sight of a gleam in his eyes.

Then he followed his father back to the hotel.

The next day they were sitting in the Alitalia plane to Copenhagen, with his father in the window seat, just as on the trip down. Wallander looked at his hands and saw that he had a tan. Not until they were on the ferry heading back to Limhamn did Wallander ask whether his father was pleased with the trip. He nodded, mumbled something unintelligible, and Wallander knew that he couldn't demand more enthusiasm than that. Gertrud was waiting for them in Limhamn and drove them home. They dropped Wallander off in Ystad, and later that night, when he called to ask if everything was all right, Gertrud told him that his father was already out in his studio painting his trademark motif, the sunset over a motionless, becalmed landscape.

Now Wallander got out of bed and went to the kitchen. It was five thirty. He brewed some coffee. Why had his father gone out into the night? Why did he sit there on the steps? What was it that gleamed in his eyes at the fountain?

He had no answers. But he had been allowed a glimpse into his father's secret interior landscape. He also had the wits to stay where he was, outside the invisible fence. And he would never ask him about his solitary promenade through Rome.

As the coffee was brewing, Wallander went into the bathroom. He noticed with pleasure that he looked healthy and energetic. The sun had bleached his blond hair. All that spaghetti might have put a few kilos on him, but he refused to step on the bathroom scale. He felt rested. That was the most important thing. He was glad they had actually made the trip.

The feeling that in just a few hours he would turn into a cop again didn't bother him. He often had trouble going back to work after a vacation, especially in recent years; he felt a strong reluctance. He had also gone through periods when he harbored serious thoughts of leaving the force and finding another job, maybe as a security officer at some corporation. But a cop was what he was. This insight had matured slowly but irrevocably. He would never be anything else.

As he showered he thought back to the events of several months before, during the hot summer and Sweden's triumphant victory in the World Cup soccer tournament. He still recalled with anguish the desperate hunt that summer for a serial axe murderer who scalped his victims. During the week in Rome, all thoughts of this had been banished from his mind. Now they came flooding back. A week in Rome hadn't changed a thing. He was coming back to the same world.

He sat at his kitchen table until after seven. The rain continued to beat on the windowpanes. The heat of Italy already seemed a distant memory. Fall had come to Skåne.

At seven thirty he left his apartment and drove to the police station. His colleague Martinsson arrived at the same time, parking next to him. They said a quick hello in the rain and hurried into the entryway of the station.

"How was the trip?" asked Martinsson. "Welcome back, by the way."

"My father was very pleased," replied Wallander.

"What about you?"

"It was a great trip. And hot."

They went inside. Ebba, who had been the receptionist at the station for more than thirty years, greeted him with a big smile.

"Can you get so tan in Italy in September?" she asked in surprise.

"You can," said Wallander, "if you stay in the sun."

They walked down the hall. Wallander realized he should have bought Ebba a little something. He was annoyed at his thoughtlessness.

"Everything's calm here," said Martinsson. "No serious cases. Almost nothing going on."

"Maybe we can hope for a calm autumn," said Wallander dubiously.

Martinsson went off to get coffee. Wallander opened the door to his office. Everything was just as he'd left it. The desk was empty. He hung up his jacket and opened the window a crack. In the in-box someone had placed a pile of memos from the National Police Board. He picked up the top one but let it drop to his desk unread.

He thought about the complicated investigation into car smuggling from southern Sweden to the former Eastern Bloc countries that he'd been working on for almost a year now. If nothing special had happened while he was gone, he'd have to go back to that investigation.

He wondered whether he'd be spending time on that case until his retirement in about fifteen years.

At quarter past eight he got up and went to the conference room. At eight thirty all the detectives in Ystad showed up to go over the work for the coming week. Wallander walked around the conference table and shook hands with everyone. They all admired his tan. Then he sat down in his usual place. The mood was normal for a Monday morning in the fall: gray and weary, everyone a little preoccupied. He wondered how many Monday mornings he had spent in this room. Since Lisa Holgersson, their new chief, was in Stockholm, Hansson led the meeting. Martinsson was right. Not much had happened during the week.

"I suppose I'll have to go back to my smuggled cars," said Wallander with no attempt to conceal his reluctance.

"Unless you want to take on a burglary," said Hansson encouragingly. "At a flower shop."

Wallander looked at him in surprise.

"A break-in at a flower shop? What did they steal, tulips?"

"Nothing, as far as we can tell," said Svedberg, scratching his balding head.

At that moment the door opened and Ann-Britt Höglund hurried in. Since her husband was a traveling machinery installer and always seemed to be overseas in some far-off country no one had ever heard of, she was often alone with their two children. Her mornings were chaotic, and she was frequently late to their meetings. She had been with the Ystad police for about a year now and was their youngest detective. At first, some of the older detectives, among them Svedberg and Hansson, had openly displayed their displeasure over having a female colleague. But Wallander, who quickly saw that she had great aptitude for police work, had come to her defense. Nobody commented anymore when she was late, at least not when he was around. She sat down on one side of the table and nodded cheerfully to Wallander, as if surprised he had come back at all.

"We're talking about the flower shop," said Hansson. "We thought Kurt might be able to take a look at it."

"The break-in happened last Thursday night," she said. "The assistant discovered it when she came in on Friday morning. The burglar came in through a back window."

"What was stolen?" asked Wallander.

"Not a thing."

Wallander frowned.

"What do you mean, not a thing?"

Höglund shrugged her shoulders.

"Not a thing means not a thing."

"There were traces of blood on the floor," said Svedberg. "And the owner is out of town."

"The whole thing sounds pretty weird," said Wallander. "Is it really worth spending so much time on?"

"The whole thing *is* weird," said Höglund. "Whether it's worth spending time on, I can't say."

Wallander had a fleeting thought that at least he'd get out of digging through the hopeless investigation into the steady stream of cars still being smuggled out of the country. He'd give himself a day to get used to not being in Rome anymore.

"I suppose I could take a look," he said.

"I've got all the info on it," said Höglund. "The flower shop is downtown."

The meeting was over. It was still raining. Wallander went and got his jacket. He and Höglund drove downtown in his car.

"How was your trip?" she asked when they stopped at a light near the hospital.

"I saw the Sistine Chapel," replied Wallander as he stared out at the rain. "And I got to see my father in a good mood for a whole week."

"Sounds like a nice trip," she said.

The light changed and they drove on. She navigated since he wasn't sure where the florist shop was.

"So how are things here?" asked Wallander.

"Nothing changes in a week," she replied. "It's been quiet."

"And our new chief?"

"She's in Stockholm discussing all the new proposed cutbacks. I think she'll be fine. At least as good as Björk."

Wallander shot her a quick look.

"I never thought you liked him."

"He did the best he could. What more can you expect?"

"Nothing," said Wallander. "Absolutely nothing."

They stopped at Västra Vallgatan, at the corner of Pottmakargränd. The flower shop was called Cymbia. Its sign was swinging in the blustery wind. They stayed in the car. Höglund gave Wallander some papers in a plastic folder. He looked at them as he listened.

"The owner of the shop is Gösta Runfeldt. He's out of town. His assistant arrived at the shop just before nine on Friday morning. She discovered that a window in the back was broken. There were shards of glass both outside on the ground and inside the window. On the floor inside the shop there were traces of blood. Nothing seems to have been stolen. And they never keep any cash in the shop at night. She called the police at 9:03. I got here just after ten. It was exactly the way she described it. A broken window. Blood traces on the floor. Nothing stolen. A little strange, the whole thing."

Wallander thought for a moment.

"Not a single flower?" he asked.

"That's what the assistant claimed."

"Could anyone really remember the exact number of flowers they have in each vase?"

He handed back the papers.

"We can always ask her," said Höglund. "The shop's open."

When Wallander opened the door an old-fashioned bell jingled. The scents inside the shop reminded him of the gardens in Rome. There were no customers. A woman in her fifties came out from a back room. She nodded when she saw them.

"I've brought along my colleague," said Höglund.

Wallander shook hands and introduced himself.

"I've read about you in the newspaper," said the woman.

"Nothing negative, I hope," said Wallander.

"Oh no," replied the woman. "Only good things."

Wallander had seen from the file Höglund gave him in the car that the woman who worked in the shop was named Vanja Andersson and that she was fifty-three years old.

Wallander moved slowly around the shop. From old, ingrained habit he watched carefully where he stepped. The humid fragrance of flowers continued to fill his mind with memories. He went behind the counter and stopped at a back door, the upper half of which was a glass window. The putty was new. This was where the burglar or burglars had entered. Wallander looked at the floor, which was covered with interlocking plastic mats.

"I presume it was here that the blood was found," he said.

"No," said Höglund. "The blood traces were in the storeroom in back."

Wallander raised his eyebrows in surprise. Then he followed her into the back among the flowers. Höglund took up a stance in the middle of the room.

"Here," she said. "Right here."

"But nothing over by the broken window?"

"Not a thing. Now do you understand why I think it's a little weird? Why is there blood in here, but not by the window? If we assume that whoever broke the window cut himself, that is."

"Who else would it be?" asked Wallander.

"That's just it. Who else would it be?"

Wallander went through the shop one more time. He tried to understand the course of events. Someone had broken the window and let himself into the shop. There was blood in the middle of the back room. Nothing had been stolen.

Every crime follows some kind of plan or reason, except those that are clearly acts of insanity. He knew this from many years of experience. But nobody would commit the insane act of breaking into a flower shop and not stealing anything, thought Wallander.

It just didn't make sense.

"I presume it was blood that had dripped," he said.

To his surprise, Höglund shook her head.

"It was a little puddle," she said. "Not drops."

Wallander pondered this fact. But he didn't say a word. He had nothing to say. Then he turned to the shop assistant, who was standing in the background, waiting.

"So nothing was stolen?"

"Nothing."

"Not even any flowers?"

"Not that I could see."

"Do you really know exactly how many flowers you have in the shop at any one time?"

"Yes, I do."

Her reply was quick and adamant. Wallander nodded.

"Do you have any explanation for this break-in?"

"No."

"You don't own the shop, is that right?"

"The owner's name is Gösta Runfeldt. I work for him."

"If I understand correctly, he's out of town. Have you been in contact with him?"

"That's not possible."

Wallander looked at her attentively.

"Why isn't it possible?"

"He's on an orchid safari in Kenya."

Wallander considered what she had said.

"Can you tell me something more? An orchid safari?"

"Gösta is a passionate orchid lover," said Vanja Andersson. "He knows everything about them. He travels all over the world looking at all the types that exist. He's been writing a book on the history of orchids. Right now he's in Kenya. I don't know where. All I know is he'll be back next Wednesday."

Wallander nodded.

"We'll definitely have to talk with him when he gets back," said Wallander. "Maybe you could ask him to call us at the police station?"

Vanja Andersson promised to pass on the message. A customer came into the shop. Höglund and Wallander went out in the rain and got into the car. Wallander waited to start the engine.

"Of course, it could be a burglar who made a mistake," he said. "A thief who smashed the wrong window. There's a computer store right next door."

"But what about the pool of blood?"

Wallander shrugged.

"Maybe the thief didn't notice he cut himself. He stood there with his arm hanging down and looked around. The blood dripped from his arm. And blood dripping in the same spot will eventually form a puddle."

She nodded. Wallander turned the ignition.

"This will be an insurance case," said Wallander, "nothing more."

They drove back to the police station in the rain.

It was eleven o'clock on Monday, the 26th of September, 1994.

In Wallander's mind the trip to Rome was slipping away like a slowly dissolving mirage.

Chapter Three

On Tuesday, the 27th of September, the rain was still falling over Skåne. The meteorologists had predicted that the hot summer would be followed by a rainy autumn. Nothing had yet occurred to contradict their prognosis.

The day before, Wallander had come home from his first workday after his trip to Italy and quickly thrown together a meal and forced it down. He made several attempts to get hold of his daughter, who lived in Stockholm. He propped open the door to the balcony when there was a brief pause in the persistent rain. He felt himself getting annoyed that Linda hadn't called to ask him how the trip had been. He tried to convince himself, without much success, that it was because she was so busy. This fall she was combining studies at a private theater school with work as a waitress at a lunch restaurant on Kungsholmen.

Around eleven he called Baiba in Riga. By that time it was raining and windy again. It was already hard for him to remember the warm days in Rome.

The one thing he had done in Rome, besides enjoy the heat and serve as a traveling companion for his father, was think about Baiba. They had taken a trip to Denmark in the summer, just a few months before, when Wallander was worn out and down in the dumps after the excruciating manhunt. On one of their last days together, he had asked Baiba to marry him. She gave him an evasive answer, without necessarily closing all the doors. Nor did she try to conceal the reasons for her reluctance. They were walking along the endless beach at Skagen where the two seas meet. Wallander had walked the same stretch many years before with his wife Mona, and alone on a later occasion when he was depressed and seriously considering quitting the police force.

The evenings in Denmark had been almost as hot as in the tropics. At one point he and Baiba realized that the World Cup had people glued to their TVs, so the beaches were unusually deserted. They strolled along, picking up pebbles and shells, and Baiba told him she didn't think she could ever live with a policeman again. Her first husband, the Latvian police major Karlis, had been murdered in 1992. That was when Wallander had met her, during that confused and unreal time in Riga. In Rome, Wallander had asked himself whether deep down he really ever wanted to get married again. Was it even necessary to be married? To tie yourself down with complicated, formal bonds which hardly had any meaning in this day and age?

He had been married to Linda's mother for a long time. Then one day five years ago she had confronted him out of the blue: she wanted a divorce. He had been totally dumbfounded. Only now did he feel able to understand and at least partially accept the reasons why she had wanted to begin a new life without him. Now he could see why things had turned out the way they had. He understood his part in the whole thing; he could even admit that because of his constant absence and his increasing lack of interest in what was important in Mona's life, he bore most of the blame. If you had to talk about blame. In life, people walked together part of the way. Then their paths diverged, so slowly and unnoticed that it wasn't clear what had happened until it was too late. And by that time they were already out of sight of each other.

He had thought a lot about it during those days in Rome. And he finally came to the conclusion that he really did want to marry Baiba. He wanted her to leave Latvia and come to live in Ystad. And he had also decided to move, to sell his apartment on Mariagatan and buy his own house. Somewhere just outside town, with a flourishing garden. An inexpensive house, but in good enough shape that he could handle the necessary repairs himself. He had also thought about getting the dog he had been dreaming about for so long.

Now he talked about all of this with Baiba as the rain fell again over Ystad. It was like a continuation of the conversation he had been having in his head in Rome. He had been talking to her then too, even though she wasn't there. On a few occasions he had started talking out loud to himself. His father, of course, hadn't let this go unnoticed, trudging along at his side in the heat. His father had sarcastically but not unkindly asked which of them was the one actually getting old and senile.

Baiba sounded happy. Wallander told her about the trip and then repeated his question from the summer. For a moment the silence bounced back and forth between Riga and Ystad. Then she said that she had been thinking too. She still had doubts; they hadn't lessened, but they hadn't increased either.

"Why don't you come over here?" said Wallander. "We can't talk about this on the phone."

"You're right," she said. "I'll come."

They didn't decide on when. They would talk about that later. She had her job at the University of Riga. Her time off always had to be planned far in advance. But when Wallander hung up the phone he had a sense of certainty that he was now on his way to a new phase of his life. She would come. He would get married again.

That night it took a long time for him to fall asleep. Several times he got out of bed, stood by the kitchen window, and stared out at the rain. He was going to miss the streetlight swinging on the wire out there, lonesome in the wind.

Even though he didn't get much sleep, he was up early on Tuesday morning. Just after seven he parked his car outside the police station and hurried through the rain and wind. When he reached his office he decided to dig into the pile of paperwork about the car thefts right away. The longer he put it off, the more his distaste and lack of inspiration would weigh him down. He hung his jacket over the visitor's chair to dry out. Then he lifted the pile of investigative material, almost half a meter high, down from the shelf. He was just starting to organize the folders when there was a knock at the door. Wallander knew it would be Martinsson. He called to him to come in.

"When you're away I'm always the first one here in the morning," said Martinsson. "Now I have to settle for second place."

"I've missed my cars," said Wallander, pointing at the folders all over his desk.

Martinsson had a piece of paper in his hand.

"I forgot to give this to you yesterday," he said. "Chief Holgersson wanted you to have a look at it."

"What is it?"

"Read it for yourself. You know that people expect us cops to make statements about all kinds of topics."

"Is it something political?"

"Something like that."

Wallander gave him an inquiring look. Martinsson didn't usually beat around the bush. Several years before, he had been active in the Liberal party and probably had hopes of a political career. As far as Wallander knew, this hope had gradually faded as the party began to dwindle. He decided not to comment on the party's showing in the election the week before.

Martinsson left. Wallander sat down and read over the paper. After he read it twice he was fuming. He went out to the hall and strode into Svedberg's office, whose door was ajar.

"Have you seen this?" asked Wallander, waving Martinsson's sheet of paper.

Svedberg shook his head.

"What is it?"

"It's from a new organization that wants to know whether the police would have any objections to its name."

"Which is?"

"They were thinking of calling themselves 'Friends of the Axe.'"

Svedberg gave Wallander a baffled look.

"Friends of the Axe?"

"That's right. And now they're wondering—considering what happened here this summer—if the name might possibly be misconstrued. This organization has no intention of going out and scalping people."

"What *are* they going to do?"

"If I understand correctly, it's some sort of home crafts association that wants to establish a museum for old-fashioned hand tools."

"That sounds all right, doesn't it? Why are you so worked up?"

"Because they think the police have time to make pronouncements about such things," Wallander said. "Personally, I think Friends of the Axe is a pretty strange name for a home crafts association. But I can't be wasting time on stuff like this."

"So tell the chief."

"I'm going to."

"Though she probably won't agree with you. Since we're all supposed to become local police again."

Wallander knew that Svedberg was right. During the years he had been a cop, the police corps had undergone endless and sweeping changes because of the always-complex relationship between the police and that vague and threatening entity called "the public." This public, which hung like a nightmare over the National Police Board as well as over the individual policeman, was characterized by one thing: fickleness. The latest attempt to satisfy the public was to change the entire Swedish police corps to a nationwide "local police." Just how this was supposed to be done, no one knew. The national commissioner had nailed his theses to every door he came across, proclaiming how important it was for the police to be *seen*. But since nobody had ever thought the police were invisible, they couldn't figure out how this liturgy was supposed to be followed. They already had beat cops walking patrols. Now the police were also riding bikes around in small, swift mini-squads. Apparently the national commissioner was talking about some kind of spiritual visibility. "Local police" sounded comfy, like a soft pillow under your head. But how it was actually going to be combined with the fact that crime in Sweden was growing more brutal and violent all the time, no one could really explain. In all probability, part of this new strategy would force them to spend time making judgment calls about whether it was proper for a home crafts organization to call itself "Friends of the Axe."

Wallander left the room to get a cup of coffee. Then he closed his office door and tried again to make some headway in the huge amount of investigative material. To start with, he was having a hard time concentrating. Thoughts of his conversation with Baiba the night before kept coming up. But he forced himself to act like a cop again. After a few hours he had reviewed the investigation and reached the point where he had left off before he went to Italy. He called up a detective in Göteborg he was collaborating with. They discussed some of the ideas they had in common. By the time he hung up it was noon, and Wallander was hungry. It was still raining. He went out to his car, drove downtown, and ate at one of the lunch restaurants. He was back at the station by one o'clock. Just as he sat down, the telephone rang. It was Ebba at the front desk.

"You have a visitor," she said.

"Who is it?"

"A man named Tyrén. He wants to talk to you."

"What about?"

"Somebody who might be missing."

"Isn't there someone else who can handle it?"

"He says he absolutely has to speak with you."

Wallander took a look at the open folders on his desk. Nothing in them was so urgent that he couldn't take a report on a missing person.

"Send him in," he said and hung up.

He opened the door and began moving the folders off his desk. When he looked up, a man was standing in the doorway. Wallander had never seen him before. He was dressed in overalls with the logo of the OK oil company. When the man entered the office Wallander could smell oil and gasoline.

He shook the man's hand and asked him to take a seat. The man was in his fifties, had thin gray hair, and was unshaven. He introduced himself as Sven Tyrén.

"You wanted to talk to me?" said Wallander.

"I've heard you're a good cop," said Sven Tyrén. His accent sounded like western Skåne, where Wallander himself had grown up.

"Most cops are good," said Wallander.

Tyrén's reply surprised him.

"You know that's not true. I've been locked up for a thing or two in

my day. And I've met a lot of cops who were real assholes, to put it
mildly."

Wallander was startled by the force of his words. He decided to drop
the topic.

"I presume you didn't come here to tell me that," he said instead.
"There was something about a missing person?"

Tyrén fidgeted with his OK cap.

"It's strange, actually," he said.

Wallander had taken out a notebook from a drawer and turned to
a blank page.

"Maybe we should take it from the top," he said. "Who might have
disappeared? And what's so strange about it?"

"Holger Eriksson."

"Who's that?"

"One of my customers."

"I'm guessing that you own a gas station."

Tyrén shook his head.

"I deliver heating oil," he said. "I take care of the district north of
Ystad. Holger Eriksson lives out between Högestad and Lödinge. He
called the office and said his tank was almost empty. We agreed on a
delivery for Thursday morning. But when I got there, nobody was
home."

Wallander jotted this down.

"You're talking about last Thursday?"

"The twenty-second."

"And when did he call?"

"Last Monday."

Wallander thought for a moment.

"Could there have been some misunderstanding about the time?"

"I've delivered oil to Holger Eriksson for more than ten years.
There's never been any misunderstanding before."

"So what happened next? When you discovered that he wasn't
home."

"His oil intake is locked, so I drove off. I left a note in his mailbox."

"Then what?"

"Nothing."

Wallander put down his pen.

"When you deliver oil," Tyrén went on, "you tend to notice people's
routines. I couldn't stop thinking about Holger Eriksson. It didn't
make sense that he'd be out of town. So I drove out there again
yesterday afternoon after work. In my own car. My note was still in the
mailbox, underneath all the other mail that had come since last Thursday. I rang the doorbell. Nobody was home. His car was still in the
garage."

"Does he live alone?"

"He's not married. He made it big selling cars. And he writes poems, too. He gave me a book once."

Suddenly Wallander recalled that at the Ystad Bookshop he had seen the name Holger Eriksson on a shelf of literature by various local writers. He'd been looking for something to give Svedberg for his fortieth birthday.

"There was something else that didn't make sense," said Tyrén. "The door was unlocked. I thought maybe he was sick. He's almost eighty. So I went inside. The house was empty, but the coffee maker in the kitchen was on. It smelled bad. The coffee had boiled dry and burned on the bottom. That's when I decided to come and see you."

Wallander could see that Sven Tyrén's concern was genuine. From experience, however, he knew that most disappearances usually solved themselves. It was very seldom that anything serious happened.

"Doesn't he have any neighbors?" asked Wallander.

"The farmhouse is pretty isolated."

"What do you think might have happened?"

Tyrén's reply came at once, quite firmly.

"I think he's dead. I think somebody killed him."

Wallander said nothing. He was waiting for Tyrén to continue. But he didn't.

"Why do you think that?"

"It doesn't make any sense," said Tyrén. "He had ordered heating oil. He was always home when I came. He wouldn't have left the coffee maker on. He wouldn't have gone out without locking the door. Even if he was just taking a little walk around his property."

"Did you get the impression the house had been broken into?"

"No, everything seemed the same as usual. Except for that coffee maker."

"So you've been in his house before?"

"Every time I delivered oil. He would usually offer me some coffee and read me some of his poems. He was probably a pretty lonely guy, so I think he looked forward to my visits."

Wallander paused to think about it.

"You said you think he's dead. But you also said you think someone killed him. Why would anyone do that? Did he have any enemies?"

"Not that I know of."

"But he was wealthy?"

"Yes."

"How do you know that?"

"Everybody knows that."

Wallander let the question drop.

"We'll take a look into it," he said. "There's probably an ordinary explanation. There usually is."

Wallander wrote down the address. To his surprise the name of the farm was "Seclusion."

Wallander accompanied Sven Tyrén out to the lobby.

"I'm sure something has happened," said Tyrén as he was leaving. "He'd never leave when I was coming with the oil."

"I'll be in touch," said Wallander.

At the same moment Hansson came into the lobby.

"Who the hell is blocking the driveway with an oil truck?" he fumed.

"Oh, that's me," said Tyrén calmly. "I'm leaving now."

"Who was that?" asked Hansson after Tyrén had gone.

"He wanted to report a missing person," said Wallander. "Have you ever heard of a writer named Holger Eriksson?"

"A writer?"

"Or a car dealer."

"Which is it?"

"He seems to have been both. And according to this oil-truck driver, he's disappeared."

They went to get coffee.

"Seriously?" said Hansson.

"The oil-truck guy seems worried, at least."

"I thought I recognized him," said Hansson.

Wallander had great respect for Hansson's memory. Whenever he forgot a name, it was usually Hansson he asked for help.

"His name is Sven Tyrén," said Wallander. "He said he'd done time for a thing or two."

Hansson searched his memory.

"I think he was mixed up in some assault cases," he said after a while. "Quite a few years ago."

Wallander listened thoughtfully.

"I think I'll take a drive out to Eriksson's place," he said after a while. "I'll log him in as reported missing."

Wallander went into his office, grabbed his jacket, and stuffed the address of "Seclusion" in his pocket. He really should have started by filling out the missing-person form, but he skipped it for the time being. It was two thirty when he left the police station. The heavy rain had changed to a steady drizzle. He shivered as he walked to his car.

Wallander drove north and had no problem finding the farmhouse. As the name implied, it lay quite isolated, high up on a hill. The brown fields sloped down toward the sea, but he couldn't see the water. A flock of rooks was cawing in a tree. He raised the lid of the mailbox. It was empty. He assumed that Sven Tyrén had taken in the mail. Wallander walked into the cobblestone courtyard. Everything was well-kept. He stood there and listened to the silence. The farm consisted of three wings. Once it had formed a complete square. One wing had either been demolished or had burned down. He admired the thatched roof. Sven Tyrén was right. Anyone who could afford to maintain a roof like that was a wealthy man.

Wallander walked up to the door and rang the bell. Then he knocked. He opened the door and stepped inside, listening. The mail lay on a stool next to an umbrella stand. There were several pairs of binoculars hanging on the wall. One of the cases was open and empty. Wallander moved slowly through the house. It still smelled from the coffee maker that had burned dry. The large living room was split-level with an exposed-beam ceiling. He stopped at the wooden desk and looked at a sheet of paper lying on it. Since the light was poor, he picked it up carefully and went over to a window.

It was a poem about a bird. A woodpecker.

At the bottom a date was written. *21 September 1994. 10:12 P.M.*

On that evening Wallander and his father had eaten dinner at a restaurant near the Piazza del Popolo.

As he stood in the silent house, Rome felt like some remote, surreal dream.

He put the paper back on the desk. At ten o'clock Wednesday night he wrote a poem and even put down what time it was. The next day Sven Tyrén was supposed to deliver oil. By then he was gone. With the door unlocked.

Struck by an idea, Wallander went outside and found the oil tank. The meter showed that it was almost empty.

He went back inside the house. He sat down in an old Windsor chair and looked around.

Something told him that Sven Tyrén was right.

Holger Eriksson had truly disappeared. He wasn't just away from home.

After a while Wallander stood up and searched through several wall cabinets until he found a set of spare keys. He locked the house and left. The rain had picked up again. Just before five he was back in Ystad. He filled out the form to report Holger Eriksson missing. Early the next morning they would start looking for him in earnest.

Wallander drove home. On the way he stopped and bought a pizza. He ate it while he watched TV. Linda still hadn't called. Just after eleven he went to bed and fell asleep almost at once.

At four in the morning on Wednesday Wallander sat up abruptly in bed with the feeling that he had to throw up. He only got halfway to the toilet. At the same time he noticed he had diarrhea. He had some sort of stomach trouble. Whether it was the pizza or a stomach flu he had brought home from Italy, he didn't know. By seven o'clock he was so exhausted that he called the police station to report in sick. He got hold of Martinsson.

"You heard what happened, I guess," said Martinsson.

"All I know is I'm puking and shitting," replied Wallander.

"A ferry boat sank last night," Martinsson went on. "Somewhere off the coast of Tallinn. Hundreds of people died, they think. And most of them were Swedes. There seem to have been quite a few police employees on board."

Wallander could feel that he was about to throw up again. But he stayed on the line.

"Police from Ystad?" he asked worriedly.

"None from here. But it's terrible, what happened."

Wallander had a hard time believing what Martinsson was saying. Several hundred people dead in a ferry accident? That just didn't happen. At least not around Sweden.

"I don't think I can talk anymore," he said. "I've got to throw up again. But there's a note on my desk about a man named Holger Eriksson. He's missing. One of you will have to look into it."

He slammed down the receiver and made it to the toilet just in time. Afterwards, as he was on his way back to bed, the phone rang again.

This time it was Mona, his ex-wife. He felt on edge at once. She never called unless something was wrong with Linda.

"I talked to Linda," she said. "She wasn't on the ferry."

It took a moment before Wallander grasped what she meant.

"You mean the ferry that sank?"

"What did you think I meant? When hundreds of people die in an accident, at least *I* call my daughter to see if she's all right."

"You're right, of course," said Wallander. "You'll have to excuse me if I'm a little slow today, but I'm sick. I'm throwing up. I've got a stomach flu. Maybe we can talk another time."

"I just didn't want you to worry," she said.

Wallander said goodbye and went back to bed.

For a moment he thought about Holger Eriksson. And about the ferry disaster that had occurred during the night.

He had a fever. Soon he was asleep.

At about the same time the rain stopped.

Chapter Four

After a few hours he began to gnaw on the rope again.

The feeling that he was about to go crazy had been with him the whole time. He couldn't see; something covered his eyes and made the world dark. He couldn't hear either. Something shoved into his ears was pressing on his eardrums. There were sounds, but they came from inside. An internal rushing noise that wanted to force its way out, not the other way around. But what bothered him most was that he couldn't move. That was what was driving him crazy. Despite the fact that he was lying down, stretched out on his back, he had the constant feeling that he was falling. A dizzy plummeting, without end. Maybe it was just a hallucination, a manifestation of the fact that he was falling apart from within. The madness was about to shatter his mind into pieces that no longer had any connection.

He tried to cling to reality. He desperately forced himself to think. Reason and the ability to remain utterly calm might give him some possible explanation for what had happened.

Why can't I move? Where am I? And why?

For the longest time he had tried to fight off the panic and the incipient madness by forcing himself to keep track of time. He counted minutes and hours, making himself stick to an impossible, endless routine. The darkness never changed, and he had woken up where he lay, fettered on his back. He had no memory of being moved, so there was no beginning. He could have been born right where he lay.

This was the source of his madness. For the brief moments he succeeded in keeping the panic at bay and thinking clearly, he tried to cling to anything that seemed related to reality.

What could he start from?

What he lay on. That wasn't his imagination. He knew that he lay on his back and that what he was lying on was hard.

His shirt had slid up just over his left hip and his skin rested directly against the hard surface. The surface was rough. He could feel that he had scraped his skin when he tried to move. He was lying on a cement floor. Why was he lying here? How had he wound up here? He thought back to the last moment of normality before the sudden darkness had fallen over him. But even that was beginning to seem vague. He knew what had happened. And yet he didn't. And it was when he started to doubt what was his imagination, and what had actually happened, that panic would seize him. Then he would start to sob. A brief outburst that stopped as quickly as it began, since no one could hear him anyway. He had never cried when no one could hear him. There are people who cry only when they're out of earshot of others, but he wasn't one of them.

Actually that was the one thing he was sure of. That no one could hear him. Wherever he was, wherever this cement floor of terror had been poured, even if it was floating freely in a universe totally unknown to him, there was no one close by. Nobody who could hear him.

Beyond the growing madness were the only things he had left to hold on to. Everything else had been taken from him, not merely his identity but also his pants.

It was the night before he was supposed to leave for Nairobi. It was almost midnight, he had closed his suitcase and sat down at his desk to go over his travel plans one last time. He could still see it all quite clearly. Without knowing it, he was waiting in death's anteroom, which some unknown person had prepared for him. His passport lay on the left side of his desk. He was holding his plane tickets in his hand. The plastic pouch with the dollar bills, credit cards, and traveler's checks was on his lap, waiting for him to inspect them too. Then the telephone rang. He put everything aside, lifted the receiver, and answered.

Since that was the last living voice he had heard, he clung to it with all his strength. It was his last link to the reality that still held madness at bay.

It was a lovely voice, soft and pleasant, and he knew at once that he was speaking to a stranger—a woman he had never met.

She asked if she could buy some roses. At first she apologized for calling him at home and disturbing him so late. But she was in desperate need of those roses. She never said why. But he trusted her at once. Who would lie about needing roses? He couldn't remember whether he actually asked her or wondered himself why she had suddenly discovered she didn't have the roses she needed, despite the fact that it was late at night and there were no florists open.

But he hadn't hesitated. He lived close to his shop, and he wasn't going to bed yet. It would take him no more than ten minutes to help her out.

Now as he lay in the dark and thought back, he realized that here was one thing he couldn't explain.

He was convinced the whole time that the woman who called was somewhere close by. There was some reason, which wasn't clear to him, why she had called him instead of someone else.

Who was she? What happened after that?

He had put on his coat and gone down to the street. He had the keys to the shop in his hand. There was no wind, and a cool scent rose up toward him as he walked down the wet street. It had rained earlier that evening, a sudden cloudburst that had passed as quickly as it arrived. He stopped outside the front door of the shop. He could remember that he unlocked the door and went inside. Then the world exploded.

He could no longer count how many times he had walked down that street in his mind, whenever the panic subsided for a moment—a fixed point in the constant, throbbing pain. There must have been someone there.

I expected a woman to be standing outside the door. But there was no one. I could have waited and then gone back home. I could have been angry because someone had played a bad joke on me. But I unlocked the shop because I knew she would come. She said that she really needed those roses.

Nobody lies about roses.

The street was deserted. He was sure of that. But one detail of the scene bothered him. Somewhere there was a car parked, with its lights on. When he turned toward the door, searching for the keyhole to unlock it, the headlights were on him. And then the world ended in a sharp white glare.

The only explanation made him hysterical with fright. He must have been attacked. Behind him in the shadows was someone he hadn't seen. But a woman who calls up at night, pleading for roses?

He never got any farther than that. That's where everything rational ended. With a tremendous effort, he had managed to wrench his bound hands up toward his mouth so he could gnaw on the rope. At first he ripped and tore at it like a ravenous beast of prey gorging on a kill. Almost at once he broke a bottom tooth on the left side. The pain was intense at first, but subsided quickly. When he began chewing on the rope again—he thought of himself as an animal in a trap who had to gnaw off its own leg to escape—he did it slowly.

Gnawing on the hard, dry rope was consoling. Even if he couldn't free himself, chewing on the rope kept him sane, and he could think relatively clearly. He had been attacked. He was being held captive, lying on a floor. Twice a day, or maybe it was twice a night, he could hear a scraping sound next to him. A gloved hand would pry open his mouth and pour water into it. Never anything else. The hand that gripped his jaw seemed more determined than brutal. Afterwards a straw was stuck into his mouth. He sucked up a little lukewarm soup and then he was again left alone in the dark and the silence.

He had been attacked and tied up. Beneath him a cement floor. Someone was keeping him alive. He figured he had already been lying here for a week. He had tried to understand why. It must be a mistake. But what kind of mistake? Why would a person be kept tied up in the dark? Somehow he sensed that the madness was based on an insight he didn't dare allow to surface. *It was no mistake.* This terrible thing had been planned specifically for him, not for anyone else. But how would it end? Maybe the nightmare would go on forever, and he would never know why.

Twice each day (or night) he was given water and food. Twice he was also dragged along the floor by his feet until he came to a hole in the floor. He had no pants on, they had disappeared. There was only his shirt, and he was dragged back to his original position when he was finished. He had nothing to wipe himself with. Besides, his hands were tied. He noticed the smell around him.

Filth. But also perfume.

Was there someone near him? The woman who wanted to buy roses? Or just a pair of hands with gloves on? Hands that dragged him to the hole in the floor. And a faint, almost imperceptible smell of perfume that lingered after the meals and visits to the latrine. The hands and perfume must come from somewhere.

Of course he had tried to speak to the hands. Somewhere there had to be ears and a mouth. Every time he felt the hands on his face and his shoulders, he tried another approach. He had pleaded, he had raged, he had tried to be his own defense attorney and speak calmly and soberly.

Everyone has rights, he had claimed, sometimes sobbing, sometimes enraged. Even a fettered man has rights. The right to know why I've lost all my rights. If you take that away from me, the universe no longer has any meaning.

He hadn't even asked to be set free. To start with, he just wanted to know why he was being held captive. That's all.

He had received no answer. The hands had no body, no ears, no mouth. Finally he had yelled and screamed in utter despair. But there was no reaction at all in the hands. Only the straw in his mouth. And a trace of some strong, pungent perfume.

He foresaw his own demise. The only thing that kept him going was his stubborn chewing on the rope. After what must have been at least a week, he still had barely gnawed through the hard surface of the rope. Yet this was the only way he could imagine his salvation. He survived because of the gnawing. In another week he was supposed to return from the journey he was now presumed to be on, if only he hadn't gone down to the shop to sell a bouquet of roses. By now he would have been deep inside an orchid jungle in Kenya, and his mind would have been filled with the most wondrous of scents. When he didn't arrive home, Vanja Andersson would start to worry. Unless she already had. There was one more possibility he couldn't ignore. The travel agency should be keeping track of its clients. He had paid for his ticket but never showed up at Kastrup Airport. Surely someone must be missing him. Vanja and the travel agency were his only hope of being rescued. Sometimes he gnawed on the rope just to keep from losing his mind—what was left of it.

He knew he was in hell. But he didn't know why.

The terror was in his teeth as they worked at the tough rope. The terror and his only possible way out.

He kept on gnawing.

Once in a while he would cry, overcome by cramps. But then he would go back to gnawing.

She had arranged the room as a place of sacrifice.

No one could guess her secret. She was the only one who carried that knowledge.

Once, the room had consisted of many small rooms with a low ceiling, and dark walls, illuminated only by the dim light that filtered through the small basement windows, set deep into the thick walls. That's how it had looked the first time she was there. She could still recall that summer. It was the last time she had seen her grandmother. By early fall her grandmother was gone, but that summer she had sat in the shade of the apple trees, slowly turning into a shadow herself. She was almost ninety and had cancer. She sat motionless all summer long, inaccessible to the world, and her grandchildren had been instructed not to bother her. Not to shout when they were near her, and to approach her only if and when she called them.

Once Grandmother had raised her hand and waved her over. She approached with trepidation. Old age was dangerous; it held diseases and death, dark graves and fear. But her grandmother had only looked at her with her kind smile, which the cancer could never corrode. Maybe she said something; if so, she couldn't remember what. But her grandmother had been alive and it was a happy summer. It must have

been 1952 or '53. A time infinitely long ago. The catastrophes were
still far off.

It wasn't until she took over the house herself in the late sixties that
she began the great remodeling. She hadn't done the work alone,
knocking down all the internal walls that could be spared without
risking collapse. She had had help from some of her cousins, young
men who wanted to show off their strength. But she had also wielded
the sledgehammer herself, and the whole house shook and the mortar
crumbled. Then from the dust this gigantic room appeared, and the
only thing she left was the big baking oven that now towered like a
strange boulder in the middle of the room. Everyone who came to her
house back then, after the great remodeling, stopped in amazement at
how beautiful it had become. It was the same old house, and yet
completely different. The light flooded in from the newly cut windows.
If she wanted it dark, she could close the shutters of massive oak that
had been installed on the outside of the house. She had exposed the
roof beams and ripped up the old floors.

Someone told her it looked like a church nave.

After that she had begun to regard the room as her private sanctu-
ary. When she was there alone she was in the center of the world. Then
she could feel completely calm, far from the dangers that otherwise
menaced her.

There had been times when she seldom visited her cathedral. The
schedule of her life had always fluctuated. On several occasions she
had also asked herself whether she shouldn't get rid of the house.
There were far too many memories that the sledgehammers could
never demolish. But she couldn't leave the room with the huge, loom-
ing baking oven, the white boulder she had kept, although it had been
remortared. It had become a part of her. Sometimes she saw it as the
last bastion she had left to defend in her life.

Then the letter had arrived from Africa.

After that, everything changed.

She never again considered abandoning her house.

On Wednesday, the 28th of September, she arrived in Vollsjö just after
three o'clock in the afternoon. She had driven from Hässleholm, and
before she drove to her house on the outskirts of town, she stopped at
the store and bought supplies. She knew what she needed. Just to be
sure, she bought an extra package of straws. The clerk nodded to her.
She smiled back and said a few words about the weather. Then they
talked about the terrible ferry accident. She paid and drove off.

Her closest neighbors weren't home. They only spent a month at
Vollsjö, in the summer. They were German, lived in Hamburg, and

only came up to Skåne in July. She and her neighbors would say hello to each other but had no other contact.

She unlocked the front door. In the entryway she stood quite still and listened. She went into the big room and stood motionless next to the baking oven. Everything was quiet. Precisely as quiet as she wanted the world to be.

The man lying down there inside the oven couldn't hear her. She knew he was alive, but she didn't need to be bothered by the sound of his breathing. Or by his sobbing.

She thought of the secret impulse that had led her to this unexpected conclusion. It began when she decided to keep the house, rather than sell it and put the money in the bank. And it was there when she decided to leave the old baking oven untouched. Only much later, when the letter from Africa came and she realized what she had to do, had the oven revealed its actual purpose.

Her thoughts were interrupted by the alarm on her watch. In an hour her guests would arrive. Before then she would have to give the man in the oven his food. He had now lain there for five days. Soon he would be so weak that he wouldn't be able to put up any resistance. She took her schedule from her handbag and saw that she had time off from next Sunday afternoon until Tuesday morning. That's when it would be. Then she would take him out and tell him what had happened.

She had not yet decided how she was going to kill him. There were several possibilities. But she still had plenty of time. She would think about what he had done and then figure out how he was supposed to die.

She went into the kitchen and heated the soup. Because she was careful about hygiene, she washed the plastic cup and lid that she used when she fed him. She poured water into another cup. Each day she reduced the amount she gave him. He would get no more than was necessary to keep him alive. When she finished preparing the meal, she pulled on a pair of latex gloves, splashed a few drops of perfume behind her ears, and went into the room where the oven stood. On the rear side was a hole that was hidden behind some loose stones. It was more like a tube almost a meter long that she could carefully pull out. Before she put him in there, she had installed a powerful loudspeaker and filled in the hole. She played music full-blast, but not a sound seeped out.

She leaned forward so she could see him. When she put her hand on one of his legs he didn't move. She briefly feared that he was dead. Then she heard him gasping.

He's weak, she thought. Soon the waiting will be over.

After she gave him his food, let him use the hole, and then pulled him back to his place again, she filled in the hole in back. When she had washed the dishes and straightened up the kitchen, she sat down at the table and had a cup of coffee. From her handbag she took out her personnel newsletter and slowly leafed through it. According to the new salary table, she would be getting 174 kronor more each month, retroactive from the first of July. She looked at the clock again. She seldom went more than ten minutes without taking a look at it. It was part of her identity. Her life and her work were held together by precisely mapped-out timetables. And nothing bothered her more than not being able to meet schedules. Excuses were unacceptable. She always regarded it as a personal responsibility. She knew that many of her colleagues laughed at her behind her back. That hurt her, but she never said a word. The silence was a part of her too. But it hadn't always been that way.

I remember my voice when I was a child. It was strong. But not shrill. The muteness had come later. After I saw all the blood. And my mother when she almost died. I didn't scream that time. I hid in my own silence. There I could make myself invisible.

That's when it happened. When my mother lay on a table and, sobbing and bleeding, robbed me of the sister I had always waited for.

She looked at the clock again. Soon they would be coming. It was Wednesday, time for their meeting. If she had her preference, it would always be on Wednesdays. That would create a greater sense of regularity. But her work schedule didn't permit it, and she knew she had no control over that schedule.

She set out five chairs. She didn't want any more people than that to visit her at any one time. Then the intimacy might be lost. It was hard enough as it was to create such great trust that these silent women would dare to speak. She went into the bedroom and started to take off her uniform. For each article of clothing she removed, she muttered a prayer. And she remembered.

It was my mother who told me about Antonio. The man she had met in her youth, long before the Second World War, on a train between Cologne and Munich. They couldn't find any seats, so they wound up squeezed close together in the smoky corridor. The lights from the boats on the Rhine had glimmered past them outside the dirty windows, and Antonio told her that he was going to be a Catholic priest. He said that the mass started as soon as the priest changed his clothes. As a prelude to the holy ritual, the priests had to undergo a cleansing procedure. For each garment they took off or put on they had a prayer. Each garment brought them a step closer to their sacred task.

She had never forgotten her mother's recollection of the meeting with Antonio in the train corridor. And since she had realized that she was a priestess, dedicated to the sacred task of proclaiming that justice was holy, she too had begun to view her change of clothes as something more than simply exchanging one set of garments for another. But the prayers she offered up were not part of a conversation with God. In a chaotic and absurd world, God was the ultimate absurdity. The mark of the world was an absent God. She directed the prayers to the child she had been. Before everything fell apart for her. Before her mother robbed her of what she wanted most of all. Before the sinister men had towered up before her with eyes like writhing, menacing snakes.

She changed her clothes and prayed herself back to her childhood. She laid her uniform on the bed. Then she dressed in soft fabrics with gentle colors. Something happened inside her. It was as if her skin altered, as if it too was shifting back to its childhood state.

Last of all she put on her wig and eyeglasses. The last prayer faded away inside her. *Ride, ride a cock-horse . . .*

She heard the first car pulling up in the courtyard. She looked at her face in the big mirror.

It wasn't Sleeping Beauty that awoke from her nightmare. It was Cinderella.

She was ready. Now she was somebody else. She placed her uniform in a garment bag, smoothed out the bedspread, and then left the room. Even though no one else would go in there, she locked the door and then tested the handle.

They gathered just before six o'clock. But one of the women was missing. One of the others told them that the missing woman had been taken to the hospital the night before with labor pains. It was two weeks too early. But the baby might already have been born.

She decided at once to visit her at the hospital the next day. She wanted to see her. She wanted to see her face after all she had gone through.

Then she listened to their stories. Now and then she pretended to write something in her notebook. But she wrote only numbers. She was making timetables. Figures, times, distances. It was an obsessive game, a game that had increasingly become an incantation. She didn't need to write anything down to remember it. All the words spoken in those frightened voices, all the pain that they now dared express, remained etched in her consciousness. She could see the way something eased up in each of them. Maybe just for a moment. But what was life except a series of moments?

The timetable again. Times that coincide, one taking over from the other. Life is like a pendulum. It swings back and forth between pain and relief. Without ceasing, endless.

She was sitting so that she could see the big oven behind the women. The light was turned down and muted. The room was bathed in a gentle dimness. She imagined the light as being feminine. The oven was like a boulder, immovable, mute, in the middle of an empty sea.

They talked for a couple of hours. Afterwards they drank tea in her kitchen. They all knew when they would meet next time. No one ever had to question the times she gave them.

It was eight thirty when she showed them out. She shook their hands, accepted their gratitude. When the last car was gone she went back inside the house. In the bedroom she changed her clothes and took off the wig and glasses. She took the garment bag with her uniform in it and left the room. In the kitchen she washed the teacups. Then she turned out all the lights and picked up her handbag.

For a moment she stood still in the dark beside the oven. Everything was very quiet.

Then she left the house. It was drizzling. She got into her car and drove toward Ystad.

Before midnight she was in her bed asleep.

Chapter Five

When Wallander woke up on Thursday morning he felt rested. His stomach trouble was gone. He got up right after six and saw by the thermometer outside the kitchen window that it was 5° Celsius. Heavy clouds covered the sky. The streets were wet, but it wasn't raining. He arrived at the police station just after seven. The morning calm still prevailed. As he walked down the hall to his office he wondered whether they had found Holger Eriksson. He hung up his jacket and sat down. There were a few telephone messages on his desk. Ebba reminded him that he had an appointment at the optometrist later in the day. He had forgotten about it, but he knew the visit was necessary. He needed reading glasses. If he sat for too long leaning over his paperwork, he got a headache; the letters would blur and run together. He was going to be forty-seven soon. There was no getting around it; his age was catching up with him.

On another message he saw that Per Åkeson wanted to get hold of him. Since Åkeson was a morning person, he phoned him right away at the prosecutor's office in another part of the building. He was told that Åkeson would be in Malmö all day. Wallander put the message aside and went to get a cup of coffee. Then he leaned back in his chair and tried to devise a strategy for tackling the car-smuggling investigation. In almost all organized crime there was some weak point, a link that could be cracked if you leaned on it hard enough. If the police were to have the faintest hope of getting to these smugglers, they would have to concentrate on striking precisely such a link.

His thoughts were interrupted by the telephone. It was Lisa Holgersson, their new chief, welcoming him home.

"How was the trip?" she asked.

"Very successful."

"You rediscover your parents that way," she said.

"And they might acquire a different view of their children," said Wallander.

She excused herself abruptly. Wallander heard someone come into her office and say something. He didn't think Björk would ever have asked him about his trip. She came back on the line.

"I've been in Stockholm for a few days," she said. "It wasn't much fun."

"What are they up to now?"

"I'm thinking about the *Estonia*. All of our colleagues who died."

Wallander sat in silence. He should have thought about that himself.

"I think you can imagine the mood," she went on. "How could we just sit there, discussing organizational problems between the national criminal police and the districts all over the country?"

"We're probably just as helpless in the face of death as everyone else," said Wallander. "Even though we shouldn't be, since we've seen so much of it. We think we're used to it, but we aren't."

"A ferry sinks one windy night and suddenly death is visible in Sweden again," she said. "After it's been hidden away and denied for so long."

"You're right, I suppose. Although I hadn't thought of it that way."

He heard her clearing her throat. After a pause she returned.

"We discussed organizational problems," she said, "along with the eternal question of what should take priority."

"I think we ought to catch crooks," said Wallander. "And bring them to justice and make sure we have enough evidence to get them convicted."

"If only it was that simple," she sighed.

"I'm glad I'm not the chief," said Wallander.

"I sometimes wonder myself," she said, and left the rest of her sentence unfinished. Wallander thought she was going to say goodbye, but she had more to say.

"I promised that you would come up to the Police Academy in early December," she said. "They want you to give a talk on the investigation we had here last summer. If I understand correctly, the cadets themselves requested it."

Wallander was shocked.

"I can't," he said. "I just can't stand up in front of a bunch of people and pretend I'm teaching. Somebody else can do it. Martinsson's good at speaking. He ought to be a politician."

"I promised you'd come," she said, laughing. "It'll be fine, really."

"I'll call in sick," said Wallander.

"It's a long time till December," she said. "We can talk more about this later. I really called to hear how your trip was. Now I can tell it turned out fine."

"And everything's quiet here," said Wallander. "All we have is a missing person. But my colleagues are handling it."

"A missing person?"

Wallander gave her a brief rundown of his conversation on Tuesday with Sven Tyrén, and Tyrén's concern that Holger Eriksson hadn't been home for his heating-oil delivery.

"How often is it ever something serious when people disappear?" she asked. "What do the statistics say?"

"I don't know what they say," said Wallander. "I do know there's very seldom a crime or even an accident involved. When it comes to old or senile people, they may have simply wandered off. With young people there's usually a rebellion against their parents or a longing for adventure behind it. It's rare that anything serious is involved."

Wallander recalled the last time it had happened. With distaste he thought about the female real-estate agent who disappeared and was later found murdered at the bottom of a well. That had happened a few years back, and it was one of his most unpleasant experiences as a police officer.

They said goodbye and hung up. Wallander was dead set against giving lectures at the Police Academy. It was flattering, of course, that they had asked for him. But his aversion was stronger. He also thought he'd be able to talk Martinsson into taking his place.

He went back to thinking about the car smuggling operation, searching his mind for a point where they could crack the organization. Just after eight he went to get some more coffee. Since he felt hungry, he also helped himself to a few rusks. His stomach no longer seemed to be upset. He had just sat down when Martinsson knocked on the door and came in.

"Are you feeling better?"

"I feel fine," said Wallander. "How's it going with Holger Eriksson?"

Martinsson gave him a baffled look.

"Who?"

"Holger Eriksson. The man I wrote a report on, who might be missing? The one I talked to you on the phone about?"

Martinsson shook his head.

"When did you tell me that?"

"Yesterday morning, when I called in sick," said Wallander.

"I guess I didn't hear you. I was pretty upset about the ferry accident."

Wallander got up from his chair.

"Is Hansson here yet? We have to get started on this right away."

"I saw him in the corridor," said Martinsson.

They went to Hansson's office. He was sitting staring at a scratch-off lottery ticket when they came in. He tore it up and dropped the pieces in his wastebasket.

"Holger Eriksson," said Wallander. "The man who may have disappeared. Do you remember the tank truck that was blocking the driveway here? On Tuesday?"

Hansson nodded.

"The driver, Sven Tyrén," Wallander went on. "You remembered that he'd been mixed up in some assaults?"

"I remember," said Hansson.

Wallander was having a hard time concealing his impatience.

"He came here to report a missing person. I drove out to the farmhouse where Holger Eriksson lives and where he apparently disappeared from. I wrote a report on it. Then I called here yesterday morning when I was sick and asked the rest of you to take on the case. I considered it serious."

"It must be lying around here somewhere," said Martinsson. "I'll take care of it myself."

Wallander knew he couldn't be angry about it.

"Things like this shouldn't happen, you know," he said. "But we can blame it on bad timing. I'll drive out to the farm one more time. If he's not there we'll have to start looking for him. I hope we don't find him dead somewhere, considering we've wasted a whole day already."

"Should we call in a search party?" asked Martinsson.

"Not yet. I'll drive out there first. But I'll let you know."

Wallander went to his office and looked up the number for OK Oil in the phone book. A girl answered on the first ring. Wallander introduced himself and said he needed to get hold of Sven Tyrén.

"He's out on a delivery," said the girl. "But he has a phone in the truck."

Wallander wrote down the number in the margin of a National Police Board memo and dialed. The connection was fuzzy when Sven Tyrén picked up the phone.

"I think you may be right," said Wallander. "That Holger Eriksson has disappeared."

"You're damn right I'm right," Tyrén shot back. "Did it take you this long to figure it out?"

Wallander didn't answer that one.

"Is there anything else you wanted to tell me about?" he asked instead.

"And what would that be?"

"You know better than I do. Doesn't he have any relatives he visits? Doesn't he ever travel? Who knows him best? Anything that might explain why he's gone."

"There isn't any reasonable explanation," said Tyrén. "I already told you that. That's why I went to the police."

Wallander thought for a moment. There was no reason for Sven Tyrén not to tell him the truth.

"Where are you?" Wallander asked.

"I'm on the road from Malmö. I was at the terminal filling up."

"I'll drive up to Eriksson's place. Can you stop off there?"

"I'll be there within an hour," said Tyrén. "I just have to unload some oil at a nursing home first. We don't want the old folks to freeze, right?"

Wallander said goodbye. Then he left the station. It was drizzling again.

He felt ill at ease driving out of Ystad. If he hadn't had that stomach trouble, the misunderstanding never would have happened.

Now he was convinced that Tyrén's worry was warranted. He had already sensed it deep inside on Tuesday. Now it was Thursday, and nothing had been done.

When he reached Holger Eriksson's farmhouse the rain was coming down harder. He pulled on the rubber boots he kept in the trunk. When he opened the mailbox he found a newspaper and a few letters. He went into the courtyard and rang the doorbell. He used the spare key to open the front door. He tried to sense whether anyone else had been there. But everything was just as he left it. The binoculars case on the wall in the entryway was still empty. The lone sheet of paper lay on the desk.

Wallander went back out to the courtyard. For a moment he stood pondering an empty dog pen. Somewhere out in the fields a flock of rooks was squawking. A dead hare, he thought absently. He went to his car and got his flashlight. He began a methodical search of the entire house. Holger Eriksson had kept everything neat and tidy. Wallander stood for a long time admiring an old, well-polished Harley-Davidson in part of one wing that served as a garage and workshop. Then he heard a truck coming down the road. He went out to greet Sven Tyrén. When Tyrén climbed down from the truck and looked at him, Wallander shook his head.

"He's not here," said Wallander.

They went into the house. Wallander took Tyrén out to the kitchen. In one of his jacket pockets he found some crumpled slips of paper, but no pen. He grabbed the one on the desk beside the poem about the middle spotted woodpecker.

"I have nothing more to say," said Sven Tyrén belligerently. "Wouldn't it be better if you started looking for him?"

"Everyone always knows more than they think," said Wallander, not hiding his irritation over Tyrén's attitude.

"So what do you think I know?"

"Did you talk to him yourself when he ordered the oil?"

"He called the office. We have a girl there. She writes up the delivery slips for me. She always knows where I am. I talk to her on the phone several times a day."

"And he sounded normal when he called?"

"You'll have to ask her about that."

"I'll do that. What's her name?"

"Ruth. Ruth Sturesson."

Wallander wrote it down.

"I stopped here one day in early August," said Tyrén. "That was the last time I saw him. And he was the same as always. He offered me coffee and read me a few new poems he'd written. He was a good storyteller too. But in a crude kind of way."

"What do you mean, crude?"

"It almost made me blush is what I mean."

Wallander stared at him. He realized that he was thinking of his father, who liked telling crude stories too.

"You never had the feeling he was getting senile?"

"He was as clear-headed as you and me put together."

Wallander looked at Tyrén as he tried to figure out whether that was an insult or not. He let it slide.

"Didn't Eriksson have any relatives?"

"He was never married. He had no kids, no lady friend. Not that I know of, anyway."

"No other relatives?"

"He never talked about any. He'd decided that some organization in Lund would inherit all his property."

"What organization?"

Tyrén shrugged.

"Some home crafts society or something, I don't know."

Uneasily Wallander was reminded of Friends of the Axe. Then he realized that Holger Eriksson must have decided to will his farm to the Cultural Association in Lund. He made a note.

"Do you know if he owned anything else?"

"Like what?"

"Maybe another farmhouse? A house in town? Or an apartment?"

Tyrén thought before he replied.

"No," he said. "There was just this farmhouse. The rest is in the bank. Handelsbanken."

"How do you know that?"

"He paid his oil bills through Handelsbanken."

Wallander nodded. He folded up his papers. He had no more questions. Now he was convinced that something had happened to Holger Eriksson.

"I'll be in touch," Wallander said, getting to his feet.

"What happens next?"

"The police have their routines."

They went outside.

"I'd be happy to stay and help you search," said Tyrén.

"I'd rather you didn't," replied Wallander. "We prefer to do this our own way."

Sven Tyrén didn't object. He climbed into his oil truck and skillfully turned around in the small space available. Wallander watched the truck leave. Then he took up a position at the edge of the fields and gazed toward a grove of trees in the distance. The flock of rooks was still making a fuss. Wallander pulled his phone from his pocket and called Martinsson at the station.

"How's it going?" Martinsson asked.

"We'll have to start with a complete search," said Wallander. "Hansson has the address. I want to get started as soon as possible. First send a couple of canine units out here."

Wallander was about to hang up when Martinsson stopped him.

"There's one more thing. I checked the computer to see if we had anything on Holger Eriksson. Just routine. And we did."

Wallander pressed the phone tighter to his ear and moved under a tree to get out of the rain.

"What was it?"

"About a year ago he reported that he had a break-in at his house. By the way, is the farmhouse called 'Seclusion'?"

"That's right," said Wallander. "Keep going."

"His report was filed on October 19th, 1993. Svedberg took the message. But when I asked him, he'd forgotten it, of course."

"What happened?"

"The burglary report was a little strange," Martinsson said hesitantly.

"What do you mean, strange?" Wallander asked impatiently.

"Nothing was stolen. But he was still certain that someone had broken into his house."

"Then what happened?"

"Nothing. The whole thing was dismissed. We never sent anyone out, since nothing was stolen. But the report is here. And it was made by Holger Eriksson."

"That's odd," said Wallander. "We'll have to take a closer look at that later. Get those canine units out here ASAP."

Martinsson laughed into the phone.

"Isn't there anything that strikes you about Eriksson's report?" he asked.

"Such as?"

"That it's the second time in a few days we're talking about break-ins where nothing was stolen."

Wallander realized that Martinsson was right. Nothing had been stolen from the flower shop on Västra Vallgatan either.

"That's where the similarities end," Wallander said.

"The owner of the flower shop is missing too," Martinsson ventured.

"No, he isn't," said Wallander. "He's on a trip to Kenya. He hasn't disappeared. But it certainly looks like Holger Eriksson has."

Wallander hung up and stuffed the phone in his pocket. He pulled his jacket tighter around him and went back to the garage to continue his search. He didn't know quite what he was looking for. Nothing serious could be done until the canine units arrived. Then they would organize the search and start talking to the neighbors. After a while he gave up and went back to the house. In the kitchen he drank a glass of water. The pipes clunked when he turned on the faucet. Another sign that no one had been in the house for several days. As he emptied the glass he absentmindedly watched the rooks making a ruckus in the distance. He put down the glass and went back outside.

It was raining steadily. The rooks were cawing. Suddenly Wallander stopped short. He thought of the empty binoculars case hanging on the wall just inside the front door. He looked at the flock of rooks. Just past them, on the hill, was a tower. He stood motionless, trying to think. Then he began walking slowly along the edge of the field. The clay stuck to his boots in clumps. He discovered a path leading straight through the field. He followed it with his eyes—it led to the little hill with the tower on it. He estimated the distance as a few hundred meters. He started to walk along the path. The clay was harder there and didn't stick to his boots. The rooks dived toward the field, vanished, and flew up again. Wallander thought there must be a hollow or a ditch there and kept walking. The tower grew clearer. He assumed that it was used in hunting hares or deer. Below the hill on the opposite side was a patch of woods. It was probably also part of Eriksson's property. Then he saw that there was a ditch in front of him. Some rough planks seemed to have fallen into it. The closer he came, the more noise the rooks made. Then they all rose up at once and flew off. Wallander continued to the ditch and looked down.

He gave a start and took a step back. Instantly he felt sick.

Later he would say that it was one of the worst things he had ever seen. And in his years as a policeman he'd looked at plenty of things he would have preferred not to see.

But as he stood there with the rain running down inside his jacket and shirt, he couldn't tell at first exactly what he was looking at. There was something alien and unreal about what lay in front of him. Something he could never have imagined.

The only thing that was completely clear was that there was a dead body in the ditch.

He carefully squatted down. He had to force himself not to look away. The ditch was deep—at least two meters. A number of sharp stakes were fixed in the bottom of it. On these stakes hung a man. The bloody stakes with their spearlike tips had pierced the body in several places. The man lay prostrate, suspended on the stakes. The rooks had attacked the back of his neck. Wallander stood up, his knees shaking. Somewhere in the distance he could hear cars approaching. He assumed they were the canine units.

He looked down again. The stakes seemed to be made of bamboo. Like thick fishing rods, with their tips sharpened to points. Then he looked at the planks that had fallen into the ditch. Since the path continued on the other side, they must have served as a footbridge. Why did they break? They were thick boards that should withstand a heavy load. Besides, the ditch was no more than two meters across.

When he heard a dog barking he turned and walked back to the farmhouse. Now he really felt sick. And he was scared too. It was one thing to discover someone murdered. But the way it had been done . . .

Someone had planted sharpened bamboo stakes in the ditch. To impale a man.

He stopped on the path to catch his breath.

Images from the summer raced through his mind. Was it starting all over again? Were there no limits to what could happen in this country? Who would impale an old man on stakes in a ditch?

He kept walking. Two officers with dogs were waiting outside the house. He could see Höglund and Hansson there too. Both of them wore rain jackets with the hoods up.

When he reached the end of the path and walked into the cobblestone courtyard, they could see at once from his face that something had happened.

Wallander wiped the rain off his face and told them. He knew that his voice was unsteady. He turned and pointed down toward the flock of rooks, which had returned as soon as he left the ditch.

"He's lying down there," he said. "He's dead. It's a homicide. Get a full team out here."

They waited for him to say something else.

But he didn't.

Chapter Six

By the time darkness fell on the evening of Thursday, the 29th of September, the police had put up a rain canopy above the place in the ditch where the body of Holger Eriksson hung impaled on nine sturdy bamboo poles. They had shoveled out the mud mixed with blood at the bottom of the ditch. The macabre work and the relentless rain made the murder scene one of the most depressing and disgusting Wallander and his colleagues had ever witnessed. The clay clumped and stuck to their boots, they tripped over electrical cables winding through the mud, and the harsh light from the floodlights they had rigged up intensified the surreal, repugnant impression. They had also gotten hold of Sven Tyrén, who identified the man caught on the stakes. It was Holger Eriksson, all right, Tyrén told them. No doubt about it. The search for the missing man had ended before it even began. Tyrén remained unusually composed, as though not fully comprehending what he saw before him. He paced restlessly outside the cordon for several hours without saying a word, until Wallander suddenly noticed he was gone.

Down in the ditch Wallander felt like a drowning rat in a trap. His closest colleagues seemed to be having a hard time handling their jobs. Both Svedberg and Hansson had left the ditch several times because of acute nausea. But Höglund, the person he most wanted to send home early, seemed strangely unperturbed.

Chief Holgersson had come out as soon as the body had been reported found. She organized the cumbersome murder scene so that people wouldn't slip and fall on top of each other. A young police trainee stumbled in the clay and fell into the ditch. He injured his hand on one of the stakes; the wound was patched up by the doctor who was trying to figure out how to remove the corpse. Wallander happened to see the trainee slip and got a sudden glimpse of what must have happened when Holger Eriksson fell.

Almost the first thing he had done with Nyberg, their technician, was to examine the rough planks. Sven Tyrén had confirmed that they had lain across the ditch as a footbridge. Holger Eriksson himself had placed them there. Tyrén had once been invited along to the tower on the hill. Eriksson had been a passionate birdwatcher. It wasn't a hunting tower, but a viewing tower. They found the missing binoculars hanging around Eriksson's neck. It took Nyberg only a few minutes to verify that the planks had been sawed through until their bearing capacity was almost nil. After hearing this, Wallander climbed up out of the ditch and went off to think. He tried to picture the sequence of events in his mind. When Nyberg discovered that the binoculars had night vision, he began to have an inkling. At the same time he found it difficult to accept his interpretation. If he was right, they were dealing with a murder that had been planned and prepared with such ghastly and cruel perfection that it was almost unbelievable.

Late in the evening they started work on removing Eriksson's corpse from the ditch. Along with the doctor and Chief Holgersson, they had to decide whether to dig out the bamboo poles, saw them off, or choose the almost unbearable alternative of yanking the body free from the stakes.

They chose the last option, on Wallander's recommendation. He and his colleagues needed to see the murder scene exactly as it was before Eriksson stepped on the planks and fell to his death. Wallander felt compelled to take part in this grisly final act as Eriksson was pulled loose and then taken away. It was past midnight by the time they finished; the rain had let up but showed no sign of stopping, and all that could be heard were an electrical generator and the sound of boots squelching through the mud.

Afterwards there was a momentary lull. Nothing happened. Somebody had brought coffee. Weary faces glowed eerily in the white light. Wallander thought he ought to formulate an overview. What had actually happened? How were they going to proceed? Everyone was exhausted now, and it was already the middle of the night. They were anxious, soaking wet, and hungry.

Martinsson stood with a phone pressed to his ear. Wallander wondered if he was talking to his wife, who was always worried. But when he hung up and put the phone back in his pocket he told them that a meteorologist on duty somewhere had promised that the rain would stop during the night. At that instant Wallander decided that the best thing to do was wait until dawn. They hadn't yet begun to hunt for the killer; they were still looking for leads to give them some starting point. The canine units at the scene hadn't picked up any scents. Wallander and Nyberg had been up in the tower but hadn't found any clues. Since Chief Holgersson was still on-site, Wallander turned to her.

"We're getting nowhere right now," he said. "I suggest we meet here again at dawn. The best thing we can do now is get some rest."

No one had any objection. They all wanted to go home. All except Sven Nyberg, of course. Wallander knew he'd want to stay. He'd keep working through the night, and he'd be there when they returned. As the others started to head up toward the cars by the farmhouse, Wallander hung back.

"What do you think?" he asked.

"I don't think anything," said Nyberg. "Except I've never in my life seen anything remotely like this."

Wallander nodded mutely. He had never been involved with anything like it either.

They stood looking down into the ditch. Plastic sheeting had been spread over it.

"What exactly are we standing here looking at?" asked Wallander.

"A copy of an Asian trap for large predators," said Nyberg, "which is also used in war. They call them pungee stakes."

Wallander nodded.

"Bamboo doesn't grow this thick in Sweden," Nyberg went on. "We import it to use for fishing rods and interior decorating."

"Besides, there aren't any large predators in Skåne," said Wallander thoughtfully. "And we're not at war. So what exactly are we looking at?"

"Something that doesn't belong here," said Nyberg. "Something that doesn't fit. Something that gives me the creeps."

Wallander watched him attentively. Nyberg was seldom this loquacious. His expression of both personal revulsion and fear was entirely out of character.

"Don't work too late," Wallander said as he left.

Nyberg didn't reply.

Wallander climbed over the barricade, nodded to the patrolmen who would be guarding the crime scene overnight, and continued up to the farmhouse. Lisa Holgersson had stopped halfway up the path to wait for him. She had a flashlight in her hand.

"We've got reporters up there," she said. "What are we going to tell them?"

"Not much," said Wallander.

"We can't even give them Eriksson's name?" she said.

Wallander pondered this before he replied.

"I think we can. I'll take the responsibility that the tank-truck driver knows what he's talking about. He told me Holger Eriksson had no relatives. If we don't have anyone to inform of his death, we might as well release his name. It might help us."

They continued walking. Far behind them the floodlights cast a spooky glow.

"Can we say anything else?" she asked.

"Tell them it's a homicide," replied Wallander. "That's one thing we can say with certainty. But we have no motive and no leads to a suspect."

"Have you formed any opinion on that yet?"

Wallander could feel how tired he was. Every thought, every word he had to say, seemed to cost him an almost insurmountable effort.

"I didn't see any more than you did. But it was very well planned. Eriksson walked straight into a trap that slammed shut. That means there are at least three conclusions we can draw easily."

They stopped again. The rain had let up considerably.

"First, we can assume that whoever did it knew Holger Eriksson and at least some of his habits," Wallander began. "Second, the perpetrator fully intended to kill him."

Wallander turned and was about to start walking again.

"You said we know three things."

He looked at her pale face in the light from the flashlight. He wondered vaguely how he looked himself. Had the rain washed away his Italian tan in the night?

"The perpetrator didn't just want to take Eriksson's life," he said. "He wanted him to suffer. Eriksson may have hung on those stakes for a long time before he died. No one heard him but the crows. Maybe the doctors can tell us how long he stayed alive."

Chief Holgersson grimaced in distaste.

"Who would do something like this?" she asked as they walked on.

"I don't know," said Wallander. "All I know is it makes me sick."

When they reached the edge of the field, two reporters and a photographer stood waiting for them, all freezing. Wallander nodded. He knew them all from previous cases. He glanced at Chief Holgersson, who shook her head. Wallander told them as briefly as he could what had happened. When they wanted to ask questions he held up his hand in dismissal, and the reporters left.

"You're a detective with a good reputation," said the chief. "Last summer you demonstrated how talented you are. There isn't a police district in Sweden that wouldn't be glad to have you on their roster."

They had stopped by her car. Wallander could tell that she meant everything she said, but he was too tired to take it in.

"Set up this investigation as you see fit," she continued. "Tell me what you need and I'll see that you get it."

Wallander nodded.

"We'll know more in a few hours. Right now we both need to get some sleep."

When Wallander arrived home at Mariagatan it was almost two in the morning. He made a couple of sandwiches and ate them at the kitchen table. Then he lay down on top of his bed. He set his alarm clock to ring just after five.

At seven o'clock in the gray dawn they gathered once more. The meteorologist had been right. The rain had stopped. Instead the wind was blowing again, and it had turned colder. Nyberg and the officers who stayed at the scene overnight had been forced to rig up temporary fixtures to keep the plastic sheeting covering the crime scene from blowing away. Later, when it suddenly stopped raining, Nyberg had a fit about the fickle weather gods. Since they didn't think another rainstorm would come right away, they took off the plastic canopy, which meant that Nyberg and the other techs were now working down in the ditch completely unprotected from the biting wind.

Driving there, Wallander had tried to figure out how to set up the investigation. They knew nothing about Holger Eriksson. The fact that he was wealthy could conceivably be a motive, of course. But Wallander was dubious. The sharp bamboo stakes in the ditch spoke another language. He couldn't interpret it and didn't know which direction it led.

As usual when he felt unsure, he returned in his thoughts to Rydberg, the old detective who had been his mentor and without whose wisdom he suspected he would have been a mediocre criminal investigator. Rydberg had died of cancer almost four years ago. Wallander shivered at the thought of how quickly the time had passed. He asked himself: What would Rydberg have done?

Patience, he thought. Rydberg would have cut straight to the heart of the matter in his Sermon on the Mount. He would have told me that now the rule about being patient was more valid than ever.

They set up temporary headquarters in Eriksson's house. Wallander tried to decide on the most important tasks and see to it that they were assigned as efficiently as possible.

At that early morning hour, with everyone still groggy, Wallander attempted the impossible task of summarizing the situation.

He actually had only one thing to say: They had nothing to go on.

"We know very little," he began. "An oil-truck driver named Sven Tyrén reported what he suspected was a disappearance. That was on Tuesday. Based on what Tyrén said and taking into account the date on the poem, we can assume that the murder took place sometime after ten o'clock last Wednesday night. Exactly when, we can't say. But it didn't happen any earlier. We'll have to wait for what the medical examiner can tell us."

Wallander paused. No one had any questions. Svedberg sniffled. His eyes were glassy. Wallander thought he probably had a fever and should be home in bed. Yet both he and Svedberg knew that right now they needed all available manpower.

"We don't know much about Holger Eriksson," Wallander went on. "A former car dealer. Wealthy, unmarried, no children. He was some sort of local poet and also clearly interested in birds."

"We do know a little more than that," Hansson broke in. "Holger Eriksson was quite well known. At least in this area, especially about ten or twenty years ago. You might say he had a reputation for being a horse trader with cars. A tough negotiator. Didn't tolerate the unions. Made money hand over fist. Mixed up in tax disputes and suspected of a number of illegalities. But he was never caught, if I remember correctly."

"In other words, he may have had enemies," said Wallander.

"It's probably safe to assume that. That doesn't mean they'd be prepared to commit murder. Especially not the way this one was done."

Wallander decided to wait to discuss the sharpened bamboo stakes and the bridge that was sawed through. He wanted to take things in order, so as to keep everything straight in his own weary mind. That was something else Rydberg had often reminded him about. *A criminal investigation is like a kind of construction site. Everything has to be done in the proper order or it won't hold up.*

"Mapping out Eriksson's life is the first thing we have to do," said Wallander. "But before we divide up the assignments I want to try and give you my impression of the chronology of the crime."

They were sitting around the big round kitchen table. In the distance they could see the barricades and the white plastic canopy flapping in the wind. Nyberg stood like a yellow-clad scarecrow in the mud, waving his arms around. In his mind Wallander could hear his weary, irritated voice. But he knew that Nyberg was talented and meticulous. If he waved his arms he had a reason for it.

Wallander felt his attention begin to sharpen. He had done this many times before. At this precise moment the investigative group was starting to track the murderer.

"I think it happened like this," Wallander began, speaking slowly and choosing his words with care. "Sometime after ten o'clock on Wednesday night, or maybe early Thursday morning, Holger Eriksson exits the house. He leaves the door unlocked because he intends to return soon. He doesn't leave empty-handed. He takes a pair of binoculars along with him. Nyberg has confirmed that they're a night-vision type. He walks down the path toward the ditch, over which he has laid a footbridge. He's probably on his way to the tower on the little hill past the ditch. He's interested in birds. Right now, in September and October, the migratory birds are heading south. I don't know much about it, but I've heard that most of them, maybe the largest flights, take off and navigate at night. That would explain the night-vision binoculars and the late hour. Unless it happened in the morning. Anyway, he steps onto the footbridge, which instantly snaps in two because the planks were sawed almost all the way through in advance. He falls into the ditch and is impaled on the stakes. That's where he dies. If he called for help, there was no one to hear him. As you've already noticed, the farm isn't called 'Seclusion' for nothing."

He poured some coffee from one of the department's thermoses before he continued.

"That's how I think it happened," he said. "We end up with considerably more questions than answers. But it's where we have to start. We're dealing with a well-planned homicide. Cruel and grisly. We have no obvious or even conceivable motive and no leads to follow up on."

They were all silent. Wallander let his gaze travel around the table. Finally Höglund broke the silence.

"One more thing is important. Whoever did this had no intention of concealing his action."

Wallander nodded. He had planned to come back to that very point.

"I think there's a chance it's even more than that," he said. "If we look at this ghastly trap we can interpret it as a display of sheer atrocity."

"Do you think we're searching for a madman?" asked Svedberg.

Everyone around the table knew what he meant. The events of the past summer were not yet that far off.

"We can't rule out that possibility," Wallander said. "In fact, we can't rule out anything at all."

"It's like a bear trap," said Hansson. "Or something you see in an old war movie from Asia. A peculiar combination: a bear trap and a bird-watcher."

"Or a car dealer," Martinsson put in, who had been silent so far.

"Or a poet," said Höglund. "We have plenty of choices."

The meeting ended. It was seven thirty. For the time being they would use Eriksson's kitchen whenever they had to meet. Svedberg drove off to have a serious talk with Sven Tyrén and the girl at the oil company who took Eriksson's order. Höglund would see to it that all the neighbors in the area were contacted and interviewed. Wallander remembered the letters in the mailbox and asked her to talk to the rural mailman too. Hansson would go over the house with some of Nyberg's technicians, while Chief Holgersson and Martinsson would work together to organize all the other tasks.

The investigative wheel had started to turn.

Wallander put on his jacket and walked through the wind down to the ditch, where the plastic sheeting fluttered. Ragged clouds chased across the sky. He bent into the wind. Suddenly he heard the distinctive sound of migrating geese. He stopped and looked up at the sky. It took a moment before he spied the birds. It was a small group high up, just below the clouds, heading southwest. He guessed that, like all other migratory birds crossing Skåne, they would leave Sweden over Falsterbo Point.

Wallander stood there thinking, watching the geese. He thought about the poem lying on the desk. Then he kept walking. He could feel his uneasiness increasing steadily.

There was something in this brutal killing that shook him to the core. It could be an act of blind hatred or insanity. But cold calculation also lay behind the murder. He couldn't decide which scared him more.

Nyberg and his techs had started extracting the bloody stakes from the clay when Wallander reached the ditch. Each pole was wrapped in plastic and carried off to a waiting vehicle. Nyberg had spots of clay on his face and worked with abrupt, irritable movements in the ditch.

Wallander felt he was looking down into a grave.

"How's it going?" he asked, trying to sound encouraging.

Nyberg muttered something unintelligible in reply. Wallander decided to save his questions. Nyberg was irascible and moody and thought nothing of starting a quarrel with anyone. The general opinion at the station was that Nyberg wouldn't hesitate for an instant to yell at the national police commissioner at the slightest provocation.

The police had built a temporary bridge across the ditch. Wallander walked toward the hill on the other side. The gusts of wind tore at his jacket. He studied the tower, which stood about three meters high. It was built of the same lumber that Holger Eriksson had used for his footbridge. A stepladder was leaning against the tower, and Wallander climbed up. The platform was no bigger than one square meter. The wind whipped at his face. Even though he was only three meters above the hill, the entire look of the landscape was changed. He could see Nyberg down in the ditch. In the distance he saw Eriksson's farm. He squatted down and began looking at the platform. Suddenly he regretted that he had climbed up the tower before Nyberg had finished his examinations, and quickly climbed down again. He tried to find a place out of the wind in the lee of the tower. He felt very tired, but something else was troubling him even more. He tried to pin down the feeling. Dejection? The happiness had been so short-lived. The trip to Italy. His personal decision to buy a house, maybe get a dog too. And Baiba, who would come to see him.

But then an old man lies impaled in a ditch, and once again the world starts slipping away beneath his feet.

He wondered how long he could keep this up.

He forced himself to fend off the gloomy thoughts. As soon as possible, they had to find whoever had set this macabre death trap for Holger Eriksson. Wallander trudged cautiously down the hill. In the distance he could see Martinsson coming along the path, in a hurry as usual. Wallander went to meet him. He still felt tentative and uncertain. How was he going to approach the investigation? He was searching for a way in, but he didn't think he'd found it yet.

Then he saw from Martinsson's face that something had happened.

"What is it?" he asked.

"You're supposed to call someone named Vanja Andersson."

Wallander had to search his memory before he remembered. The florist's shop on Västra Vallgatan.

"Damn it, we don't have time for that now."

"I'm not so sure," said Martinsson, seeming hesitant to contradict him.

"Why is that?"

"It seems the owner of the flower shop never left for Nairobi. Gösta Runfeldt."

Wallander didn't understand what Martinsson was talking about.

"Apparently his assistant called the travel agency to find out the exact arrival time of his plane. That's when she found out."

"Found out what?"

"That Gösta Runfeldt never made it to Kastrup. He never flew to Africa. Even though he had picked up his ticket."

Wallander stared at Martinsson.

"So this means another person seems to have disappeared," Martinsson said uncertainly.

Wallander didn't answer.

The time was nine o'clock on Friday morning, the 30th of September.

Chapter Seven

I
t took two hours for Wallander to realize that Martinsson was
actually right. On the way in to Ystad, after he had decided to visit
Vanja Andersson by himself, he also remembered something
someone had said earlier, that there was another similarity between the
two cases. Holger Eriksson had reported a break-in to the Ystad police
a year before, and nothing had been stolen. And there had been a
break-in at Gösta Runfeldt's shop in which nothing seemed to have
been taken. Wallander drove toward Ystad with a growing sense of
dread.

The murder of Holger Eriksson was more than enough. They didn't
need another disappearance, especially not one that seemed to have a
connection with Eriksson. They didn't need any more ditches with
sharpened stakes in them. Wallander was driving much too fast, as if
trying to leave behind the thought that once again he was heading
straight into a nightmare. Now and then he stomped hard on the
brake, as if to give the car and not himself an order to take it easy and
start thinking rationally. What evidence was there that Gösta Runfeldt
had really disappeared? There could be some reasonable explanation.
What had happened to Holger Eriksson was extraordinary, after all,
and it certainly wouldn't happen twice. At least not in Skåne and
definitely not in Ystad. There had to be an explanation, and Vanja
Andersson would provide it.

But Wallander never succeeded in convincing himself. Before he
drove to the flower shop on Västra Vallgatan he stopped at the police
station. He found Höglund in the corridor and pulled her into the
lunchroom, where some tired traffic cops were sitting half-asleep over
their lunchboxes. They got some coffee and sat down at a table. Wallander told her about the phone call Martinsson had received, and her

reaction matched his own: disbelief. It had to be pure coincidence. But Wallander asked Höglund to find a copy of the burglary report Eriksson had filed the year before. He also wanted her to see if there was any connection between Holger Eriksson and Gösta Runfeldt in the computers. He knew she had plenty of other things to do, but it was important that this be taken care of right away. It was a matter of *cleaning up before the guests arrived,* he said. Even he could hear how lame this metaphor was. He didn't even know where it came from. She gave him a quizzical look and waited for the follow-up that never came.

"We'll have to hurry," he went on. "The less energy we have to spend on searching for a connection, the better."

He was in a rush and about to get up from the table. But she stopped him with a question.

"Who could have done it?" she asked.

Wallander sank back in his chair. He could picture the bloody· stakes, an unbearable sight.

"I don't know," he said. "It's so sadistic and macabre that I can't imagine any normal motive. If there is such a thing for taking someone's life."

"There is," she replied firmly. "Both you and I have felt enough rage to imagine someone dead. For some people, the usual barriers don't exist, so they kill."

"What scares me is that it must have been so well planned. Whoever did this took his time. He also knew Holger Eriksson's habits in detail. He probably stalked him."

"Maybe that gives us an opening right there," she said. "Eriksson didn't seem to have any close friends. But the person who killed him must have had some proximity to him. He sawed through the planks. In any case, he must have come there and he must have left. Somebody might have seen him, or maybe a car that didn't belong out there. People keep an eye on what happens around them. People in villages are like deer in the forest. They watch us, but we don't notice them."

Wallander nodded distractedly. He wasn't listening with as much concentration as usual.

"We'll have to talk more about this later," he said. "I'm driving over to the flower shop now."

"I'll see what I can find out," she said.

They parted at the door to the lunchroom. On his way out of the station Ebba called to him and said his father had called.

"Later," said Wallander, "not now."

"It's terrible what happened," said Ebba. Wallander thought it sounded as if she felt personally sorry for some sorrow he had suffered.

"I bought a car from him once," she said. "A Volvo PV 444."

It took Wallander a moment before he grasped that she was talking about Holger Eriksson.

"Do you drive?" he asked, surprised. "I didn't even know you had a license."

"I've had a flawless driving record for thirty-nine years," replied Ebba. "And I still have that Volvo."

Wallander recalled that over the years he had occasionally noticed a well-kept black Volvo in the police parking lot, without ever wondering whose it was.

"I hope you got a good deal," he said.

"Holger Eriksson got a good deal," she replied firmly. "I paid way too much for that car. But since I've taken care of it for all these years, I suppose in the end I'm the one who came out ahead. It's a collector's item now."

"I've got to go," said Wallander. "But sometime you'll have to take me for a ride in it."

"Don't forget to call your father."

Wallander stopped in his tracks and thought a moment. Then he decided.

"You call him, would you? Do me a favor. Call him back and explain what I'm doing. Tell him I'll call as soon as I can. I presume it wasn't anything urgent, right?"

"He just wanted to talk about Italy," she said.

Wallander nodded.

"We'll talk about Italy, but I can't right now. Tell him that."

Wallander drove straight to Västra Vallgatan. He parked hastily, half-way up the narrow sidewalk, and went into the shop. There were a few customers inside. He gestured to Vanja Andersson that he could wait. After about ten minutes the shop emptied out. Vanja Andersson printed a note and taped it to the glass of the front door and locked it. They went into the tiny office in back. The scent of flowers made Wallander feel sick. As usual, he had nothing to write on, so he picked up a stack of gift cards and started making notes on the back. The clock on the wall showed five minutes to eleven.

"Let's take it from the beginning," Wallander said. "You called the travel agency. Why did you do that?"

He could see that she was confused and upset. A copy of the local newspaper, *Ystad's Allehanda,* was lying on the table, with a big headline about the murder of Holger Eriksson. At least she doesn't know why I'm here, Wallander thought. That I'm here hoping there won't be a connection between Eriksson and Gösta Runfeldt.

"Gösta wrote me a note saying when he would be coming back," she began. "I couldn't find it anywhere. So I called the travel agency. They told me he was supposed to leave on the 23rd, but he never showed up at Kastrup Airport."

"What's the name of the travel agency?"

"Special Tours. It's in Malmö."

"Who did you talk to there?"

"Anita Lagergren."

Wallander wrote it down.

"When did you call?"

She told him the time.

"And what else did Ms. Lagergren say?"

"Gösta never left. He never went to the check-in counter at Kastrup. They called the phone number he'd given them, but nobody answered. The plane had to leave without him."

"And they didn't do anything else after that?"

"Ms. Lagergren said they sent a letter explaining that Gösta could not expect a refund for any of the travel costs."

Wallander could tell she was about to say something else, but she stopped herself.

"You were thinking of something," he coaxed.

"The trip was extremely expensive," she said. "Ms. Lagergren told me the price."

"How much was it?"

"Almost 30,000 kronor. For two weeks."

Wallander agreed. The trip really was quite expensive. Never in his life would he consider taking such an expensive trip. He and his father together had spent about a third of that amount for their week in Rome.

"I don't get it," she said suddenly. "Gösta would never do anything like this."

Wallander followed her lead.

"How long have you worked for him?"

"Almost eleven years."

"And things have gone well?"

"Gösta is very nice. He truly loves flowers. Not just orchids."

"We'll come back to that later. How would you describe him?"

She thought about it.

"Considerate and friendly," she said. "A little eccentric. A recluse."

Wallander thought uneasily that this description might also fit Holger Eriksson. Aside from the hints that Holger Eriksson had not been a particularly considerate person.

"He wasn't married?"

"He was a widower."

"Did he have children?"

"Two. Both of them are married and have their own children. Neither of them lives in Skåne."

"How old is Gösta Runfeldt?"

"Forty-nine."

Wallander looked at his notes.

"A widower," he said. "So his wife must have been quite young when she died. Was it an accident?"

"I'm not sure. He never talked about it. But I think she drowned."

Wallander dropped the line of questioning. They would go over it all in detail soon enough, if it proved necessary. Which was the last thing he was hoping for.

Wallander put his pen down on the table. The scent of flowers was strong.

"You must have thought about this," he said. "You must have wondered about two things in the past few hours. First, why he didn't get on the plane to Africa. Second, where he is now instead of in Nairobi."

She nodded. Wallander suddenly noticed she had tears in her eyes.

"Something must have happened," she said. "As soon as I talked to the travel agency I went over to his apartment. It's right down the street, and I have a key. I was supposed to water his flowers. After I thought he'd left on his trip I was there twice. Put his mail on the table. Now I went back. But he wasn't there. And he hasn't been there, either."

"How do you know that?"

"I would have noticed."

"So what do you think happened?"

"I have no idea. He was looking forward to this trip so much. This winter he was planning to finish writing his book about orchids."

Wallander could feel his own anxiety increasing steadily. A warning bell had started ringing inside him. He recognized the silent alarm.

He gathered up the gift cards he had used for his notes.

"I'll have to take a look at his apartment," he said. "And you need to open the shop again. I'm sure all of this has a reasonable explanation."

She sought assurance in his eyes that he really meant what he said. But Wallander knew she probably wouldn't find it.

He took the keys to the apartment. It was on the same street, one block closer to the center of town.

"I'll drop the keys off when I'm done," he said.

When he came out onto the narrow street, an elderly couple was trying with difficulty to squeeze past his haphazardly parked car. They gave him an imploring look. But he ignored them and walked away.

The apartment was on the third floor of a building that Wallander assumed dated from around the turn of the century. There was an elevator, but Wallander took the stairs. Several years ago he had considered trading his own apartment for one in a building like this. He no longer understood what he had been thinking of. If he sold the apartment on Mariagatan, it would have to be for a house with a garden. Where Baiba could live. And maybe a dog too.

He unlocked the door and entered Runfeldt's apartment. He suddenly wondered how many times in his life he had trod the foreign ground of an unknown individual's living quarters. He stopped just inside the door and stood motionless. Every apartment had its own character. Over the years Wallander had perfected his habit of listening for traces of the people who lived there. He slowly walked through the apartment. That was the first step, and often the most important: the first impression, which he would return to later. Here lived a man named Gösta Runfeldt, who early one morning did not show up where he was expected, at Kastrup Airport. Wallander thought about what Vanja Andersson had said. About Runfeldt's eager anticipation of his trip. He could feel his own uneasiness growing.

After going through all four rooms and the kitchen, Wallander stopped in the middle of the living room. It was a large, bright apartment. He had a vague feeling that it was furnished with indifference. The only room that had any personality was the study. A comfortable chaos prevailed there. Books, papers, lithographs of flowers, maps. A work table piled with clutter. A computer. A few photographs on a windowsill. Children and grandchildren. A photo of Gösta Runfeldt somewhere in an Asian landscape, surrounded by giant orchids. On the back someone had written in ink that it was taken in Burma in 1972. Runfeldt was smiling at the unknown photographer. A friendly smile from a suntanned man. The colors had faded, but not Runfeldt's smile. Wallander put back the photo and looked at a map of the world hanging on the wall. With a little effort he located Burma. Then he sat down in the desk chair. Gösta Runfeldt was supposed to leave on a trip, but he never left. At least not for Nairobi on the charter flight from Special Tours.

Wallander got out of the chair and went into the bedroom. The bed was made, a narrow single bed. There was a stack of books on the nightstand. Wallander looked at the titles. Books about flowers. The only one that stood out was a book about the international currency market. Wallander put the book back. He was looking for something else. He bent down and looked under the bed. Nothing. He opened the doors to the wardrobe. On a shelf at the top of the wardrobe lay two suitcases. He stood on tiptoe and lifted them down. Both were empty. Then he went to the kitchen and got a chair. He looked at the top shelf. Now he found what he was looking for. A single man's apartment is seldom completely free of dust. Gösta Runfeldt's apartment was no exception. The outline of dust was quite clear. A third suitcase had been there. Because the other two he had already taken down were old, and one of them even had a broken lock, Wallander imagined that Runfeldt had used the third suitcase. If he had gone on the trip. If it wasn't somewhere else in the apartment. He hung his jacket over the back of a chair and opened all the cupboards and storage spaces where a suitcase might be kept. He found nothing. Then he returned to the study.

If Runfeldt had left on the trip, he would have had to take his passport with him. Wallander searched through the desk drawers, which weren't locked. In one of them was an old herbarium. He opened it. *Gösta Runfeldt 1955.* Even during his school days he had pressed flowers. Wallander looked at a forty-year-old cornflower. The blue color was still present, or at least a pale memory of it. He had pressed flowers himself once. He kept on searching. He couldn't find a passport. He frowned. A suitcase was gone, and the passport too. He hadn't found the tickets, either. He left the study and sat down in an armchair in the living room. Sometimes changing to a different chair helped him to formulate his thoughts. There were plenty of signs that Runfeldt had actually left his apartment. With his passport, tickets, and a packed suitcase.

He let his thoughts roam. Could something have happened on the way to Copenhagen? Could he have fallen into the sea from one of the ferries? In that case, his suitcase would have been found. He pulled out one of the gift cards he had in his pocket. He had written the phone number of the shop on it. He went to the kitchen to make the call. Through the window he could see the tall grain elevator in Ystad harbor. Over there one of the ferries to Poland was on its way out past the stone jetty. Vanja Andersson answered the phone.

"I'm still here at the apartment," he said. "I've got a couple of questions. Did he tell you how he was traveling to Copenhagen?"

Her reply was firm and precise.

"He always went via Limhamn and Dragør."

So now he knew that much.

"One more thing. Do you know how many suitcases he owned?"

"No. How should I know that?"

Wallander saw that he ought to ask the question in a different way.

"What did his suitcase look like? The one you may have seen?"

"He didn't usually take a lot of luggage," she replied. "He knew how to travel light. He had a shoulder bag and a larger suitcase with wheels that folded out."

"What color was it?"

"It was black."

"Are you sure about that?"

"Yes, I am. I'm sure. I picked him up a few times after his trips. At the train station or at Sturup Airport. Gösta never threw anything away. If he'd had to buy a new suitcase I would have known about it, because he would have complained about how expensive it was. He could be stingy sometimes."

But the trip to Nairobi cost 30,000 kronor, Wallander thought. And that money was just thrown away. I'm sure it wasn't voluntarily.

He could feel his discomfort growing stronger. He told her he'd come by the shop with the keys within half an hour and said goodbye.

After he hung up he thought that she probably locked up the shop during lunch hour. Then he thought about what she had said. A black suitcase. The two he had found in the wardrobe were gray. He hadn't seen a shoulder bag either. Besides, now he knew that Runfeldt traveled out into the world via Limhamn. He stood by the window and looked out over the rooftops. The Poland ferry was gone.

It doesn't make sense, he thought. Gösta Runfeldt didn't disappear voluntarily. There may have been an accident. But even that wasn't certain.

To follow up on one of the most important questions, he called information and asked for the number of the ferry line between Limhamn and Dragør. He was lucky and got hold of the person right away who was responsible for lost-and-found on the ferries. The man spoke Danish. Wallander told him who he was and asked about the black suitcase. He told him the date. Then he waited. It took a few minutes before the Dane, who had introduced himself as Mogensen, came back.

"Nothing," he said.

Wallander tried to think. Then he asked his question truthfully.

"Do people ever disappear from your boats? Fall overboard?"

"Hardly ever," replied Mogensen. Wallander thought he sounded convincing.

"But it does happen?"

"It happens in all boat traffic," said Mogensen. "People commit suicide. People get drunk. Some of them are nuts and try to balance on the railing. But it doesn't happen very often."

"Have you got any statistics on whether the people who fall overboard are recovered? Either drowned or alive?"

"I don't have any statistics," said Mogensen. "But you hear about it. Most of them float ashore, dead. Some get caught in fishing nets. Some disappear for good, but there aren't many of those."

Wallander had no more questions. He thanked Mogenson for his help and said goodbye.

He had nothing tangible to go on, and yet now he was convinced. Gösta Runfeldt had never gone to Copenhagen. He had packed his bag, taken his passport and ticket, and left his apartment.

Then he had disappeared.

Wallander thought about the puddle of blood inside the flower shop. What did that mean? Maybe they had figured it all wrong. It might well be that the break-in was no mistake.

He paced around the apartment, trying to understand. It was almost a quarter past twelve. The telephone in the kitchen rang. The first ring made him jump. He hurried over to answer it. It was Hansson, calling from the homicide scene.

"I heard from Martinsson that Runfeldt has disappeared," he said. "How's it going?"

"He's not here, at any rate," said Wallander.

"You have any ideas?"

"No. I think he did intend to take his trip, but something prevented him."

"You think there's a connection? With Holger Eriksson?"

Wallander thought about it. What did he actually believe? He didn't know, and so that's how he replied.

"We can't rule out the possibility," was all he said. "We can't rule out anything."

Then he changed the subject and asked if anything had happened out there. But Hansson had nothing new for him. After he hung up, Wallander walked through the apartment one more time. He had a feeling there was something he should be noticing. Finally he gave up. He looked through the mail out in the entryway. There was the letter from the travel agency. An electric bill. There was also a slip for a package from a mail-order firm in Borås. It had to be paid for C.O.D. at the post office. Wallander stuck the slip in his pocket.

Vanja Andersson was waiting for him at the shop when he arrived with the keys. He asked her to get in touch with him if she thought of anything else that might be important.

Then he drove to the station. He left the C.O.D. slip with Ebba and asked her to have someone pick up the package.

At one o'clock he closed the door to his office.

He was hungry. But he was more anxious than hungry. He recognized the feeling. He knew what it meant.

He doubted they would ever find Gösta Runfeldt alive.

Chapter Eight

At midnight, Ylva Brink finally sat down to have a cup of coffee. She was one of the two midwives working the night of September 30th in the maternity ward of Ystad's hospital. Her colleague, Lena Söderström, was with a woman who had just started to have contractions. Until then it had been a busy night—without drama, but with a steady stream of tasks that had to be done.

They were understaffed. Two midwives and two nurses had to handle all the work. As backup there was an obstetrician they could call if there was serious hemorrhaging or any other complication. But it used to be worse, thought Ylva Brink as she sat down on the couch with her coffee cup in her hand. A few years ago she had been the only midwife on duty all night long. Occasionally this had resulted in difficult situations when she couldn't be in two places at once. They had finally managed to talk some sense into the hospital administration and push through their demand for at least two midwives on duty every night.

Her office was in the middle of the large ward. The glass walls allowed her to see what was going on outside her office. In the daytime there was constant activity in the corridors. But now, at night, everything was different. She liked working nights. A lot of her colleagues preferred other shifts. They had families, and they couldn't get enough sleep during the day. But Ylva Brink's children were grown, and her husband was chief engineer on an oil tanker making contract trips between ports in the Middle East and Asia; she had nothing against the night shift. For her it was peaceful to work while everyone else was asleep.

She drank her coffee with pleasure and took a piece of sugar cake from a tray on her desk. One of the nurses came in and sat down, and then the other one joined them. A radio was playing softly over in the corner. They started talking about autumn and the persistent rain. One of the nurses had heard from her mother, who could predict the weather, that it was going to be a long, cold winter.

Ylva Brink thought back on the times Skåne had been snowed in. It didn't happen often. But when it did, dramatic situations could arise for women who were in labor but couldn't get to the hospital. She remembered one time she had sat freezing in an ice-cold tractor that crept along through the blizzard and snowdrifts to an isolated farm north of town. The woman was hemorrhaging. It was the only time in all her years as a midwife that she had been seriously afraid of losing a patient. And that couldn't be allowed to happen. Sweden was a country where women giving birth simply did not die.

But still, it was fall now. Time of the red mountain-ash berries. Ylva, who came from the far north of Sweden, sometimes missed the melancholy Norrland forests. She had never gotten used to living in the open landscape of Skåne, where the wind reigned supreme. But her husband's wishes had been stronger. He was born in Trelleborg and couldn't imagine living anywhere but in Skåne. Whenever he had time to stay home for a while, that is.

Her musings were interrupted when Lena Söderström came into the room. She was about thirty years old. She could be my daughter, Ylva had thought. I'm twice as old, sixty-two.

"She probably won't deliver before early morning," said Lena. "We'll get to go home."

"It'll be quiet tonight," said Ylva. "Take a nap if you're tired."

The nights could be long. Sleeping for fifteen minutes, maybe half an hour, could make all the difference. The acute weariness vanished. But Ylva never slept. After she turned fifty-five she noticed that her need for sleep had gradually diminished. She regarded it as a reminder that life was both short and finite. You shouldn't sleep it away for no good reason.

A nurse hurried by in the corridor. Lena Söderström was drinking her tea. The other two nurses sat bent over a crossword puzzle. The time was nineteen minutes past twelve.

Already October, Ylva thought. The middle of fall already. Soon winter will be here. In December Harry has a vacation, a month off. Then we'll remodel the kitchen. Not because it needs it, but so he can have something to do. Harry's not wild about vacations. He gets restless.

Someone had pressed a call button. A nurse got up and left. After a few minutes she came back.

"Maria in Room 3 has a headache," she said, sitting back down to her crossword puzzle. Ylva sipped her coffee. All at once she noticed she was sitting there wondering about something, without knowing exactly what it was. Then it came to her.

The nurse who had walked past in the corridor.

Something didn't add up. Hadn't all the women working in the ward been here in the office? And no call bells had rung from intensive care.

She shook her head. She must have been imagining things.

But at the same time she knew she hadn't been. A nurse who shouldn't have been there had walked past in the corridor.

"Who just walked by?" she asked softly.

The two nurses gave her curious looks.

"What?" said Lena Söderström.

"A nurse walked past out in the corridor a few minutes ago. While we were sitting here."

They still couldn't understand what she was talking about. She didn't understand it herself. Another bell rang. Ylva quickly set down her cup.

"I'll get it."

It was the woman in Room 2 who was feeling bad. She was about to have her third child. Ylva suspected that the child hadn't exactly been planned. After she gave the woman something to drink she went out in the corridor. She looked around. The doors were all closed. But a nurse had walked past. She hadn't imagined it. All of a sudden she felt uneasy. Something wasn't quite right. She stood still in the corridor and listened. The muted radio could be heard in the office. She went back and picked up her coffee cup.

"It was nothing," she said.

At that instant the nurse she had seen before went by in the corridor. This time Lena saw her too. They both gave a start as they heard the door to the main corridor close.

"Who was that?" asked Lena.

Ylva shook her head. The two nurses at their crossword puzzle looked up from their newspaper.

"Who are you talking about?" asked one of them.

"The nurse who just walked past."

The one sitting with a pen in her hand, filling in the crossword, started to laugh.

"But we're right here. Both of us."

Ylva got up quickly. When she pulled open the door to the outer corridor, which connected the maternity ward to the rest of the hospital, it was empty. She listened. Far off she could hear a door close. She went back to the nurses' station, shaking her head. She hadn't seen anyone.

"What's a nurse from another ward doing here?" asked Lena. "Without even saying hello?"

Ylva didn't know. But she knew it hadn't been her imagination.

"Let's take a look in all the rooms," she said, "and see if everything's all right."

Lena gave her a searching look.

"What could be wrong?"

"Just for safety's sake, that's all."

They went into all the rooms. Everything seemed normal. At one o'clock a woman started bleeding. The rest of the night was taken up with work.

At seven o'clock, after briefing the day shift, Ylva Brink went home. She lived in a house right near the hospital. When she got home she started thinking again about the strange nurse she had glimpsed in the hall. Suddenly she was sure it hadn't been a nurse at all. Even if she did have a uniform on. A nurse wouldn't have entered the maternity ward at night, especially not without saying hello and telling them what she was doing there.

Ylva kept thinking about it. She grew more and more anxious. The woman must have had some purpose in mind. She stayed for ten minutes. Then she vanished.

Ten minutes. She must have been in a room visiting someone. Who? And why?

Ylva lay there trying to sleep, but it was no use. The strange woman from last night kept appearing in her thoughts. At eleven o'clock she gave up. She got out of bed and made some coffee. She thought she'd better talk to somebody.

I've got a cousin who's a policeman. I'm sure he could tell me if I'm worrying about this for nothing.

She picked up the phone and dialed his home number. His voice on the answering machine said he was on duty. Since it wasn't far to the police station, she decided to take a walk. Scattered clouds were racing across the sky. She thought maybe the police didn't take visitors on Saturdays. She had also read in the paper about the terrible thing that happened outside Lödinge. A car dealer who was murdered and tossed in a ditch. Maybe the police wouldn't have time for her. Not even her cousin.

She went to the front desk and asked if Inspector Svedberg was in. He was, but he was very busy.

"Tell him it's Ylva," she said. "I'm his cousin."

A few minutes later Svedberg came out to meet her. Since he liked his relatives, especially his cousin, he couldn't resist giving her a few minutes of his time. He got coffee for both of them and they sat down in his office. Then she told him about what had happened the night before. Afterwards Svedberg said that it was odd, of course, but hardly anything to worry about. She let herself be reassured.

She had three days off and soon forgot about the nurse who had walked through the maternity ward on the night of September 30th.

Late Friday evening Wallander called his weary colleagues together for a meeting of the investigative team at the police station. They closed the doors at ten o'clock, and the meeting dragged on till far past midnight. He began by explaining in detail that they now had another missing person to worry about. Martinsson and Höglund had finished their preliminary check of the available records, but the results were negative. The police had nothing to indicate a connection between Holger Eriksson and Gösta Runfeldt. Nor could Vanja Andersson re-call that Runfeldt had ever talked about Eriksson. Wallander made it clear that all they could do was keep on working without assuming anything. Gösta Runfeldt might show up at any time with a reasonable explanation for his disappearance. But they couldn't ignore the omi-nous signs.

Wallander asked Höglund to take responsibility for the Runfeldt investigation. But that didn't mean she was released from the Holger Eriksson case. Wallander was often opposed to asking Stockholm for reinforcements in complex criminal investigations, but this time he had a feeling that maybe they should do so right from the start. He'd also mentioned this to Hansson. They agreed to wait to take up the question until early next week. After all, they might get a break in the investigation sooner than they expected.

They sat around the conference table and went over what they had learned so far. As usual, Wallander started by asking if anyone had anything important to report. His gaze wandered around the table. They all shook their heads. Nyberg sniffled quietly at the end of the table, where he usually sat all by himself. Wallander let him have the first word.

"Nothing at all so far. You've all seen exactly what we've seen. The planks were sawed through to their breaking point. He fell and was impaled. We didn't find anything in the ditch. We don't know yet where the bamboo stakes came from."

"What about the tower?" asked Wallander.

"We didn't find anything there," said Nyberg. "But of course we're nowhere near finished yet. It would be a big help if you could talk about what we should be looking for."

"I don't know. But whoever did this must have come from some-where. We have the path leading from Eriksson's house. There are fields all around it. And a patch of woods behind the hill."

"There's a tractor path up to the woods," said Höglund, "with tracks from car tires. But none of the neighbors noticed anything unusual."

"Apparently Eriksson owned a lot of land," Svedberg put in. "I spoke with a farmer named Lundberg. He sold off more than fifty hectares to Eriksson ten years ago. Since it was Eriksson's property, there was no reason for anyone else to be on it. Which means not many people ever paid much attention to it."

"We still have a lot of people to talk to," said Martinsson as he shuffled through his papers. "By the way, I got in touch with the forensics lab in Lund. They think they'll probably have something to tell us by Monday morning."

Wallander made a note. Then he turned back to Nyberg.

"How's it going with Eriksson's house?"

"We can't do everything at once," Nyberg hedged. "We've been out in the mud because it might start raining again soon. I think we can start on the house in the morning."

"That sounds good," said Wallander soothingly. Most of all he didn't want to make Nyberg mad. That could create a bad mood that would affect the whole meeting. At the same time he couldn't get over his irritation at Nyberg's continual grouchiness. He also saw that Lisa Holgersson, sitting near the middle of the table, had noticed Nyberg's surly reply.

They continued their review of the case, still in the introductory phase of the investigative work. Wallander often compared it to clearing a field. They proceeded carefully. As long as they didn't have any leads, everything was of equal importance. It wasn't until some things appeared more important than others that they would seriously begin to head in one or more directions.

Near one in the morning, Wallander realized that they were still plodding along. The interviews with Ruth Sturesson and Sven Tyrén hadn't taken them any farther. Holger Eriksson had placed his order for fuel oil, four cubic meters. There was nothing disquieting about that. The mysterious break-in which he had reported the year before remained unexplained. Their charting of Eriksson's life and the sort of person he was had barely started. They were still involved in the most elementary routines of a criminal investigation. The search had not yet begun to take on a life of its own. They had few facts to go on. Sometime after ten o'clock on Wednesday night, the 21st of September, Eriksson had gone outside with a pair of binoculars around his neck. By that time the trap was set. He walked out onto the footbridge and fell straight to his death.

When no one had any more to say, Wallander tried to sum up. During the whole meeting he'd had a feeling that he'd seen something at the homicide scene that should have prompted a discussion. Something he couldn't explain.

The M.O., he thought. There's something about those bamboo stakes. A killer uses a language that he deliberately chooses. Why would he impale a person? Why would he go to all that trouble?

For the time being he kept his thoughts to himself. They were still too vague to present to the team.

He poured himself a glass of mineral water and shoved aside the papers in front of him.

"We're still searching for a way in," he began. "What we have here is a murder unlike anything we've ever seen. This may mean that the motive and the perpetrator are unlike anything we've ever encountered. In a way, it reminds me of the situation we were in last summer. We solved that case by refusing to get hung up on one thing. And we can't afford to do that now, either."

He turned to face Chief Holgersson.

"We'll have to work hard. It's already Saturday, but it can't be helped. Everyone will continue working today and tomorrow on the tasks at hand. We can't wait till Monday."

Holgersson nodded. She made no objections.

The meeting was adjourned. They were all tired. The Chief stayed behind, as did Höglund. Soon they were alone in the conference room. Wallander thought that now, for once, women were in the majority in his world.

"Per Åkeson wants to get hold of you," said Holgersson.

Wallander remembered that he had forgotten to call. He shook his head in resignation.

"I'll call him tomorrow."

Holgersson had put on her coat, but Wallander could tell that she wasn't finished with him.

"Isn't it possible that this murder might have been committed by an insane person?" she asked. "Impaling someone on stakes! It sounds like the Middle Ages to me."

"Not necessarily," Wallander objected. "Stake pits were used during the Second World War. Atrocity and insanity don't always go hand in hand."

Holgersson didn't seem satisfied with his answer. She leaned against the doorjamb and looked at him.

"I'm still not convinced. Maybe we could call in that forensic psychologist who was here last summer. If I understood correctly, he was a big help to you."

Wallander couldn't deny that Mats Ekholm had been important to the successful investigation. He had helped them draw up a credible profile of the killer. But Wallander didn't think it was time to call him in yet. In fact, he was afraid to draw parallels.

"Maybe," he said hesitantly. "But I think we should wait a while."

She studied him closely.

"You aren't afraid it'll happen again, are you? A new pit with sharpened stakes in it?"

"No."

"What about Gösta Runfeldt, the other missing person?"

Wallander was suddenly unsure whether he might be speaking against his better judgment. But he shook his head. He didn't think it would be repeated. Or was that only what he hoped?

He didn't know.

"Holger Eriksson's murder must have required a lot of preparation," he said. "Something you do only once. Something that depends on a special set of circumstances. Like a ditch that's deep enough, for instance. And a footbridge. And an intended murder victim who goes out at night or at dawn to look at birds. I'm aware that I'm the one who linked Gösta Runfeldt's disappearance with what happened in Lödinge. But that's mainly for reasons of caution."

"I think I understand what you're getting at," she said. "But think about calling in Ekholm."

"I will," said Wallander. "I don't deny that you may be right, but I think it's too early. Timing often determines the success of certain efforts."

Holgersson nodded and buttoned her coat.

"You need to get some sleep too. Don't stay here too long," she said as she left.

Wallander began gathering up his papers.

"I have some things to figure out for myself," he said to Höglund. "Do you remember when you first came here? You said you thought I had a lot I could teach you. Now maybe you can see how wrong you were."

She was sitting on the table, looking at her nails. Wallander thought she looked pale and tired and definitely not beautiful. But she was talented. And that rarity: a dedicated cop. In that they were alike.

He dropped the stack of papers on the table and plopped into his chair.

"Tell me what you see," he said.

"Something that scares me."

"How come?"

"The savagery. The calculation. Besides, we don't have a motive."

"Holger Eriksson was rich. Everyone says he was a tough businessman. He may have had enemies."

"That doesn't explain why he would be impaled on bamboo stakes."

"Hate can blind people. The same way envy can. Or jealousy."

She shook her head.

"When I arrived at the scene I got a feeling that we were looking at something more than the murder of an old man," she said. "I can't explain it any better than that. But the feeling was there. And it was strong."

Wallander snapped out of his weariness. He knew she had said something important. Something that vaguely touched on thoughts that had crossed his own mind.

"Keep going," he said. "Think harder!"

"There isn't that much more. The man was dead. Nobody who saw the scene could forget how it happened. It was a murder. But there was also something else."

"Every murderer has his own language," said Wallander. "Is that what you mean?"

"More or less."

"You mean he wanted to tell us something?"

"Could be."

A code, Wallander thought. A code we haven't cracked yet.

"You may be right," he said.

They sat in silence. Wallander got up from the chair and went back to gathering his papers. He discovered something that didn't belong to him.

"Is this yours?"

She glanced at the paper.

"That looks like Svedberg's writing."

Wallander tried to make out what was written in pencil. It was something about a maternity ward. About some woman he didn't know.

"What the hell is this?" he said. "Is Svedberg having a baby? He isn't even married. Is he even dating anyone?"

She took the note out of his hand and read through it.

"Evidently somebody reported that an unknown woman was wandering around in the maternity ward dressed like a nurse," she said, handing back the paper.

"We'll have to check it out when we have time," replied Wallander sarcastically. He considered tossing the note in the wastebasket but changed his mind. He'd give it to Svedberg the next day.

They parted in the corridor.

"Who's taking care of your kids?" he asked. "Is your husband home?"

"He's in Mali."

Wallander didn't know where Mali was, but he didn't ask.

She left the empty police station. Wallander put the piece of paper on his desk and picked up his jacket. On the way out to the front desk he stopped at the dispatch office, where a lone officer sat reading a newspaper.

"Anybody call about Lödinge?" he asked.

"Not a peep."

Wallander continued out to his car. It was windy outside. He didn't think Ann-Britt had answered his question about her child-care problems. He searched through all his pockets before he found his car keys. Then he drove home. Even though he was tired, he sat on his couch and thought through everything that had happened during the day. Most of all he worried about what Höglund had said just before she left. That the murder of Holger Eriksson was something more. Something else.

But could a murder be more than a murder?

It was almost three in the morning when he went to bed. Before he fell asleep he remembered that he had to call his father and Linda the next day.

He woke up with a start at six o'clock. He had been dreaming. Holger Eriksson was alive. He was standing on the wooden footbridge leading across the ditch. Just as it collapsed, Wallander woke up. He forced himself to get out of bed. Outside it had started raining again. In the kitchen he discovered he was out of coffee. Instead he took a couple of headache tablets and then sat for a long time at the table with his head propped on one hand.

At a quarter to seven he arrived at the station. On the way to his office he got a cup of coffee.

When he opened the door he noticed something he hadn't seen the night before. There was a package on the chair by the window. When he looked more closely at it he remembered the C.O.D. notice he had found in Gösta Runfeldt's apartment. Ebba had seen to it that the package was picked up. He hung up his jacket and started to open it. He wondered for a second whether he actually had the right to do that. Then he pulled off the paper and opened the box. He looked at the contents with a frown.

The door to his office was open. Martinsson walked past.

Wallander called to him. Martinsson stopped in the doorway.

"Come here," said Wallander. "Come and take a look at this."

Chapter Nine

They stood leaning over Gösta Runfeldt's package.

To Wallander it all seemed like a bunch of junk, coupling relays and tiny black boxes whose purpose he couldn't guess. But to Martinsson it was obvious what Gösta Runfeldt had ordered and the police had paid for. "This is state-of-the-art bugging equipment," he said, picking up one of the boxes.

Wallander shot him a skeptical look.

"Can you really buy bugging equipment from a mail-order company in Borås?" he asked.

"You can buy anything you want by mail order," replied Martinsson. "The days are long gone when mail-order companies didn't sell top-of-the-line goods. Maybe there are a few like that still around. But this is the real thing. Whether it's totally legal or not is something we'll have to check out. Importing stuff like this is strictly regulated."

They unpacked the carton on Wallander's desk. It turned out that there was more than eavesdropping equipment in it. To their undisguised amazement they also found a box containing a magnetic brush and iron filings. That could only mean one thing. Runfeldt intended to test for fingerprints.

"What do you make of this?" asked Wallander.

Martinsson shook his head. "It seems pretty strange."

"What's a florist doing with eavesdropping equipment? Is he going to spy on his competitors in the tulip business?"

"The fingerprint stuff is even weirder."

Wallander frowned. He didn't get it at all. The equipment was expensive. It was certainly bona fide technically. Wallander relied on Martinsson's judgment. The company that had sold it was called Secure, with an address on Getängsvägen in Borås.

"Let's call them up and see if Runfeldt bought anything else," said Wallander.

"I suspect they won't be too willing to give out information on their customers," Martinsson replied. "Besides, it's early Saturday morning."

"They have a 24-hour order line," Wallander said, pointing to the brochure that came with the carton.

"It's probably just an answering machine," said Martinsson. "I've bought gardening tools through a mail-order company in Borås. They don't have operators sitting there around the clock, if that's what you think."

Wallander stared at one of the tiny microphones.

"Is this stuff really legal? You're right, we've got to check it out."

"I think I can tell you right now," said Martinsson. "I've got some reference material in my office that deals with this sort of thing."

He strode down the corridor and came right back. In his hand he had a few thin booklets.

"From the information unit of the National Police Board," he said. "A lot of the things they publish are pretty good."

"I read them whenever I get a chance," said Wallander. "But sometimes I wonder if they aren't publishing too much."

"Take a look at this: 'Bugging as a coercive method in criminal interrogations,'" said Martinsson, placing one of the pamphlets on the desk. "But maybe that's not quite what we're looking for. How about this one: 'Memorandum re: eavesdropping equipment.'"

Martinsson leafed through it, then stopped and read aloud. "'According to Swedish law it is illegal to possess, sell, or install eavesdropping equipment.' Which probably means that it's also forbidden to manufacture it."

"That means we ought to ask our colleagues in Borås to clamp down on that mail-order business," Wallander said. "It means they're making illegal sales. And importing illegal goods."

"Mail-order businesses are usually completely legitimate," said Martinsson. "I suspect this is a rotten apple that the industry itself would like to be rid of."

"Get hold of Borås," said Wallander. "Do it ASAP."

He thought back on his visit to Gösta Runfeldt's apartment. He hadn't seen any technical equipment like this when he went through the desk drawers and wardrobes.

"I think we should ask Nyberg to take a look at this stuff. That should be good enough for now. But it does seem strange."

Martinsson agreed. He couldn't understand either why an orchid lover would have bugging equipment. Wallander put everything back in the box.

"I'm going to drive out to Lödinge."

"I managed to track down a salesman who sold cars for Holger Eriksson for more than twenty years," said Martinsson. "I'll be meeting him over in Svarte in half an hour. He should be able to give us some idea of who Eriksson was, if anyone can."

They parted out in the lobby. Wallander was carrying Runfeldt's box of electronics under his arm. He stopped at Ebba's desk.

"What did my father say?" he asked.

"He just asked me to tell you to call if you had time."

Wallander was instantly suspicious.

"Did he sound sarcastic?"

Ebba gave him a stern look.

"Your father is a very nice man. He has great respect for your work."

Wallander, knowing the truth, just shook his head. Ebba pointed at the carton.

"I paid for that out of my own pocket. There isn't any petty cash in the department at the moment."

"Just give me a bill," said Wallander. "Is it all right if I get you the money by Monday?"

Ebba agreed, and Wallander left the police station. It had stopped raining and the cloud cover was breaking up. It was going to be a clear, beautiful fall day. Wallander put the carton on the back seat and drove out of Ystad. Now that the sun was shining, the countryside was less oppressive. For a moment he felt less worried. Then Holger Eriksson's murder rose up before him like a nightmare. But the fact that Gösta Runfeldt was also suspected missing didn't necessarily mean that anything else bad had happened. Although Wallander had no idea why Runfeldt would have ordered eavesdropping apparatus, it could be taken as a sign, paradoxically enough, that he was still alive. Wallander had entertained the thought that Runfeldt might have taken his own life. But he dismissed the notion. The joy that Vanja Andersson spoke of was no portent of a dramatic disappearance and subsequent suicide. As Wallander drove through the bright fall countryside he thought that sometimes he gave in to his inner demons much too easily.

He turned in at Holger Eriksson's place and parked. A man Wallander recognized as a reporter from *Arbetet* was walking toward him. Wallander was carrying Runfeldt's box under his arm. They said hello, and the reporter nodded at the box.

"Are you carrying the solution in there?"

"No, nothing like that."

"But honestly, how's it going?"

"There'll be a press conference on Monday. Until then we don't have much to say."

"But he was impaled on sharpened steel pipes?"

Wallander gave him an astonished look.

"Who said that?"

"One of your colleagues."

Wallander had a hard time believing this was true.

"That must be a misunderstanding. There weren't any steel pipes."

"But he was impaled?"

"That's correct."

"It sounds like some kind of torture chamber dug into a field in Skåne."

"Those are your words, not mine."

"What are your words, then?"

"That there will be a press conference on Monday."

The reporter shook his head.

"You've got to give me something."

"We're still in the preliminary stage of this investigation. We can confirm that a homicide has been committed. But we don't have any leads."

"Nothing?"

"Until further notice I have no comment."

The reporter reluctantly gave up. Wallander knew he would quote him accurately. He was one of the few reporters who never distorted any of Wallander's statements.

He went into the cobblestone courtyard. In the distance the abandoned plastic canopy fluttered down by the ditch. The crime scene tape was still there. A patrolman suddenly appeared near the tower. Wallander thought they could safely stop guarding the site now. Just as he got to the house the door opened. Nyberg stood there with plastic covers on his shoes.

"I saw you from the window," he said.

Wallander saw that Nyberg was in a good mood. That was a good omen for the day's work.

"I've got a box for you," said Wallander as he entered. "Take a look at this."

"Does it have something to do with Eriksson?"

"No, Runfeldt. The florist."

Wallander set the carton down on the desk. Nyberg moved the poem aside to make room to unpack the box. His comments were the same as Martinsson's. It was definitely bugging equipment. And it was state-of-the-art. Nyberg put on his glasses and searched for the manufacturer's stamp.

"It says Singapore. But it was probably made somewhere else."

"Where?"

"The U.S., or Israel."

"So why does it say Singapore?"

"Some of these manufacturers try to maintain as low a profile as possible. They're involved in one way or another with the international arms trade. And they don't reveal any secrets to each other unless they have to. The technical components are fabricated in various countries. Assembly is done somewhere else. And a third country might contribute the stamp of origin."

Wallander pointed at the apparatus.

"What could you use this for?"

"You could bug an apartment. Or a car."

Wallander shook his head in resignation.

"Gösta Runfeldt is a florist. What would he need this for?"

"Find him and ask him yourself," said Nyberg.

They put everything back in the box. Nyberg sniffled. Wallander saw he had a bad cold.

"Try and take it a little easier," he said. "You have to get some sleep sometime."

"It's that goddamn mud," said Nyberg. "I get sick from standing out in the rain. I don't understand why it should be so hard to design a portable rain shelter that would hold up under the weather conditions in Skåne."

"Write an article about it for *Swedish Police*," Wallander suggested.

"When am I going to have time for that?"

The question was left unanswered. They went through the house.

"I haven't found anything remarkable," said Nyberg. "At least not yet. But the house has a lot of nooks and crannies."

"I'll hang around for a while," Wallander said. "I want to take a look around."

Nyberg went back to his technicians. Wallander sat down by the window. A ray of sun warmed his hand. He was still tan.

He looked around the large room. He thought about the ditch. What kind of man writes poems about a woodpecker? He picked up the sheet of paper and read again what Holger Eriksson had written. He could see that there were some beautiful turns of phrase. Wallander himself had been known to write verse in the autograph books of his female classmates when he was young. But he had never really read poetry. Linda had complained that there were never any books in the house when she was growing up. Wallander couldn't argue with her. He let his eyes scan the walls.

A wealthy car dealer, almost eighty years old. Who writes poems. And is interested in birds. So much so that he goes out late at night and stares at the invisible migrating night birds. Or in the early dawn.

His eyes kept wandering. The ray of sunshine was still warming his left hand. Suddenly he remembered something from the report of the break-in he had dug out of the archives.

According to Eriksson, the front door was forced open with a crowbar or the like. But nothing seemed to have been stolen. There was something else. Wallander searched his memory. Then he remembered. The safe was untouched. He stood up and went to find Nyberg, who was in one of the bedrooms. Wallander stopped in the doorway.

"Did you find a safe anywhere?"

"No."

"We have to find it," said Wallander. "Let's start looking."

Nyberg was on his knees next to the bed. When he stood up, Wallander saw that he had put on knee protectors.

"Are you sure?" asked Nyberg. "I would have found it."

"Yes, I am. Somewhere there's a safe."

They searched the house methodically. It took them half an hour before they found it. One of Nyberg's assistants discovered it behind a false oven door in a serving area of the kitchen. The door could be swung open laterally. The safe was built into the wall and had a combination lock.

"I think I know where the combination is," said Nyberg. "Eriksson was probably afraid his memory might fail him in his old age."

Wallander followed Nyberg back to the desk. In one of the drawers Nyberg remembered seeing a little box containing a slip of paper with a row of numbers on it. When they tried it on the safe, the tumblers clicked into place. Nyberg stepped aside so Wallander could open it.

Wallander peered into the safe. Then he gave a start. He took a step back and trod on Nyberg's toes.

"What is it?" Nyberg asked.

Wallander nodded for him to look. Nyberg leaned forward. He gave a start too, but less violently than Wallander.

"It looks like a human head," said Nyberg.

He turned to one of his assistants, who had blanched when he heard that. Nyberg asked him to get a flashlight. They stood there waiting uneasily. Wallander was getting dizzy. He took a few deep breaths. Nyberg gave him a curious look. The flashlight arrived. Nyberg shone it into the safe. There really was a head in there, cut off at the neck. The eyes were open. But it was no ordinary head. It was shrunken and dried. Neither Nyberg nor Wallander could tell whether it was an ape or a human. Besides the head there were only a few pocket calendars and notebooks. At that moment Ann-Britt Höglund entered the room. From the tense atmosphere she knew that something had happened. She didn't ask what, but stood quietly in the background.

"Should we call in the photographer?" asked Nyberg.

"No, just take a few pictures yourself," replied Wallander. "The most important thing is to get it out of the safe."

He turned to Höglund.

"There's a head in there," he said. "A shrunken human head. Or maybe it's an ape."

She leaned forward and looked. Wallander noticed that she didn't flinch. They left the serving area to give Nyberg and his assistants room to work. Wallander could feel himself sweating.

"A safe with a head in it," she said. "Possibly shrunken, possibly an ape. How do we interpret that?"

"Holger Eriksson must have been a much more complex man than we imagined," said Wallander.

They waited for Nyberg and his team to empty the safe. It was nine o'clock. Wallander told Höglund about the package from the mail-order company in Borås. She looked through the box and asked what it could mean. They decided that someone ought to go through Gösta Runfeldt's apartment more methodically than Wallander had had time to do. It would be best if Nyberg could spare some of his techs. Höglund called the station and was told that the Danish police had reported that no male bodies had drifted ashore recently. The Malmö police and the Sea Rescue Unit had no information on floaters, either.

At nine thirty Nyberg came out carrying the head and the other things he had found in the safe. Wallander moved the poem about the woodpecker aside, and Nyberg set down the head. In the safe there had also been some old diaries, a notebook, and a box with a medal in it. But it was the dried shrunken head that captured their full attention. In the daylight there was no longer any doubt. It was a human head. A black head. Maybe a child. Or at least a young person. When Nyberg looked at it with a magnifying glass he could see that moths had gotten at the skin. Wallander grimaced with disgust when Nyberg leaned close to the head and sniffed it.

"Who do we know that might know about shrunken heads?" asked Wallander.

"The Ethnographic Museum," said Nyberg. "These days it's called the Museum of World Peoples. The National Police Board issued a little booklet that's actually quite excellent. It lists where you can find information on the most peculiar phenomena."

"Then we'll get in touch with them," said Wallander. "It'd be great if we could find someone who could answer our questions now, during the holidays."

Nyberg began wrapping up the head in a plastic bag. Wallander and Höglund sat down at the desk and started examining the other items. The medal, which rested on a little silk pillow, was foreign. It had an inscription in French. None of them could read it. Wallander knew it was no use to ask Nyberg. His English was poor, his French no doubt nonexistent. They started going through the books. The pocket calendars were from the early sixties. On the half-title page they could make out a name: *Harald Berggren.* Wallander shot Höglund a questioning glance. She shook her head. That name hadn't come up in the investigation so far. There were very few entries in the calendars. A few times of day. Initials. In one place the initials *HE.* It was dated February 10, 1960—more than thirty years ago.

Wallander began to leaf through the notebook. It was a diary, crammed with entries. The first one was made in November of 1960, the last in July of 1961. The handwriting was cramped and hard to read. He realized he had forgotten to keep his appointment with the optician. He borrowed a magnifying glass from Nyberg and read a line here and there.

"It's about the Belgian Congo," he said. "Somebody who was there during the war. As a soldier."

"Holger Eriksson or Harald Berggren?"

"Harald Berggren. Whoever that is."

He put down the book. He knew it might be important and he'd have to read it carefully. They looked at each other. Wallander knew they were thinking the same thing.

"A shrunken human head," he said. "And a diary about a war in Africa."

"A pungee pit," said Höglund. "A reminder of the war. In my mind shrunken heads and impaled people go together."

"Mine too," said Wallander. "The question is whether we've found a lead or not."

"Who is Harald Berggren?"

"That's one of the first things we have to find out."

Wallander recalled that at this moment Martinsson was presumably visiting a person in Svarte who had known Holger Eriksson for many years. He asked Höglund to call him on his cell phone. Starting right now, the name Harald Berggren would be mentioned and examined in all conceivable connections. She punched in the number. Waited. Then she shook her head.

"His phone isn't working," she said.

Wallander was annoyed.

"How are we supposed to conduct an investigation if we aren't all accessible?"

He knew he often broke the accessibility rule himself. He was probably the hardest to reach of any of them. At least sometimes. But she didn't say a word.

"I'll find him," she said, getting to her feet.

"Harald Berggren," said Wallander. "The name is important. That goes for everyone."

"I'll see that word gets out," she replied.

When Wallander was alone in the room, he turned on the desk

lamp. He was just about to open the diary when he noticed that something was stuck inside the leather cover. Carefully he coaxed out a photograph. It was black-and-white, well-thumbed and stained. One corner was torn off. The photo showed three men posing for an unknown photographer. They were young, laughing toward the camera, and dressed in some sort of uniform. Wallander remembered the photo he had seen in Gösta Runfeldt's apartment, where he stood somewhere in a tropical landscape, surrounded by giant orchids. The landscape in this picture wasn't Sweden either. He studied the photograph with the magnifying glass. The sun must have been high in the sky when the picture was taken. The men were very tanned. Their shirts were unbuttoned and the sleeves rolled up. There were rifles at their feet. The men were leaning against an oddly shaped boulder. Behind the boulder there was open countryside with no distinguishable features. The ground was crushed gravel or sand.

He looked at their faces. The men were in their early twenties. He turned the picture over. He imagined that it was taken at about the same time the diary entries were made. Early sixties. If nothing else, the men's haircuts would attest to that. None of them had long hair. Their age meant that he could eliminate Holger Eriksson. In 1960 he would have been between forty and fifty years old.

Wallander put down the photo and opened one of the desk drawers. He remembered that he had seen some loose passport photos in an envelope there earlier. He placed one of the photos of Holger Eriksson on the desk. It was taken relatively recently. On the back it was dated 1989 in pencil. Holger Eriksson, age seventy-three. Wallander stared at his face. The pointed nose, the thin lips. He tried to imagine away the wrinkles and see a younger face. He went back to the photo with the three men posing. He studied their faces one by one. The man on the left had some features that resembled Holger Eriksson. Wallander leaned back in his chair and closed his eyes.

Holger Eriksson lies dead in a ditch. In his safe we find a shrunken head, a diary, and a photograph.

Suddenly Wallander sat up straight in the chair, his eyes wide. He was thinking about the break-in that Eriksson had reported the year before.

The safe was untouched. Let's assume, thought Wallander, that whoever broke in had an equally hard time finding the hidden safe. And assume the contents were the same then as they are now. That's precisely what the thief was looking for. He failed and apparently didn't repeat the attempt. But Holger Eriksson died a year later.

He realized that his thoughts made sense, at least partially. But there was one point that presented a serious contradiction to his attempt to find a link between the two events. After Holger Eriksson's death, his safe would be found sooner or later. If by no one else, then by one of the executors of the estate. The thief must have been aware of this.

Still, this was something. A lead.

He looked at the photo one more time. The men were smiling. They had been smiling in this picture for over thirty years. Wallander wondered fleetingly whether the photographer could have been Holger Eriksson. But Eriksson had successfully sold cars in Ystad, Tomelilla, and Sjöbo. He hadn't taken part in some far-off African war. Or had he? They still knew about only a fraction of his life.

Wallander pensively regarded the diary lying in front of him. He slipped the photograph into his jacket pocket, picked up the book, and went in to Nyberg, who was busy with a technical examination of the bathroom.

"I'm taking this diary. I'll leave the pocket calendars."

"You think there's something there?" asked Nyberg.

"I think so," said Wallander. "If anyone wants me I'll be at home."

When he came out into the courtyard he could see that some patrol officers were busy taking down the crime-scene tape by the ditch. The rain canopy was already gone.

An hour later he was sitting at his kitchen table. He opened the diary.

The first entry was from November 20, 1960.

Chapter Ten

It took Wallander almost six hours to read Harald Berggren's diary from cover to cover. Of course, he was interrupted several times. The telephone rang again and again. Just after four in the afternoon, Ann-Britt dropped by for a quick visit. Wallander tried to keep the interruptions brief. The diary was one of the most fascinating yet frightening things he had ever come across. It was a record of several years in a man's life, and for Wallander it was like stepping into an utterly foreign world. Although Harald Berggren, whoever he was, couldn't be described as a master of language—in fact, he often expressed himself sentimentally or with an uncertainty that sometimes gave way to helplessness—the entries, his experiences, had a force that was always stronger than the linguistic difficulties he managed to struggle through. Wallander sensed that it was important for them to decipher the diary in order to understand what had happened to Holger Eriksson. And yet inside himself he could hear an admonishing voice: This could also lead them in a completely wrong direction. Wallander knew that most truths were both expected and unexpected at the same time. It was simply a matter of knowing how to interpret the connection. Besides, one criminal investigation never resembled another, at least not deep down, once they got past the superficial similarities.

Harald Berggren's diary was a war journal. As Wallander read it, he learned the names of the other two men in the photograph. But when he had finished the book, he still couldn't tell exactly which was which. The picture was of Harald Berggren flanked by an Irishman, Terry O'Banion, and a Frenchman, Simon Marchand. It was taken by a man called Raul whose nationality was unknown. They had been mercenaries in a war in Africa for more than a year. At the beginning of the diary, Berggren described how somewhere in Stockholm he had heard about a café in Brussels where contacts could be made with the mysterious world of mercenaries. He mentioned that he first heard of it around New Year's, 1958. He didn't write anything about what eventually drove him to go there a few years later. Berggren stepped into his own diary out of nowhere: no past, no parents, no background. The only sure things were that he was twenty-three years old and desperate over Hitler's defeat in the war that had ended fifteen years earlier.

Wallander stopped at this point. That was Berggren's exact word: *desperate.* Wallander read the passage again: *the desperate defeat that Hitler was subjected to by his treacherous generals.* Wallander tried to understand. The use of the word *desperate* said something crucial about Berggren. Was he expressing a political conviction? Or was he high-strung and confused? Wallander found no clues to indicate any of these things. Harald Berggren didn't mention it again either.

In June of 1960 he had left Sweden by train and stayed a day in Copenhagen so he could go to Tivoli. There he danced in the warm summer night with a girl named Irene. He noted that she was *sweet but much too tall.* The next day he was in Hamburg. The day after that—June 12, 1960—he arrived in Brussels. After about a month he achieved his goal: a contract as a mercenary. He noted proudly that now he was drawing a salary and would be going off to war. Wallander thought he sounded as though he was nearing the goal of his dreams. He wrote all this down much later, under the date November 20, 1960. In this first entry in the diary, which was also the longest, he summarized the events that had led him to the place where he now found himself. He was in Africa. When Wallander read the name of the place, Omerutu, he got up and looked for his old school atlas, which he found at the bottom of a cardboard box in the back of a closet. Omerutu wasn't on the map. Still, he left the old map open on the kitchen table as he continued reading the diary.

Together with Terry O'Banion and Simon Marchand, Berggren joined a fighting company that consisted solely of mercenaries. Their leader, about whom Berggren was quite reticent, was a Canadian who was never called anything but Sam. Berggren didn't seem particularly interested in what the war was actually about. Wallander himself was extremely hazy about the war in what was then called the Belgian Congo, as it was on his old map. Berggren didn't seem to have any need to justify his presence as a hired soldier. He noted merely that they were fighting for freedom. But whose? That was never made clear. On several occasions, including December 11, 1960 and January 19, 1961, he noted that he would not hesitate to use his weapon if he wound up in a combat situation with Swedish UN soldiers confronting him.

Berggren also made a careful note of every time he received his pay. He did some minor bookkeeping on the last day of each month. How much he was paid, how much he spent, and how much he saved. He also noted with satisfaction every item of booty he managed to grab. In a particularly unpleasant section of the diary, in which the mercenaries arrived at an abandoned, burned-out plantation, he described the half-rotted corpses, swarming with flies, of the Belgian plantation owner and his wife. They lay in their beds with their arms and legs hacked off. The stench was unbelievable. But the mercenaries still searched the house and found several diamonds and pieces of gold jewelry, which a Lebanese jeweler later appraised at more than 20,000 Swedish kronor.

Berggren then noted that the war was justified because the profits were good. In a personal reflection which had no counterpart elsewhere in the diary, he asked himself whether he could have achieved the same wealth if he had stayed in Sweden working as an auto mechanic. His answer was no. Living that sort of life, he never would have advanced in any way. With great zeal he continued to participate in his war.

Apart from his obsession with making money and keeping precise accounts, Berggren was also meticulous about his other entries.

Harald Berggren killed people in his African war. He wrote down the times and the body count. Whenever possible he also indicated whether he later had a chance to approach the people he had killed. He noted whether they were men or women or children. He also recorded coolly where the shots he fired had struck them. Wallander read these regularly recurring passages with growing distaste and anger. Harald Berggren had nothing to do with this war. He was paid to kill. It was unclear who was paying him. And the people he killed were seldom in uniform. The mercenaries raided villages that were thought to oppose the freedom they were supposedly fighting to preserve. They murdered and plundered and then retreated. They were a death squad, all Europeans, and they didn't regard the people they killed as equals. Berggren didn't hide his contempt for the blacks. He noted delightedly that they *ran like bewildered goats when we approached. But bullets fly faster than people can jump or run.*

At those lines Wallander almost threw the book across the room. But he forced himself to read on, after taking a break and washing his irritated eyes. More than ever he wished he had already gone to the optometrist and gotten the glasses he needed.

Harald Berggren killed an average of ten people a month, assuming he wasn't lying in his diary. After seven months of war he fell ill and was transported by airplane to a hospital in Léopoldville. He had contracted amoebic dysentery and was apparently quite sick for several weeks. The diary entries stopped completely during this period. By the time he was admitted to the hospital he had already killed more than fifty people in this war he was fighting instead of becoming an auto mechanic in Sweden.

When Berggren recovered, he returned to his company. A month later they were in Omerutu. They posed in front of a big boulder, which was not really a rock but a termite mound, and the unknown Raul took a picture of Berggren, Terry O'Banion, and Simon March- and. Wallander went over to the kitchen window with the photograph. He had never seen a termite mound before, but he understood that it was this very picture the diary was talking about. He returned to his reading.

Three weeks later they got caught in an ambush and Terry O'Banion was killed. They were forced to withdraw without planning the retreat. It turned into a panicked rout. Wallander tried to sense the fear in Harald Berggren. He was convinced it was there, but Berggren concealed it. He wrote only that they had buried their dead in the bush and marked their graves with simple wooden crosses. The war went on. On one occasion they used a group of apes for target practice. Another time they gathered crocodile eggs on the bank of a river. Berggren's savings were now up to almost 30,000 kronor.

But then, in the summer of 1961, everything was over. The end of the diary came unexpectedly. Wallander thought it must have been the same way for Harald Berggren. He must have imagined that this pe- culiar jungle war would go on forever. In his last entries he described how they fled the country at night, in a cargo plane with no lights. One of its engines started coughing just after they lifted off from the runway they had cleared in the bush. The diary ended abruptly, as though Berggren had grown tired of it, or else no longer had anything to say. It stopped with him on board the cargo plane, in the night, and Wallander didn't even find out where the plane was headed. Harald Berggren was flying through the African night, the engine noise died away, and he no longer existed.

It was now five in the afternoon. Wallander stretched and went out onto the balcony. A cloudy front was on its way in from the sea. It was going to rain again. He thought about what he had read. Why was the diary kept inside Eriksson's safe along with a shrunken human head? If Berggren was still alive, he would be at least fifty years old. Wallander felt cold standing out on the balcony. He went inside and shut the door. Then he sat down on the couch. His eyes hurt. Who was Berg- gren writing the diary for? Himself or someone else?

There was also something missing.

Wallander hadn't yet figured out what it was. A young man keeps a diary of a distant war. Often what he describes is rich in detail, but it is also constrained in some way. There was something missing. Something that Wallander couldn't read even between the lines.

Not until Höglund rang the doorbell for the second time did it dawn on him what it was. He saw her in the doorway and suddenly knew what was missing in everything Berggren had written. The diary described a world completely dominated by men. The women Berggren wrote about were either dead or fleeing in panic. Except for Irene, the woman he met at Tivoli in Copenhagen. The one who was sweet but much too tall. Otherwise he didn't mention any women. He wrote about furloughs in various cities in the Congo, about how he got drunk and got into fights. But there were no women.

Wallander couldn't help thinking that this was significant somehow. Harald Berggren was a young man when he went off to Africa. The war was an adventure. In a young man's world, women are an important part of the adventure.

He was starting to wonder. But for the time being he kept his thoughts to himself.

Höglund had come to tell him that she had gone through Gösta Runfeldt's apartment along with one of Nyberg's techs. The result was negative. They had found nothing that would explain why he had bought bugging equipment.

"Gösta Runfeldt's world consists of orchids," she said. "I get the impression of a kindly and intense widower."

"His wife seems to have drowned," said Wallander.

"She was quite beautiful," said Höglund. "I saw their wedding picture."

"Maybe we ought to find out what happened," said Wallander. "Sooner or later."

"Martinsson and Svedberg are working on contacting his children."

Wallander had already talked to Martinsson on the phone. He had been in touch with Runfeldt's daughter. She was utterly baffled by the idea that her father might have disappeared on purpose. She was extremely worried. She knew he was supposed to fly to Nairobi and had assumed that's where he was.

Wallander agreed. Starting now, Gösta Runfeldt's disappearance was an important matter for the police.

"There's too much that doesn't add up," he said. "Svedberg was supposed to call when he got hold of the son. He was apparently out at a farm somewhere in Hälsingland where there wasn't any phone."

They decided to hold a meeting of the investigative team early Sunday afternoon. Höglund promised to make the arrangements. Then Wallander told her about the contents of the diary. He took his time and tried to be thorough. Telling her about it was like reviewing it in his own mind.

"Harald Berggren," she said when he was through. "Could he be the one?"

"I don't know, but at any rate, earlier in his life he committed atrocities on a regular basis and for money," said Wallander. "The diary is horrifying reading. Maybe these days he's living his life in fear that the contents might be divulged."

"In other words, we'll have to find him," she said. "That's the first thing to do. The question is where to start looking."

Wallander nodded.

"The diary was in Eriksson's safe. For the moment that's the clearest lead we have. Still, we have to keep investigating with an open mind."

"You know that's impossible," she said, surprised. "When we find a clue it shapes the search."

I'm just reminding you," he replied evasively, "that we can be wrong in spite of everything."

She was just about to leave when the telephone rang. It was Svedberg, who had gotten hold of Gösta Runfeldt's son.

"He was pretty upset," said Svedberg. "He wanted to jump on a plane and come here right away."

"When was the last time he heard from his father?"

"A few days before he left for Nairobi. Or was supposed to leave, I should say. Everything was normal. According to the son, his father always looked forward to his trips."

Wallander nodded.

"So, we know that, anyway."

Then he handed the phone to Höglund, who set a time for the meeting of the investigative team the next day. Wallander didn't remember until she hung up that he had a note that was written to Svedberg. A report of a woman acting strange at the Ystad maternity ward.

Höglund hurried home to her children. When Wallander was alone he called his father. They decided he would come out on Sunday morning. The pictures that his father had taken with his ancient camera had been developed.

Wallander devoted the rest of Saturday evening to writing up a summary of Holger Eriksson's murder. As he worked he mulled over Gösta Runfeldt's disappearance in his mind. He was uneasy and restless and had a hard time concentrating.

His foreboding that they were still just skirting something very big was growing stronger all the time.

The feeling of anxiety wouldn't let up. By nine o'clock he was so tired that he couldn't think any longer. He shoved his notebook aside and called his daughter Linda. The ringing of the phone vanished into a vacuum. She wasn't home. He put on one of his heavier jackets and walked downtown, where he ate dinner at a Chinese restaurant on the square. The place was unusually packed. He reminded himself that it was Saturday night, and indulged in a carafe of wine, which gave him an instant headache. When he went home later it had started to rain again.

That night he dreamed about Harald Berggren's diary. He was in a huge dark place, it was very hot, and somewhere in the dense darkness Berggren was pointing a gun at him.

He woke up early.

The rain had stopped; it was clear again. At seven fifteen he got in his car and drove out to visit his father in Löderup. In the morning light, the curves of the countryside were sharp and clear. Wallander thought he would try to tempt his father and Gertrud to come along with him down to the beach. Soon it would be too cold to go anymore.

He thought with displeasure about the dream he'd had. As he drove he also thought that at the investigative meeting that afternoon they had to make a timetable for the order in which various questions had to be answered. Locating Harald Berggren was important. Especially if it turned out that they were following a trail that led nowhere.

When Wallander turned into the courtyard, his father was standing on the steps waiting for him. They hadn't seen each other since they'd gotten back from Rome. They went into the kitchen, where Gertrud had set out some breakfast. They looked through the photos his father had taken. Many of them were blurry, and in some cases the subject had wound up partly outside the frame. But since his father was both pleased and proud of them, Wallander merely nodded appreciatively.

There was one picture that stood out from the rest. It was taken by a waiter on their last night in Rome. They had just finished their dinner. Wallander and his father were squeezed close together. A half-empty bottle of red wine stood on the white tablecloth. Both of them were smiling straight at the camera.

For an instant the faded photograph from Harald Berggren's diary flashed into Wallander's mind. But he pushed it away. Right now he wanted to look at himself and his father. He realized that the picture confirmed once and for all what he had discovered on the trip.

They resembled each other in appearance. They were even a lot alike.

"I'd like to have a copy of this picture," said Wallander.

"I've already taken care of it," his father replied contentedly. He handed him an envelope containing the picture.

After lunch they went over to his father's studio. He was just finishing up work on a landscape with a grouse in it. The bird was always the last thing he painted.

"How many pictures have you painted in your life?" Wallander asked.

"You ask me that every time you come here," said his father. "How am I supposed to keep track? What would be the point? The main thing is that they're all the same. Every last one of them."

Long ago Wallander had realized that there was only one explanation for why his father kept painting the same motif over and over. It was his way of keeping at bay all the things that were changing around him. In his paintings he even controlled the path of the sun. It was motionless, locked in time, always at the same height above the forested ridges.

"It was a great trip," Wallander said as he looked at his father, who was busy mixing colors together.

"I told you it would be," said his father. "Otherwise you would have gone to your grave without ever seeing the Sistine Chapel."

Wallander wondered briefly whether he should ask his father now about the solitary walk he took on that night in Rome. But he decided not to. It was nobody's business but his father's.

Wallander suggested that they drive down to the sea. To his surprise his father agreed at once. Gertrud preferred to stay home. At just after ten they got into Wallander's car and drove down to Sandhammaren. There was almost no breeze. They headed for the beach. His father took him by the arm when they passed the last cliff. The sea spread itself out before them. The beach was almost deserted. In the distance they could see some people playing with a dog. That was all.

"It's beautiful," said his father.

Wallander sneaked a look at him. It was as though the trip to Rome had made a fundamental change in his mood. Maybe it would also end up having a positive effect on the insidious disease the doctors had discovered his father was suffering from. But he realized that he would never fully understand what the trip had meant to his father. It had been the journey of a lifetime, and Wallander had been given the honor of accompanying him.

Rome was his father's Mecca.

They took a long walk on the beach. Wallander thought that maybe now he could talk to him about the old days. But there was no hurry.

Suddenly his father stopped short.

"What is it?" Wallander asked.

"I've been feeling bad for a few days," he said. "But it'll pass."

"You want me to drive you back home?"

"I said it'll pass."

Wallander could hear his father starting to fall back into his old bad habit of replying peevishly to his questions. He kept his mouth shut.

They continued their walk. A flight of migratory birds passed overhead, flying west. They were on the beach more than two hours before his father thought they had walked enough. Wallander, who had forgotten the time, knew that now he'd have to hurry so he wouldn't be late for the meeting at the police station.

After he dropped off his father in Löderup he returned to Ystad with a feeling of relief. Even though his father couldn't escape his insidious disease, the trip to Rome had obviously meant a lot to him. Maybe now they could finally regain the contact they had lost many years before when Wallander decided to become a policeman. His father had never accepted his choice of profession. But he hadn't ever managed to explain what he had against it, either. On the way back Wallander thought that now he finally might get an answer to the question he had spent far too much of his life worrying about.

At two thirty they closed the door to the conference room. Even Chief Holgersson showed up. When Wallander saw her he remembered that he still hadn't called Per Åkeson. He wrote a reminder to himself in his notebook so he wouldn't forget again.

Then he reported on finding the shrunken head and Harald Berggren's diary. When he finished there was general agreement that this really did look like a lead. After they divided up the various tasks, Wallander shifted the discussion to Gösta Runfeldt.

"We have to assume that something has happened to Gösta Runfeldt," he said. "We can't rule out either an accident or foul play. Naturally there's always the possibility that it's a voluntary disappearance. On the other hand, I think we can discount the existence of any sort of connection between Holger Eriksson and Gösta Runfeldt. There might be one, but it's highly unlikely. There's nothing to indicate it."

Wallander wanted to end the meeting as soon as possible. After all, it was Sunday. He knew that all his colleagues were putting a lot of effort into completing their assignments. But he also knew that sometimes the best way to work meant taking a break. The hours he had spent with his father that morning had given him renewed energy. When he left the police station just after four o'clock, he felt more rested than he had in days. The anxiety inside him had also abated for a while.

If they did find Harald Berggren, there was a good chance they would find the solution. The murder was too well planned not to have an extremely unusual perpetrator.

Harald Berggren might be just that perpetrator.

On his way home to Mariagatan Wallander stopped and bought groceries in a store that was open on Sundays. He couldn't resist the impulse to rent a video. It was a classic, "Waterloo Bridge." He had seen it in a theater in Malmö with Mona, some time in the early years of their marriage. But he had only a vague recollection of what it was about.

He was in the middle of the movie when Linda called. When he heard it was her he said he'd call her right back. He turned off the video and sat down in the kitchen. They talked for almost half an hour. She didn't say a word about feeling guilty that she hadn't called in such a long time. He didn't mention it either. He knew they were a lot alike. They could both be absentminded, but they knew how to concentrate if there was a task to be done. She told him that everything was going fine; she was waiting tables at a lunch restaurant on Kungsholmen and going to classes at a theater school. He didn't ask her about that. He had the definite impression that she still doubted her talent.

Just before they finished their conversation, he told her about his morning on the beach.

"It sounds like you had a great day together," she said.

"We did. It feels like something has changed."

When they hung up, Wallander went out on the balcony. There was still almost no wind, a rare occurrence in Skåne.

For a moment all his worries were gone. Now he had to get some sleep. Tomorrow he'd have to get down to work again.

When he turned out the light in the kitchen, the diary was in his mind again.

He wondered where Harald Berggren was at that very moment.

Chapter Eleven

When Wallander woke up on Monday morning, October 3rd, he had a feeling that he ought to have another talk with Sven Tyrén right away. Whether he had dreamed about this insight he couldn't tell, but he was positive. That's why he didn't even wait until he got to the station. As he waited for his coffee to brew he called information and got Tyrén's home phone number. Tyrén's wife answered the phone; her husband had already left. Wallander took down his cell-phone number. The connection was crackling and raspy when Tyrén answered. In the background Wallander could hear the muffled sound of the tanker truck's diesel engine.

Tyrén told him he was on the road outside Högestad. He had two deliveries to make before he went back to the terminal in Malmö. Wallander asked him to come to the Ystad police station as soon as he could. When Tyrén asked whether they had caught the person who killed Holger Eriksson, Wallander told him it was just a routine conversation. They were still in the early stages of the investigation, he explained. They were bound to catch the murderer. It might happen soon, but it could also take time. Sven Tyrén promised to be at the station by nine.

"Please don't park in front of the driveway," added Wallander. "It causes problems."

Tyrén muttered something inaudible in reply.

At quarter past seven Wallander arrived at the station. Walking toward the glass doors, he changed his mind and turned left, toward the prosecutor's office, which had its own entrance. He knew that the person he wanted to see usually got to work as early as he did. When he knocked on the door, a voice told him to come in.

Per Åkeson was sitting behind his desk, which was piled high with work as always. The entire office was a chaos of papers and file folders. But appearances were deceiving. Åkeson was an extraordinarily efficient and methodical prosecutor, and Wallander enjoyed working with him. They had known each other for a long time, and over the years they had developed a relationship that went beyond the purely professional. Sometimes they would share confidences and seek each other's advice or help. Still, there was an invisible boundary between them that they never overstepped. They would never really be close friends; they were not enough alike for that.

Per Åkeson nodded amiably when Wallander stepped into the room. He got up and moved a box of documents for a case that was coming up in district court that day, making room on a chair. Wallander sat down. Åkeson told the switchboard to hold his calls.

"I've been waiting to hear from you," he said. "Thanks for the card, by the way."

Wallander had forgotten about the postcard he had sent Åkeson from Rome. He seemed to recall it was a view of the Forum Romanum.

"It was a great trip. For both of us."

"I've never been to Rome. How does that proverb go? See Rome and then die? Or is it Naples?"

Wallander shook his head. He didn't know. "I'd been hoping for a calm autumn. So I come home and find an old man impaled in a ditch."

Åkeson grimaced. "I've seen some of the photos. And Chief Holgersson told me about it. Have you got anything to go on?"

"Maybe," said Wallander and gave him a brief report on what they had found in Holger Eriksson's safe. He knew that Åkeson respected his ability to lead an investigation. He seldom disagreed with Wallander about his conclusions or the way he handled a case.

"Of course it sounds like pure insanity to set out sharpened bamboo stakes in a ditch," said Åkeson. "On the other hand, these days it's getting harder and harder to distinguish between what's insane and what's normal."

"How's it going with Uganda?" asked Wallander.

"I assume you mean the Sudan," said Åkeson.

Wallander knew that Åkeson had applied for service with the UN High Commission on Refugees. He wanted to get away from Ystad for a while. See something else before it was too late. Åkeson was several years older than Wallander. He was over fifty.

"The Sudan," said Wallander. "Have you talked about it with your wife?"

Åkeson nodded.

"I got up the courage last week. She was considerably more understanding than I could have hoped. I got the distinct feeling she wouldn't mind getting me out of the house for a while. I'm still waiting for official notification, but I'd be surprised if I didn't get the post. As you know, I have my connections."

Over the years Wallander had learned that Åkeson had a highly developed knack for acquiring information under the table. Wallander had no idea how he did it. Åkeson was always well informed, for instance, about what was being discussed in the various committees in Parliament, or in the most elite and confidential circles of the National Police Board.

"If all goes well, I'll be leaving at New Year's," he said. "I'll be away for at least two years."

"Let's hope we solve this Eriksson case before then. Do you have any directives you want to give me?"

"You're the one who should tell me what you want, if there is anything."

Wallander thought a moment before replying. "Not yet. Chief Holgersson mentioned that we ought to call in Mats Ekholm again. You remember him from this summer, the guy who does psychological profiles? He hunts crazy people by trying to catalog them. I think he's quite talented."

Per Åkeson remembered him well.

"But I still think we should wait," Wallander went on. "I'm not so sure we're dealing with a crazy person."

"If you think we should wait, then so be it," said Åkeson, getting to his feet. He pointed at the box.

"I have a particularly complicated case today," he excused himself. "I have to prepare."

Wallander got ready to leave.

"What is it you're actually going to do in the Sudan?" he asked. "Do refugees really need Swedish legal help?"

"Refugees need all the help they can get," replied Åkeson as he accompanied Wallander to the lobby. "Not just in Sweden."

Suddenly he said, "I was in Stockholm for a few days while you were in Rome. I ran into Anette Brolin. She asked me to say hello to everyone down here. But especially to you."

Wallander gave him a doubtful look, but he didn't say a word. A few years before, Anette Brolin had filled in for Åkeson. Despite the fact that she was married, Wallander had made personal advances that did not end well. It was something he preferred to forget.

He walked out of the prosecutor's wing. There was a gusty wind blowing. The sky was gray. Wallander guessed that it was no more than 8° Celsius. In the entryway to the police station he ran into Svedberg, who was on his way out. He remembered he had a note that belonged to him.

"I took one of your notes with me by mistake from a meeting the other day," he said.

Svedberg looked baffled. "I didn't notice anything missing."

"It was something about a woman behaving strangely in the maternity ward at the hospital."

"Oh, you can toss that," said Svedberg. "It was just someone who saw a ghost."

"Toss it yourself," said Wallander. "I'll put it on your desk."

"We're still talking to people in the area around Eriksson's farm," said Svedberg. "I'm also going to have a talk with the rural-delivery mailman."

Wallander nodded. They went their separate ways.

As Wallander entered his office he had already forgotten about Svedberg's note. He took Harald Berggren's diary from his inside jacket pocket and put it in a desk drawer. He left the photograph lying on his desk of the three men posing by the termite mound. As he waited for Sven Tyrén he read quickly through a stack of papers the other investigators had left for him. At quarter to nine he went to get some coffee. Höglund passed him in the hall and told him that Gösta Runfeldt's disappearance had now been formally recorded and was being given priority.

"I spoke to one of Runfeldt's neighbors," she said. "A high-school teacher who seemed extremely credible. He claimed he had heard Runfeldt in his apartment on Tuesday night. But not after that."

"Which indicates he left that night," said Wallander. "But not for Nairobi."

"I asked the neighbor whether he had noticed anything unusual about Runfeldt. But he seems to have been a reserved man with regular, discreet habits. Polite but no more than that. And he seldom had any visitors. The only thing out of the ordinary was that Runfeldt sometimes came home late at night. This teacher lives in the apartment below Runfeldt's, and the building is not well insulated. I think we can believe what he says."

Wallander stood there with his coffee cup in his hand, thinking about what she had said.

"We have to figure out what the stuff in that box means," he said. "It would be great if someone could call the mail-order company today. I also hope our colleagues in Borås have been informed. What was the name of that company? 'Secure'? Nyberg knows. We have to find out if Runfeldt bought other things from them. He must have placed the order because he was going to use it for something."

"Bugging equipment," she said. "Fingerprints. Who's interested in that? Who uses things like that?"

"We do."

"But who else?"

Wallander saw that she was thinking of something in particular.

"Of course a bugging device could be used for unauthorized purposes."

"I was thinking more of the fingerprints."

Wallander nodded. Now he got it.

"A private investigator," he said. "A private eye. The thought crossed my mind too. But Runfeldt is a florist who devotes his life to orchids."

"It was just an idea," she said. "I'll call that mail-order company myself."

Wallander went back to his office. The telephone rang. It was Ebba. Sven Tyrén was waiting in the lobby.

"He didn't park his truck across the driveway, did he?" Wallander asked. "Hansson will have a fit."

"I don't see a truck," said Ebba. "Are you coming to get him? And Martinsson wants to talk to you."

"Where is he?"

"In his office, I should think."

"Ask Tyrén to wait a few minutes while I talk to Martinsson."

Martinsson was on the phone when Wallander walked in. He cut his conversation short. Wallander assumed his wife had called. She talked to Martinsson innumerable times every day, nobody knew what about.

"I got in touch with the forensic medicine division in Lund," Martinsson said. "They have some preliminary results. The problem is, they're having a hard time determining what we most want to know."

"Time of death?"

Martinsson nodded.

"None of the stakes went through his heart. And none of the main arteries was perforated. That means he could have hung there for quite a while before he died. The immediate cause of death can be defined as drowning."

"What's that supposed to mean?" Wallander asked in surprise. "He was hanging in a ditch, right? He couldn't have drowned there."

"The doctor I talked to was full of gruesome details," said Martinsson. "He told me that Eriksson's lungs were so full of blood that finally he couldn't breathe. Technically, he drowned."

"We have to find out when he died," said Wallander. "Call them back. They have to tell us something."

"I'll see to it you get the report as soon as it comes in."

"I'll believe it when I see it. Considering how stuff keeps disappearing around here."

He didn't mean to criticize Martinsson. When Wallander was out in the corridor he realized that his words could have been misunderstood. But by then it was too late to do anything about it. He went out to the lobby and greeted Sven Tyrén, who was sitting on a vinyl sofa and staring at the floor. He was unshaven and had bloodshot eyes. The smell of oil and gasoline was strong. They went to Wallander's office.

"Why haven't you arrested whoever killed Holger?" Tyrén asked.

Wallander could feel himself getting annoyed again at Tyrén's attitude. "If you can tell me who did it, I'll drive out and arrest him right now," he said.

"I'm not a cop."

"You don't have to tell me that. If you were, you wouldn't have asked such a dumb question."

When Tyrén opened his mouth to protest, Wallander held up his hand. "At the moment I'm the one asking the questions."

"Am I under suspicion for something?"

"Not a thing. But I'll ask the questions. And you have to answer them. That's all."

Tyrén shrugged his shoulders. Wallander suddenly sensed that he was on his guard. He could feel his police instincts sharpening. His first question was the only one he had prepared.

"Harald Berggren," he said. "Does that name mean anything to you?"

Tyrén looked at him.

"I don't know any Harald Berggren. Should I?"

"Are you sure?"

"Yes, I am."

"Think!"

"I don't have to think. If I'm sure, I'm sure."

Wallander shoved the photograph over and pointed. Tyrén leaned forward.

"See if you recognize any of these men. Look closely. Take your time."

Tyrén picked up the photo in his greasy fingers. He looked at it for a long time. Wallander was beginning to feel vaguely hopeful when Tyrén put it back on the table.

"I've never seen any of them before."

"You looked at it for a long time. Did you think you recognized one of them?"

"You told me to take my time. Who are they? Where was it taken?"

"Are you sure?"

"I've never seen them before."

Wallander sensed that Tyrén was telling the truth.

"They're mercenaries," he said. "It was taken in Africa over thirty years ago."

"The Foreign Legion?"

"Not exactly, but almost. Soldiers who fight for whoever pays the most."

"Gotta make a living."

Wallander gave him a puzzled look, but he didn't ask what Tyrén actually meant.

"Did you ever hear that Holger Eriksson may have had contact with mercenaries?"

"Holger Eriksson sold cars. I thought you knew that."

"Holger Eriksson also wrote poems and watched birds," said Wallander, not hiding his irritation. "Have you or have you not ever heard Eriksson talk about mercenaries? Or about a war in Africa?"

Tyrén stared at him. "Why do cops have to be so unpleasant?"

"Because we deal with unpleasant things," replied Wallander. "Starting right now, please just answer my questions. That's all. Don't make any personal comments that have nothing to do with the case."

"What happens if I do?"

Wallander felt on the verge of misconduct. But he didn't care. There was something about this man across the desk that he just couldn't stand.

"Then I'd have to call you in for a talk every single day for the foreseeable future. And I'd have to request a warrant from the prosecutor to search your apartment."

"What do you think you'd find there?"

"That's beside the point. Do you understand what's at stake now?"

Wallander knew he was taking a big risk. Sven Tyrén might see right through him. But apparently he preferred to comply with Wallander's demands.

"Holger was a peaceful man. Even though he could be tough when it came to business. But he never talked about any mercenaries. Although he certainly could have."

"What do you mean?"

"Mercenaries fight against revolutionaries and communists, don't they? And Holger was a conservative, I'd say. To put it mildly."

"Conservative how?"

"He thought society was going straight to hell. He thought we should bring back flogging and we should hang murderers. If it were up to him, whoever killed him would wind up with a rope around his neck."

"And he spoke to you about this?"

"He talked like that to everybody. He stood up for his beliefs."

"Was he in contact with any conservative organization?"

"How should I know?"

"If you know one thing, you might know something else. Answer the question!"

"I don't know."

"No neo-Nazis?"

"No idea."

"Was he a Nazi himself?"

"I don't know anything about them. He thought society was going to hell. He didn't see any difference between Social Democrats and Communists. The People's Party was probably the most radical one he would accept."

Wallander considered what Tyrén had said for a moment. It both modified and deepened his picture of Eriksson. He was obviously an unusually complex and contradictory person. Poet and ultra-conservative, birdwatcher and advocate of capital punishment. Wallander recalled the poem on the desk, in which Eriksson grieved that a bird was about to disappear from Sweden. But violent felons should be hanged.

"Did he ever mention that he had any enemies?"

"You already asked me that."

"I know. I'm asking you again."

"He never came right out and said so. But he did lock his doors at night."

"Why?"

"Maybe he had enemies."

"But you don't know of any?"

"No."

"Did he say why he might have enemies?"

"He never said he had any. How many times do I have to tell you that?"

Wallander raised a hand in admonition.

"If I feel like it I can ask you the same question every day for the next five years. No enemies? But he locked his doors at night?"

"Right."

"How do you know?"

"He told me. How the hell else would I know? I didn't drive out there and try his door at night! In Sweden today you can't trust anybody. That's what he said."

Wallander decided to conclude the discussion for the time being. He'd get back to it soon enough. He had a feeling that Tyrén knew more than he was telling him, but he wanted to proceed cautiously. If he scared Tyrén into a corner he'd have a hard time coaxing him out again.

"That'll be all for now," Wallander said.

"For now? Does that mean I have to come back here again? When am I going to have time to do my job?"

"We'll be in touch. Thanks for coming," said Wallander, getting to his feet. He extended his hand.

The courtesy surprised Tyrén. He had a powerful handshake, Wallander thought.

"I think you can find your way out."

After Tyrén left, Wallander called Hansson. He was lucky and got hold of him at once.

"Sven Tyrén," he said. "The tank-truck driver. The one you thought had been mixed up in some spousal-abuse cases? Remember?"

"Yes, I remember."

"See what you can find out about him."

"Is it urgent?"

"No more than anything else, but no less either."

Hansson promised to take care of it.

It was ten o'clock. Wallander got some coffee. Then he wrote down a report of his conversation with Tyrén. The next time the investigative group met, they would discuss in detail what had come out in that conversation. Wallander was convinced it was important.

When he closed his notebook, he discovered the note that he had forgotten to return to Svedberg several times. Now he was going to do it before he got involved in anything else. He took the slip of paper and left the office. Out in the corridor he heard his telephone start to ring. He hesitated for a second, then went back and picked it up.

It was Gertrud. She was crying.

"You have to come right away," she sniffled.

Wallander felt a cold chill.

"What's happened?" he asked.

"Your father is dead. He's lying in his studio in the middle of his paintings."

It was a quarter past ten, Monday the 3rd of October, 1994.

Chapter Twelve

Kurt Wallander's father was buried in the New Churchyard in Ystad on October 11th. It was a blustery day of heavy downpours interspersed with occasional sunbreaks. A week after Wallander had received the news of his death, he still had a hard time understanding what had happened. A sense of denial had been with him from the moment he hung up the phone. It was unthinkable that his father would die. Not now, just after their trip to Rome. Not when they had recaptured the closeness they had lost so many years before.

Wallander left the police station without speaking to anyone. He was convinced that Gertrud was mistaken. But when he arrived in Löderup and ran to the studio where it always smelled of turpentine, he knew instantly that Gertrud was right. His father lay prone across the painting he had been working on. At the moment of death he had shut his eyes and held on tight to the paintbrush he had just used to add tiny dabs of white to the grouse. Wallander saw that his father had been finishing up the painting he was working on the day before, when they took that long walk along the beach at Sandhammaren. Death had come suddenly. Later, after Gertrud had calmed down enough to talk coherently, she told him that his father had eaten breakfast as usual. Everything was normal. At six thirty he went out to his studio. When he didn't come back to the kitchen at ten for coffee as he usually did, she went out to remind him. By then he was already dead. It occurred to Wallander that no matter when death comes, it disrupts everything. Death always arrives at the wrong time—a cup of morning coffee is left untouched, or something else is left undone.

They waited for the ambulance. Gertrud stood and held tightly to his arm. Wallander felt completely empty inside. He was incapable of feeling any grief. He didn't feel anything at all, other than a vague sense that it was unfair. He couldn't feel sorry for his dead father.

The ambulance arrived. Wallander knew the driver. His name was Prytz and he understood at once that it was Wallander's father they were picking up.

"He wasn't sick," said Wallander. "Yesterday we were out walking on the beach. He complained about feeling bad, that's all."

"It was probably a stroke," said Prytz with compassion in his voice. "That's what it looks like."

That was also what the doctor told Wallander later. It had happened very quickly. His father probably had no idea he was dying. A blood vessel had burst in his brain and he was dead before his head hit the unfinished painting. For Gertrud the sorrow and the shock were mixed with relief that it happened so quickly; that he was spared a slow wasting-away into a no-man's-land of confusion.

Wallander was thinking completely different thoughts. His father had been alone when he died. No one should be alone in his final hour. He felt guilty because he hadn't reacted to his father's complaint of feeling bad. That was something that might indicate an impending heart attack or stroke. But even worse was that it had happened now. Even though his father had been eighty years old, it was too early. It should have happened later. Not now. Not like this. When Wallander stood in the studio he had tried to shake life back into his father. But there was nothing he could do. The grouse would never be finished.

In the midst of the chaos that death always causes, Wallander had still retained his ability to act calmly and rationally. Gertrud went along in the ambulance. Wallander returned to the studio, stood there in the silence and the smell of turpentine, and wept at the thought that his father wouldn't have wanted to leave the grouse before it was finished. As a gesture of understanding of the invisible border between life and death, Wallander took the paintbrush and filled in the two white points that were still missing in the grouse's plumage. It was the first time in his life that he had touched any of his father's paintings with a brush. Then he cleaned the brush and put it back with the others in an old jam crock. He couldn't comprehend what had happened; he had no idea what it would mean to him. He didn't even know how to act.

He went back to the house and called Ebba. She was upset and sad, and Wallander had a hard time talking. Finally he asked her just to tell the others what had happened. They should go on as usual without him. All they had to do was keep him informed if anything important happened in the investigation. He wouldn't be coming back to work that day. He didn't know what he was going to do tomorrow. Then he called his sister Kristina and told her the news. They talked for a long time. To Wallander it seemed as though she had prepared herself in a completely different way for the possibility that their father might die suddenly. She would help him locate Linda, since he didn't have the phone number of the lunch restaurant where she worked.

Then he called Mona. She worked at a beauty shop in Malmö whose name he didn't remember. But a friendly information operator helped him find it when he told her what had happened. He could hear that Mona was surprised when he called. At first she was afraid that something had happened to Linda. When Wallander told her that it was his father who had died, he could hear that she was at least partially relieved. That made him mad. But he didn't say anything. He knew that Mona and his father had gotten along well. It was only natural that she would be worried about Linda. He remembered the morning that the *Estonia* had sunk.

"I know what you're going through," she said. "You've been afraid of this moment your whole life."

"We had so much to talk about," he replied. "We were finally getting along again. And now it's too late."

"It's always too late," she said.

She promised to come to the funeral and help out if he needed her. After they hung up he felt a lingering emptiness. He dialed Baiba's number in Riga, but she didn't answer. He called back again and again. But she wasn't home.

Then he went back out to the studio. He sat down on the old rickety sled where he used to sit, a coffee cup always in his hand. There was a tentative drumming on the roof. It had started raining again. Wallander felt that he was holding his own fear of death in his hands. The studio was already transformed into a crypt. He got up quickly and went back to the kitchen. The phone rang. It was Linda, and she was crying. Wallander started crying too. She wanted to come home as soon as possible. Wallander asked if he should call her employer and talk to him. But Linda had already talked to the restaurant owner. She would take a bus to Arlanda and try to get on a plane that afternoon. He offered to pick her up at the airport, but she told him to stay with Gertrud. She would manage to get to Ystad and out to Löderup on her own.

That evening they all gathered in the house in Löderup. Wallander noticed that Gertrud was very calm. They began to discuss the funeral arrangements. Wallander doubted that his father would have wanted a clergyman to officiate. But it was Gertrud who decided. She was his widow, after all.

"He never talked about death," she said. "I can't tell you if he was afraid of it or not. He didn't talk about where he wanted to be buried. But I want to have a pastor."

They agreed that it would be at the New Churchyard in Ystad. A simple funeral. His father hadn't had a lot of friends. Linda said she would read a poem, Wallander promised that he wouldn't give a eulogy, and they chose "Wondrous Is the Earth" as the hymn they would sing.

Kristina arrived the next day. She stayed with Gertrud, and Linda stayed at Wallander's apartment in Ystad. It was a week in which death brought them together. Kristina said that now that their father had passed on, the two of them were next in line. Wallander noticed the whole time that his fear of death was growing, but he didn't talk about it. Not to anyone. Not to Linda, not even to his sister. Maybe he could with Baiba sometime. She had reacted with deep feeling when he finally managed to get hold of her and tell her what had happened. They talked for almost an hour. She told him about her feelings when her own father had passed away ten years before, and she also talked about how she felt when her husband Karlis was murdered. Afterwards Wallander felt relieved. She was there and she wasn't going away.

The day the obituary was printed in *Ystad's Allehanda*, Sten Widén called from his horse farm outside Skurup. It had been a few years since Wallander last talked to him. Once they had been close friends. They had shared an interest in opera and had high hopes for the future together. Widén had a beautiful voice, and Wallander would be his impresario. But everything changed when Widén's father died suddenly and he was forced to take over the farm, where they trained racehorses. Wallander became a policeman, and they gradually drifted apart. But now Sten Widén called to offer his condolences. After their conversation, Wallander wondered whether Widén had ever even met his father. But he was grateful that he had called. Someone outside the immediate family hadn't forgotten him.

In the midst of all this, Wallander forced himself to continue to be a cop. The day after his father died, Tuesday the 4th of October, he returned to the police station. He had spent a sleepless night in the apartment. Linda slept in his old room. Mona had also come to visit and brought dinner so she could get them to think of something else for a while. For the first time since the devastating divorce five years ago, Wallander could now feel that his marriage was definitively over. For far too long he had pleaded with her to come back and clung to unrealistic dreams that someday everything would be the way it had been before. But there was no going back. And now it was Baiba he was closest to. Somehow his father's death had shown him that the life he had led with Mona was over for good.

Despite sleeping badly the whole week before the funeral, he gave his colleagues the impression that everything was perfectly normal. They expressed their condolences and he thanked them. He returned immediately to the investigation. When Chief Holgersson took him aside in the corridor and suggested that he take a few days off, he turned down her offer: His grief for his father eased somewhat while he was working.

Still, the investigation moved slowly during the week before the funeral. The other case they were concentrating on, always overshadowed by the murder of Holger Eriksson, was Gösta Runfeldt's disappearance. No one could figure out what had happened. He had simply vanished. None of the detectives believed any longer that there was a natural explanation. On the other hand, they hadn't been able to find any connection between Eriksson and Runfeldt. The only thing that seemed perfectly clear about Runfeldt was that his great passion in life was orchids.

"We ought to take a look at his wife's death," said Wallander at one of the investigative meetings that week. Höglund promised to take care of it.

"How about the mail-order company in Borås?" Wallander asked later. "What's happening with that? What do our colleagues there say?"

"They got on it right away," said Svedberg. "It obviously wasn't the first time the company was involved in illegal importing of bugging devices. According to the Borås police, the company would pop up and then vanish, only to reappear with a new name and address. Sometimes even with different owners. They've already made some headway there. We're waiting for a written report."

"The most important thing is to find out if Runfeldt had ever bought anything else from them," said Wallander. "We don't have to worry about the rest of it now."

"Their list of customers is incomplete, to say the least. But the Borås police have evidently found prohibited and very advanced equipment at their business locations. If I'm interpreting what they said correctly, Runfeldt could practically be a spy."

Wallander pondered this for a moment.

"Why not?" he said finally. "We can't rule anything out. He must have had some reason for buying the stuff."

Aside from Runfeldt's disappearance, they were totally focused on the Eriksson murder. They searched for Harald Berggren without finding the slightest trace of him. The museum in Stockholm informed them that the shrunken head they had found in Eriksson's safe was definitely human and probably came from the Congo. So far so good. But who was this Harald Berggren? They had already spoken with people who had known Holger Eriksson during different periods of his life, but none had ever heard him speak of Berggren, and none had ever heard that he had contact with the mercenary underground, in which mercenaries moved like wary rats and wrote their contracts with various messengers of the Devil. At last it was Wallander who came up with the idea that got the investigation moving again.

"There's a lot of fishy stuff surrounding Holger Eriksson," he said. "Particularly the fact that there isn't a woman in his life. Not anywhere, not ever. That made me start to wonder whether there was a homosexual relationship between Eriksson and this Harald Berggren. There are almost no women in Berggren's diary either."

There was silence in the conference room. No one seemed to have considered this possibility.

"It sounds a little strange that homosexual men would choose such a macho occupation as being soldiers," Höglund ventured.

"Not at all," replied Wallander. "It's not unusual for gay men to become soldiers. They could do it to hide their preference. Or just to be around other men."

Martinsson sat studying the photo of the three men by the termite mound.

"I get a feeling you might be right," he said. "These men have something feminine about them."

"Like what?" asked Höglund curiously.

"I don't know," said Martinsson. "Maybe the way they're leaning on the termite mound. Their hair."

"It doesn't do us any good to sit here guessing," interrupted Wallander. "I'm only pointing out one more possibility. We should keep it in mind just like everything else."

"In other words, we're looking for a gay mercenary," said Martinsson dourly. "Where would we find one?"

"That's not exactly what we're doing," said Wallander. "But we have to evaluate this possibility alongside the rest of the material."

"Nobody I spoke to so much as intimated that Holger Eriksson might have been gay," said Hansson, who until now had sat in silence.

"It's not really something people talk about openly," said Wallander. "At least not men in the older generation. If Eriksson was gay, then he can remember the time when blackmail was used against people of that persuasion in this country."

"So you mean we have to start asking people if Eriksson may have been homosexual?" said Svedberg, who hadn't said much during the meeting either.

"You have to decide how you want to proceed," said Wallander. "I don't even know if this is the right track. But we can't ignore the possibility."

Wallander could see that this was the moment when the investigation entered another phase. It was as if they all suddenly understood that there wasn't anything simple or easily accessible about the murder of Holger Eriksson. They were dealing with one or more cunning perpetrators, and now they began to suspect that the motive for the murder lay hidden in the past, a past well shielded from view.

They continued with the laborious basic tasks. They charted everything they had access to about Eriksson's life. Svedberg even sat for several long nights reading slowly and carefully through the nine books of poetry Eriksson had published. At last Svedberg thought he would go nuts from all the spiritual complexities that evidently existed in the world of birds. But he didn't seem to understand any more about Holger Eriksson.

Martinsson took his daughter Terese to Falsterbo Point one windy afternoon and walked around talking to various birdwatchers who stood straining their necks and staring at the gray clouds. The only thing he got from the trip, apart from spending time with his daughter, who had expressed interest in becoming a member of the Field Biologists, was that the night Eriksson was murdered, huge flocks of red-winged blackbirds had departed from Sweden. Martinsson conferred later with Svedberg, who claimed that there were no poems about red-winged blackbirds in any of the nine books.

"On the other hand, there are three long poems about the single snipe," said Svedberg hesitantly. "Is there anything called a double snipe?"

Martinsson didn't know. The investigation continued.

Finally the day of the funeral arrived. They were all meeting at the crematorium. A few days before, Wallander had learned to his surprise that it was a female minister who would officiate. It wasn't just any minister. He had met her on a memorable occasion this last summer. Afterwards he would be glad that she was the one; her words were simple, and she never drifted into the grandiose or sentimental. The day before, she had called to ask whether his father had been religious. Wallander said no. Instead he told her about his paintings. And their trip to Rome. The funeral was not as unbearable as Wallander had feared. The casket was made of dark wood with a simple decoration of roses. Linda was the one who showed her emotions most openly. No one doubted that her sorrow was genuine. She was probably the one who missed the deceased man most.

After the ceremony they drove to Löderup. Now that the funeral was over Wallander felt relieved. How he would react later he had no idea. He still felt as though he didn't really understand what had happened. He thought he belonged to a generation that was particularly ill-prepared to accept that death was always nearby. In his own case the feeling was intensified by the odd fact that he had to deal with dead people so often in his work. But now he turned out to be as defenseless as anyone else. He thought about the conversation he had had with Chief Holgersson the week before.

The night of the funeral he and his daughter stayed up late and talked. She was going back to Stockholm early the next morning. Wallander wondered cautiously whether she was going to visit him less often now that her grandfather was gone. But she promised that she would come more often than ever. In turn, Wallander promised that he wouldn't neglect Gertrud.

When he went to bed that night he felt that now he had to get back to work at full speed. For a week he had been distracted. Only when he had put some distance between himself and his father's sudden death could he begin to understand what it meant. To get that distance he had to work. There was no other way.

I never did find out why he didn't want me to be a cop, he thought before he went to sleep. And now it's too late. Now I'll never know.

If there is a spirit world, which I basically doubt, then my father and Rydberg can keep each other company. Even though they met very seldom when they were alive, I think now they would find a lot to talk about.

She had made an exact and detailed timetable for Gösta Runfeldt's last hour. He was so weak now that he wouldn't be able to put up any resistance. She had broken him down at the same time that he had broken himself down from the inside. *The worm hidden in the flower portends the flower's death,* she thought as she unlocked the doors to the house in Vollsjö. She had noted in her timetable that she would arrive at four in the afternoon. She was now three minutes ahead of schedule. She had to wait until dark. Then she would pull him out of the oven. For safety's sake she thought she'd put handcuffs on him. And a gag. But nothing over his eyes. Even though he'd have a hard time getting used to the light after so many days spent in utter darkness, after a few hours he would start to see again. Then she wanted him to really see her. And she would show him the photographs. The pictures that would make him understand what was happening to him. And why.

There were some elements she couldn't completely ignore which might affect her planning. One was the risk that he might be so weak that he couldn't stand up. That's why she had borrowed a little, easily maneuverable baggage cart from the Central Station in Malmö. No one had noticed when she put it in her car. She still hadn't decided whether to return it or not. She could use it to roll him out to the car if necessary.

The rest of the timetable was quite simple. Just before nine she would drive him out to the woods. She would tie him to the tree she had already picked out. And show him the photos.

Then she would strangle him. Leave him where he was. She would be home in bed no later than midnight. Her alarm clock would ring at 5:15. At 7:15 she would be at work.

She loved her timetable. It was perfect. Nothing could go wrong. She sat down in a chair and looked at the mute oven which towered like a sacrificial altar in the middle of the room. My mother would have understood, she thought. If no one does it, it won't get done. Evil must be driven out with evil. Where there is no justice, it must be created.

She took her timetable out of her pocket and looked at the clock. In three hours and fifteen minutes, Gösta Runfeldt would die.

Lars Olsson didn't really feel much like training on the evening of October 11th. For a few hours he had been wondering whether he should go out on his run or forget about it. It wasn't just that he felt tired. TV2 was showing a movie he wanted to see. It wasn't until he considered taking his run after the movie, even though it would be late, that he made up his mind. Lars Olsson lived in a house near Svarte. He was born on that farm and still lived with his parents although he was over thirty years old. He was part-owner of a backhoe and was the one who knew best how to operate it. This week he was busy digging a ditch for a new drainage system on a farm in Skårby.

But Lars Olsson was also a devoted orienteer. He lived to run in the Swedish woods with a map and compass. He ran for a team in Malmö that was now preparing for a big national night-orienteering run. He had often asked himself why he spent so much time at his orienteering. What was the point of running around in the woods with a map and compass looking for hidden signs? It was often cold and wet; his body ached and he never felt his performance was good enough. Was that really something to devote your life to? On the other hand, he knew he was a good orienteer. He had a feeling for the terrain, as well as both speed and endurance. On several occasions he had led his team to victory with a strong effort on the final leg. He was still below national-team status, but he hadn't yet given up hope of someday taking a step up and representing Sweden in international competition.

He watched the film on TV, but it wasn't as good as he expected. Just after eleven he started out on his run. He headed for the woods just north of the farm, on the boundary of Marsvinsholm's huge fields. He could choose to run either five or eight kilometers, depending on which path he took. Since he felt tired and had to go out early with the backhoe the next day, he chose the shorter route. He strapped his running light to his head and started off. It had rained that day, heavy showers followed by sunshine. Tonight it was 6° Celsius. He could smell the wet earth. He ran along the path into the woods. The tree trunks glistened in the light from his headlamp. In the midst of the densest part of the forest there was a little creek. If he kept close to it, the creekbed made a good shortcut. He decided to do that. He turned off the path and ran up a small hill.

Suddenly he stopped short. In the light of his lamp he had discovered someone. At first he didn't understand what he was looking at. Then he realized that he was facing a half-naked man tied to a tree ten meters in front of him. Lars Olsson stood quite still. He was breathing hard and felt very frightened. He took a quick look around. The lamp cast its glow over trees and bushes. But he was alone. Cautiously he took a few steps forward. The man was hanging over the ropes tied around his body. His torso was bare.

He didn't have to go any closer. He could see that the man was dead. Without really knowing why, he glanced at his watch. It showed nineteen minutes past eleven.

Then he turned around and ran home. He had never run so fast in his life. Without even taking the time to remove his headlamp he called the police in Ystad from the telephone hanging on the wall in the kitchen.

The officer who took the call listened attentively.

Afterwards he didn't hesitate. He pulled up Kurt Wallander's name on his computer screen and then punched in his home number.

By this time it was ten minutes to midnight.

Skåne

12—17 October 1994

Chapter Thirteen

Wallander still hadn't slept and was thinking about his father and Rydberg lying in the same cemetery when the telephone rang next to his bed. He grabbed it before the ringing could wake Linda. With a feeling of growing helplessness he listened to what the officer on duty had to say. Information was still sparse. The first police patrol hadn't yet reached the scene in the woods south of Marsvinsholm Castle. Of course there was a chance that the night orienteer had been mistaken, but that was a long shot. The officer thought he sounded unusually lucid even though he was excited. Wallander said he'd come at once. He tried to get dressed as quietly as he could, but Linda came out in her nightgown as he sat at the kitchen table writing a note to her.

"What's happened?" she asked.

"They found a dead man in the woods," he replied. "That means they call me."

She shook her head.

"Don't you ever get scared?"

He gave her a curious look.

"Why should I be scared?"

"About all the people who are dying."

He sensed rather than understood what she was trying to say.

"I can't. It's my job. Somebody has to deal with it."

He promised to be back in plenty of time to drive her to the airport in the morning. It wasn't quite one in the morning when he got into his car. Not until he was on his way out to Marsvinsholm did it occur to him that it might be Gösta Runfeldt who had been found in the woods. He had just left the town behind him when his cell phone rang. The patrol that was sent out had confirmed the report. There really was a dead man in the woods.

"Any ID on him?" asked Wallander.

"No. Sounds like he barely had any clothes on. It looks pretty bad."

Wallander felt his stomach tying itself in knots. But he didn't say anything.

"They'll meet you at the crossroads. Take the first exit toward Mars-vinsholm."

Wallander hung up and stomped on the gas pedal. He was already dreading the sight that awaited him.

He saw the squad car at a distance and slowed to a stop. An officer was standing outside the car. He recognized Peters. Wallander rolled down his window and gave him an inquiring look.

"It's not a pretty sight," said Peters.

Wallander knew what that meant. Peters had plenty of experience. He wouldn't use those words without a reason.

"Has he been identified?"

"He barely has a stitch on. Go see for yourself."

"And the guy who found him?"

"He's there too."

Peters went back to his car. Wallander drove behind him. They reached a clearing south of the castle. The road ended near the remains of a logging operation.

"We'll have to walk the last stretch," said Peters.

Wallander got his boots out of the trunk. Peters and his partner, a young patrolman named Bergman that Wallander didn't really know, had brought powerful flashlights. They followed a path that led upwards, to a little creek deep in the woods. There was a strong smell of autumn in the air. Wallander thought he should have worn a heavier sweater. If he had to stay out in the woods all night he was going to get cold.

"We're almost there," said Peters.

Wallander knew he said it to warn him about what was waiting.

The sight still took him by surprise. The two flashlights shone with macabre precision on a man who hung half-naked, tied to a tree. The beams of light quivered. Wallander stood quite still. Somewhere close by a night bird cried. He cautiously went closer. Peters shone his light so Wallander could see where he was putting his feet. The man's head and torso had fallen forward. Wallander got down on his knees to look at his face. He already thought he knew. The man's face gave him his confirmation. Even though the photos he had seen in Runfeldt's apartment were several years old, there was no doubt. Gösta Runfeldt had never made it to Nairobi. Now they knew the outcome of what had happened instead.

Wallander got to his feet and took a step back. There was no longer any doubt in his mind about one other thing. There was a connection between Holger Eriksson and Gösta Runfeldt. The killer's language was the same, even if the choice of words was different this time. A pungee pit and a tree. It simply couldn't be a coincidence.

He turned toward Peters. "Get the team," he said.

Peters nodded. Wallander discovered he had left his own telephone in the car. He asked Bergman to get it for him, and to bring the flashlight from the glove compartment.

"Where's the guy who found him?" he asked then.

Peters shone his flashlight to one side. On a rock sat a man in a jogging suit with his face buried in his hands.

"His name is Lars Olsson," said Peters. "He lives on a farm near here."

"What was he doing out in the woods in the middle of the night?"

"He's apparently an orienteer."

Wallander nodded. Peters gave him his flashlight. Wallander went up to the man, who looked up at him quickly when the beam struck his face. He was very pale. Wallander introduced himself and sat down on a rock next to him. He noticed it was cold and involuntarily shivered.

"So you're the one who found him."

Lars Olsson told his story. About the bad movie on TV. About his nightly training run. About how he decided to take a shortcut. And how the man was suddenly caught in the beam of his headlamp.

"You've given a very exact time," said Wallander, remembering what the officer on duty had said.

"I looked at my watch," replied Olsson. "It's a habit of mine. Or rather a bad habit. When something important happens I look at my watch. If I could have, I would have looked at my watch when I was born."

Wallander nodded.

"If I understand correctly, you take a run out here almost every night. When you're training in the dark."

"I ran here last night. But earlier. I ran two routes. The long one first. Then the short one. Then I took a shortcut."

"What time was that?"

"Between 9:30 and 10:00."

"And you didn't see anything then?"

"No."

"Could he have been here by the tree without you seeing him?"

Lars Olsson thought about it. Then he shook his head.

"I always pass close by that tree. I would have seen him."

Wallander had no more questions. He got up from the rock. There were flashlights approaching through the woods.

"Leave us your name and phone number," he told the man. "You'll be hearing from us."

"Who would do something like this?" asked Olsson.

"That's what I'm wondering too," replied Wallander.

Then he left Lars Olsson. He gave Peters his flashlight back when he was handed his own along with his cell phone. As Bergman took down Olsson's name and phone number, Peters talked to the station. Wallander took a deep breath and approached the man hanging in the ropes. It astonished him for a moment that he wasn't thinking about his father at all, now that he was in the presence of another death. But deep inside he knew why. He had been through it so many times before. Dead people weren't just dead. They had nothing human left in them. After the first wave of disgust passed, it was simply like approaching any other lifeless object.

Wallander cautiously felt the back of Runfeldt's neck. All body heat was gone. He hadn't really expected there to be any. Trying to determine the time of death, outdoors, with constantly changing temperature, was a complicated process. Wallander looked at the man's bare chest. The color of the skin didn't tell him anything about how long he had been hanging there either. There were no signs of injuries. Not until Wallander shone his flashlight at Rundfeldt's throat did he see the blue discolorations. That could mean that he had been hanged. Then Wallander started to inspect the ropes. They were wound around his body from his thighs up to his ribs. The knots were simple. The ropes weren't tied very tight either. It surprised him.

He took a step backward and shone his light on the whole body. Then he walked around the tree. The whole time he watched where he was putting his feet. He made only one circuit. He assumed that Peters had told Bergman not to tramp around unnecessarily. Lars Olsson was gone. Peters was still talking on the phone. Wallander needed another sweater. He knew he should always keep a spare in his car, the way he kept boots in the trunk. It was going to be a long night.

He tried to imagine what had happened. The loosely tied ropes made him nervous. He thought about Holger Eriksson. It was possible that Runfeldt's murder might provide the solution. When they resumed the investigative work it would force them to develop double vision. The clues would keep pointing in two directions at the same time. But Wallander was also aware that just the opposite could occur. The confusion could increase. The focal point could get harder and harder to pin down, with the landscape of the investigation more and more difficult to define and interpret.

For a moment Wallander turned off his flashlight and thought in the dark. Peters was still talking on the phone. Bergman stood motionless somewhere nearby. Gösta Runfeldt hung dead in his loosely tied ropes.

Is this a beginning, a middle, or an end? thought Wallander. Or is it so bad that we have a new serial killer on our hands? An even more difficult chain of events to unravel than we had in the summer?

He had no answers. He simply didn't know. It was too early. It was way too early.

There was engine noise in the distance. Peters had gone to meet the various emergency vehicles that were approaching. Wallander thought quickly of Linda and hoped she was asleep. Whatever happened, he would drive her to the airport in the morning. Suddenly a great wave of grief for his dead father surged through him. He longed for Baiba. And he was exhausted. He felt burnt out. All the energy he had felt on his return from Rome was gone. There was nothing left.

He had to marshal all his forces to dispel the dismal thoughts. Martinsson and Hansson came tramping through the woods, followed by Höglund and Nyberg. After them came the ambulance men and crime-scene technicians. Then Svedberg. And finally a doctor. They gave the impression of a poorly organized caravan that had wound up in the wrong place. Wallander started by gathering his closest colleagues around him in a circle. A floodlight hooked up to a portable generator was already aiming its eerie light on the man tied to the tree. Wallander was suddenly reminded of the macabre experience they had had by the ditch on Holger Eriksson's property. Now it was being repeated. The framework was different, and yet the same. The killer's stage sets were related.

"It's Gösta Runfeldt," said Wallander. "There's no doubt about it. We'll have to wake up Vanja Andersson and bring her out here. We have to have a positive ID as soon as possible. We can wait until we take him down from the tree. She doesn't need to see that."

He gave a brief report on how Lars Olsson had found Runfeldt.

"He's been missing for almost three weeks," he went on. "But if I'm not completely mistaken, and if Lars Olsson is right, he's been dead for less than twenty-four hours. At least he hasn't been tied to this tree any longer than that. So the question is: Where has he been all this time?"

Then he answered the question that no one had asked yet—the only obvious question.

"I have a hard time believing it's a coincidence. It has to be the same perpetrator we're searching for in the Eriksson case. Now we've got to find out what these two men have in common. Actually, there are three investigations: Holger Eriksson, Gösta Runfeldt, and the two of them together."

"What happens if we don't find any connection?" asked Svedberg.

"We will," replied Wallander firmly. "Sooner or later. The planning of both of these homicides seems to exclude the possibility that the victims were chosen at random. This is no run-of-the-mill nut case at work. Both of these men were killed with a specific aim in mind, for specific reasons."

"Gösta Runfeldt couldn't have been a homosexual," said Martinsson. "He was married with two kids."

"He could have been bisexual," said Wallander. "It's too soon for those questions. We have other things to do that are more urgent."

The circle broke up. They didn't need a lot of talking to organize their work. Wallander went over and stood by Nyberg, who was waiting for the doctor to finish.

"So it's happened again," Nyberg said in a weary voice.

"Yes," said Wallander, "and we have to get through it one more time."

"Just yesterday I decided to take a couple of weeks' vacation," said Nyberg. "As soon as we find out who killed Eriksson. I thought I'd go to the Canary Islands. Not particularly imaginative, maybe—but warmer."

Nyberg seldom talked about personal matters. Wallander knew he was disappointed that his trip would now be postponed indefinitely. He could see that Nyberg was tired and harried. His workload was often unreasonable. Wallander decided to take it up with Chief Holgersson as soon as possible. They didn't have the right to exploit Nyberg's dedication any longer.

At the same moment he had this thought, he discovered that the chief had arrived at the crime scene. She stood talking to Hansson and Höglund.

The chief probably had a lot on her plate right from the start, thought Wallander. With this second homicide the media are going to have a field day. Björk never could handle the stress. Now we'll see if she can take it.

Wallander knew that Holgersson was married to a man who worked for an international export firm in the computer field. They had two grown children. After moving to Ystad they had bought a house in Hedeskoga, north of town. Wallander hoped her husband gave her plenty of support. She'd need it.

The doctor got to his feet. Wallander had met him before but couldn't remember his name.

"It looks like he was strangled," the doctor said.

"Not hanged?"

The doctor held out his hands.

"Strangled with bare hands," he said. "It causes different types of pressure wounds than a rope. You can see the marks from the thumbs quite clearly."

A strong man, Wallander thought instantly. A person in good shape. Who has no qualms about killing with his bare hands.

"How long ago?" he asked.

"Impossible to say for sure. Within the last twenty-four hours, no longer. You'll have to wait for the ME's report."

"Can we take him down?"

"I'm done," said the doctor.

"Then I can get started," muttered Nyberg.

Höglund came up beside them. "Vanja Andersson is here. She's waiting in a car down there."

"How did she take the news?" asked Wallander.

"It's a hell of way to be woken up, of course. But I got the feeling she wasn't surprised. She's probably been worrying that he might be dead."

"I have too," said Wallander. "And you?"

She nodded but didn't say a word.

Nyberg had unwound the ropes. Runfeldt's body lay on a stretcher.

"Bring her up here," said Wallander. "Then she can go home."

Vanja Andersson was very pale. Wallander noticed she was dressed in black. Had she set those clothes out ready to wear? She looked at the dead man's face, took a deep breath, and nodded.

"You can identify him as Gösta Runfeldt?" asked Wallander. He moaned inwardly at how clumsy this sounded.

"He's so thin," she murmured.

Wallander pricked up his ears. "What do you mean, thin?"

"His face is all sunken in. He didn't look like this three weeks ago."

Wallander knew that death could alter a person's face dramatically. But he had a feeling that Vanja Andersson was talking about something else.

"You mean he's lost weight since the last time you saw him?"

"Yes. He's grown terribly thin."

Wallander knew that what she was saying was important. But he still couldn't figure out how to interpret it.

"You don't have to stay here any longer," he said. "We'll drive you home."

She gave him a helpless and forlorn look.

"What am I supposed to do with the shop?" she asked. "And all the flowers?"

"Tomorrow you can leave it closed, I'm sure," said Wallander. "Start with that. Don't think any farther ahead than that."

She nodded mutely. Höglund followed her to the police car that would drive her home. Wallander thought about what she had said. For almost three weeks Runfeldt had been missing without a trace. When he reappeared, tied to a tree and possibly strangled, he was inexplicably thin. Wallander knew what that meant: imprisonment.

He stood still and followed his internal thought process attentively.

Imprisonment too could be related to a wartime situation. Soldiers take prisoners.

He was interrupted when Chief Holgersson stumbled over a rock and almost fell as she walked over to him. He thought he'd better prepare her right away for what awaited her.

"You look like you're freezing," she said.

"I forgot to bring a heavier sweater," replied Wallander. "Some things you never learn."

She nodded at the stretcher where the remains of Runfeldt lay. It was being carried off toward the ambulance that waited somewhere down by the logging site.

"What do you think of all this?" she asked.

"Same perp that killed Holger Eriksson. It wouldn't make sense to think otherwise."

"It seems he was strangled."

"I try not to draw conclusions too soon," said Wallander. "But I think I can imagine how it all happened. He was alive when he was tied to the tree. Maybe unconscious. But he was strangled here and then left behind. And he didn't put up any resistance."

"How can you be sure of that?"

"The rope was tied loosely. If he wanted to, he could have wriggled free."

"Couldn't the loose rope be a sign of that?" she asked. "That he did try to resist and tried to wriggle out of it?"

Good question, thought Wallander. Lisa Holgersson is a cop, all right.

"That could be," he replied. "But I don't think so. Because of something Vanja Andersson said. That he had grown terribly thin."

"I don't get the connection."

"I just think that rapid emaciation would also have involved increasing weakness."

She understood.

"He was left hanging on the ropes," Wallander went on. "The perp had no need to conceal his action. Or the body. It reminds me of what happened to Holger Eriksson."

"Why here?" she asked. "Why tie a person to a tree? Why this brutality?"

"When we understand that, maybe we'll know why this happened in the first place," said Wallander.

"Have you got any ideas?"

"I've got plenty of ideas. I think the best thing we can do now is let Nyberg and his people work in peace. It's more important to have a meeting and run-through back in Ystad than to wander around out here wearing ourselves out. There's nothing left to see here, anyway."

She had no objections. At two o'clock they left Nyberg and his techs alone out in the woods. By that time it had started to drizzle and the wind came up. Wallander was the last to leave the scene.

What do we do now? he asked himself. How do we proceed? We don't have a motive or a suspect. All we have is a diary that belonged to a man named Harald Berggren. A birdwatcher and a passionate orchid lover have been killed. With consummate savagery.

He tried to remember what Höglund had said. It was important. Something about the specifically macho. Which had then started him thinking more and more about a perpetrator with a military background. Harald Berggren had been a mercenary, to be sure. He had been more than a soldier. A person who defended neither his country nor a cause. He had been a man who killed people for a monthly wage in cold cash.

At least we have a starting point, he thought. We have to stick with it until it collapses.

He went over to say goodbye to Nyberg.

"Is there anything special you want us to look for?" he asked.

"No. Just look for anything that may remind you of what happened to Eriksson."

"I think everything does," replied Nyberg. "Except for the bamboo stakes."

"I want dogs up here early tomorrow," Wallander went on.

"I'll probably still be here," said Nyberg dismally.

"I'm going to bring up your work situation with Lisa," Wallander said, hoping it would at least offer him a modicum of encouragement.

"It probably won't do any good."

"Well, it won't do any good not to try," said Wallander, putting an end to the conversation.

At quarter to three in the morning they were gathered at the station. Wallander was the last to enter the conference room. He saw tired, sallow faces all around him and realized that his main task was to infuse the investigative team with renewed energy. From experience he knew that there were always moments in an investigation when all their self-confidence seemed to be used up. The only difference now was that the moment had arrived unusually early this time.

We could have used a calm fall, thought Wallander. The summer wore us out.

He sat down and Hansson brought him a cup of coffee.

"This isn't going to be easy," he began. "What we probably feared most has turned out to be true. Gösta Runfeldt has been murdered. Apparently by the same perpetrator who killed Holger Eriksson. We don't know what this means. For example, we don't know whether we're going to have more unpleasant surprises. We don't know if this will be similar to what we went through this summer. We shouldn't draw any other parallels than that the same man has evidently been at work again. There are also a lot of things that are different about these two crimes. More differences than similarities."

He paused for comments. No one had anything to say.

"We'll have to continue working on a wide front. Without making assumptions but with determination. We have to track down Harald Berggren. We have to find out why Gösta Runfeldt wasn't on that plane to Nairobi. We have to figure out why he ordered a sophisticated bugging device just before he disappeared and then died. We have to find a connection between these two men, who seem to have lived their lives with no apparent connection to each other. Since the victims were not chosen at random, there simply has to be some kind of link."

Still nobody had any comments. Wallander decided to adjourn the meeting. What they needed more than anything was a few hours' sleep. They would meet again early in the morning.

They broke up quickly.

Outside, the wind and rain had gotten worse. As Wallander hurried across the wet parking lot to his car he thought about Nyberg and his techs.

But he also thought about what Vanja Andersson had said. That Gösta Runfeldt had grown so thin in the three weeks he was missing. Wallander knew that was important.

He had a hard time imagining any other cause but imprisonment. But where had he been held captive?

And why? By whom?

Chapter Fourteen

That night Wallander slept under a blanket on the couch in his living room, since he had to get up in a few hours. It had been quiet in Linda's room when he came in the wee hours. He had woken up abruptly, drenched in sweat, after a nightmare he could only vaguely recall. He had dreamed about his father; they were in Rome again, and something frightening happened. What it was vanished into the darkness. Maybe in the dream, death had already been with them on their trip to Rome, like a warning. He sat up on the couch with the blanket wrapped around him. It was five o'clock. The alarm clock would ring any minute now. He sat there heavy and unmoving. The exhaustion was like a dull ache in his whole body. It seemed to take all his strength to get up and go to the bathroom. After a shower he felt a little better. He made breakfast and woke Linda at quarter to six. By six thirty they were on their way out to the airport. She was groggy and didn't say much during the ride. She didn't seem to wake up until they turned off E65 for the last few kilometers to Sturup.

"What happened last night?" she asked.

"Someone found a dead man in the woods."

"Can't you tell me any more than that?"

"The body was found by an orienteer who was out running. He practically tripped over it."

"Who was it?"

"The orienteer or the dead man?"

"The dead man."

"A florist."

"Did he commit suicide?"

"No, unfortunately."

"What do you mean, unfortunately?"

"He was murdered. And that means a lot of work for us."

She sat silent for a while. Now they could see the yellow airport terminal up ahead.

"I don't see how you stand it," she said.

"Me neither. But I have to. Somebody has to."

The question she now asked astonished him.

"Do you think I would make a good cop?"

"I thought you had other plans."

"I do. Answer the question."

"I don't know," he said. "You might."

They didn't say any more. Wallander pulled into the parking lot. She had only a backpack, which he lifted out of the trunk. When he wanted to follow her in, she shook her head.

"Go home now," she said. "You're so tired you can hardly stand up."

"I have to work," he replied. "But you're right, I am tired."

Then there was a moment of sadness. They talked about his father, her grandfather, who was no longer with them.

"It's strange," she said. "I was thinking about it in the car. That you have to be dead so long."

He mumbled something vague in response. They said goodbye. She promised to buy an answering machine. He watched her vanish through the glass doors that slid open and closed.

He sat in the car and thought about what she had said. Was that what made death so terrifying? That you had to be dead so long?

He started the engine and drove off. The countryside was gray and seemed just as dismal as the entire investigation they were working on. Wallander thought about the events of the past week. A man lies impaled in a ditch. Another man is tied to a tree and strangled. Could death be any more repellent than that? Of course, it wasn't any better seeing his father lying in the middle of his paintings. He needed to see Baiba again soon. He was going to call her that night. He couldn't stand the loneliness anymore. It had been going on long enough. He had been divorced for five years. He was on the way to becoming an old, shaggy dog, scared of people. And that's not what he wanted to be.

Soon afterwards he arrived at the police station. The first thing he did was get some coffee. Then he called Gertrud. Her voice was unexpectedly cheerful. His sister Kristina was still there. Since Wallander was so busy with the investigations, they had agreed that Gertrud and his sister would take inventory of the meager estate his father had left. His assets consisted mainly of the house in Löderup. But there were almost no debts. Gertrud asked if there was anything special that Wallander wanted to have. At first he said no. Then he suddenly changed his mind and said he'd take a painting with a grouse from the stacks of finished canvases leaning against the walls of the studio. For some reason that he couldn't explain, he didn't want the painting his father had almost finished when he died. For the time being he would keep the painting he chose in his office at the station. He still hadn't decided where to hang it. Or whether he would hang it at all.

He turned into a cop again.

He started by quickly reading through a report on a conversation that Höglund had had with the female rural letter-carrier who delivered the mail to Holger Eriksson. He saw that Höglund wrote well, without awkward sentences or irrelevant details. Apparently police officers nowadays at least learned to write better reports than his generation had.

But there was nothing that seemed to have direct significance for the investigation. The last time Holger Eriksson had hung out the little sign on his mailbox that meant he needed to talk to the letter-carrier was several months ago. As far as she could remember, it was a matter of some simple money orders. She hadn't noticed anything unusual lately at Eriksson's farm, or any strange cars or people in the area either.

Wallander put the report aside, pulled over his notebook, and wrote some notes to remind himself what should take priority. Someone had to have an in-depth conversation with Anita Lagergren at the travel agency in Malmö. When had Gösta Runfeldt reserved his trip? What was this orchid safari all about, anyway? Now they had to chart his life, the same way they had for Eriksson. It was particularly necessary to have detailed discussions with his children. Wallander also wanted to know more about the equipment Runfeldt had bought. What was it supposed to be used for? Why would a florist have these things? He was convinced that it was crucial to understanding what had happened. Wallander pushed the notebook away and sat hesitantly with his hand on the telephone. It was a quarter past eight. There was a chance that Nyberg was asleep. But it couldn't be helped. He dialed the number of his cell phone. Nyberg answered at once. He was still out in the woods. Wallander asked him how it was going.

"We've got dogs out here right now," said Nyberg. "They've picked up the scent from the rope down by the logging site. But that's not so strange, since it's the only way up here. I think we can assume that Runfeldt didn't walk out here. There must have been a car."

"Any tire tracks?"

"Quite a few. But I can't tell you which is which yet."

"Anything else?"

"The rope is from a rope factory in Denmark."

"Denmark?"

"I should think it could be purchased just about anywhere that sells rope. Anyway, it seems brand-new. Bought for the occasion."

Wallander reacted with disgust. Then he asked Nyberg the question he had called about.

"Have you been able to find the slightest sign that he put up any resistance when he was tied to the tree? Or that he tried to work his way loose?"

Nyberg's answer was firm.

"No. It doesn't seem that he did. First, I haven't found any traces of a struggle nearby. The ground would have been disturbed. There would have been something to see. Second, there are no chafing marks, either on the rope or the tree trunk. He was tied up there. And he stood still."

"How do you interpret that?"

"There are two possibilities," replied Nyberg. "Either he was already dead, or at least unconscious, when he was tied up, or else he chose not to resist. But that's hard to believe."

Wallander thought about it.

"There's a third possibility," he said finally. "Runfeldt simply didn't have the strength to put up any resistance."

Nyberg agreed. That was also a possibility, and maybe the most likely.

"Let me ask one more thing," Wallander went on. "I know you can't tell me for sure. But we always imagine how something might have happened. Nobody guesses more often than cops do. Even though we always deny it. Was there more than one person there, you think?"

"I thought of that," said Nyberg. "There are plenty of reasons why there should have been more than one. Dragging a man into the woods and tying him up isn't that easy. But I have my doubts."

"How come?"

"I don't honestly know."

"Go back to the ditch in Lödinge. What sort of feeling did you have there?"

"The same. There should have been more than one. But I'm not sure."

"I have that feeling too," said Wallander. "And it bothers me."

"At any rate, I think it's a person with a great deal of physical strength," said Nyberg. "There are plenty of indications."

Wallander had nothing more to ask.

"Otherwise nothing, then?"

"A couple of beer cans and a press-on nail. That's it."

"A press-on nail?"

"Women use them. But it could have been here quite a while."

"Try to get a few hours' sleep," said Wallander.

"And when would I have time for that?" asked Nyberg. Wallander could hear him suddenly getting annoyed. He hurried to end the conversation and hung up. The phone rang instantly. It was Martinsson.

"Can I come and see you?" he asked. "When were we supposed to have another meeting?"

"Nine o'clock. We've got time."

Wallander hung up. Martinsson must have come up with something. He could feel the tension. What they needed most of all right now was a real breakthrough.

Martinsson came in and sat down in Wallander's guest chair. He got straight to the point.

"I've been thinking about all that mercenary stuff. And Harald Berggren's diary. This morning when I woke up it struck me that I've actually met a person who was in the Congo at the same time as Harald Berggren."

"As a mercenary?" asked Wallander in surprise.

"No. As a member of the Swedish UN contingent which was supposed to disarm the Belgian forces in Katanga province."

Wallander shook his head. "I was twelve or thirteen when all that happened. I don't remember much about it. Actually, nothing except that Dag Hammarskjöld crashed in a plane."

"I wasn't even born yet," said Martinsson. "But I remember something about it from school."

"Who was it you met?"

"Several years ago I was going to meetings of the People's Party," Martinsson continued. "Afterwards there was often some sort of get-together with coffee. I got a bad stomach from all the coffee I drank in those days."

Wallander drummed his fingers impatiently on the desk.

"At one of the meetings I wound up sitting next to a man who was about sixty. How we got to talking about it I don't know, but he told me he'd been a captain and adjutant to General von Horn, who was commander of the Swedish UN force in the Congo. I remember he mentioned there were mercenaries involved."

Wallander listened with growing interest.

"I made a few calls this morning when I got up. One of my fellow party members knew who that captain was. His name is Olof Hanzell, and he's retired. He lives in Nybrostrand."

"Great," said Wallander. "Let's pay him a visit as soon as possible."

"I've already called him. He said he'd gladly talk to the police if we thought he could help. He sounded lucid and claimed he has an excellent memory."

Martinsson placed a slip of paper with a phone number on Wallander's desk.

"We have to try everything," Wallander said. "The meeting we're having this morning will be short."

Martinsson stood up to go. He stopped in the doorway.

"Did you see the papers?" he asked.

"When would I have time for that?"

"They say Björk went through the roof. People in Lödinge and other areas have been talking to the press. After what happened to Eriksson they've started talking about the need for a citizen militia."

"They've always done that," Wallander replied dismissively. "That's nothing to worry about."

"I'm not so sure," said Martinsson. "There's something different about the stories today."

"What's that?"

"They aren't speaking anonymously anymore. They're giving out their names and photos. That's never happened before. The idea of a citizen militia is acceptable all of a sudden."

Wallander knew that Martinsson was right. But he still had a hard time believing that it was anything but the usual manifestation of fear when a brutal crime had been committed. It even made some sense to Wallander.

"There'll be more articles tomorrow," was all he said. "Once the news about Runfeldt gets out. It would probably be a good idea for us to prepare Chief Holgersson for what's coming."

"What's your impression?" asked Martinsson.

"Of Lisa Holgersson? I think she seems first-rate."

Martinsson stepped back into the room. Wallander saw how tired he was. He thought Martinsson had aged rapidly during his years as a cop.

"I thought what happened this summer was the exception," he said. "Now I realize it wasn't."

"There aren't many similarities," said Wallander. "We shouldn't draw parallels that aren't there."

"That's not what I was thinking about. It's all this violence. As if nowadays it's necessary to torture the people you've decided to kill."

"I know. But I can't tell you how we're supposed to deal with it."

Martinsson left the room. Wallander thought about what he had heard. He decided to make the drive himself to talk to retired Captain Olof Hanzell that very day.

As Wallander had predicted, the meeting was brief. Even though no one had gotten much sleep, they all seemed determined and energized. They knew that they were faced with a complex investigation. Per Åkeson had also showed up to listen to Wallander's summary. Afterwards he had very few questions.

They divided up the various tasks and discussed what should be given priority. The question of calling in extra manpower was left on the table for the time being. Chief Holgersson had released more patrol officers from other assignments so they could take part in the homicide investigation, which would now involve twice as much work. When the meeting neared its conclusion after about an hour, they all had far too many assignments to handle.

"One more thing," said Wallander in closing. "We have to expect that these murders are going to get a lot of press. What we've seen so far is just the tip of the iceberg. As I understand it, people out in the surrounding areas have started to talk again about organizing night patrols and a citizen militia. We'll have to wait and see if things develop the way I think they will. For now, it's easier if the chief and I handle the contact with the press. And I'd be grateful if Ann-Britt could help out at our press conferences."

At ten past ten the meeting broke up. Wallander talked to Chief Holgersson for a while. They decided to hold a press conference at five thirty. Wallander went out in the corridor to find Per Åkeson, but he had already left. Wallander went back to his office and called the number written on Martinsson's note, remembering that he still hadn't put Svedberg's note on his desk. At that instant someone picked up the phone. It was Olof Hanzell himself. He had a friendly voice. Wallander introduced himself and asked if he could come out and see him that morning. Captain Hanzell said he was welcome to, and gave him directions.

When Wallander left the station the sky had cleared up again. It was windy, but the sun was shining between the scattered clouds. He reminded himself to put a sweater in his car for the coming cool days. In spite of his haste to get to Nybrostrand, he stopped at a real-estate office downtown and stood looking at the window notices about properties for sale. At least one of the houses interested him. If he'd had more time he would have gone in and picked up a photocopy of the info sheet. He memorized the sale number and went back to his car. He wondered whether Linda had managed to get on a plane to Stockholm or was still waiting out at Sturup.

Then he drove east toward Nybrostrand. He passed the golf course and then turned right and started looking for Skrakvägen, where Olof Hanzell lived. All the streets in the area were named after birds. He wondered if it was a coincidence that meant something. He was searching for a person who had killed a birdwatcher. Maybe someone lived on Skrakvägen who could help him find the perpetrator.

After taking several wrong turns, he finally found the correct address. He parked the car and walked through the gate of a villa that must have been less than ten years old. Still, it seemed somehow dilapidated. Wallander thought it was the type of house he would never feel comfortable in. The front door was opened by a man dressed in a sweatsuit. He had close-cropped gray hair, a thin mustache, and seemed to be in good physical shape. He smiled and held out his hand in greeting. Wallander introduced himself.

"My wife died years ago," said Olof Hanzell. "Since then I've lived alone. Please forgive the mess. But come on in!"

The first thing Wallander noticed was a large African drum in the entryway. Hanzell followed his gaze.

"The year I was in the Congo was the journey of my life. I never traveled again. The children were small and my wife didn't want to. And then one day it was suddenly too late."

He invited Wallander into the living room, where coffee cups were set out on a table. There too, African mementos hung on the walls. Wallander sat down on a sofa and said yes to coffee. Actually, he was hungry and could use something to eat. Hanzell had put out a tray of rusks.

"I bake them myself," he said, nodding at the rusks. "It's a good pastime for an old soldier."

Wallander wanted to get to the point. He took the photograph of the three men out of his pocket and handed it across the table.

"I want to start by asking whether you recognize any of these men. I can tell you that the picture was taken in the Congo during the same time the Swedish UN force was there."

Olof Hanzell took the photograph. Without looking at it he stood up and got a pair of reading glasses. Wallander remembered the visit he would have to make to the optician as soon as he could. Hanzell took the photo over to the window and looked at it for a long time. Wallander listened to the silence that filled the house. He waited. Then Hanzell came back from the window. Without a word he laid the photograph on the table and left the room. Wallander ate another rusk. He had almost decided to go look for Hanzell when he returned with a photo album in his hand, went back to the window, and starting leafing through it. Wallander kept waiting. Finally Hanzell found what he was looking for. He came back to the table and handed the open photo album to Wallander.

"Look at the picture at the lower left," Hanzell said. "It's not very good, I'm afraid. But I think it might interest you."

Wallander looked. He gave an inward start. The photos showed some dead soldiers. They lay lined up with bloody faces, arms blown off, their torsos torn up by bullets. The soldiers were black. Behind them stood two white men holding rifles. They stood posing as if for a hunting photo. The dead soldiers were their trophies.

Wallander recognized one of the white men at once. It was the one on the left in the photograph he had found stuffed into the binding of Harald Berggren's diary. There was absolutely no doubt.

"I thought I recognized him," said Hanzell. "But I couldn't be sure. It took me a while to find the right album."

"Who is he? Terry O'Banion or Simon Marchand?"

He saw Hanzell react with surprise.

"Simon Marchand," replied Hanzell. "I must admit I'm curious how you knew that."

"I'll explain in a minute. But first tell me how you got hold of these pictures."

Hanzell sat down.

"How much do you know about what was going on in the Congo in those days?" he asked.

"Practically nothing."

"Let me give you some background. I think it's necessary so you can understand."

"Take all the time you need," said Wallander.

"Let me start in 1953. At that time there were four independent countries in Africa that were members of the United Nations. Seven years later that number had climbed to twenty-six. Which means that the entire African continent was in turmoil at the time. Decolonization had entered its most dramatic phase. New countries were proclaiming their independence in a steady stream. The birth pangs were often severe. But not always as severe as they were in the Belgian Congo. In 1959, the Belgian government worked out a plan for making the transition to independence. The date for the transfer of power was set for June 30th, 1960. The closer that day came, the more the unrest in the country grew. Tribes took different sides, and acts of politically motivated violence happened every day. But independence came, and an experienced politician named Kasavubu became president, while Lumumba became prime minister. Lumumba is a name you've heard before, I presume."

Wallander nodded doubtfully.

"For a few days you might have thought there would be a peaceful transition from colony to independent state, in spite of everything. But after only a few weeks, the Force Publique, the country's regular army, mutinied against their Belgian officers. Belgian paratroopers were dropped in to rescue their own men. The country quickly sank into chaos. The situation became uncontrollable for Kasavubu and Lumumba. At the same time, Katanga province, the southernmost in the country and the richest because of its mineral wealth, proclaimed its own secession and independence. Their leader was Moise Tshombe.

Kasavubu and Lumumba requested help from the UN. Dag Hammarskjöld, who was General Secretary at the time, mustered an intervention force of UN troops in a short time, including troops from Sweden. Our role was to serve as police only. The Belgians who were left in the Congo supported Tshombe in Katanga. With money from the big mining companies, they hired assorted mercenaries. And that's where this photograph comes in."

Hanzell paused and took a sip of coffee.

"That might give you some idea how tense and complex the situation was back then."

"I can see it must have been extremely confusing," replied Wallander, waiting impatiently for him to go on.

"Several hundred mercenaries were involved during the conflict in Katanga," said Hanzell. "They came from many different countries: France, Belgium, the French colonies in Africa. Fifteen years after the end of the Second World War, there were still plenty of Germans who could never accept that the war had ended the way it did. They took their revenge on innocent Africans. There were also a number of Scandinavians. Some of them died and were buried in graves that can no longer be located. On one occasion an African came to the Swedish UN encampment. He had papers and photos of a number of mercenaries who had fallen. But no Swedes."

"Why did he come to the Swedish encampment?"

"We Swedes were known to be polite and generous. He came with a cardboard box and wanted to sell the contents. God knows where he got hold of it."

"And you bought it?"

Hanzell nodded.

"I think I paid the equivalent of ten kronor for the box. I tossed most of it. But I kept a few of the photographs. Including this one."

Wallander decided to go one step further.

"Harald Berggren," he said. "One of the other men in the photograph is Swedish and that's his name. He must be either the one in the middle or the one on the right. Does that name mean anything to you?"

Hanzell thought about it. Then he shook his head.

"No. But on the other hand, that's not so surprising."

"Why not?"

"Many of the mercenaries changed their names. Not just the Swedes. You took a new name for the time of your contract. When it was all over and you were lucky enough to be alive, you could assume your old name again."

Wallander thought for a moment.

"So that means Harald Berggren could have been in the Congo under a completely different name?"

"Exactly."

"That also means that he could have written the diary under his real name. Which would have functioned as a pseudonym?"

"Right."

"That could also mean that Harald Berggren may have been killed under another name?"

"Yes."

Wallander gave Hanzell a searching look.

"In other words, it means that it's almost impossible to say whether he's alive or dead. He could be dead under one name and alive under another."

"Mercenaries are skittish people. Which is understandable."

"That means it would be almost impossible to find him, if he didn't want to be found."

Hanzell nodded. Wallander stared at the tray of rusks.

"I know that many of my former colleagues had another view," said Hanzell. "But for me, mercenaries were always despicable. They killed for money. Even if they claimed they were fighting for an ideology. For freedom. Against communism. But the truth was something else. They killed indiscriminately. They took orders from whoever was paying the most at the moment."

"A mercenary must have had considerable difficulty returning to normal life," said Wallander.

"Many of them never managed to. They turned into what you might call cold shadows, on the periphery of society. Or else they drank themselves to death. And some of them were probably mentally un-balanced to start with."

"How do you mean?"

Hanzell's reply came quickly and firmly.

"Sadists and psychopaths."

Wallander nodded. He understood. Harald Berggren was a man who both existed and didn't exist. How he might fit into the picture was far from obvious. But his gut feeling was quite clear.

He was stuck. He had no idea how to proceed.

Chapter Fifteen

Wallander stayed in Nybrostrand until late in the afternoon. But he didn't spend all his time with Olof Hanzell. He left the house at one o'clock. When he came out into the autumn air after the long conversation, he felt at a loss. Instead of returning to Ystad he drove down to the sea. He decided to take a walk. Maybe it would help him think. But when he got down to the beach and felt the biting fall wind, he changed his mind and went back to the car. He sat in the front on the passenger side and leaned the seat back as far as it would go. Then he closed his eyes and started going over in his mind all the events that had taken place since the morning two weeks ago when Sven Tyrén came into his office and reported Holger Eriksson missing. Today, on October 12th, they had another murder and were looking for another killer.

Wallander tried to analyze the chronology. Among all the things he had learned from Rydberg over the years, one of the most important was that the events that seem to have occurred first were not necessarily the earliest in the chain of causality. Holger Eriksson and Gösta Runfeldt had both been killed. But were they killed out of revenge? Or was it a crime committed for gain, even though he couldn't figure out what kind of gain that might be?

He opened his eyes and looked at a tattered string of flags whipping in the stiff breeze. Holger Eriksson had been impaled in a meticulously prepared pit full of sharpened stakes. Gösta Runfeldt had been held prisoner and then strangled.

There were too many bothersome details. Why the explicit display of cruelty? And why was Runfeldt held prisoner before he was killed? Wallander tried to go over the basic assumptions that the investigative

group had to start with. The perpetrator must have known both victims. He was familiar with Eriksson's routines. And he must have
known that Runfeldt was going to take a trip. These were both assumptions they could start from. Another one was that the murderer wasn't
at all concerned that the dead men would be found. There were signs
that the opposite was true.

Why put something on display? he thought. So that somebody will
notice what you've done. Did the murderer want other people to see
what he had accomplished? If so, what was it he wanted to show? That
those two particular men were dead? But not only that. He also wanted
it to be clear how it had happened. That they had been killed in a
gruesome and premeditated way.

That was a possibility, he thought with growing distaste. In that case
the murders of Eriksson and Runfeldt were part of something much
bigger, something whose scope he couldn't grasp yet. It didn't necessarily mean that more people would die. But it definitely meant that
Holger Eriksson, Gösta Runfeldt, and the person who had killed them
had to be looked for among a larger group of people. Some type of
community. Such as a group of mercenaries in a remote African war.

Wallander suddenly wished he had a cigarette. Even though it had
been unusually easy for him to quit several years back, there were times
when he wished he still smoked. He got out of the car and switched to
the back seat. Changing seats was like changing perspective. He soon
forgot the cigarettes and went back to what he was thinking about.

The most important thing was to find a connection between Eriksson and Runfeldt. It was there somewhere, he was convinced of that.
To find this connecting link they needed to know more about the two
men. Outwardly they had very little in common. The differences began
with their ages. They belonged to different generations. There was an
age gap of thirty years. Eriksson could have been Runfeldt's father. But
somewhere there was a point where their tracks crossed. The search for
that point had to be the focus of the investigation now. Wallander
couldn't see any other route to take.

The phone rang. It was Höglund.

"Has something happened?" he asked.

"I have to admit I'm calling out of sheer curiosity," she replied.

"The talk with Captain Hanzell was productive," said Wallander.
"One of the many things he had to say that could be important was that
Harald Berggren might be living under an assumed name. Mercenaries often used phony names when they signed their contracts or made
verbal agreements."

"That's going to make it harder for us to find him."

"That was my first thought, too. It's like dropping the needle back
into the haystack. But maybe it doesn't have to be that way. How many

people actually change their names during their lifetimes? Even though it's going to be a tedious task, it should be possible to solve it."

"Where are you?"

"At the beach. In Nybrostrand."

"What are you doing there?"

"As a matter of fact, I'm sitting in the car thinking." He noticed the sharpness in his voice, as if he felt the need to defend himself. He wondered why.

"Then I won't bother you," she said.

"You're not bothering me. I'm heading back to Ystad now. I'm thinking of driving past Lödinge on the way."

"Any special reason?"

"I need to refresh my memory. Later I'm going over to Runfeldt's apartment. I plan on getting there by three. It would be good if Vanja Andersson could meet me there."

"I'll see to it."

They said goodbye. Wallander started the car and drove toward Lödinge. He was far from done with his thinking. He had made a little progress. In his mind the investigation had been given an outline. He had begun to plumb depths that were deeper than he imagined.

It wasn't completely true, as he had claimed to Höglund, that he went back to Eriksson's house because he felt the need to refresh his memory. Wallander wanted to see the house right before he went back to Runfeldt's apartment. He wanted to see if there were any similarities. He wanted to know where the differences lay.

When he turned into the driveway to Eriksson's house, two cars were already there. Surprised, he wondered who the visitors could be. Reporters devoting an autumn day to taking gloomy pictures of a murder scene? He had his answer as soon as he entered the courtyard. Standing there was a lawyer from Ystad whom Wallander had met on previous occasions. There were also two women, one elderly and one about Wallander's age. The lawyer, whose name was Bjurman, shook hands and said hello.

"I'm in charge of Holger Eriksson's will," he said. "We thought the police were done with their investigations out here. I called and asked at the police station."

"We won't be done until we catch the perpetrator," replied Wallander. "But we have nothing against you going through the house."

Wallander remembered noticing in the investigative report that Bjurman was Eriksson's executor. He also seemed to recall that it was Martinsson who had been in contact with him.

Bjurman introduced Wallander to the two women. The older one shook his hand in a noticeably leery manner, as if it was beneath her dignity to have anything to do with the police. Wallander, who was extremely sensitive to other people's snobbishness, was instantly riled, but he held himself in check. The other woman was friendly.

"Mrs. Mårtensson and Ms. von Fessler are from the Cultural Association in Lund. Holger Eriksson willed most of his estate to the association. He kept meticulous accounts of his property. We were just about to start going through everything."

"Let me know if anything's missing," said Wallander. "Otherwise I won't disturb you. I'm not staying long."

"Is it true the police haven't found the murderer?" said Ms. von Fessler, the older woman. Wallander took her words to be a statement of ill-concealed criticism.

"That's right," said Wallander. "The police have not."

He realized he had to end the conversation before he got angry. He turned around and walked up to the house, where the front door stood open. To insulate himself from the conversation going on out in the courtyard, he shut the door behind him. A mouse raced right by his feet and disappeared behind an old wardrobe that stood against the wall. It's fall, thought Wallander. The field mice are making their way into the walls of the house. Winter is on its way.

He went through the house slowly, paying close attention. He wasn't looking for anything in particular; he wanted to memorize the house. It took him about twenty minutes. Bjurman and the two women were in one of the other two wings when he went out the door. Wallander decided to leave without saying anything. He looked out toward the fields as he walked to his car. No crows clamoring over by the ditch. Just as he reached the car he stopped. It was something that Bjurman had said. At first he couldn't recall what it was. It took him a moment to remember. He went back to the house. Bjurman and the two women were still in the outbuilding. He pushed open the door and beckoned Bjurman over.

"What was it you said about the will?" he asked.

"Holger Eriksson willed most of his estate to the Cultural Association in Lund."

"Most? So that means not everything is going there?"

"There's a grant of 100,000 kronor allocated to another recipient. That's all."

"What other recipient?"

"A church in Berg parish. Svenstavik Church. As a gift. To be used in accordance with the decision of the church authorities."

Wallander had never heard of the place.

"Is Svenstavik in Skåne?" he asked dubiously.

"It's up in southern Jämtland," replied Bjurman. "Near the border of Härjadal."

"What did Holger Eriksson have to do with Svenstavik?" asked Wallander in surprise. "I thought he was born here in Ystad."

"Unfortunately I have no information on that," replied Bjurman. "Eriksson was a very secretive man."

"Did he give any explanation for the gift?"

"The will is an exemplary document, brief and precise," said Bjurman. "No explanations of an emotional nature are included. Svenstavik Church, according to his last wish, is to receive 100,000 kronor. And that is what it shall receive."

Wallander had no more questions. When he got back to his car he called the station. Ebba answered. She was the one he wanted to talk to.

"I want you to find the phone number for the parsonage at Svenstavik," he said. "Or it might be in Östersund. I assume that's the nearest city."

"Where is Svenstavik?" she asked.

"Don't you know?" said Wallander. "In southern Jämtland."

"Very funny," she replied.

Wallander admitted that he hadn't known either until Bjurman told him.

"When you get the number, let me know," he said. "I'm on my way to Runfeldt's apartment now."

"Chief Holgersson wants to talk to you right away," said Ebba. "Reporters keep calling here. But the press conference was postponed until 6:30 tonight."

"That suits me fine," said Wallander.

"Your sister called, too," Ebba went on. "She'd like to talk to you before she goes back to Stockholm."

The reminder of his father's death was both swift and harsh. But he couldn't give in to his feelings. At least not right now.

"I'll call her," he said. "But the parsonage in Svenstavik is top priority."

He drove back to Ystad. He stopped at a fast-food stand and ate a flavorless hamburger. He was about to get back in his car but turned around and went back to the counter. This time he ordered a hot dog. He ate quickly, as if he were committing an illegal act and was afraid someone would catch him. Then he drove to Västra Vallgatan. Höglund's old car was parked outside the door to Gösta Runfeldt's building.

The wind was still gusting. Wallander was cold. He hunched up his shoulders as he hurried across the street.

It wasn't Höglund but Svedberg who opened the door to Runfeldt's apartment when Wallander rang the bell.

"She had to go home," said Svedberg when Wallander asked for her.

"One of her kids is sick. Her car wouldn't start, so she took mine. But she'll be back soon."

Wallander went into the apartment's living room and looked around.

"Is Nyberg done already?" he asked in surprise.

Svedberg gave him a baffled look.

"Didn't you hear?" he asked.

"Hear what?"

"About Nyberg's foot."

"I haven't heard a thing," said Wallander. "What happened?"

"He slipped on a patch of oil outside the station. He fell so hard that he tore a muscle or a tendon in his left foot. He's at the hospital right now. He called and said he can still work. But he'll have to use a crutch to walk. He was really pissed off."

Wallander thought about Sven Tyrén's oil truck parked outside the front door of the station. He decided not to mention it.

They were interrupted by the doorbell. It was Vanja Andersson. She was very pale. Wallander nodded to Svedberg, who disappeared into Runfeldt's study. He took Ms. Andersson into the living room. She seemed frightened to be in the apartment, and hesitated when he invited her to sit down.

"I know this is unpleasant," he said. "But I wouldn't have asked you to come here if it wasn't absolutely necessary."

She nodded. Wallander doubted whether she really understood. Everything that was happening must be just as incomprehensible to her as the fact that Runfeldt never went to Nairobi and was found dead in the woods outside Marsvinsholm instead.

"You've been to this apartment before," said Wallander. "And you have a good memory. I know that because you remembered the color of his suitcase."

"Have you found it?" she asked.

Wallander realized that they hadn't even started looking for it. In his own mind it had disappeared. He excused himself and went to find Svedberg, who was methodically searching the contents of a bookshelf.

"Have you heard anything about Gösta Runfeldt's suitcase?"

"Did he have a suitcase?"

Wallander shook his head. "It's nothing. I'll talk to Nyberg."

He went back to the living room. Vanja Andersson was sitting uneasily on the couch. Wallander saw that she wanted to get out of there as soon as possible. She looked as if she had to force herself to breathe the air in the apartment.

"We'll come back to the suitcase," he said. "What I'd like to ask you now is to go through the apartment and try to see if anything is missing."

She gave him a terrified look.

"How could I tell? I haven't been here very often."

"I know," said Wallander. "But you still might notice something missing. Right now everything is important, if we're going to find the person who did this. I'm sure you want that as much as we do."

Wallander was expecting it, yet it still came as a surprise.

She burst into tears. Svedberg appeared in the doorway. As usual in these kinds of situations, Wallander felt helpless. He wondered if the present-day police cadets were trained in how to comfort people. He had to remember to ask Höglund about it.

Svedberg came back from the bathroom and handed a tissue to Vanja Andersson. She stopped crying as suddenly as she had started.

"I'm terribly sorry," she said. "It's so difficult."

"I know," said Wallander. "There's nothing to be sorry about. I don't think people cry often enough."

She looked at him.

"That goes for me too," said Wallander.

After a brief pause she got up from the couch. She was ready to begin.

"Take your time," Wallander told her. "Try to remember how it looked the last time you were here to water the flowers. Take your time."

He followed her but kept his distance. When he heard Svedberg cursing in the study, he went in and held a finger to his lips. Svedberg nodded; he understood. Wallander had often thought that significant moments in complicated investigations occurred either during conversations or during periods of absolute and intense silence. He had seen it happen countless times. Right now, silence was essential. He could see that she was really making an effort.

Still, nothing came of it. They returned to their starting point, the couch in the living room. She shook her head.

"I think everything looks the same as usual," she said. "I can't see that anything is missing or different."

Wallander was not surprised. He would have noticed if she had paused during her survey of the apartment.

"You haven't thought of anything else?" he asked.

"I thought he had gone to Nairobi," she said. "I watered his flowers and took care of the shop."

"And you did both of those things very well," said Wallander. "Thank you for coming. We'll probably be contacting you again."

He escorted her to the door. Svedberg came out of the bathroom just as she left.

"Nothing seems to be missing," said Wallander.

"He seems to have been a complicated man," said Svedberg

thoughtfully. "His study is a strange mixture of chaos and meticulous order. When it comes to his flowers, there's perfect order. I never imagined there were so many books about orchids. But when it comes to his personal life, his papers are a big mess. In his account books from the flower shop for 1994, I found a tax return from 1969. By the way, that year he declared a dizzying income of 30,000 kronor."

"I wonder how much we made back then," said Wallander. "Probably not much more than that. Most likely less. I seem to remember that we were getting about 2,000 kronor a month."

They pondered this until Wallander said, "Let's keep searching."

Svedberg went back to what he was doing. Wallander stood by the window and looked out over the harbor. The front door opened. It was Höglund. He met her out in the entryway.

"Nothing serious, I hope?"

"A fall cold," she said. "My husband is over in what used to be called the East Indies. My neighbor rescued me."

"I've often wondered about that," said Wallander. "I thought helpful neighbor women went extinct back in the '50s."

"That's probably true. But I've been lucky. She's in her fifties and has no children. Of course she doesn't do it for free. And sometimes she says no."

"Then what do you do?"

She shrugged her shoulders in resignation.

"I improvise. If it's in the evening I might be able to find a babysitter. Sometimes I wonder myself how I do it. But you know there are times when I can't. Then I come in late. I don't think men really understand what a complicated process it is to figure out how to handle your job when you have a sick child, for example."

"Probably not," replied Wallander. "Maybe we should see to it that your neighbor gets some kind of medal."

"She's been talking about moving," said Höglund gloomily. "What I'll do then, I don't even dare think about."

The conversation died out.

"Has she been here?" asked Höglund.

"Vanja Andersson has come and gone. Nothing seems to have disappeared from the apartment. But she reminded me about something completely different. Runfeldt's suitcase. I have to admit I forgot all about it."

"Me too," she said. "As far as I know, they didn't find it out in the woods. I talked to Nyberg right before he broke his foot."

"Is it that bad?"

"Well, it's badly sprained, anyway."

"Then he's going to be in a bad mood for a while. Which is not good at all."

"I'll invite him over for dinner," said Höglund cheerfully. "He likes boiled fish."

"How do you know that?" asked Wallander in surprise.

"I've invited him over before," she replied. "He's a very nice dinner guest. He talks about all kinds of things, and never about his job."

Wallander wondered briefly whether he would be considered a nice dinner guest. He knew that he too tried not to talk about work. But when was the last time he had been invited somewhere for dinner? It was so long ago that he couldn't even remember.

"Runfeldt's children have arrived," said Höglund. "Hansson is handling them. A daughter and a son."

They were now in the living room. Wallander looked at the photograph of Runfeldt's wife.

"We should find out what happened to her," he said.

"She drowned."

"More of the details."

"Hansson understands that. He's usually thorough in his interviews. He'll ask them about their mother."

Wallander knew she was right. Hansson had many bad traits, but one of his best skills was interviewing witnesses. Gathering information. Interviewing parents about their children. Or vice versa, as in this case.

Wallander told Höglund about his conversation with Olof Hanzell. She listened attentively. He skipped a lot of the details. The most important part was his conclusion that Harald Berggren might be living under a different name. He had mentioned it before when they talked on the phone. He noticed that she had been thinking more about this.

"If he changed his name legally we can track it down through the Patent and Registration Office," she said.

"I doubt that a mercenary soldier would follow such a formal process," Wallander objected. "But of course we'll look into it, like everything else. It'll be a lot of trouble."

He told her about his meeting with the women from Lund and Attorney Bjurman out at Holger Eriksson's farm.

"My husband and I drove through the interior of Norrland once," she said. "I have a distinct memory of passing through Svenstavik."

"Ebba should have called to give me the number of the parsonage," Wallander remembered, taking his phone out of his pocket. It was turned off. He swore at his own carelessness. Ann-Britt tried to hide her smile but couldn't. Wallander realized he was acting like a child. Embarrassed, he called the police station. He borrowed a pen from Höglund and wrote down the number on a corner of the newspaper. It turned out that Ebba had tried to call him several times.

At that moment, Svedberg came into the living room with a stack of papers in his hand. Wallander saw that they were receipts.

"This might be something," said Svedberg. "It looks as if Gösta Runfeldt has a place on Harpegatan here in town. He pays rent once a month. As far as I can tell, he keeps it totally separate from any payments that have to do with the flower shop."

"Harpegatan?" asked Höglund. "Where's that?"

"Over by Nattmanstorg," replied Wallander. "Right downtown."

"Has Vanja Andersson ever mentioned that he had another place?"

"The question is whether she knew about it," said Wallander. "I'll find out right now."

Wallander left the apartment and walked the short distance over to the flower shop. The wind was now blowing hard. He bent over and held his breath in the wind. Vanja Andersson was alone in the shop. As before, the scent of flowers was strong. A brief feeling of homelessness came over Wallander as he thought about the trip to Rome, and his father, who was no longer alive. But he pushed aside the thoughts. He was a cop. He would grieve on his own time, not now.

"I have a question," he said. "You can probably give me a straight yes-or-no answer."

She looked at him with her pale, frightened face. Wallander thought that certain people always gave the impression of being prepared for the worst. Vanja Andersson seemed to be one of those people. Right now he could hardly blame her.

"Did you know that Gösta Runfeldt was renting a place on Harpegatan here in town?" he asked.

She shook her head.

"Are you sure?"

"Gösta didn't have any other place but this one."

Wallander suddenly felt in a big hurry.

"That's all then," he said. "Thanks."

When he got back to the apartment, Svedberg and Höglund had gathered all the keys they could find. They took Svedberg's car to Harpegatan. It was an ordinary apartment building. Runfeldt's name wasn't on the list of residents in the entryway.

"It says on the receipts that it's in the basement," said Svedberg.

They made their way down the half-flight of stairs to the floor below ground. Wallander noticed the sharp fragrance of winter apples. Svedberg started trying the keys. The twelfth one worked. They went into a corridor from which red-painted steel doors led to various store-rooms.

Höglund was the one who found it.

"I think this is it," she said, pointing to a door.

Wallander and Svedberg went to stand next to her. On the door there was a sticker with a floral motif.

"An orchid," said Svedberg.

"A secret room," replied Wallander.

Svedberg tried the keys again. Wallander noticed that an extra lock was set into the door.

Finally the first lock clicked. Wallander felt the tension inside him swell. Svedberg kept on trying the keys. He had only two left when he looked at them and nodded.

"Let's go in," said Wallander.

Svedberg opened the door.

Chapter Sixteen

The terror sank into Wallander like a claw.

When the thought came it was already too late. Svedberg had opened the door. In that brief instant when terror replaced time, Wallander waited for the explosion to come. But all that happened was that Svedberg felt with one hand along the wall and muttered, wondering where the light switch was. Afterwards, Wallander felt embarrassed about his fear. Why would Runfeldt have booby-trapped his cellar room with a bomb?

Svedberg turned on the light. They entered the room and looked around. Since it was underground, there was only a thin row of windows along the top of the wall. The first thing Wallander noticed was that the windows had iron gratings on the inside. That was unusual, something Runfeldt must have paid for himself.

The room was set up as an office. There was a desk, and file cabinets along the walls. On a small table next to the wall stood a coffee maker and some cups on a towel. The room had a telephone, fax machine, and photocopier.

"Should we look around or wait for Nyberg?" asked Svedberg.

Wallander heard him, but waited to reply. He was still trying to understand his first impressions. Why had Gösta Runfeldt rented this room and kept the payments separate from his other bookkeeping? Why hadn't Vanja Andersson known about it? And most important: What did he use the room for?

"No bed," Svedberg continued. "It doesn't seem to be a secret love nest."

"No woman could get romantic down here," said Höglund skeptically.

Wallander still hadn't answered Svedberg. The most important

154

question, without a doubt, was why Runfeldt had kept this office secret. Because it was an office. There was no doubt about that.

He let his gaze wander along the walls. There was another door. He nodded to Svedberg, who walked over and tried the handle. The door was open. He looked inside.

"It looks like a darkroom," said Svedberg. "With all the necessary equipment."

Wallander started to wonder if there was some simple, logical reason why Runfeldt had this space. He took a lot of photographs. They could see that in his apartment. He had a big collection of orchid photos from all over the world. There were seldom any people in his pictures, and they were often black-and-white, although the colors of orchids were beautiful and should have tempted a man with a camera.

Wallander and Höglund went and looked over Svedberg's shoulder. It was indeed a tiny darkroom. Wallander decided they didn't have to wait for Nyberg. They could go through the room themselves.

The first thing he looked for was a suitcase, but he found none. He sat down at the desk chair and started leafing through the papers on the desk. Svedberg and Höglund concentrated on the file cabinets. Wallander remembered vaguely that Rydberg, way back in the beginning, on one of those frequent evenings when they sat on his balcony drinking whiskey, had said that the work of a policeman and an auditor was quite similar. They spent a good deal of their time going through papers. If that's correct, then right now I'm auditing a dead man; and in the books, like in a secret account, there's an office located on Harpegatan in Ystad.

Wallander pulled out the desk drawers. In the top one was a laptop computer. Wallander's computer literacy was limited. He often had to ask for help when he had to work on the computer in his office at the station. He knew that both Svedberg and Höglund were comfortable with computers and viewed them as essential working tools.

"Let's see what's hiding in here," he said, lifting the computer to the desktop.

He got up from the chair. Höglund sat down. There was an outlet in the wall by the desk. She opened the lid and turned on the laptop. After a moment the screen lit up. Svedberg was still searching through one of the file cabinets. She logged on to the computer.

"No passwords," she muttered. "I'm in."

Wallander leaned forward to watch, so closely that he could smell the discreet perfume she wore. He thought about his eyes. He couldn't wait any longer. He had to get reading glasses.

"It's a directory," she said. "A list of names."

"See if Harald Berggren is on it," said Wallander.

She gave him a look of surprise.

"You think?"

"I don't think anything. But we can try."

Svedberg had left the file cabinet and now stood next to Wallander while Höglund searched through the directory. Then she shook her head.

"Holger Eriksson?" Svedberg suggested.

Wallander nodded. She searched. Nothing.

"Just browse through the directory at random," said Wallander.

"Here's a man named Lennart Skoglund," she said. "Should we try him?"

"That's Nacka, damn it!" Svedberg exclaimed.

They gave him a puzzled look.

"There's a famous soccer player named Lennart Skoglund," said Svedberg. "His nickname is Nacka. Haven't you heard of him?"

Wallander nodded. Höglund didn't know who he was.

"Lennart Skoglund sounds like a common name," said Wallander. "Let's look him up."

She pulled up the record on him. Wallander squinted his eyes and managed to read the brief text.

Lennart Skoglund. Started 10 June 1994. Ended 19 August 1994. No steps taken. Case closed.

"What does that mean?" Svedberg wondered.

"It's almost as if one of us had written it," said Höglund.

At that instant Wallander knew what the explanation might be. He thought about the technical equipment Runfeldt had bought. And about the photo lab, and the secret office. The whole thing had seemed improbable, yet now, as they stood leaning over the directory in the little computer, it did seem likely.

Wallander stretched his back.

"The question is whether Runfeldt was interested in other things besides orchids. The question is whether Runfeldt might also have been a private detective."

There were plenty of counter-arguments. But Wallander wanted to follow this track, and he wanted to do it at once.

"I think I'm right," he went on. "Now you two have to try and convince me that I'm wrong. Go through everything you find here. Keep your eyes peeled and don't forget Holger Eriksson. And I want one of you to get hold of Vanja Andersson. Without knowing it, she might have seen or heard things that have to do with this little operation. I'm going back to the station and talk to Runfeldt's kids."

"What do we do about the press conference at 6:30?" Höglund asked. "I promised to be there."

"It's better if you stay here."

Svedberg handed his car keys to Wallander, who shook his head.

"I'll get my own car. I need a walk anyway."

When he reached the street level he regretted it at once. The wind was strong and it seemed to be getting colder all the time. Wallander hesitated a moment, wondering whether to go home and get a heavier sweater. He decided to skip it. He was in a hurry. Besides, he was uneasy. They had made some new discoveries, but they didn't fit into the picture. Why had Gösta Runfeldt been a private detective? Wallander hurried through town and got his car. He noticed that the fuel gauge was near empty and the red light was on, but he didn't have time to get gas. His uneasiness made him impatient.

He reached the police station just before 4:30. Ebba handed him a stack of phone messages, which he stuffed in his jacket pocket. When he got to his office he started by tracking down Chief Holgersson. She reminded him that the press conference was at 6:30. Wallander promised to take care of it. It wasn't something he liked to do. He was too easily annoyed by what he regarded as impertinent and insinuating questions from the reporters. On several occasions there had been complaints about his uncooperativeness, even from the top police echelons in Stockholm. At those moments Wallander realized that he was actually known outside his own circle of colleagues and friends. For better or worse, he had become one of Sweden's national police.

He gave the chief a quick rundown about the discovery of Runfeldt's basement office on Harpegatan. For the time being, though, he didn't mention his idea that Runfeldt could have been a part-time private detective. He hung up and called Hansson. Gösta Runfeldt's daughter was in his office. They agreed to meet briefly out in the hallway.

"I'm done with the son," said Hansson. "He's staying at the Hotel Sekelgården."

Wallander nodded. He knew where it was.

"Any luck?"

"Not much. You could say he confirmed the picture of Runfeldt as a man passionately interested in orchids."

"And his mother? Runfeldt's wife?"

"A tragic accident. You want the details?"

"Not now. What does the daughter say?"

"I was just about to talk to her. It took some time with the son. I'm trying to do this as thoroughly as I can. The son lives in Arvika, by the way, and the daughter in Eskilstuna."

Wallander looked at his watch. Quarter to five. He should be preparing for the press conference. But he could talk to the daughter for a few minutes.

"Do you have any objections if I start by asking her a few questions?"

"No, go right ahead."

"I don't have time to explain right now, but the questions might sound strange to you."

They went into Hansson's office. The woman sitting in the guest chair was young—Wallander guessed no more than twenty-three or twenty-four. He could see that she resembled her father. She stood up when he came in, Wallander smiled and shook hands. Hansson leaned against the doorjamb while Wallander sat down in his chair. He noticed that the chair seemed to be brand-new. He wondered how Hansson had managed to get a new office chair. His own was in very poor shape.

Hansson had written down a name, Lena Lönnerwall. Wallander gave Hansson a quick glance, and he nodded. He took off his jacket and put it on the floor next to the chair. She followed his movements with her eyes the whole time.

"I should start by saying how sorry we are that this happened," he said. "My condolences."

"Thank you."

Wallander could see that she was composed. With some relief he could tell that she wasn't about to burst into tears.

"Your name is Lena Lönnerwall and you live in Eskilstuna," Wallander said. "You are the daughter of Gösta Runfeldt."

"That's correct."

"All the other personal information that is unfortunately necessary will be taken by Inspector Hansson. I have only a few questions. Are you married?"

"Yes."

"What's your profession?"

"I'm a basketball coach."

Wallander pondered her answer.

"Does that mean you're a gym teacher?"

"It means I'm a basketball coach."

Wallander nodded. He left the follow-up questions to Hansson. He had never met a female basketball coach in his life.

"Your father was a florist?"

"Yes."

"All his life?"

"In his youth he went to sea. When he and Mamma got married he stayed ashore."

"If I understand correctly, your mother was drowned?"

"That's right."

The instant of hesitation that preceded her reply hadn't escaped Wallander. He sharpened his attention at once.

"How long ago did that happen?"

"About ten years ago. I was just thirteen."

Wallander sensed that she was stressed. He continued cautiously.

"Can you give me a little more detail about what happened, and where?"

"Does this really have something to do with my father?"

"It's a basic police routine to do a chronological rundown," said Wallander, trying to sound authoritative. Hansson stared at him in amazement from his place by the door.

"I don't know that much about it," she said.

Wrong, thought Wallander. You know, but you don't want to talk about it.

"Tell me what you do know," he went on.

"It was in the winter. For some reason they took a drive out to Älmhult to take a Sunday walk. She fell through a hole in the ice. Pappa tried to save her. But it was no use."

Wallander sat motionless. He was thinking about what she had said. Something was related to the investigation they were working on. Then it occurred to him what it was. It wasn't about Runfeldt, but about Holger Eriksson. A man who falls into a visible hole in the ground and is impaled. Lena Lönnerwall's mother falls through a hole in the ice. All Wallander's police instincts told him that there was some connection here. But he couldn't say what it was. Or why the woman sitting across from him didn't want to talk about her mother's death.

He left the accident and went right to the main question.

"Your father had a flower shop. And he had a passion for orchids."

"That's the first thing I remember about him. The way he told me and my brother about flowers."

"Why was he such a passionate orchid lover?"

She looked at him with sudden surprise.

"Why does anyone become passionate about something? Can you answer that?"

Wallander shook his head without replying.

"Did you know that your father was a private detective?"

Over by the door Hansson gave a start. Wallander kept his gaze steady on the woman in front of him. Her astonishment seemed genuine.

"My father was a private detective?"

"Yes. Didn't you know that?"

"That can't be true."

"Why not?"

"I don't get it. I don't even know exactly what a private detective is. Do we really have them in Sweden?"

"That's a different question altogether," said Wallander. "But your father quite obviously spent time doing business as a private detective."

"Like Ture Sventon? That's the only Swedish detective I've ever heard of."

"Forget about the comic books," said Wallander. "I'm serious about this."

"I am too. I've never heard a word about my father being involved in anything like this. What did he do?"

"It's too early to tell."

Wallander was now convinced that she didn't know what her father had been doing in secret. Of course there was the possibility that Wallander was completely wrong, that his assumption was a mistake. Yet he already felt deep inside that he was right. The discovery of Runfeldt's secret room was a breakthrough in the investigation, but they couldn't yet see all the consequences. The secret room on Har-pegatan might merely lead them on to other secret rooms. But Wallander had a feeling that it had shaken up the entire investigation. A barely perceptible earthquake had occurred. Everything had been set in motion.

He got up from the chair. "That's all for now," he said, holding out his hand. "I'm sure we'll meet again."

She gave him a somber look.

"Who did it?" she asked.

"I don't know," said Wallander. "But I'm convinced we'll catch the person or persons who killed your father."

Hansson followed him out to the hallway. "Private detective? Is that supposed to be a joke?"

"No," said Wallander. "We found a secret office that belonged to Runfeldt. You'll hear more about it later."

Hansson nodded. "Ture Sventon wasn't a comic-book character," he said. "He was in a series of mystery novels."

But Wallander had already left. He got a cup of coffee and closed the door to his office. The phone rang. He picked it up without answering. Most of all he wanted to get out of that press conference. He had too many other things to think about. With a grimace he pulled over a notebook and wrote down the most important things to tell the press.

He leaned back and looked out the window. The wind was howling.

If the killer speaks a language, then we can attempt to answer him, he thought. If it's the way I think it is, he wants to show other people what he's doing. So we have to acknowledge that we've seen. But we haven't let ourselves be scared off.

He made some more notes. Then he got up and went into Chief Holgersson's office. He gave her a brief rundown on what he had been thinking. She listened attentively and then nodded. They would do as he suggested.

The press conference was held in the largest conference room in the police building. Wallander got the feeling that he had been dragged back to last summer and that tumultuous press conference when he had walked out in a rage. He recognized many of the same faces.

"I'm glad you're handling this," Chief Holgersson whispered.

"Somebody has to do it."

"I'll make the opening remarks. The rest is yours."

They went up to the podium at one end of the room. Lisa Holgersson welcomed everyone and then turned it over to Wallander, who could already feel himself starting to sweat.

He gave a thorough run-through of the murders of Holger Eriksson and Gösta Runfeldt. He gave them a select number of details and his own view that these were among the most savage crimes he and his colleagues had ever investigated. The only significant information he held back was the discovery that Runfeldt had probably worked secretly as a private detective. He also didn't mention that they were looking for a diary-writing man who had once been a mercenary in a remote African war and called himself Harald Berggren.

Instead he said something completely different. What he and Lisa Holgersson had agreed on.

He said that the police had some clear leads to follow. He couldn't go into details at this time. But there were clues and indications. The police were on a specific track that they couldn't talk about yet. For reasons crucial to the investigation.

This thought had been born when he noticed that the investigation had been shaken up. Movement deep down inside, almost impossible to register, but there nevertheless. It was there.

The thought that came to him was quite simple.

When there is an earthquake, people flee from the epicenter in a hurry. The perpetrator, or perpetrators, wanted the world to see that the murders were sadistic and well-planned. Now the investigators could confirm that they were aware of this. But they could also give a more detailed answer. They had seen more than what might have been intended.

Wallander wanted to get the perpetrator moving. A quarry in motion was easier to see than one who held still and hid in his own shadow.

Naturally Wallander realized that the whole tactic could backfire. The perpetrator might make himself invisible. Still, he thought it was worth a try. He had also received Chief Holgersson's permission to say something that was not altogether true.

They had no leads. All they had were unrelated fragments.

When Wallander finished, the questions started up. He was ready for most of them. He had heard and replied to them before, and he would keep on hearing them as long as he was a cop.

Not until the press conference was almost over, when Wallander had started to grow impatient and Chief Holgersson had nodded to him to wind it up, did everything turn in another direction. The man who raised his hand and then stood up had been sitting far back in a corner. Wallander didn't see him and was just about to adjourn the conference when Holgersson drew his attention to the fact that there was one more question.

"I'm from the *Observer* magazine," said the man. "I have a question I'd like to ask."

Wallander searched his memory. He'd never heard of a magazine called the *Observer.* His impatience was growing.

"What magazine did you say you were from?"

"The *Observer.*"

The crowd started to fidget.

"I have to admit that I've never heard of your magazine. What's the question?"

"The *Observer* has roots that go way back," replied the man in the corner, unfazed. "There was a magazine in the early nineteenth century with that name. A magazine of social criticism. We plan to publish our first issue shortly."

"One question," said Wallander. "After you come out with the first issue I'll answer two questions."

There was tittering in the room. But the man in the corner remained unfazed. He had the air of a preacher about him. Wallander began to wonder whether the *Observer,* the magazine that had not yet come out, might be religious. Cryptoreligious, he thought. New-age spirituality has finally reached Ystad. The southern plain of Sweden has been conquered, and Österlen is all that's left.

"What do the Ystad police think about the fact that the residents of Lödinge have decided to set up a citizen militia?" asked the man in the corner.

Wallander had a hard time seeing his face.

"I haven't heard that the people of Lödinge have considered committing any collective stupidities," replied Wallander.

"Not only in Lödinge," continued the man in the corner calmly. "There are plans to start a people's movement in this country. An umbrella organization for the citizen militia. A popular-police cadre that will protect the populace. Which will do everything the police don't want to do. Or can't do. One of the starting points will be the Ystad district."

There was a sudden silence in the room.

"And why was Ystad chosen for this honor?" asked Wallander. He was still unsure whether to take the man from the *Observer* seriously.

"Within the past few months there have been a large number of brutal murders. It is acknowledged that the police succeeded in solving the crimes from this summer. But now it seems to have started again. People want to live out their lives. The Swedish police have capitulated to the criminal elements that are creeping out of their holes today. That's why the citizen militia is the only way to solve the problem of security."

"It never solves anything for people to take the law into their own hands," said Wallander. "There can only be one response to this from the Ystad police. And it is clear and unequivocal. No one can misunderstand it. We will regard all private initiatives to establish an adjunct security force as illegal, and participants will be prosecuted."

"Should I interpret that to mean you are against the citizen militia?" asked the man in the corner.

Now Wallander could see his pale, emaciated face. He decided to memorize it.

"Yes," he said. "You can interpret it this way: We are opposed to any attempt to organize a citizen militia."

"Don't you wonder what the people in Lödinge are going to say about that?"

"I may wonder, but I'm not afraid of the answer."

Then he quickly adjourned the press conference.

"Do you think he was serious?" asked Chief Holgersson when they were alone in the room.

"Maybe. We should probably keep an eye on what's happening in Lödinge. If it's true that people are starting to publicly demand a citizen militia, then there's been a change in the situation. And we might have problems."

It was now seven o'clock. Wallander said goodbye to Holgersson and went back to his office. He sat down in his chair. He needed to think. He couldn't remember the last time he had had so little time for reflection and summarizing during a criminal investigation.

The phone rang. He picked it up at once. It was Svedberg.

"How did the press conference go?"

"A little worse than usual. How's it going with you two?"

"I think you ought to come over here. We found a camera with a roll of film in it. Nyberg's here. We thought we should develop it."

"Can we nail down the fact that he lived a double life as a private eye?"

"We think so. But there's something else too."

Wallander waited tensely for the rest.

"We think the film contains pictures from his last case."

Last, thought Wallander. Not latest. But last.

"I'm coming," he said.

He left the station in the gusty wind. Racing clouds filled the sky. As he walked toward his car he wondered if migratory birds flew at night in wind this strong.

On the way to Harpegatan he stopped and filled the car with gas. He felt tired and drained. He wondered when he would have time to look for a house. And think about his father. He wondered when Baiba would come to visit.

He looked at his watch. Was it time or his life that was passing? He was too tired to decide which was which.

He started the engine. His watch said twenty-five minutes to eight.

A few minutes later he parked on Harpegatan and went down to the basement.

Chapter Seventeen

They watched tensely as the picture began to emerge in the developing bath. Wallander wasn't sure what he was expecting, or at least hoping for, as he stood next to his colleagues in the dimly lit room. The red light made him feel like he was waiting for something indecent to happen. Nyberg was in charge of the developing. He was hobbling around on a crutch after his fall outside the police station. When Wallander returned to Harpegatan, Höglund had whispered to him that Nyberg was in an unusually grumpy mood.

But they had made progress while Wallander was busy with the reporters. There was no longer any doubt that Gösta Runfeldt had been working as a private detective. In the various client records they had discovered, they could see that he'd been doing it for at least ten years. The oldest entries were from September 1983.

"His activities were limited," said Höglund. "At most he had seven or eight cases a year. It seems likely that this was something he did in his spare time."

Svedberg had made a cursory survey of the types of assignments Runfeldt had taken on.

"About half the cases have to do with suspected infidelity," he said after consulting his notes. "Strangely enough, it was mostly men who suspected their wives."

"Why is that strange?" asked Wallander.

Svedberg realized that he didn't have a good response to that.

"I just didn't think it would be that way," was all he said. "But what do I know?"

Svedberg wasn't married and had never mentioned any relationships with women. He was over forty and seemed to be content with life as a bachelor.

Wallander nodded for him to continue.

"There are at least two cases per year in which an employer suspects an employee of embezzling," said Svedberg. "We've also come across a number of surveillance assignments that are rather vague in nature. In general, a quite tedious picture. His notes aren't particularly extensive. But he was well paid."

"So now we know how he could take those expensive trips," said Wallander. "It cost him 30,000 kronor for the trip to Nairobi that he never took."

"He was working on a case when he died," said Höglund.

She opened an appointment calendar on the desk. Wallander thought about the reading glasses that he still hadn't bought. He didn't bother to look at the calendar.

"It seems to have been his usual sort of assignment. Someone referred to only as 'Mrs. Svensson' suspects her husband of being unfaithful."

"Here in Ystad?" asked Wallander. "Or did he work in other areas too?"

"In 1987 he had a case in Markaryd," said Svedberg. "There's nothing further north than that. Since then only cases in Skåne. In 1991 he went to Denmark twice and once to Kiel. I haven't had time to look into the details. But it had something to do with a chief engineer on a ferry who seemed to be having an affair with a waitress who worked on the ferry too. His wife in Skanör was apparently right about her suspicions."

"But otherwise he only took cases in the Ystad area?"

"I wouldn't say that," replied Svedberg. "Southern and eastern Skåne is probably closer to the truth."

"Holger Eriksson?" asked Wallander. "Have you come across his name?"

Höglund looked at Svedberg, who shook his head.

"Harald Berggren?"

"Not him either."

"Have you found anything that might indicate a connection between Eriksson and Runfeldt?"

Again the answer was negative. They hadn't found anything. It has to be there, thought Wallander. It doesn't make sense that there would be two different perpetrators. Just as it doesn't make sense that there would be two random victims. The connection is there. We just haven't found it yet.

"I can't figure him out," said Höglund. "There's no doubt he had a passion for flowers. But he spent his spare time as a private detective."

"People are seldom what you think they are," replied Wallander, wondering suddenly whether this also applied to himself.

"He seems to have made a bundle from his work," said Svedberg. "But if I'm not mistaken, he didn't report any of the income when he filed his tax returns. Could the explanation be that simple? He kept it secret so the tax authorities wouldn't find out what he was up to?"

"Hardly," said Wallander. "In the eyes of most people, being a private detective is a rather shady occupation."

"Or childish," said Höglund. "A game for men who have never grown up."

Wallander felt a vague urge to protest. But since he didn't know what to say, he let it drop.

The image that emerged was that of a man. The photo had been taken outdoors. None of them could identify the background. The man was in his fifties. He had thin, close-cropped hair. Nyberg guessed that the pictures had been taken from a great distance. Some of the negatives were blurry, which might mean that Runfeldt had used a telephoto lens sensitive to the slightest movement.

"Mrs. Svensson contacted him the first time on September 9th," said Höglund. "On September 14th and 17th, Runfeldt noted that he had 'worked on the case.'"

"That's only a few days before he was supposed to leave for Nairobi," said Wallander.

They had come out of the darkroom. Nyberg was sitting at the desk, going through a number of file folders with photographs in them.

"Who is his client?" asked Wallander. "This Mrs. Svensson?"

"His client records and notes are vague," said Svedberg. "He seems to have been a detective of few words when it came to writing. There isn't even an address for Mrs. Svensson."

"How does a private detective find clients?" asked Höglund. "He must advertise his services somehow."

"I've seen ads in the papers," said Wallander. "Maybe not in *Ystad's Allehanda*. But in national newspapers. It must be possible to track down this Mrs. Svensson somehow."

"I talked to the doorman," said Svedberg. "He thought Runfeldt had some kind of storeroom here. He never saw anybody come down here to visit."

"He must have met his clients somewhere else," said Wallander. "This was the secret room in his life."

They silently mulled over what he had said. Wallander tried to decide what was most important right now. At the same time he could feel the press conference still haunting his thoughts. The man from the *Observer* had upset him. Could it really be true that a national citizen militia was being formed? If it was, then Wallander knew it wouldn't be long before these people began meting out punishment. He felt a need to tell Höglund and Svedberg what had happened, but he let it go. It was probably better if they all discussed it together at the next meeting at the station. And Chief Holgersson was really the one who should tell them.

"We have to find Mrs. Svensson," said Svedberg. "The question is how?"

"We'll find her," said Wallander. "We'll put a tap on the phone and go through all the papers here again. We'll find her somewhere. I'm sure of that. I'm thinking of leaving it to you, while I go have a talk with Runfeldt's son."

He left Harpegatan and drove out along Österleden. The wind was still gusting. The town seemed deserted. He turned up Hamngatan and parked near the post office. He stepped out into the wind again. He saw himself as a pathetic figure, a police officer in a thin sweater, battling the wind in a desolate Swedish town in the fall. The Swedish criminal justice system, he thought. What's left of it. This is how it looks. Freezing police officers in thin sweaters.

He turned left at the Savings Bank and walked to the Hotel Sekel-gården. He had made a note that the man he was looking for was named Bo Runfeldt. A young man was sitting at the front desk reading. Wallander nodded.

"Hello," said the desk clerk.

Wallander suddenly realized that he recognized him. It took him a moment before he remembered that he was the oldest son of former police chief Björk.

"It's been a long time," said Wallander. "How's your father?"

"He's unhappy in Malmö."

He's not unhappy in Malmö, thought Wallander. He's unhappy being chief.

"What are you reading?" asked Wallander.

"About fractals."

"Fractals?"

"It's a mathematical term. I'm studying at Lund University. This is just a part-time job."

"That sounds good," said Wallander. "I'm not here to get a room. I'm here to talk to one of your guests, Bo Runfeldt."

"He just came in."

"Is there someplace we can sit and talk in private?"

"We don't have many guests tonight," said the boy. "You can sit in the breakfast room."

He pointed toward the corridor.

"I'll wait there," said Wallander. "Call his room and tell him I'm waiting to see him."

"I saw it in the paper," said the boy. "Why is it that everything is getting so much worse?"

Wallander looked at him with interest.

"What do you mean by that?"

"Worse. More brutal."

"I don't know," replied Wallander. "I honestly don't know why things have gotten so bad. At the same time, I don't really believe what I just said. I think I do know. I think everybody knows why things are this way."

Björk's son wanted to continue the discussion. But Wallander raised his hand to cut him off and pointed to the phone. Then he went into the breakfast room and sat down. He thought about the unfinished conversation. Why everything was getting worse and more brutal. He wondered why he was so unwilling to reply. He knew quite well what the explanation was. The Sweden that was his, the country he had grown up in, that was built after the war, was not as rock-solid as they had thought. Under it all was quagmire. Even back then the high-rise suburbs that were erected were described as "inhuman." How could people who lived there be expected to keep their "humanity" intact? Society had grown cruel. People who felt they were unwanted or out-right unwelcome in their own country reacted with aggressiveness and contempt. There was no meaningless violence. Wallander knew that. Every violent act had a meaning for the person who committed it. Only when you dared accept this truth could you hope to turn the development in another direction.

He also asked himself how it could be possible to function as a police officer in the future. He knew that many of his colleagues were seriously considering finding other professions. Martinsson had talked about it several times; Hansson had mentioned it once when they were sitting in the lunchroom. And a few years ago Wallander himself had cut out an ad in the paper about job openings for security personnel at a large company in Trelleborg.

He wondered what Ann-Britt thought. She was still young. She could be a police officer for at least thirty more years.

He thought about asking her. He needed to know in order to figure out how he was going to stand it himself.

At the same time he knew that the picture he was drawing was incomplete. Among young people the interest in police jobs had risen sharply during the past few years. And the increase seemed to be holding steady. Wallander had become more and more convinced that it was all a generational question.

He had a vague feeling that he had been right for a long time. Back

\ in the early '90s he had often sat on Rydberg's balcony on warm, late-summer evenings while they talked about what the cops of the future would be like. They continued their discussions during Rydberg's illness and his last days. They never reached any conclusions. But they didn't always agree either. What they did agree on was that police work ultimately had to do with being able to decipher the signs of the times. To understand change and interpret trends in society.

Back then Wallander already thought that although he was right for the most part, he was mistaken about one essential point: It was no harder being a police officer today than it was in the past.

It was harder for *him*. Which was not the same thing.

Wallander's thoughts were interrupted when he heard steps in the corridor coming from the lobby. He stood up and greeted Bo Runfeldt. He was a tall, well-built man. Wallander judged his age to be twenty-seven or twenty-eight. He had a strong grip. Wallander invited him to sit down. At the same time he realized that as usual he had forgotten to bring his notebook. It was doubtful that he even had a pen. He considered going out to the front desk to borrow pen and paper from Björk's son. But he decided to skip it. He would have to rely on his memory. His carelessness was inexcusable. It annoyed him.

"Let me start by offering my condolences," said Wallander.

Bo Runfeldt nodded. He didn't say anything. His eyes were an intense blue, his gaze rather squinting. Wallander thought he might be nearsighted.

"I know you've had an extensive conversation with my colleague, Inspector Hansson," continued Wallander. "But I need to ask you a few questions myself."

Runfeldt remained silent. Wallander noticed that his gaze was piercing.

"If I understand right, you live in Arvika," said Wallander. "And you're an accountant."

"I work for Price Waterhouse," said Runfeldt. His voice indicated a person who was used to expressing himself.

"That doesn't sound particularly Swedish."

"It's not. Price Waterhouse is one of the world's largest accounting firms. It's easier to list the countries where we don't do business than where we do."

"But you work in Sweden?"

"Not all the time. I often have assignments in Africa and Asia."

"Do they need accountants from Sweden?"

"Not just from Sweden, but from Price Waterhouse. We audit many relief projects. To ensure the money has really ended up where it's supposed to go."

"And does it?"

"Not always. Is this really relevant to what happened to my father?"

Wallander noticed that the man sitting across from him was having a hard time hiding his feeling that talking with a policeman was beneath his dignity. Under normal circumstances this would have made Wallander mad, but he felt uncertain in relation to Bo Runfeldt. Something made him hold back. He wondered fleetingly whether it was because he had inherited the submissiveness that his father had so often exhibited in his life. Especially toward the men who had come in their shiny American cars to buy his paintings. He had never thought about this until now. Maybe that was his inheritance from his father. A feeling of inferiority, concealed beneath a thin democratic veneer.

He regarded the man with the blue eyes.

"Your father was murdered," he said. "Right now I'm the one who decides which questions are relevant."

Bo Runfeldt shrugged his shoulders. "I have to admit that I don't know much about police work."

"I spoke to your sister earlier today," Wallander continued. "One question I asked her may have great significance. Now I'm going to ask you too. Did you know that your father, besides being a florist, also worked as a private detective?"

Runfeldt sat motionless. Then he burst out laughing.

"That's got to be the most idiotic thing I've heard in a long time," he said.

"Idiotic or not, it's true."

"Private detective?"

"Private investigator, if you prefer. He had an office. He took on various types of investigative assignments. He'd been doing it for at least ten years."

Runfeldt saw that Wallander meant what he said. His surprise was genuine.

"He must have started his business about the same time that your mother drowned."

Wallander got the same feeling he had had when he talked to Bo Runfeldt's sister earlier that day. An almost invisible shift in his face, as if Wallander had entered an area that he really should have kept out of.

"You knew that your father was supposed to go to Nairobi," he continued. "One of my colleagues spoke to you on the phone. You seemed quite incredulous that he never showed up at Kastrup Airport."

"I talked to him the day before."

"How did he seem then?"

"The same as usual. He talked about his trip."

"He didn't show any sign of apprehension?"

"No."

"You must have been worried about what happened. Can you come up with any conceivable explanation for why he would voluntarily give up his trip? Or mislead you?"

"There's no reasonable explanation for it."

"It looks as if he packed his suitcase and left the apartment. That's where the trail ends."

"Someone must have picked him up."

Wallander paused briefly before asking the next question.

"Who?"

"I don't know."

"Did your father have any enemies?"

"None that I know of. Not anymore."

Wallander gave a start.

"What do you mean by that? Not anymore?"

"Exactly what I said. I don't think he's had any enemies for a long time."

"Could you be a little more precise?"

Runfeldt took a pack of cigarettes out of his pocket. Wallander noticed that his hand was shaking slightly.

"Do you mind if I smoke?"

"Not at all."

Wallander waited. He knew there would be more. He also had a premonition that he was getting close to something important.

"I don't know if my father had any enemies," he said. "But I do know there's one person who had reason to hate him."

"Who?"

"My mother."

Runfeldt waited for Wallander to ask him a question. But it didn't come. He kept on waiting.

"My father was a man who sincerely loved orchids," said Runfeldt. "He was also a knowledgeable man. A self-taught botanist, you might say. But he was also something else."

"What's that?"

"He was a brutal man. He abused my mother throughout their marriage. Sometimes so badly that she had to seek treatment at the hospital. We tried to get her to leave him, but it did no good. He beat her. Afterwards he would be contrite, and she would give in. It was a nightmare that never seemed to end. The brutality didn't stop until she drowned."

"As I understand it, she fell through a hole in the ice?"

"That's as much as I know too. That's what Gösta said."

"You don't sound totally convinced."

Runfeldt stubbed out his half-smoked cigarette in the ashtray.

"Maybe she went out there beforehand and sawed a hole in the ice. Maybe she decided to put an end to it all."

"Is that a possibility?"

"She talked about committing suicide. Not often; a few times during the last years of her life. But none of us believed her. People usually don't. Suicides are fundamentally inexplicable to those who should have paid attention and understood what was happening."

Wallander thought about the pungee pit. The partially sawed-through planks. Gösta Runfeldt had been a brutal man. He had abused his wife. He tried hard to figure out the significance of what Bo Runfeldt was telling him.

"I don't grieve for my father," continued Runfeldt. "I don't think my sister does either. He was a cruel man. He tortured the life out of our mother."

"He was never cruel toward the two of you?"

"Never. Only toward her."

"Why did he mistreat her?"

"I don't know. You shouldn't speak badly about the dead, but he was a monster."

Wallander thought for a moment.

"Has it ever crossed your mind that your father might have killed your mother? That it wasn't an accident?"

Runfeldt's reply was swift and firm.

"Many times. But of course there's no way to prove it. There were no witnesses. They were alone on the ice that winter day."

"What's the name of the lake?"

"Stång Lake. It's not far from Älmhult. In southern Småland."

Wallander thought for a moment. Did he really have any other questions? It felt as if the investigation had taken a stranglehold on itself. There ought to be plenty of questions. And there were. But there was no one to ask.

"Does the name Harald Berggren mean anything to you?"

Runfeldt gave it careful thought before he answered.

"No. Nothing. But I could be mistaken. It's a common name."

"Has your father ever had contact with mercenary soldiers?"

"Not as far as I know. But I remember that he often talked about the Foreign Legion when I was a kid. Not to my sister. Just to me."

"What did he tell you?"

"Adventure stories. Maybe joining the Foreign Legion was some kind of teenage dream he once had. But I'm positive he never had anything to do with them. Or other mercenaries."

"Holger Eriksson? Have you ever heard that name?"

"The man who was murdered the week before my father? I saw it in the newspapers. But as far as I know, my father never had anything to do with him. I could be wrong, of course. We didn't keep in close contact."

Wallander nodded. He had no further questions.

"How long are you staying in Ystad?"

"The funeral will be as soon as we can make all the arrangements. We have to decide what to do with the flower shop."

"It's very possible that you'll hear from me again," said Wallander, getting to his feet.

He left the hotel. It was almost nine. He noticed that he was hungry. The wind tugged and pulled at his clothes. He stood in the shelter of a building and tried to decide what to do. He should eat, he knew that. But he also knew that he had to sit down soon and try to collect his thoughts. The intertwining investigations were starting to spin. There was now a big chance that they would lose their footing. He was still looking for the point where the lives of Eriksson and Runfeldt formed a tangent. It's there somewhere, in the dim background, he told himself. Maybe I've even seen it already, or walked past it without noticing.

He got his car and drove over to the station. While he was still sitting in the car he called Höglund on her cell phone. She told him that they were still going through the office, but they had sent Nyberg home because his foot was hurting badly.

"I'm on my way to the office after an interesting conversation with Runfeldt's son," said Wallander. "I need some time to go over it."

"It's not enough for us to shuffle our papers," replied Höglund. "We also need someone to do the thinking."

Afterwards he wasn't sure if she meant this last remark to be sarcastic. But he pushed the thought aside.

Hansson was sitting in his office going over parts of the investigative material that was starting to pile up. Wallander stood in the doorway. He had a coffee cup in his hand.

"Where are the forensic medical reports?" he asked suddenly. "They must have come in by now. At least the ones about Holger Eriksson."

"They're probably in Martinsson's office. I seem to recall he mentioned something about it."

"Is he still here?"

"He went home. He copied a file to a disk and was going to keep working on it at home."

"Is that really allowed?" Wallander wondered absentmindedly. "Taking investigative materials home?"

"I don't know," replied Hansson. "For me, it's never come up. I don't even have a computer at home. But maybe that's a breach of duty these days."

"What's a breach of duty?"

"Not having a computer at home."

"In that case, we're both guilty," said Wallander. "I'd like to see those reports early tomorrow morning."

"How did it go with Bo Runfeldt?"

"I have to write up my notes tonight. But he said some things that might be important. And now we know for sure that Gösta Runfeldt spent some of his time working as a private detective."

"Svedberg called. He told me."

Wallander took his phone out of his pocket.

"What did we do before we had these things?" he asked. "I can hardly remember anymore."

"We did the exact same thing," replied Hansson. "But it took longer. We searched for phone booths. We spent a lot more time in our cars. But we did exactly the same things that we do now."

Wallander walked down the corridor to his office, nodding to a few patrol officers coming out of the lunchroom. He went into his office and sat down. More than ten minutes passed before he pulled over an unused note pad.

It took him more than two hours to put together a thorough summary of the two murders. He had been trying to steer two vessels at the same time. The whole time he was looking for the point of contact that he knew had to exist. When it was past eleven, he threw down his pen and leaned back in his chair. He had reached a point where he could see nothing more.

But he was positive. The contact was there. They just hadn't found it yet.

There was also something else.

Time after time he came back to the observation that Höglund had made. *There's something blatant about the M.O.* Both in terms of Eriksson's death on the sharpened bamboo stakes and Runfeldt, who was strangled and left tied to a tree.

I see something, he thought. I just haven't managed to see through it.

He brooded over what it could be, but couldn't come up with an answer.

It was almost midnight when he turned off the light in his office. He stood there in the dark. It was still just a hunch, a vague fear deep inside his brain.

He thought the perpetrator would strike again. He seemed to have detected a signal as he worked at his desk.

There was something incomplete about everything that had happened so far.

What it was, he didn't know.

But still he was sure.

Chapter Eighteen

She waited until 2:30 in the morning. From experience she knew that was when the fatigue would creep up on her. She thought back on all the nights when she had been at work. That's how it always was. The greatest danger of dozing off was between two and four o'clock.

She had been waiting in the linen-supply room since nine in the evening. Just as on her first visit, she had walked right in through the main entrance of the hospital. No one had noticed her. A nurse in a hurry. Maybe she had been out running an errand, or had gone out to get something she had left in her car. No one had noticed her because there was nothing unusual about her. She had contemplated disguising herself in some way, maybe changing her hair. But that would have been a sign of exaggerated caution. In the linen room, which reminded her vaguely of her childhood with its scent of newly washed and ironed sheets, she had plenty of time to think. She sat there in the dark, though it wouldn't have made any difference if the light had been on. After midnight she finally took out her flashlight, the one she always used at work, and read the last letter her mother had written to her. It was unfinished. But it was in this letter that her mother had suddenly started talking about herself. About the events that lay behind her attempt to take her own life. She realized that her mother had never gotten over her bitterness. *I wander around the world like a ship without a captain,* she wrote. *I'm a cursed Flying Dutchman forced to atone for someone else's guilt. I thought that age would add enough distance, that the memories would grow dim, fade, and maybe finally vanish altogether. But now I see that won't happen. Only with death can I put an end to it. And since I don't want to die, not yet, I choose to remember.*

The letter was dated the day before her mother had moved in with the French nuns, the day before shadows had detached themselves from the darkness and murdered her.

After she read the letter she turned off the flashlight. Everything had grown quiet. Only twice had someone walked past in the corridor. The linen supply was located in a wing that was only partially in use.

She had had plenty of time to think. There were now three free days entered in her timetable. She wouldn't have to go back on duty for 49 hours, at 5:44 P.M. She had some time and she was going to use it. Until now everything had gone the way it was supposed to. Women only made mistakes when they tried to think like men. She had known that for a long time, and in her view she had already proved it.

But there was something that bothered her, something that threw off her timetable. She had closely followed everything that had been written in the newspapers. She listened to the news on the radio and watched it on various TV channels. It was quite clear to her that the police didn't understand a thing. And that had been her intention, not to leave any traces, to lead the dogs away from the track they should really be following. But now she was impatient with all this incompetence. The police were never going to figure out what happened. By her actions she was adding riddles to the story. In their minds the police would be looking for a male perpetrator. She didn't want it to be that way any longer.

She sat in the dark closet and devised a plan. In the future she would make some minor changes. Nothing that would reveal her timetable, of course. There was always a built-in margin, even if it couldn't be seen from the surface.

She would give the riddle a face.

At 2:30 in the morning she left the linen closet. The corridor was deserted. She straightened her white uniform and headed for the stairway up to the maternity ward. She knew that there were usually only four people on duty. She had been there in the daytime, asking about a woman she knew had already gone home with her baby. Over the nurse's shoulder she could see in the log that all the rooms were occupied. She had a hard time understanding why women had babies this time of year, when fall was turning to winter. But she knew women still didn't choose when to have their children.

When she reached the glass doors of the maternity ward, she stopped and took a careful look at the nurses' station. She held the door slightly ajar and heard no voices. That meant the midwives and nurses were busy. It would take her less than fifteen seconds to reach the room of the woman she intended to visit. She probably wouldn't run into anybody, but she had to be careful. She pulled the glove out of her pocket. She had sewn it herself and filled the fingers with lead, shaped to follow the contours of her knuckles. She put it on her right hand, opened the door, and quickly entered the ward. The nurses' station was empty; there was a radio playing somewhere. She walked rapidly and soundlessly to the designated room. She slipped inside and closed the door noiselessly behind her.

Taking off her glove, she approached the woman lying in the bed; she was awake. She stuffed the glove in her pocket, the same pocket where she had put the letter from her mother. She sat down on the edge of the bed. The woman was very pale, and her belly pushed up the sheet. She took the woman's hand.

"Have you decided?" she asked her.

The woman nodded. It didn't surprise her, and yet she felt a sort of triumph. Even the women who were most cowed could be turned toward life again.

"Eugen Blomberg," the woman said. "He lives in Lund. He's a researcher at the university. I don't know any better way to describe what he does."

She patted the woman's hand.

"I'll take care of it. Don't worry about a thing."

"I hate that man," she said.

"Yes," said the woman sitting on the edge of the bed. "You hate him and you have every right to."

"I would have killed him if I could."

"I know. But you can't. Think of your baby instead."

She leaned forward and stroked the woman's cheek. Then she got up and put on her glove. She had been in the room no more than two minutes. Carefully she pushed open the door. None of the midwives or nurses was around. She walked back toward the exit.

Just as she was passing the station a woman came out. It was bad luck. The woman stared at her. It was an older woman, presumably one of the midwives.

She kept walking toward the exit doors. The woman behind her yelled and started running toward her. Her only aim was to keep going out those doors. But the woman behind her grabbed her left arm and asked who she was and what she was doing there. It was a shame that this woman had to be so meddlesome, she thought. She spun around and hit her with the glove. She didn't want to hurt her; she took care not to hit her on the temple, which could be fatal. She struck her hard on one cheek—enough to knock her out. The woman groaned and fell to the floor.

She turned around to be on her way. Then she felt two hands gripping her leg. When she looked back she realized she hadn't struck hard enough. At the same time she heard a door open somewhere in the distance. She was about to lose control of the situation. She yanked her leg away and bent down to deliver another blow. The woman scratched her in the face. Now she struck her without worrying if it was too hard or not. Right in the temple. The woman sank to the floor.

She fled through the glass doors, her cheek stinging where the midwife's nails had torn her skin. She ran down the corridor. No one called after her. She wiped her face, and her white sleeve showed streaks of blood. She stuffed the glove in her pocket and took off her clogs so she could run faster. She wondered whether the hospital had some kind of internal alarm. But she got out without meeting anyone. When she reached her car and looked at her face in the rearview mirror, she saw that she had only a few superficial scratches.

Things hadn't gone the way she had planned. But you couldn't always expect them to. What was important was that she had succeeded in persuading the pregnant woman to reveal the name of the man who had caused her so much grief.

Eugen Blomberg.

She still had forty-eight hours to begin her investigation and draw up a plan and a timetable. She was in no hurry. It would take as long as it took. She didn't think she'd need more than a week.

The oven was empty. It was waiting.

Just after eight o'clock on Thursday morning the investigative team was assembled in the conference room. Wallander had also asked Per Åkeson to attend. Just as he was about to begin, he noticed someone was missing.

"Where's Svedberg? Didn't he come in today?"

"He's been in but he left again," said Martinsson. "Evidently there was an assault up at the hospital last night. He said he'd probably be back soon."

A vague memory flitted through Wallander's head, but he couldn't pin it down. It had something to do with Svedberg. And the hospital.

"This brings the need for additional personnel to a head," said Per Åkeson. "We can't avoid the issue any longer, I'm afraid."

Wallander knew what he meant. On several earlier occasions he and Åkeson had clashed when it came to evaluating whether they should request extra manpower or not.

"We'll take up that question at the end of the meeting," said Wallander. "Let's start with where we actually stand in this mess."

"Stockholm has called a few times," said Chief Holgersson, "and I don't think I need to tell you who it was. These violent events are clouding the image of the friendly local police force."

A mixture of resignation and mirth swept through the room. But no one commented on what Lisa Holgersson had said. Martinsson yawned audibly. Wallander seized on that as a starting point.

"We're all tired. A policeman's curse is lack of sleep. At least during certain periods."

He was interrupted by the door opening, and Nyberg came in. Wallander knew that he had been talking on the phone to the forensic lab in Linköping. He hobbled up to the table using his crutch.

"How's your foot?" asked Wallander.

"It's better than being impaled on bamboo from Thailand, anyway," he replied.

Wallander gave him an inquiring look.

"Do we know that for sure? That it's from Thailand?"

"We do. It's imported for fishing rods and decorative material by a company in Bremen. We talked to their Swedish agent. They bring in over a hundred thousand bamboo poles a year. It's impossible to say where in Sweden they were purchased. But I just talked to Linköping. At least they can help us by determining how long the bamboo has been in Sweden. Bamboo is imported once it reaches a certain age."

Wallander nodded.

"Anything else?" he asked, still facing Nyberg.

"With regard to Eriksson or Runfeldt?"

"Either one."

Nyberg opened his notebook.

"The planks for the footbridge came from the Building Warehouse in Ystad. If that makes any difference. The murder scene is clean of any objects that might have helped us. On the back side of the hill where he had his birdwatching tower there's a tractor path that we can assume the killer used. If he came by car, which he probably did. We've taken impressions of all the tire tracks we found. But the whole scene is extraordinarily devoid of clues."

"And the house?"

"The problem is, we don't know what we're looking for. Everything seems to be in good order. The break-in he reported a few years ago is a riddle too. The only thing that might be worth noting is that Eriksson had a couple of extra locks installed recently, on the doors leading directly into the residence."

"That might mean he was afraid of something," said Wallander.

"I thought so too," said Nyberg. "On the other hand, everybody's putting on extra locks these days, aren't they? We live in the age of armored doors."

Wallander glanced around the table.

"Neighbors," he said. "Various tips. Who was Holger Eriksson? Who might have had a reason to kill him? What about Harald Berggren? It's about time we did a complete run-through. No matter how long it takes."

Later, Wallander would think back on that Thursday morning as an endless uphill climb. All of them presented the results of their work, and the only conclusion was that there was no sign of a break-in anywhere. The uphill slope grew steeper. Holger Eriksson's life seemed impregnable. When they did manage to puncture it, there was nothing inside. But they kept at it while the hill got higher and steeper. No one had seen a thing, no one even seemed to have known this man who sold cars, watched birds, and wrote poems. Finally Wallander began to think he was mistaken; that Holger Eriksson might have run afoul of an indiscriminate killer, who just happened to pick his ditch and saw through his footbridge. Deep inside he knew that couldn't be true. The killer had spoken a specific language—there was a logic and consistency to his method of killing Holger Eriksson. Wallander knew he wasn't mistaken. The problem was, that was as far as he got.

They were completely mired down by the time Svedberg returned from the hospital. Afterwards Wallander thought that his appearance was like a savior in the midst of their great struggle. Because when Svedberg sat down at the table and laboriously sorted out his papers, they finally seemed to reach a point where the investigation began to open the door a crack.

Svedberg started by apologizing for his absence. Wallander thought he ought to ask what had happened at the hospital.

"The whole thing is pretty weird," said Svedberg. "Just before three o'clock this morning a nurse appeared in the maternity ward. One of the midwives, Ylva Brink, who happens to be my cousin, was working there last night. She didn't recognize the nurse and tried to find out what she was doing there. Then she was struck to the ground. It seems this nurse was carrying some kind of blackjack. Ylva was knocked out. When she came to, the woman was gone. Everybody was quite upset, of course. No one knew what she was doing there. They asked all the patients, but none of them had seen her. I was there and talked to all the personnel on duty last night. They were all very upset."

"How's your cousin doing?" asked Wallander.

"She has a concussion."

Wallander was just about to return to Eriksson when Svedberg spoke up again. He seemed embarrassed and scratched his head nervously.

"What's even stranger is that this woman was there once before. One night about a week ago. Ylva happened to be working that night too. She's positive that the woman wasn't really a nurse. She was in disguise."

Wallander frowned. At the same time he remembered the note that had been lying on his desk all week.

"You talked to Ylva Brink that time too. And took some notes."

"I threw out that piece of paper," said Svedberg. "Since nothing happened the first time I didn't think it was anything to worry about. We've got more important things to do."

"I think it's creepy," said Höglund. "A phony nurse who enters the maternity ward at night. And has no qualms about using violence. It has to mean something."

"My cousin didn't recognize her. But she gave me a very good description. She was stocky and obviously very strong."

Wallander said nothing about having Svedberg's note on his desk.

"That sounds odd," was all he said. "What kind of precautions did the hospital take?"

"For the time being they're hiring a security service. Then they'll see if the phony nurse shows up again or not."

They left the night's events behind. Wallander looked at Svedberg and thought despondently that he was probably just going to reinforce the feeling that the investigation was going nowhere. But he was wrong. It turned out that Svedberg had some news.

"Last week I talked to one of Holger Eriksson's employees. Ture Karlhammar, seventy-three years old, lives in Svarte. I wrote up a report about it which you may have read. He worked as a car salesman for Eriksson for more than thirty years. At first he just sat there saying that he was sorry about what had happened. And that no one had anything but good things to say about Eriksson. Karlhammar's wife was making coffee. The door to the kitchen was open. Suddenly she came in, slammed the coffee tray on the table so the cream sloshed over, and said Holger Eriksson was a crook. Then she walked out."

"Then what happened?" asked Wallander, surprised.

"It was a little embarrassing, of course. But Karlhammar stuck to his version. I went out to talk to his wife, but by then she was gone."

"What do you mean, gone?"

"She had taken the car and driven off. Later I called several times, but nobody answered. But this morning I got a letter. I read it before I drove over to the hospital. It's from Karlhammar's wife. And if what she writes is correct, it's very interesting reading."

"Sum it up for us," said Wallander. "Then you can make copies."

"She claims that Eriksson showed signs of sadism many times in his life. He treated his employees badly. He would harass anyone who quit. She repeated over and over that she can provide as many examples as we want to prove what she writes is true."

Svedberg scanned the letter.

"She writes that he had little respect for other people. He was hard-hearted and stingy. Toward the end of the letter she indicates that he made trips to Poland quite often. Apparently to visit some women there. According to Mrs. Karlhammar, they would be able to tell us stories too. But it might all be gossip. How would she know about what he did in Poland?"

"She doesn't say anything about the fact he might have been homosexual?" asked Wallander.

"No. And this part about the trips to Poland certainly doesn't give that impression."

"And Karlhammar had never heard of anyone named Harald Berggren, I suppose?"

"No."

Wallander felt a need to get up and stretch his legs. What Svedberg had said about the contents of the letter was important, without a doubt. He realized that this was the second time in twenty-four hours he had heard a man described as brutal.

He suggested a short break so they could get some air. Per Åkeson stayed behind.

"It's all set now. With the Sudan, I mean."

Wallander felt a pang of jealousy. Åkeson had made a decision and dared to resign. Why didn't he do the same thing himself? Why did he settle for looking for a new house? Now that his father was gone, he had nothing keeping him in Ystad anymore. Linda could take care of herself.

"They don't need any cops to keep order among the refugees, do they? I've got some experience in that field here in Ystad."

Åkeson laughed.

"I can ask. Swedish cops usually go into various foreign brigades under the UN. There's nothing stopping you from putting in an application."

"Right now I've got a homicide investigation to take care of. But maybe later. When are you leaving?"

"Between Christmas and New Year's."

"And your wife?"

Åkeson threw his arms wide.

"Actually I think she'll be glad to get rid of me for a while."

"What about you? Will you be glad to get away from her?"

Åkeson hesitated before answering.

"Yes. I think it'll be great to get away. Sometimes I get the feeling that I might never come back. I'll never get to sail to the West Indies in a boat I built myself. I've never even dreamed about it. But I am going to the Sudan. And I have no idea what'll happen after that."

"Everybody dreams about escaping," said Wallander. "People in Sweden are always looking for the latest hideouts in paradise. Sometimes I think I don't even recognize my own country anymore."

"Maybe I'm escaping too. But the Sudan is no paradise, believe me."

"At least you're doing the right thing by trying. I hope you write once in a while. I'll miss you."

"That's actually something I'm looking forward to. Writing personal letters, not just official ones. Maybe that way I'll figure out how many friends I actually have: the ones who answer the letters I hope to write."

The short break was over. Martinsson, still worried about catching a cold, shut the window. They all sat down again.

"Let's hold the summation till later," said Wallander. "Instead, let's switch over to Gösta Runfeldt."

He had Höglund describe their discovery of the basement room on Harpegatan and the fact that Runfeldt was a private detective. When she, Svedberg, and Nyberg had no more to say, and after the photographs that Nyberg had developed and printed had made their way around the table, Wallander told them about his conversation with Runfeldt's son. He noticed that the investigative team now showed an entirely different level of concentration than when they started the long meeting.

"I can't shake the feeling that we're close to something crucial," Wallander concluded. "We're still looking for a point of contact. So far we haven't found one. What could it mean that both Eriksson and Runfeldt are described as brutal men? And what does it mean that this has never come out before?"

He broke off to allow for comments and questions. No one said a word.

"It's time we started digging even deeper," he went on. "There's way too much we have to find out more about. Starting now, all the material has to be run back and forth between these two men. It's Martinsson's assignment to see that this gets done. Then there are a number of items that seem more important than others we have to deal with. I'm thinking about the accident when Runfeldt's wife drowned. I can't get over the feeling that this might be crucial. Then there's the money that Eriksson donated to the church in Svenstavik. I'll take care of that myself. Which means it might be necessary to take a few trips. For example, to the lake up in Småland, outside Älmhult, where Runfeldt's wife drowned. There's something weird about all this, as I said before. I realize that I may be wrong. But we can't ignore it. It might also be necessary to take a trip to Svenstavik."

"Where's that?" asked Hansson.

"In southern Jämtland. About fifty kilometers from the border of Härjedal."

"What did Holger Eriksson have to do with that place? He was from Skåne, wasn't he?"

"That's precisely what we have to find out," said Wallander. "Why didn't he donate money to a church in this area? What does it mean that he chose that particular church? I want to know why. There must have been some definite reason."

No one had any objections when he had finished. They were all supposed to keep digging in the haystacks. None of them expected that the solution would be found any other way than by long hours and painstaking work.

They had been in the meeting for several hours when Wallander decided to bring up the need for more manpower. He also recalled that he ought to mention the suggestion about bringing in a forensic psychologist to help.

"I have nothing against getting some help in the form of reinforcements. We have plenty to investigate, and it's going to take a lot of time."

"I'll take care of it," said Chief Holgersson.

Per Åkeson nodded without saying anything. In all the years Wallander had worked with him, he had never known Åkeson to repeat anything unnecessarily. Wallander vaguely imagined that this might be an advantage for the position he was about to take on in the Sudan.

"On the other hand, I doubt we actually need a psychologist to read over our shoulders," Wallander continued when the matter of reinforcements was decided. "I'm the first to agree that Mats Ekholm, who was here last summer, was a good discussion partner. He brought up arguments and angles that were helpful. The situation is different today. My suggestion is that we send summaries of the investigative material to him and study his comments. Let's leave it at that for now. If anything dramatic happens, we can reevaluate the situation."

No one had any objections to this either.

They adjourned the meeting at just past one o'clock. Wallander left the station hastily. The long meeting had made him feel heavy-headed. He drove to one of the lunch restaurants downtown. As he ate, he tried to decide what had actually developed during the meeting. Since he kept coming back to the question of what had happened on that winter day at the lake outside Älmhult ten years ago, he decided to follow his intuition. When he finished eating he called the Hotel Sekelgården. Bo Runfeldt was in his room. Wallander asked the receptionist to tell him he was coming over just after two. Then he drove back to the police station. He found Martinsson and Hansson and took them to his office. He asked Hansson to call Svenstavik.

"What am I supposed to ask about?"

"Go straight to the point. Why did Holger Eriksson make this exception in his will? Why did he want to give money to this particular congregation? Was he looking for forgiveness of his sins? If so, what sins? And if someone starts hemming and hawing about confidentiality, tell them we need the information so we can try and stop more murders from happening."

"You really want me to ask if he was looking for forgiveness of his sins?"

Wallander burst out laughing. "Just about. Find out whatever you can. I think I'll take Bo Runfeldt with me to Älmhult. Ask Ebba to book us a couple of hotel rooms there."

Martinsson seemed dubious. "Just what, exactly, do you think you're going to figure out by looking at a lake?"

"I don't know," Wallander replied candidly. "But the trip will at least give me time to talk to Runfeldt. I've got a hunch there's some hidden information that's important for us, and that we can get it if we're persistent enough. We have to scrape hard enough to break through the surface. And there might be someone up there who was present when the accident happened. I want you to do a little footwork. Call up our colleagues in Älmhult. It happened about ten years ago. You can find out the exact date from the daughter, who's a basketball coach. A drowning accident. I'll give you a call when I get there."

The wind was still gusting when Wallander walked out to his car. He drove down to Sekelgården and went into the lobby. Bo Runfeldt was sitting in a chair waiting for him.

"Get your overcoat," said Wallander. "We're going on a field trip."

"Where to?"

"Once you're in the car I'll tell you all about it."

They left Ystad at once.

Not until they had passed the turnoff to Höör did Wallander tell him where they were headed.

Chapter Nineteen

Right after they passed Höör, it started to rain. By then Wallander had already begun to doubt the whole undertaking. Was it really worth the trouble of driving all the way to Älmhult? What did he actually think he would achieve? Anything important to the murder investigation?

Yet deep down he had no doubts. What he wanted was not a solution, but to move a step farther along.

When he told Bo Runfeldt where they were headed, Runfeldt acted annoyed and asked if this was some kind of joke. What did his mother's death have to do with the murder of his father?

"Both you and your sister seem reluctant to talk about what happened," he said. "In a way, I can understand it. People don't like to talk about a tragic accident unless they have to. But why don't I believe that it's the tragedy of the event that's making you unwilling to talk about it? If you give me a good answer, we'll turn around and drive back. And don't forget, you're the one who brought up your father's brutality."

"There you have my answer," said Runfeldt. Wallander noticed an almost imperceptible change in his voice. A hint of weariness, of a defense beginning to crumble.

Wallander cautiously used his questions to probe deeper as they drove through the monotonous landscape.

"So your mother talked about committing suicide?"

It took a while before Runfeldt answered.

"Actually it's strange that she didn't do it earlier. I don't think you can imagine what a hell she was forced to live in. I can't. No one can."

"Why didn't she divorce him?"

"He threatened to kill her if she left him. She had every reason to believe he would do it. On several occasions he beat her so badly that

188

she had to be taken to the hospital. I didn't know anything back then, but later on I understood."

"If the doctors suspect abuse, they're obligated to report it to the police."

"She always came up with explanations. And she was convincing. She would even debase herself to protect him. She might say she was drunk and fell down. My mother never touched liquor. But of course the doctors didn't know that."

The conversation ceased as Wallander veered around a bus. He noticed that Runfeldt seemed tense. Wallander wasn't driving fast, but his passenger was apparently nervous in traffic.

"I think what kept her from committing suicide was me and my sister," he said when the bus was behind them.

"That's natural," replied Wallander. "Let's go back instead to what you said earlier. That your father had threatened to kill your mother. When a man abuses a woman, he usually doesn't intend to kill her. He does it to control her. Sometimes he hits too hard, and the abuse leads to death even though that wasn't the intention. But usually there's a different reason for actually killing someone. It's taking it one step farther."

Runfeldt replied with a surprising question.

"Are you married?"

"Not anymore."

"Did you ever hit her?"

"Why would I do that?"

"I just wondered."

"We're not talking about me here."

Runfeldt was silent. Wallander remembered with horrifying clarity the one time he had struck Mona in a moment of uncontrollable rage. She had fallen, hit the back of her head against the door frame, and blacked out for a few seconds. She almost packed her bags and left, but Linda was still so young back then. And Wallander had begged and pleaded. They had sat up all night talking. He had implored her. In the end she had stayed. The incident had been etched into his memory, but he had a hard time recalling what had brought the whole thing on. What were they fighting about? Where had the rage come from? He didn't know anymore. He realized that he had repressed it. There were few things in his life that he was more ashamed of than what had happened that day. He understood his own reluctance to be reminded of it.

"Let's get back to that day ten years ago," said Wallander after a while. "What happened?"

"It was a winter Sunday," said Runfeldt. "February 5th, 1984. It was a beautiful, cold winter day. They used to go out on Sunday excursions.

Take a walk in the woods, walk along the beach. Or across the ice on the lake."

"It sounds idyllic," said Wallander. "How am I supposed to make this fit with what you said before?"

"Of course it wasn't idyllic. It was just the opposite. My mother was always terrified. I'm not exaggerating. She had long ago crossed the boundary where fear takes over and dominates your whole life. She must have been mentally exhausted. But he wanted to take a Sunday walk, and so they did. The threat of a clenched fist was always present. I'm convinced my father never saw her terror. He probably thought all was forgiven and forgotten each time. I assume he regarded his abuse of her to be chance incidents of rash behavior. Hardly anything more than that."

"I think I understand. So what happened?"

"Why they had gone up to Småland that Sunday, I don't know. They parked on a forest road. It had been snowing, but it wasn't particularly deep. They walked along the logging road and out to the lake, where they went out onto the ice. Suddenly it gave way and she fell in. He couldn't manage to pull her out. He ran back to the car and went to get help. She was dead, of course, when they found her."

"How did you hear about it?"

"He called me himself. I was in Stockholm at the time."

"What do you remember of the phone conversation?"

"Naturally he was very upset."

"In what way?"

"Can you be upset in more than one way?"

"Was he crying? Was he in shock? Try to describe it more clearly."

"He wasn't crying. I can only remember my father having tears in his eyes when he talked about rare types of orchids. It was more that he was trying to convince me he had done everything in his power to rescue her. But that shouldn't be necessary, should it? If someone's in trouble, you try to help, don't you?"

"What else did he say?"

"He asked me to try to get hold of my sister."

"So he called you first?"

"Yes."

"Then what happened?"

"We came down here to Skåne. Just like now. The funeral was a week later. I spoke to a policeman on the phone. He said that the ice must have been unexpectedly thin. My mother wasn't a big person."

"Is that what he said? The police officer you spoke to? That the ice must have been 'unexpectedly thin'?"

"I have a good memory for details. Maybe because I'm an accountant."

Wallander nodded. They passed a sign for a nearby café and decided to stop. During the brief meal, Wallander asked Runfeldt about his work in international accounting. He listened without paying much attention. Instead, he went over in his mind the conversation they had had in the car. There was some part of it that was important, but he hadn't quite pinned it down. Just as they were about to leave the café, his cell phone rang. It was Martinsson. Runfeldt stepped aside to give Wallander some privacy.

"We seem to be out of luck," said Martinsson. "Of the officers who were working in Älmhult ten years ago, one of them is dead and the other one has retired to Örebro."

Wallander was disappointed. Without a reliable informant, the trip would lose much of its purpose.

"I don't even know how to find the lake," he complained. "Aren't there any ambulance drivers? Wasn't the fire department called in to pull her out?"

"I've located the man who offered to help Gösta Runfeldt," said Martinsson. "I know his name and where he lives. The problem is that he doesn't have a phone."

"Is there really somebody in this country today who doesn't have a phone?"

"Apparently. Do you have a pen?"

Wallander searched his pockets. As usual he didn't have either a pen or paper. He waved over Runfeldt, who handed Wallander a gold-plated pen and one of his business cards.

"The man's name is Jacob Hoslowski," said Martinsson. "He's some sort of town eccentric and lives alone in a cottage not far from that lake. It's called Stång Lake and it's due north of Älmhult. I talked to a friendly woman at the Town Hall. She said that there's a road sign to Stång Lake posted next to his driveway. But she couldn't give me exact directions to Hoslowski's place. You'll have to stop at a house and ask."

"Do we have somewhere to stay overnight?"

"IKEA has a hotel, and you have rooms reserved."

"Doesn't IKEA sell furniture?"

"Yes, they do. But they also have a hotel. The IKEA Inn."

"Anything happening?"

"Everybody's really busy. But it sounds as if Hamrén's going to come down from Stockholm to help out."

Wallander remembered the two police detectives from Stockholm who had assisted them during the summer. He had nothing against meeting them again.

"Not Ludwigsson?"

"He was in a car accident; he's in the hospital."

"Serious?"

"I'll find out. I didn't get that impression."

Wallander hung up and returned the pen.

"It looks valuable," he said.

"Being an accountant for Price Waterhouse is one of the best jobs around," said Runfeldt. "At least in terms of salary and future prospects. Wise parents today advise their children to become accountants."

"What's the average salary?" asked Wallander.

"Most people who are employed above a certain level have individual contracts. Which are confidential, of course."

Wallander understood this to mean that the salaries were extremely high. He was often amazed at various disclosures about severance pay, salary levels, and golden parachutes. His own salary as a detective with many years of experience was quite low. If he had taken a position in the private-security sector, he could have earned at least double what he was making. But he had made his choice. He would stay with the police, at least as long as he could survive on his salary. Yet he had often thought that the picture of Sweden today was based on a comparison of unequal contracts.

They reached Älmhult at five o'clock. Bo Runfeldt asked if it was really necessary to stay overnight. Wallander didn't have a good answer. Runfeldt could have taken the train back to Malmö. But Wallander maintained that they wouldn't be able to visit the lake until the following day because it would soon be dark, and he wanted Runfeldt to go with him.

After they checked into the hotel, Wallander set off at once to find Jacob Hoslowski's house before nightfall. He stopped at the road sign posted at the entrance to the town and made a note of Stång Lake's location. He headed away from town. It was already dusk. He turned left and then left again. The forest was dense. The open landscape of Skåne was far behind him. He stopped when he saw a man fixing a gate near the road. The man explained which way he should go to find Hoslowski's house. Wallander drove on. The engine started to knock. He was going to have to get a new car soon. His Peugeot was getting old. He wondered how he would afford it. He had bought his present car after his first one was blown up on highway E65 one night. It had also been a Peugeot. Wallander had the feeling that his next car would be the same make. The older he got, the harder it was for him to break his habits.

He stopped when he reached the next turnoff. If he understood the directions correctly, he was supposed to turn right. Then he would come to Hoslowski's house after another 800 meters or so. It was a rough dirt road, poorly maintained. After 100 meters Wallander stopped and backed up, afraid he might get stuck. He got out of the car and started walking. There was a rustling in the trees, which stood close together along the narrow forest road. He walked briskly to keep warm.

The house stood right next to the road. It was an old-fashioned cottage. The yard was full of junked cars. A solitary rooster was sitting on a stump, staring at him. There was a light in one window. Wallander saw that it was a kerosene lamp. He wondered whether he should postpone his visit until the following day, but he had come so far. The investigation demanded that he waste no time. He went up to the front door. The rooster sat motionless on the stump. He knocked. After a moment he heard a shuffling sound. The door opened. The man standing there in the dim light was younger than Wallander had expected, maybe about forty. Wallander introduced himself.

"Jacob Hoslowski," replied the man. Wallander could hear a faint, almost imperceptible accent in his voice. The man was unwashed. He smelled bad. His long hair and beard were matted. Wallander started breathing through his mouth.

"I wonder if I might disturb you for a few minutes," he said. "I'm from the police in Ystad."

Hoslowski smiled and stepped aside.

"Come in. I always let in anyone who knocks on my door."

Wallander stepped inside the dark entryway and almost tripped over a cat. The whole house was full of them. He'd never in his life seen so many cats in one place before. It reminded him of the Forum Romanum. But in contrast to the outdoor location in Rome, the stench here was appalling. He had to open his mouth wide to be able to breathe at all. He followed Hoslowski into the larger of the two rooms in the old house. There was almost no furniture, just mattresses and cushions, piles of books, and a single kerosene lamp on a stool. And cats, everywhere. Wallander had an uneasy feeling that they were all staring at him with alert eyes and might hurl themselves at him at any moment.

"I don't often visit a house without electricity," said Wallander.

"I live outside of time," Hoslowski replied simply. "In my next life I'm going to be reincarnated as a cat."

Wallander nodded. "I see," he said without conviction. "If I've understood correctly, you were living here ten years ago?"

"I've lived here ever since I left time behind."

Wallander realized the futility of his next question, but he asked it anyway.

"When did you leave time behind?"

"A long time ago."

Wallander could see this was the most complete answer he was going to get. With some difficulty he sank down onto one of the cushions and hoped it wasn't full of cat piss.

"Ten years ago a woman went out onto the ice at Stång Lake near here and drowned," he went on. "Do you remember the incident? Even though, as you say, you live outside of time?"

Wallander noticed that Hoslowski reacted positively to having his talk about a timeless existence accepted.

"A winter Sunday ten years ago," said Wallander. "According to the report, a man came here and asked for help."

Hoslowski nodded. "A man came and pounded on my door. He wanted to borrow my telephone."

Wallander looked around the room. "But you don't have a phone?"

"Who would I talk to?"

Wallander nodded. "What happened then?"

"I directed him to my nearest neighbors. They have a telephone."

"Did you go with him?"

"I went over to the lake to see if I could pull her out."

Wallander paused and backed up a bit.

"The man who pounded on your door—I presume he was upset?"

"Maybe."

"What do you mean by 'maybe'?"

"I remember him as being very collected in a way that might seem unexpected."

"Did you notice anything else?"

"I forget. It took place in a cosmic dimension that has changed many times since then."

"Let's move on. You went over to the lake. What happened then?"

"The ice was smooth. I saw the hole. I walked over to it. But I didn't see anything in the water."

"You say that you walked? Weren't you afraid the ice would crack?"

"I know what it can hold. Besides, I can make myself weightless when I have to."

You can't talk sense with a crazy man, thought Wallander, resigned. He kept on with his questions.

"Can you describe the hole in the ice for me?"

"It was probably cut by a fisherman. Maybe it froze over, but the ice hadn't had a chance to get thick."

Wallander thought for a moment.

"Don't ice fishermen drill small holes?"

"This one was almost rectangular. Maybe they used a saw."

"Are there usually ice fishermen on Stång Lake?"

"The lake is full of fish. I fish there myself. But not in the winter."

"Then what happened? You stood next to the hole in the ice. You didn't see anything. What did you do then?"

"I took off my clothes and got into the water."

Wallander stared at him.

"Why in God's name did you do that?"

"I thought I might be able to feel her body with my feet."

"But you could have frozen to death."

"I can make myself insensitive to extreme cold or heat if necessary."

Wallander realized he should have anticipated this answer.

"But you didn't find her?"

"No. I pulled myself back out of the water and got dressed. Right after that people came running. A car with ladders. Then I left."

Wallander began to get up from the uncomfortable cushion. The stench in the room was unbearable. He had no further questions and didn't want to stay any longer than he had to. At the same time he had to admit that Jacob Hoslowski had been obliging and friendly.

Hoslowski followed him out to the yard. "They pulled her out later," he said. "My neighbor usually stops by to tell me what he thinks I should know about the outside world. He's a very nice man. He keeps me informed about everything that goes on in the local shooting club. Most of what happens other places in the world he considers less important. That's why I don't know much about what's happening. Maybe you'd permit me to ask whether at the present time there's any kind of extensive war going on?"

"Nothing big," said Wallander. "But lots of small ones."

Hoslowski nodded. Then he pointed.

"My neighbor lives right nearby," he said. "You can't see his house. It's maybe three hundred meters from here. Earthly distances are hard to calculate."

Wallander thanked him and left. It was quite dark now. He had brought his flashlight along and used it to light his way. Lights flickered between the trees. He thought about Jacob Hoslowski and all his cats.

The house he came to seemed relatively new. In front stood a van with the words "Plumbing Services" painted on the side. Wallander rang the bell. A tall, barefoot man wearing a white undershirt tore open the door as if Wallander was the latest in an endless line of people who had come to disturb him. But the man had an open and friendly face. In the background was the sound of a child crying. Wallander explained briefly who he was.

"And it was Hoslowski who sent you over?" said the man with a smile.

"What makes you think that?"

"I can tell by the smell," said the man. "It goes away with a good airing. Come on in."

Wallander followed the man into the kitchen. The crying was coming from upstairs. There was a TV on somewhere too. The man said his
name was Rune Nilsson and he was a plumber. Wallander declined a
cup of coffee and told him why he was there.

"You don't forget something like that," Nilsson said as Wallander
fell silent. "That was before I was married. There was an old house here
that I tore down when I built the new one. Was it really ten years ago
that it happened?"

"Exactly ten years ago, give or take a few months."

"He came and pounded on my door. It was the middle of the day."

"How did he seem?"

"He was upset, but in control. He called the police while I put on my
coat. Then we took off. We took a short cut through the woods. I did
a lot of fishing back then."

"He gave you the impression of being in control the whole time?
What did he say? How did he explain the accident?"

"She had fallen in. The ice broke."

"But the ice was quite thick, wasn't it?"

"You never know about ice. There can be invisible cracks or weak-
nesses. But it did seem a little strange."

"Jacob Hoslowski said the hole in the ice was rectangular. He
thought it might have been cut with a saw."

"I don't remember whether it was rectangular or not. Only that it
was big."

"But the ice around it was strong. You're a big man but you weren't
afraid to go out on the ice?"

Rune Nilsson nodded.

"I thought a lot about that afterwards," he said. "It was a strange
thing, a woman disappearing into a hole in the ice like that. Why
couldn't he have pulled her out?"

"What was his own explanation?"

"He said he tried, but she vanished too fast. Pulled in under the ice."

"Was that true?"

"They found her several meters away from the hole. Right under the
ice. She hadn't sunk down. I was there when they pulled her out. I'll
never forget it. I never would have believed that she could weigh so
much."

Wallander gave him a surprised look.

"What do you mean by that? That she could have 'weighed so
much'?"

"I knew Nygren, who was the police officer back then. He's dead
now. He told me several times that the man claimed she weighed
almost 80 kilos. That was supposed to explain why the ice broke. I

never understood that. But I guess you always brood over accidents. About what happened. How it could have been prevented."

"That's probably true," said Wallander and stood up. "Thanks for your time. Tomorrow I'd like you to show me where it happened."

"Are we going to walk on water?"

Wallander smiled. "That's not necessary. But maybe Jacob Hoslowski has that power."

Nilsson shook his head.

"He's harmless," he said. "That man and all his cats. But he's nuts."

Wallander walked back along the forest road. The kerosene lamp was burning in Hoslowski's window. Rune Nilsson had promised to be home around eight the next morning. Wallander started up his car and headed back to Älmhult. The knocking in the engine was gone now. He was hungry. It might be opportune to suggest to Runfeldt that they have dinner together. For Wallander the trip no longer seemed pointless.

When Wallander reached the hotel there was a message for him at the front desk. Bo Runfeldt had rented a car and gone to Växjö. He had good friends there, and intended to spend the night. He promised to return to Älmhult early the next day. Wallander felt briefly annoyed. He might have needed Runfeldt for something during the evening. He had left a phone number in Växjö. But Wallander had no reason to call him. He was also slightly relieved that he would have the evening to himself. He went to his room, took a shower, and realized he didn't have a toothbrush with him. He got dressed and went in search of a shop open at night where he could buy what he needed. He ate dinner at a pizzeria he passed. The whole time he was thinking about the drowning accident. He was slowly managing to piece together a picture. Back in his hotel room, he called Höglund at home just before nine. He hoped her children were in bed asleep. When she picked up the phone, he quickly outlined what had happened. What he wanted to know was whether they had succeeded in tracking down Mrs. Svensson, presumably Gösta Runfeldt's last client.

"Not yet," she told him. "But I'm sure we will."

He kept the conversation short. Then he turned on the TV and listened distractedly to a discussion program. Eventually he fell asleep.

When Wallander woke up just after six in the morning, he felt well rested. By seven thirty he had eaten breakfast and paid for his room. He sat down in the lobby to wait. Runfeldt arrived a few minutes later. Neither of them mentioned that he had spent the night in Växjö.

"We're going on an expedition," said Wallander. "To the lake where your mother drowned."

"Has the trip been worth the trouble?" asked Runfeldt. Wallander noticed that he was irritable.

"Yes," he replied. "And your presence has actually been of crucial importance. Whether you want to believe it or not."

Wallander wasn't sure of this, of course, but he spoke the words so firmly that Runfeldt, if not totally convinced, at least looked pensive.

Rune Nilsson was waiting for them. They walked along a path through the woods. There was no wind; the temperature was close to freezing. The ground was hard under their feet. The water spread out before them. It was an oblong lake. Nilsson pointed to a spot in about the middle of the lake. Runfeldt looked uncomfortable about being there. Wallander assumed he had never been there before.

"It's hard to imagine the lake covered with ice," said Nilsson. "Everything changes when winter arrives. Especially your sense of distance. What seems far away in the summer can suddenly seem much closer. Or the other way around."

Wallander walked down to the shore. The water was dark. He thought he caught a glimpse of a little fish moving next to a rock. Behind him he could hear Runfeldt asking if the lake was deep. He didn't catch Nilsson's reply.

What happened? he asked himself. Did Gösta Runfeldt make up his mind ahead of time to drown his wife on that particular Sunday? That's what he must have done. Somehow he must have prepared the hole in the ice. The same way someone had sawed through the planks over the pit at Holger Eriksson's place. And had held Runfeldt prisoner.

Wallander stood there a long time, looking at the lake spread out before them. But what he saw was in his mind.

They walked back through the woods. At the car they said goodbye to Nilsson. Wallander thought they should be back in Ystad well before noon.

He was mistaken. Just south of Älmhult the car stopped running. The engine just quit. Wallander called the local emergency number for the road service he belonged to. The man came in less than twenty minutes, but quickly concluded that the car had a major problem that couldn't be repaired on the spot. There was nothing else to do but leave the car in Älmhult and take the train to Malmö.

The tow-truck driver drove them to the station. As Wallander settled the account, Runfeldt offered to buy the tickets. He bought first-class seats. Wallander said nothing. At 9:44, the train left for Hässleholm and Malmö. By then Wallander had called the police station and asked for someone to come to Malmö and pick them up. There was no good connection by train to Ystad. Ebba promised to see to it that someone was there.

"Don't the police have better cars than that?" Runfeldt asked suddenly after the train had left Älmhult behind. "What if there'd been an emergency?"

"That was my own car," replied Wallander. "Our emergency vehicles are in much better shape."

The landscape slid past outside the window. Wallander thought about Jacob Hoslowski and his cats. But he also thought about how Gösta Runfeldt had presumably murdered his wife. What it meant, he didn't know. Now Gösta Runfeldt himself was dead. A brutal man, probably a murderer, had now been killed in an equally gruesome way.

Wallander thought that the most obvious motive was revenge. But who was taking revenge? And how did Holger Eriksson fit into the picture? Wallander had no answers.

His thoughts were interrupted by the arrival of the conductor. It was a woman. She smiled and asked for their tickets with a distinct Skåne accent. Wallander had the feeling she was looking at him as if she recognized him. Maybe she'd seen his picture in some newspaper.

"When do we get to Malmö?" he asked.

"12:15," she replied. "Hässleholm 11:13."

Then she left.

She knew the timetable by heart.

Chapter Twenty

Peters was waiting for them at the Central Station in Malmö. Bo Runfeldt excused himself saying that he'd stay in Malmö for a few hours. In the afternoon he would return to Ystad, so he and his sister could start going through his father's estate and decide what to do about the flower shop.

On the way back to Ystad, Wallander sat in the back seat and made notes about what had happened in Älmhult. He had bought a pen and a little notebook at the station in Malmö and balanced it on his knee as he wrote. Peters, a taciturn man, didn't say a single word during the drive, since he could see that Wallander was busy. It was a sunny, windy day. Already the 14th of October. His father hadn't been in the ground even a week. Wallander suspected, or maybe feared, that he was only beginning a long grieving process that lay ahead of him.

They reached Ystad and went straight to the police station. Wallander had eaten some outrageously expensive sandwiches on the train and didn't need any lunch. He stopped at the front desk to tell Ebba what had happened to his car. Her well-kept old Volvo stood out in the parking lot as usual.

"I'm going to have to buy a new car," he said. "But how am I going to afford it?"

"It's shameful how little they pay us," she replied. "But it's best not to think about it."

"I'm not so sure about that," said Wallander. "It's not going to get any better if we just forget about it."

"I suppose you may have a secret parachute agreement," said Ebba.

"Everybody's got a parachute," said Wallander. "Except possibly you and me."

On the way to his office he peeked into his colleagues' rooms.

Everyone was out but Nyberg, who had an office at the very end of the corridor. He was seldom there. A crutch was leaning against his desk.

"How's the foot?" asked Wallander.

"As well as can be expected," replied Nyberg crossly.

"You didn't happen to find Gösta Runfeldt's suitcase, by any chance?"

"No, but at least it's not in the Marsvinsholm Woods. The dogs would have tracked it down."

"Did you find anything else?"

"We always do. The question is whether it has anything to do with the murder or not. We're in the process of comparing tire tracks from the tractor path behind the hill with Eriksson's tower on it to the ones we found in the woods. I doubt we'll be able to say anything with certainty. It was rainy and muddy at both places."

"Anything else you think I should know about?"

"The shrunken head," said Nyberg. "We got a long, detailed letter from the Ethnographic Museum in Stockholm. I understand about half of what it says. But the most important thing is, they're positive it comes from the Belgian Congo. They think it's between forty and fifty years old."

"That fits with the time period," said Wallander.

"The museum is interested in acquiring it."

"That's something the authorities will have to decide after the investigation is over."

Nyberg suddenly gave Wallander an inquiring look.

"Are we going to catch the people who did this?"

"We have to."

Nyberg nodded without saying anything more.

"You said 'the people.' When I asked you before you said it was probably a lone perpetrator."

"Did I say 'the people'?"

"Yes."

"I still think it was someone acting alone. But I can't explain why."

Wallander turned to go. Nyberg stopped him.

"We managed to get Secure, the mail order company in Borås, to tell us what Gösta Runfeldt actually bought from them. He ordered things three other times. The company hasn't been in business long. He bought night-vision binoculars, several flashlights, and a bunch of other unimportant things. Nothing illegal. We found the flashlights at Harpegatan. But the night-vision binoculars weren't there or at the flower shop."

Wallander thought for a moment.

"You think he packed them in his suitcase to take with him to Nairobi? Do people spy on orchids at night?"

"Well, we haven't found them, at any rate," said Nyberg.

Wallander went into his own office. He thought about getting a cup of coffee but changed his mind. He sat down at his desk and read through what he had written during the drive from Malmö. He was looking for similarities and differences between the two murder cases.

Both men had been described as brutal, though in different ways. Holger Eriksson had treated his employees badly, while Gösta Runfeldt had beaten his wife. There was a similarity. They had both been murdered in a premeditated way. Wallander was still convinced that Runfeldt had been held prisoner. There was no other reasonable explanation for his long absence. Eriksson, on the other hand, had walked straight to his death. That was one difference. But Wallander also thought there were other similarities, even though they were still unclear. Why was Runfeldt held prisoner? Why did the perpetrator wait to kill him? For some reason the perpetrator wanted to wait. Which in turn gave rise to new questions. Could it be that the perpetrator hadn't had the opportunity to kill him right away? If that was the case, why? Or was it part of the plan to hold Runfeldt captive, starving him until he was powerless?

Once again the only motive that Wallander could see was revenge. But revenge for what? They still hadn't found any definite clues.

Wallander moved on to the perpetrator. They had guessed that it was probably a lone man with great physical strength. They could be wrong, of course; there could be more than one, but Wallander didn't think so. There was something about the planning that pointed to a single perpetrator.

Careful planning was one of the prerequisites, he thought. If the perpetrator wasn't alone, the planning would have been much less meticulous.

Wallander leaned back in his chair. He tried to decipher the churning uneasiness that never left him. There was something about the picture that he wasn't seeing. Or was interpreting all wrong. He just couldn't figure out what it was.

After about an hour he went to get the cup of coffee he had decided against earlier. He called the optician who had waited in vain for him. He could come in whenever he liked. After going through his jacket twice, Wallander found the phone number for the car-repair shop in Älmhult in his pants pocket. The repairs were going to cost a lot. But Wallander had no alternative if he wanted to get anything for the car as a trade-in.

He hung up and called Martinsson.

"I didn't know you were back. How'd it go in Älmhult?"

"I thought we should talk about that. Who's here right now?"

"I just saw Hansson," said Martinsson. "We talked about having a short meeting at five o'clock."

"So we'll wait till then."

Wallander put down the phone and suddenly thought about Jacob Hoslowski and his cats. He wondered when he would have time to look for a house for himself. He doubted that it would ever happen. The police workload was constantly increasing. In the past there were always moments when their work slacked off in intensity. That almost never happened anymore. And no one was talking about it getting any better. Whether crime was on the rise, he didn't know. He did know it was getting more violent and more complicated. And fewer officers were involved with real police work. More and more of them had administrative jobs. It was impossible for Wallander to think of himself with a desk job. When he did sit there, as he was doing now, it was a break in his ordinary routine. They'd never be able to find the perpetrator they were after from inside the police station. The development of forensic technology was steadily progressing, but it could never replace field work.

He returned in his thoughts to Älmhult. Had Gösta Runfeldt made a murder look like an accident? There were indications that he had. There were too many details that didn't fit with an accident. Somewhere in the archives it must be possible to dig up the police investigation that had been done. Even though it had probably been sloppy, he had a hard time criticizing the officers who had done it. What could they have suspected? Why would they have had any suspicions at all?

Wallander picked up the phone and called Martinsson back. He asked him to contact Älmhult and ask for a copy of the investigative report on the drowning accident.

"Why didn't you do that yourself?" asked Martinsson in surprise.

"I never talked to any police there," replied Wallander. "On the other hand, I did sit on the floor in a house teeming with cats and a man who could make himself weightless whenever he felt like it. It'd be good to get that copy ASAP."

He hung up before Martinsson had a chance to ask any questions. It was three o'clock. Through the window he could see that it was still nice outside. He decided that he might as well go see the optician right away. The meeting was scheduled for five o'clock. There wasn't much else he could do before then. Besides, his brain was tired. He had a headache in both temples. He put on his jacket and left the station. Ebba was busy on the phone. He wrote a note telling her he'd be back by five.

He stood in the parking lot looking for his car for a minute before he remembered it was in the shop. It took him ten minutes to walk downtown. The optician's shop was on Stora Östergatan near Pilgränd.

He was told he had to wait a few minutes. He leafed through the newspapers lying on a table. There was a picture of him in one that must have been taken at least five years back. He hardly recognized himself. There was a lot of coverage about the murders. "The police are following up solid leads." That's what Wallander had told the press. Which wasn't true. He wondered if the perpetrator read the papers. Was he keeping track of the police work? Wallander turned some more pages. He stopped at a story inside, read it with growing astonishment, and studied the pictures. The journalist from the *Observer*, which hadn't come out yet, had been right. People from all over the country had gathered in Ystad to form a national organization for a citizen militia. If necessary, they wouldn't hesitate to commit illegal acts. They supported the work of the police, but they refused to accept any cutbacks. Above all, they refused to accept any insecurity regarding civil rights. Wallander kept reading with a growing mixture of bitterness and distaste. Something had happened, all right. The spokesmen for armed and organized citizen militias were no longer hiding in the shadows. They were coming out into the open. Their names and faces were in the papers and they were gathering in Ystad.

Wallander tossed the paper aside. We're going to end up fighting on two fronts, he thought. This is much more serious than all the neo-Nazi organizations they write about, whose purported threat is always being exaggerated. Not to mention the motorcycle gangs.

Then it was his turn. Wallander sat with a strange apparatus in front of his eyes and stared at blurry letters. He suddenly started to worry that he might be going blind. He felt like he couldn't see anything at all. But afterwards, when the optometrist set a pair of glasses on his nose and held up a newspaper page in front of him, a page on which there was also an article about the citizen militia and the future national organization, he could read the text without straining his eyes. For a moment this took away the unpleasantness of the article's contents.

"You need reading glasses," said the optometrist kindly. "Not unusual at your age. Plus 1.5 should be enough. You'll probably have to increase the power every few years or so."

Wallander went over to look at the display of frames. He was shocked when he saw the prices. When he heard that it was also possible to get cheaper plastic frames, he decided at once on this option.

"How many pairs?" asked the optometrist. "Two? So you'll have a spare?"

Wallander thought about all the pens he was constantly losing. He couldn't stand the thought of having glasses on a string around his neck.

"Five pairs," he said.

When he left the shop it was still only four o'clock. He strolled over to the realtor's office whose window he had stood in front of a few days earlier. This time he went inside, sat down at a table, and looked through the house listings. Two of the properties interested him. He got copies and promised to let them know if he wanted to see them. He went back outside. He still had some time left. He decided to try to get an answer to a question that had been on his mind ever since Holger Eriksson died. He went into a bookshop near Stortorget. He asked for a bookseller he knew, and was told he was in the stockroom in the basement. He went down a half flight of stairs and found his acquaintance unpacking boxes of schoolbooks. They greeted each other.

"You still owe me 19 kronor," said the bookseller with a smile.

"For what?"

"This summer you woke me up at six in the morning because the police needed a map of the Dominican Republic. The officer who came over to get it paid 100 kronor. But it cost 119."

Wallander stuck his hand under his jacket to take out his wallet. The bookseller put up his hand to stop him.

"It's on me," he said. "I was just kidding."

"Holger Eriksson's poems," said Wallander. "Which he self-published. Who bought them?"

"He was an amateur, of course," said the bookseller. "But he wasn't a bad poet. The problem was, he wrote only about birds. Or rather, that was the only thing he was any good at writing about. Whenever he tried some other subject, it didn't work."

"Who bought his poems?"

"He didn't sell many copies through the bookshop. Most of these regional writers don't generate a lot of sales, you know. But they're important for another reason."

"So who bought them?"

"I honestly don't know. Maybe an occasional tourist who came to Skåne? I think some bird lovers discovered his books. Maybe collectors of regional literature."

"Birds," said Wallander. "That means he never wrote anything that people might get upset about."

"Of course not," said the bookseller in surprise. "Did someone say that?"

"I was just wondering."

Wallander left the bookshop and went back up the hill to the police station.

When he entered the conference room and sat down in his usual place, he put on his new glasses. A certain merriment was evident in the room, but no one said a word.

"Who's missing?" he asked.

"Svedberg," said Höglund. "I don't know where he is."

She had barely finished her sentence before Svedberg tore open the door to the conference room. Wallander could see at once that something had happened.

"I've found Mrs. Svensson," he said. "Gösta Runfeldt's last client. If we're right about it."

"Good," said Wallander, feeling the suspense rise.

"I thought that at some time she might have been in the florist shop," Svedberg continued. "She might have gone to see Runfeldt there. I took along the picture we had developed. Vanja Andersson remembered seeing a picture of the same man on the table in the back room. She also knew that a woman named Svensson had been to the flower shop a couple of times. Once she bought flowers to be delivered. The rest was simple. Her address and phone number were on file. She lives on Byabacksvägen in Sövestad. I went out there. She runs a little produce store. I took along the picture and told her the truth, that we believed she had hired Runfeldt as a private detective. She told me at once that I was right."

"Good," Wallander repeated. "What else did she say?"

"I left her there. She was busy with the contractors working in the house. I thought it'd be better if we interviewed her together."

"I'll talk to her this evening," said Wallander. "Let's keep this meeting as brief as possible."

They were there for about half an hour. During the meeting Chief Holgersson came in and sat down silently at the table. Wallander reported on his trip to Älmhult. He concluded by telling them what he thought, that they shouldn't ignore the possibility that Runfeldt had murdered his wife. They should wait for a copy of the investigative report made at the time. Afterwards they would decide how to proceed.

When Wallander stopped talking, no one else said anything. Everyone understood that he might be right. But no one was sure what it actually meant.

"The trip was important," said Wallander after a moment. "I also think the trip to Svenstavik could be productive."

"With a stop in Gävle," said Höglund. "I don't know whether it means anything, but I asked a good friend in Stockholm to go to a special bookshop and get me a few issues of a paper called *Terminator*. They came today."

"What kind of paper is that?" asked Wallander, who had a vague recollection of hearing the name before.

"It's published in the States," she continued. "It's a poorly disguised trade paper, you might say. For people looking for contracts as mercenaries or bodyguards, or any kind of assignments as soldiers. It's not a pleasant paper. For one thing, it's extremely racist. But I found a little classified ad that should interest us. There's a man in Gävle who advertises that he can arrange assignments for what he calls 'battle-ready and unbiased men.' I called our colleagues in Gävle. They knew who he was but have never dealt with him directly. They thought he had contact with men in Sweden who have backgrounds as mercenaries."

"This could be important," said Wallander. "He's someone we definitely need to make contact with. It should be possible to combine a trip to Svenstavik and Gävle."

"I've checked the map," she said. "You can fly to Östersund, then rent a car. Or ask for help from our colleagues up there."

Wallander closed his notebook.

"Get someone to make me a reservation," he said. "If possible, I'd like to go tomorrow."

"Even though it's Saturday?" asked Martinsson.

"The people I have to see should still be able to meet with me," said Wallander. "There's no time to waste if we can help it. I suggest that we break up the meeting now. Who wants to go along to Sövestad?"

Before anyone could reply, Chief Holgersson tapped her pencil on the table.

"Just a minute," she said. "I don't know whether you realize that there's some kind of meeting going on here in town of people who have decided to form a national organization of citizen militias. I think it'd be good if we discussed as soon as possible how we're going to handle this."

"The NPB has sent out lots of flyers about these so-called citizen militias," said Wallander. "I think it's very clear what Swedish law says about vigilante activities."

"No doubt you're right," she replied. "But I have a strong feeling that things are changing. I'm afraid that pretty soon we're going to see a burglar get shot to death by someone from one of these groups. And then they'll start shooting each other."

Wallander knew she was right. But at that moment he had a hard time thinking about anything other than the two murder investigations they were working on. "I agree it's important. In the long run, it's crucial of course if we don't want to be inundated by people playing police. Let's talk about it on Monday when we meet."

Holgersson let it go at that. The meeting broke up. Höglund and Svedberg were going to accompany Wallander to Sövestad. It was six o'clock by the time they left the station. Clouds had moved in, and it would probably rain later that night. They took Höglund's car. Wallander got into the back seat. He wondered suddenly whether he still smelled from his visit to Jacob Hoslowski's house of cats.

"Maria Svensson," said Svedberg. "She's thirty-six years old and has a little produce shop in Sövestad. If I understood her right, she sells only organic vegetables."

"You didn't ask her why she got in contact with Runfeldt?"

"After she confirmed the connection, I didn't ask her anything else."

"This should be interesting," said Wallander. "In all my years on the force, I've never met anyone who had asked for help from a private detective."

"The photo was of a man," said Höglund. "Is she married?"

"I've told you everything I know," said Svedberg. "From this point on, you know as much as I do."

"Or as little," Wallander corrected him. "We know almost nothing."

They reached Sövestad in about twenty minutes. Wallander had been there once many years ago to cut down a man who had hanged himself. It was the first suicide he had ever encountered. He thought back on the incident with distaste.

Svedberg stopped the car in front of a building with a storefront and an attached greenhouse. A sign said "Svensson's Produce." They climbed out of the car.

"She lives in the building," said Svedberg. "I assume that she's closed up the shop for the day."

"A florist shop and a greengrocer," said Wallander. "Does that mean anything? Or is it just a coincidence?"

He didn't expect an answer, and didn't get one. When they had gone halfway up the gravel pathway the front door opened.

"Maria Svensson," said Svedberg. "She's been waiting for us."

Wallander looked at the woman standing on the steps. She was wearing jeans and a white blouse. She had clogs on her feet. There was something odd about her appearance. He noticed that she wore no makeup. Svedberg introduced them. Maria Svensson invited them in. They sat down in her living room. It occurred to Wallander that there was also something odd about her house. As if she wasn't particularly interested in the decor.

"May I offer you some coffee?" she asked.

All three of them declined.

"As you already know, we've come to find out a little more about your relationship to Gösta Runfeldt."

She gave him a surprised look.

"Am I supposed to have had a relationship with him?"

"As a private detective and client," Wallander clarified.

"That's true."

"Gösta Runfeldt has been murdered. It took a while for us to discover that he wasn't only a florist, but also ran a business as a private detective. So my first question is: How did you happen to contact him?"

"I saw an ad in *Arbetet.* This past summer."

"How did you first make contact?"

"I went to his flower shop. Later the same day we met at a café in Ystad. It's near Stortorget. I don't remember what it's called."

"What was your reason for contacting him?"

"I'd rather not say."

She sounded quite firm. Wallander was surprised because up to that point her answers had been so straightforward.

"I think you're going to have to tell us," he said.

"I can assure you that it has nothing to do with his death. I'm just as horrified and shocked as everybody else by what happened."

"Whether it has anything to do with it or not is something for the police to decide," said Wallander. "I'm afraid you'll have to answer the question. You can choose to do so here. Then anything that isn't directly connected with the investigation will just be between us. If we're forced to take you in for a more formal interrogation, it will be more difficult to avoid letting the details leak out to the media."

She sat in silence for a long time. They waited. Wallander took out the photograph they had developed on Harpegatan. She looked at it without expression.

"Is this your husband?" asked Wallander.

She stared at him. Suddenly she burst out laughing.

"No," she said. "He's not my husband. But he stole my lover away from me."

Wallander didn't understand. Höglund figured it out at once.

"What's her name?"

"Annika."

"And this man came between you?"

She had regained her composure.

"I was starting to suspect it. Finally I didn't know what I should do. That's when I thought of contacting a private detective. I had to find out if she was thinking of leaving me. Or switching. Going with a man. In the end I realized that's what she had done. Gösta Runfeldt came here and told me about it. The next day I wrote to Annika to tell her I never wanted to see her again."

"When did this happen?" asked Wallander. "When was he here to tell you about it?"

"September 20th or 21st."

"Did you have any contact with him after that?"

"No. I paid him through his post-office account."

"What was your impression of him?"

"He was very friendly. He was very fond of orchids. I think we got along well because he seemed just as reserved as I am."

Wallander thought for a moment.

"I only have one other question. Can you think of any reason why he was killed? Anything he said or did? Anything you noticed?"

"No," she replied. "Nothing. And I've really thought a lot about it."

Wallander glanced at his colleagues and stood up. "Then we won't disturb you any further. And none of this will get out. I promise."

"I'm grateful for that," she said. "I wouldn't want to lose my customers."

They said goodbye at the door. She closed it before they reached the street.

"What did she mean by that last remark?" asked Wallander. "That she was afraid of losing her customers?"

"People out in the country are conservative," said Höglund. "Homosexuality is still considered something dirty by many people. I think she has all the reason in the world not to want this to get out."

They got into the car. Wallander thought it would start raining soon.

"Where does this get us?" asked Svedberg.

"It doesn't lead us backwards or forwards," Wallander said. "The truth about these two investigations is simple. We know nothing for certain. We have a number of loose ends. But we don't have a single good clue to go on. We've got nothing."

They sat in the car in silence. For a moment Wallander felt guilty. He felt as if he'd stabbed the entire investigation in the back. But he knew that what he'd said was the truth.

They had nothing to go on.

Absolutely nothing.

Chapter Twenty-one

That night Wallander had a dream.

He had returned to Rome. He was walking along a street with his father; the summer was suddenly over and it was fall, a Roman fall. They were talking about something, he couldn't remember what. All of a sudden his father disappeared. One minute he was right next to him, the next minute he was gone, swallowed up by the swarm of people on the street.

He woke up from the dream with a start. In the silence of the night, the dream had seemed perfectly obvious and clear. It was his grief over his father's death, over never being able to finish the conversation they had started. He couldn't feel sorry for his father, who was dead; only for himself, who was left behind.

He couldn't manage to go back to sleep. He had to get up early anyway.

When they had gone back to the station in the evening after visiting Maria Svensson in Sövestad, there was a message telling Wallander that he had been booked on the seven o'clock flight from Sturup the next morning, with arrival in Östersund at 9:50, after changing planes at Arlanda Airport. He had looked over the itinerary and noticed that he could choose between spending Saturday night in Svenstavik or Gävle. A rental car would be waiting for him at the airport in Frösön. He could then decide for himself where to spend the night. He looked at the map of Sweden hanging on the wall next to the big map of Skåne. That gave him an idea. He went into his office and called Linda. For the first time he got an answering machine. He recorded his question for her: Could she take the train to Gävle, a trip that wouldn't take more than two hours, and spend the night there? Then he went looking for Svedberg. He finally found him in the exercise room on the lower level where he usually took a sauna by himself on Friday nights. Wallander asked Svedberg to do him a favor, to book two rooms at a nice hotel in Gävle for Saturday night. The next day he could be reached on his cell phone.

After that he went home. When he fell asleep he had the dream about the street in Rome in the fall.

At six A.M. the cab he had ordered was waiting outside. He picked up his tickets at Sturup Airport. Since it was Saturday morning, the plane to Stockholm was no more than half-full. The plane to Öster-sund left on time. Wallander had never been to Östersund before. His visits to that part of the country north of Stockholm had been few and far between. He realized that he was looking forward to the trip. For one thing, it would give him some distance from the dream he'd had during the night.

It was a cool morning at the airport in Östersund. The pilot had said it was +1 °C. The cold feels different, Wallander thought as he walked toward the airport terminal. He drove across the bridge from Frösön and thought the landscape was beautiful. The town rested gently along the slope of Storsjön. He headed south. It was a liberating feeling to be sitting in a rented car, driving through an unfamiliar landscape.

He reached Svenstavik at 11:30. He had heard from Svedberg along the way that he was supposed to contact a man named Robert Melander. He was the person in the church administration with whom attorney Bjurman had been in contact. Melander lived in a red house next to the old district courthouse in Svenstavik, which was now used by the Labor Educational Association, among others. Wallander parked his car outside an ICA grocery store in the middle of town. It took him a while to figure out that the old courthouse was on the other side of the newly built shopping center. He left his car where it was and walked. It was overcast but not raining. He entered the front yard of Melander's house. A Norwegian elkhound was chained to a small shed. The front door stood open. Wallander knocked. No one answered. Suddenly he thought he heard sounds from the other side of the house. He walked around the side of the well-maintained wooden house. There was a large garden with a potato patch and currant bushes. Wallander was surprised to see currants growing so far north. At the back of the house stood a man about Wallander's age, wearing boots and sawing branches off a tree that lay on the ground. When he caught sight of Wallander, he stopped at once and stretched his back. He smiled and put down the saw.

"I suppose you're the detective from Ystad," he said, putting out his hand.

His dialect is quite melodic, thought Wallander as he greeted the man.

"When'd you leave?" asked Melander. "Last night?"

"The plane left at seven o'clock," replied Wallander. "This morning."

"Imagine, it can go that fast," said Melander. "I was in Malmö several times back in the sixties. I'd gotten it into my head that it might be nice to move around a bit. And there was work at that big shipyard."

"Kockums," said Wallander. "But it doesn't exist anymore."

"Nothing exists anymore," replied Melander philosophically. "Back then it took four days to drive down there."

"But you didn't stay," said Wallander.

"No, I didn't," replied Melander cheerfully. "It was beautiful and pleasant enough down there in the south. But it wasn't for me. If I'm going to travel anywhere in my life, it's going to be north. Not south. You don't even have any snow down there, they tell me."

"Occasionally we do," replied Wallander. "When it does snow, it snows a lot."

"There's lunch waiting for us inside," said Melander. "My wife works at the welfare center, but she fixed something for us."

"It's beautiful here," said Wallander.

"Very," replied Melander. "And the beauty remains. Year after year."

They sat down at the kitchen table. Wallander ate heartily. There was plenty of food. Melander was also a good talker. He seemed to be a man who combined a large number of diverse activities to make his living. Among other things, he gave folk-dancing lessons in the winter. Not until they were having coffee did Wallander mention why he was there.

"Of course it came as a great surprise to us," said Melander. "A hundred thousand kronor is a lot of money. Especially when it's a gift from a stranger."

"You mean no one knows who Holger Eriksson was?"

"He was completely unknown to us. A car dealer from Skåne who was murdered. That was very strange. Those of us who are connected with the church began asking around. We also saw to it that a notice with his name was placed in the newspapers. It said that we were seeking information. But no one got in touch with us."

Wallander had remembered to bring along a photo of Holger Eriksson, one that they had found in one of his desk drawers. Robert Melander studied the picture while he filled his pipe. He lit it without taking his eyes off the photo. Wallander's hopes started to rise. But then Melander shook his head.

"The man is still a stranger to me," he said. "I have a good memory for faces. But I've never seen him before. Maybe someone else might recognize him. But I don't."

"I'm going to tell you two names," said Wallander. "The first one is Gösta Runfeldt. Does that name mean anything to you?"

Melander thought for a moment. But not for long.

"Runfeldt is not a name from around here," he said. "It almost sounds like an assumed or made-up name."

"Harald Berggren," said Wallander. "The second name."

Melander's pipe had gone out. He put it down on the table.

"Maybe," he said. "Let me make a call."

A telephone stood on the wide window ledge. Wallander felt his excitement rise. What he wanted most of all was to be able to identify the man who had written the diary from the Congo.

Melander spoke to a man named Nils.

"I have a guest here from Skåne," he said into the phone. "A man named Kurt who's a policeman. He's asking about someone named Harald Berggren. I don't think there's anyone alive here in Svenstavik by that name. But isn't there someone with that name buried in the cemetery?"

Wallander's heart sank. But not completely. Even a dead Harald Berggren might be of help to them.

Melander listened to the answer. Then he ended the conversation by asking how someone named Artur was doing after some kind of accident. It sounded like his state of health was unchanged. Melander came back to the kitchen table.

"Nils Enman is in charge of the cemetery," he said. "And there's a gravestone with the name Harald Berggren on it. But Nils is young. And the man who took care of the cemetery before is now lying there himself. Maybe we should go over there and have a look?"

Wallander stood up. Melander was surprised by his haste.

"Someone once told me that people from Skåne are laid-back. But that doesn't apply to you."

"I have my bad habits," replied Wallander.

They headed out into the clear autumn air. Robert Melander said hello to everyone they met. They reached the cemetery.

"His grave is supposed to be over by the grove of trees," said Melander.

Wallander walked between the graves, following Melander and thinking about the dream he'd had during the night. It suddenly seemed unreal to him that his father was dead. He hadn't fully comprehended it yet.

Melander stopped and pointed. The gravestone stood upright, with a gold inscription. Wallander read what it said and realized at once that there was no help to be found here. The man named Harald Berggren who lay buried in front of him had died in 1949. Melander noticed his reaction.

"Not the one?"

"No," replied Wallander. "It's definitely not him. The man we're looking for was still alive at least until 1963."

"A man you're looking for?" said Melander with curiosity. "A man the police are looking for must have committed some type of crime."

"I don't know," said Wallander. "It's too complicated to explain. Often the police look for people who haven't done anything illegal."

"So your trip here was in vain," said Melander. "The church has received a gift of a great deal of money. But we don't know why. And we still don't know who this Eriksson is."

"There must be an explanation," said Wallander.

"Would you like to see the church?" asked Melander suddenly, as if he wanted to give Wallander some encouragement.

Wallander nodded.

"It's a lovely place," said Melander. "We were married there."

They walked up to the church and went inside. Wallander noted that the door wasn't locked. Light shone in through the side windows.

"It's beautiful," said Wallander.

"But I don't think you're particularly religious," said Melander and smiled.

Wallander didn't reply. He sat down on one of the wooden pews. Melander stayed standing in the center aisle. Wallander searched his mind for some way to proceed. There had to be an answer, he knew that. Holger Eriksson would never have left a gift to the church in Svenstavik without a reason. A serious reason.

"Holger Eriksson wrote poetry," said Wallander. "He was what they call a regional poet."

"We have poets like that too," said Melander. "To be quite honest, what they write isn't always very good."

"He was also a bird lover," continued Wallander. "At night he went out to watch the birds heading south. He couldn't see them. But he knew they were there overhead. Maybe it's possible to hear the rushing of thousands of wings."

"I know some people who keep pigeons," said Melander. "But I guess we've only had one ornithologist."

"Had?" asked Wallander.

Melander sat down on the pew on the other side of the aisle. "It's an odd story," he said. "A story without an ending." He laughed. "Almost like your story. It doesn't have an ending either."

"I'm sure we'll find the perpetrator," said Wallander. "We usually do. So what about your story?"

"Sometime back in the mid-sixties a Polish woman came here," he said. "Where exactly she came from, I don't think anybody knew. But she worked at the local inn. Rented a room. Kept to herself. Even though she quickly learned to speak Swedish, she didn't seem to have any friends. Later she bought a house. Out towards Sveg. I was quite young back then. So young that I often thought about how beautiful she was. Even though she kept to herself. And she was interested in birds. At the post office they said she got letters and cards from all over Sweden. They were postcards with information about ringed owls and God knows what else. She wrote lots of cards and letters herself. She sent almost as much mail as City Hall. In the store they had to stock extra postcards for her. She didn't care what the picture was of. They bought up postcards that stores in other towns couldn't sell."

"How do you know all this?" asked Wallander.

"In a small town you know about a lot of things, whether you want to or not," said Melander. "That's the way it is."

"Then what happened?"

"She disappeared."

"Disappeared?"

"What's that expression? She went up in smoke. Vanished."

Wallander wasn't sure he had understood correctly. "Did she go on a trip?"

"She traveled a great deal, but she always came back. When she disappeared, she was here. She had gone for a walk through town one afternoon in October. She often took walks. Strolls. After that day she was never seen again. There was a lot written about it back then. She hadn't packed her bags. People started to wonder when she didn't show up at the inn. They went over to her house. She was gone. They searched for her. But she was never found. That happened about twenty-five years ago. They've never found anything. But there have been rumors. That she was seen in South America or Alingsås. Or as a ghost in the woods outside Rätansbyn."

"What was her name?" asked Wallander.

"Krista. Her last name was Haberman."

Wallander remembered the case. There'd been a lot of speculation. He vaguely recalled the newspaper headline: "The Polish Beauty."

Wallander thought for a moment.

"So she corresponded with other birdwatchers," he said. "And sometimes she visited them?"

"Yes."

"Do the letters still exist?"

"She was declared dead years ago. A relative from Poland suddenly turned up and made claims. Her belongings disappeared. And the house was later torn down for a new building."

Wallander nodded. It would have been too much to expect to find the letters and postcards. "I have a hazy recollection of the whole thing," he said. "But weren't there ever any suspicions? That she had committed suicide or been the victim of a crime?"

"Of course there were plenty of rumors. And I think the police who investigated the case did a good job. They were people from the area who could tell the difference between gossip and the truth. There were rumors about mysterious cars. That she'd had secret visitors in the night. And no one knew what she did when she went traveling. The case was never cleared up. She disappeared. And she's still missing. If she's alive, she's twenty-five years older. Everyone gets older. Even people who disappear."

It's happening again, thought Wallander. Something from the past is coming back. I come up here to try to figure out why Holger Eriksson willed his money to the church in Svenstavik. I don't find an answer to my question. On the other hand, I find out that there was also a birdwatcher here, a woman who disappeared over twenty-five years ago. The question is whether I've actually found an answer to my question after all. Even though I don't fully understand it.

"The investigative material is still in Östersund," said Melander. "It probably weighs several kilos."

They left the church. Wallander looked at a bird sitting on the cemetery wall.

"Have you ever heard of a bird called a middle spotted wood-pecker?" he asked.

"Isn't it extinct?" said Melander. "At least in Sweden?"

"It's close to extinction," said Wallander. "In this country it's been gone for fifteen years."

"I may have seen one a few times," said Melander doubtfully. "But woodpeckers are scarce these days. With all the clearcutting, the old trees have disappeared. That's where they usually lived. And on tele-phone poles, of course."

They had walked back to the shopping center and stopped at Wal-lander's car. It was 2:30.

"Are you going farther?" asked Melander. "Or are you heading back to Skåne?"

"I'm going to Gävle," replied Wallander. "How long does it take? Three, four hours?"

"Closer to five. There's no snow and it's not slippery. The roads are good. But it'll take you that long. It's almost four hundred kilometers."

"I want to thank you for all your help," said Wallander. "And for the nice lunch."

"But you didn't get any answers to your questions."

"Maybe I did," said Wallander. "We'll see."

"The officer who handled Krista Haberman's disappearance was an old man," said Melander. "He started when he was middle-aged. Stayed with the police until he retired. They say it was the last thing he talked about on his deathbed. About what had happened to her. He could never let it go."

"There's always that danger," said Wallander.

They said goodbye.

"If you ever come south, stop in," said Wallander.

Melander smiled. His pipe had gone out.

"I think my travels will take me mostly north," he said. "But you never know."

"I'd be grateful if you'd get in touch with me," said Wallander, "if anything happens that might explain why Holger Eriksson left the money to the church."

"It's strange," said Melander. "If he'd seen the church, it might be understandable. It's so beautiful."

"You're right," replied Wallander. "If he'd ever been here, it might be understandable."

"Maybe he went through here sometime? Without anyone knowing about it?"

"Or maybe only one person," replied Wallander.

Melander looked at him.

"You have something in mind?"

"Yes," replied Wallander. "But I don't know what it means."

They shook hands. Wallander got into his car and drove off. In the rearview mirror he saw Melander standing there, gazing after him.

He drove through endless forests.

By the time he reached Gävle it was already dark. He made his way to the hotel that Svedberg had told him about. When he asked at the front desk, he was told that Linda had already arrived.

They found a little restaurant that was cozy and quiet, with only a few guests even though it was Saturday night. He was glad that Linda had agreed to come. When they found themselves in this town that was unfamiliar to both of them, Wallander decided, without having planned it, to talk about his ideas for the future.

But first, of course, they talked about his father, her grandfather.

"I often wondered about the good relationship the two of you had," said Wallander. "Maybe it was envy, plain and simple. I would see you together, and I saw something that I remembered from my own childhood, but that had totally disappeared."

"Maybe it's good to have a generation in between," said Linda. "It's not uncommon for grandparents and grandchildren to get along better than parents and children."

"How do you know that?"

"I can see it's true for me. And a lot of my friends say the same thing."

"But I've always had a feeling that it was unnecessary," said Wallander. "I've never understood why he couldn't accept the fact that I joined the police. If only he'd told me why. Or given me an alternative. But he never did."

"Grandpa was pretty eccentric," she said. "And temperamental. But what would you say if I suddenly came and told you in all seriousness that I was thinking of becoming a cop?"

Wallander started to laugh.

"I honestly don't know what I'd say. We've talked about this before."

After dinner they went back to the hotel. On a thermometer outside a hardware store Wallander saw that it was −2°C. They sat down in the lobby. The hotel didn't have many guests, and they had the place to themselves. Wallander cautiously asked Linda how it was going with her acting aspirations. He saw at once that she didn't want to talk about it. At least not right then. He let the topic drop, but it made him uneasy. Over the course of the past few years Linda had changed tracks and interests several times. What made Wallander nervous was how quickly she made these changes. It gave him the impression they were rash decisions.

Linda poured herself some tea from a thermos and suddenly asked him why it was so difficult to live in Sweden.

"Sometimes I think it's because we've stopped darning our socks," said Wallander.

She gave him a perplexed look.

"I mean it," he continued. "When I was growing up, Sweden was still a country where people darned their socks. I even learned how to do it in school myself. Then suddenly one day it was over. Socks with holes in them were thrown out. No one bothered to repair them anymore. The whole society changed. 'Wear it out and toss it' was the only rule that really applied to everybody. I guess there were some people who kept on darning their socks. But they were never seen or heard from. As long as it was just a matter of our socks, the change didn't make much difference. But then it started to spread, until finally it became a kind of invisible but ever-present moral code. I think it changed our view of right and wrong, what you were allowed to do to other people and what you weren't. Everything has gotten so much more difficult. More and more people, especially young people like you, feel unneeded or even unwelcome in their own country. How do they react? With aggression and contempt. The most frightening thing is that I think we're only at the beginning of something that's going to get a lot worse. A generation is growing up right now, the kids who are younger than you, who are going to react with even greater violence. And they have absolutely no memory of a time when we darned our socks. When we didn't wear out or throw away anything, whether it was our woolen socks or human beings."

Wallander couldn't think of anything else to say, even though he could see that she was expecting him to continue. "Maybe I'm not expressing myself clearly," he said.

"Maybe," she said. "I still think I know what you're trying to say."

"It's also possible I've got it all wrong. Maybe every age seems worse than the ones that came before."

"I never heard Grandpa say anything about it."

Wallander shook his head. "I think he lived a lot in his own world. He painted his pictures so he could decide where the sun would be in the sky. It always hung in the same place, above the fields, with or without the grouse, for almost fifty years. Sometimes I don't think he knew what was going on outside that studio of his. He had put up an invisible wall of turpentine around himself."

"You're wrong," she said. "He knew a lot."

"If he did he never let me know about it."

"He even wrote poems once in a while."

Wallander looked at her in disbelief. "He wrote poems?"

"He showed me some of them once. Maybe he burned them later on. But he wrote poems."

"Do you write poetry too?" asked Wallander.

"Maybe," she replied. "I don't know whether they're really poems. But sometimes I write. Just for myself. Don't you?"

"No," replied Wallander. "Never. I live in a world of poorly written police reports and forensic medical records full of unpleasant details. Not to mention all the memos from the NPB."

She changed the subject so fast that afterwards he thought that she must have planned it all out.

"How's it going with Baiba?"

"It's going fine with her. How it's going with us, I'm not so sure. But I'm hoping that she'll come here to live."

"What would she do in Sweden?"

"She'd live with me," replied Wallander in surprise.

Linda slowly shook her head.

"Why wouldn't she?"

"Don't be offended," she said. "But I hope you realize you're a difficult person to live with."

"Why is that?"

"Just think about Mamma. Why do you think she wants to live a different life?"

Wallander didn't answer. In a vague way he felt he was being judged unfairly.

"Now you're mad," she said.

"No, I'm not," he replied. "I'm not mad."

"What, then?"

"I don't know. I guess I'm tired."

She got up from her chair and sat down next to him on the sofa.

"This doesn't mean I don't love you," she said. "It just means that I'm growing up. Our conversations are going to be different."

He nodded. "I probably just haven't gotten used to it yet," he said. "I suppose it should be simple enough."

When the conversation petered out, they watched a movie on TV. Linda had to go back to Stockholm early the next morning. Wallander thought he had had a glimpse of how the future would be. They would meet whenever they both had time. From now on she would also say whatever she really thought.

Just before one o'clock they said good night in the hotel corridor. Afterwards Wallander lay in bed for a long time, trying to decide whether he had lost something or gained something. His child was gone. Linda had grown up.

They met for breakfast at seven o'clock. Afterwards he accompanied her the short distance to the train station. As they stood on the platform, she suddenly started to cry. Wallander stood there bewildered. Only a moment ago she hadn't shown any signs of being upset.

"What is it?" he asked. "Did something happen?"

"I miss Grandpa," she replied. "I dream about him every night."

Wallander gave her a hug. "I do too."

The train arrived. He stood on the platform until it pulled away. The station seemed terribly desolate. For a moment he felt like someone who was lost or abandoned, utterly powerless.

He wondered how he could go on.

Chapter Twenty-two

When Wallander got back to the hotel there was a message waiting for him. It was from Robert Melander in Svenstavik. He went up to his room and dialed the number, and Melander's wife answered. Wallander introduced himself, careful to thank her for the nice dinner she had prepared the day before. Then Melander himself came to the phone.

"I couldn't help thinking about things some more last night," he said. "I called the old postmaster too. Ture Emmanuelsson is his name. He confirmed for me that Krista Haberman received postcards regularly from Skåne, a lot of them. From Falsterbo, he thought. I don't know if this means anything. But I thought I'd tell you anyway. She had a lot of bird-related mail."

"How did you find me?" Wallander asked.

"I called the police in Ystad and asked them. It wasn't difficult."

"Skanör and Falsterbo are well-known meeting places for birdwatchers," said Wallander. "That's the only reasonable explanation for why she got so many postcards from there. Thanks for taking the time to call me."

"I just keep wondering," said Melander, "why that car dealer donated money to our church."

"Sooner or later we'll find out why. But it might take time. Anyway, thanks for calling."

Wallander stayed where he was after he hung up. It wasn't eight o'clock yet. He thought about the sudden attack of powerlessness he had experienced at the train station. The feeling that something insurmountable stood before him. He also thought about the conversation with Linda the night before. Most of all, he thought about what Melander had said and what he now faced. He was in Gävle because he had an assignment. It was six hours before his plane left. He had to turn in the rental car at Arlanda.

He grabbed some papers from a plastic folder in his suitcase. Höglund had written that he could start by getting in touch with a police inspector named Sten Wenngren. He would be home all day Sunday and was expecting Wallander's call. She had also written down the name of the man who had advertised in the legionnaire's magazine: Johan Ekberg, who lived out in Brynäs. Wallander stood by the window. The weather was dismal. A cold autumn rain had started falling. Wallander wondered whether it would turn to slush, and if there were snow tires on the rental car. But most of all he thought about what he actually had to do in Gävle. With each step he took he felt himself moving farther and farther away from a center—it was unknown to him, but it must be there somewhere.

The feeling that there was something he hadn't discovered; that he had misinterpreted a fundamental structure in the pattern of the crime, came back as he stood by the window. The feeling led to the same question: Why the deliberate brutality? What is it the perpetrator wants to tell us?

The killer's language. The code he hadn't been able to crack.

He shook his head, yawned, and packed his suitcase. Since he didn't know what he would talk to Sten Wenngren about, he decided to go straight to Johan Ekberg. If nothing else, he might be able to get a glimpse into the murky world where soldiers were for sale to the highest bidder. He took his bag and left the room. Paying the bill at the front desk, he asked how to get to Södra Fältskärsgatan in Brynäs. He took the elevator down to the garage. When he got into his car he was overcome by that feeling of weakness again. He sat there without starting the engine. Was he coming down with something? He didn't feel sick—not even particularly tired.

He realized it had to do with his father. It was a reaction to everything that had happened. Maybe part of the grieving process. Trying to adjust to a new life that had been changed in a dramatic way.

There was no other explanation. Linda had her reaction, while he was dealing with his father's passing through recurrent attacks of powerlessness.

He started the engine and drove out of the garage. The desk clerk had given him clear directions. Still, Wallander got lost right away. The city was deserted on Sunday. He felt like he was driving around aimlessly in a labyrinth. It took him twenty minutes to find the right street. It was already 9:30. He stopped outside an apartment building in what he thought was the old section of Brynäs. Absentmindedly he wondered whether mercenaries slept late on Sunday mornings. He wondered if Johan Ekberg was a mercenary at all. Just because he advertised in *Terminator* didn't mean he had done any military service.

Wallander sat in the car looking at the building. The rain was falling. October was the most disconsolate month. Everything turned to gray. The colors of fall faded away.

For a moment he felt like giving up the whole thing and driving away. He might as well go back to Skåne and ask some of the others to call this Johan Ekberg on the phone. Or else he could do it himself. If he left Gävle now he might be able to catch an earlier flight to Sturup.

But of course he didn't leave. Wallander had never been able to conquer the sergeant inside him who made sure he did what he was supposed to do. He hadn't taken this trip on the taxpayers' money just to sit in his car and stare at the rain. He got out of the car and crossed the street.

Johan Ekberg lived on the top floor. There was no elevator in the building. There was cheerful accordion music coming from one of the apartments. Someone was singing. Wallander stopped on the stairs and listened. It was a schottische. He smiled to himself. Whoever was playing the accordion wasn't sitting around staring at the miserable rain, he thought, and he continued up the stairs.

Johan Ekberg's door had an inset steel frame and extra locks. Wallander rang the bell. Instinctively he felt someone looking at him through the peephole. He rang again, as if to announce that he wasn't giving up. The door opened. It had a safety chain. The entryway was dark. The man he glimpsed inside was very tall.

"I'm looking for Johan Ekberg," said Wallander. "I'm a detective from Ystad. I need to talk to you, if you are Ekberg. You're not suspected of anything, I just need some information."

The voice that answered him was sharp, almost shrill.

"I don't talk to cops. Whether they're from Gävle or anywhere else."

Wallander's earlier powerlessness was gone at once. He reacted instantly to the man's stubborn attitude. He hadn't come this far just to be turned away at the door. He took out his badge and held it up.

"I'm working on solving two homicides in Skåne. You probably read about them in the paper. I didn't come all the way up here to stand outside your door and argue. You are fully entitled to refuse me entry. But I'll be back. And then you'll have to come downtown to the Gävle police station. Take your pick."

"What do you want to know?"

"Either you let me in or else come out in the hall," said Wallander. "I'm not going to talk through a crack in the door."

The door closed, then opened. The safety chain was off now. A harsh lamp went on in the entryway. It surprised Wallander. It was purposely mounted to shine right in the eyes of a visitor. Wallander followed the man, whose face he had still not seen. They came to a living room. The drapes were drawn and the lamps were on. Wallander stopped in the doorway. It was like walking into another time. The room was like a relic of the '50s. There was a jukebox against one wall. A Wurlitzer. The glittering neon colors danced inside its plastic hood. Movie posters were on the walls; he saw James Dean on one of them, but the others were mostly war movies. *Men in Action.* American marines fighting the Japanese on the beach. There were weapons hanging on the walls too: bayonets, swords, old cavalry pistols. There was also a black leather sofa group in the room.

Johan Ekberg stood looking at him. He had a crewcut and could have stepped right off one of the posters on his walls. He was tall, dressed in khaki shorts and a white T-shirt. He had tattoos on his arms. His muscles bulged. Wallander saw he was dealing with a bodybuilder. Ekberg's eyes were wary.

"What do you want?"

Wallander pointed inquiringly at one of the chairs. The man nodded. Wallander sat down while Ekberg remained standing. He wondered if Ekberg was even born when Harald Berggren was fighting his despicable war in the Congo.

"How old are you?" he asked.

"Did you come all the way from Skåne to ask me that?"

Wallander made no attempt to hide his irritation. "Among other things," he replied. "If you don't answer my questions we'll stop right now. Then you'll have to come downtown."

"Am I suspected of committing some crime?"

"Have you?" Wallander shot back. He knew he was breaking all the rules of police behavior.

"No," said Ekberg.

"Then we'll start over," said Wallander. "How old are you?"

"Thirty-two."

Wallander was right. Ekberg wasn't even born when Dag Hammarskjöld's plane crashed outside Ndola.

"I came to talk to you about Swedish mercenaries. I'm here because you've openly hung out your shingle. You advertise in *Terminator.*"

"There's no law against that, is there? I advertise in *Combat & Survival* and *Soldier of Fortune* too."

"I didn't say there was. This interview will go a lot faster if you just answer my questions and don't ask any of your own."

Ekberg sat down and lit a cigarette. Wallander saw he smoked non-filters. He lit the cigarette with a Zippo lighter, like the ones Wallander had seen in old movies. He wondered whether Johan Ekberg was living in a different era altogether.

"Swedish mercenaries," Wallander repeated. "When did it all start? With the war in the Congo in the early sixties?"

"A little earlier," said Ekberg.

"When?"

"Try the Thirty Years' War, for instance."

Wallander wondered if Ekberg was needling him. Then he saw that he shouldn't be misled by Ekberg's appearance or the fact that he seemed to be fixated on the fifties. If there could be passionate orchid researchers, then Ekberg could well be an expert on mercenaries. Besides, Wallander had vague memories from his school days that the Thirty Years' War was actually fought by armies made up of soldiers who were paid to fight.

"Let's stick to the years after World War II," he said.

"Then it started with the Second World War. There were Swedes who volunteered in all the armies fighting each other. There were Swedes in German uniforms, Russian uniforms, Japanese, American, British, and Italian."

"I always thought that volunteering wasn't the same as being a mercenary."

"I'm talking about the will to fight," said Ekberg. "There have always been Swedes who were ready to take up arms."

Wallander sensed something of the hopeless enthusiasm that usually marked men with delusions of a Greater Sweden. He cast a quick glance along the walls to see if he had overlooked any Nazi symbols. But he saw none.

"Forget about volunteers," he said. "I'm talking about mercenaries. Men for hire."

"The Foreign Legion," said Ekberg. "It's a classic starting point. There have always been Swedes enlisted in it. Many of them lie buried in the Sahara."

"The Congo," said Wallander. "Something else started there, right?"

"There weren't many Swedes there. But some fought the whole war on the side of Katanga province."

"Who were they?"

Ekberg gave him a surprised look. "Are you looking for names?"

"Not yet. I want to know what kind of men they were."

"Former military men. Men looking for adventure. Others convinced they were fighting for a just cause. Here and there, a cop who'd been kicked off the force."

"What cause?"

"The fight against communism."

"They killed innocent Africans, didn't they?"

Ekberg was suddenly on his guard again.

"I don't have to answer questions about political views. I know my rights."

"I don't care about your views. I want to know who they were. And why they became mercenaries."

"Why do you want to know that? Let's say it's my only question. And I want an answer to it." Ekberg watched him with his wary eyes.

Wallander had nothing to lose by going straight to the point.

"It's possible that someone with a past among Swedish mercenaries had something to do with at least one of these murders. That's why I'm asking all these questions. That's why your answers might be significant."

Ekberg nodded. He understood now. "Would you like something to drink?" he asked.

"Such as?"

"Whiskey? Beer?"

Wallander was aware that it was only ten in the morning. He shook his head. Even though he wouldn't have minded a beer.

"I'll pass."

Ekberg got up and came back a moment later with a glass of whiskey.

"What kind of work do you do?" asked Wallander.

Ekberg's reply surprised him. He didn't know what he expected. But certainly not what Ekberg told him.

"I own a consulting firm that works in the personnel-administration sector. I concentrate on developing methods for conflict resolution."

"That sounds interesting." Wallander still wasn't sure if Ekberg was pulling his leg or not.

"I also have a stock portfolio that's doing well. My liquidity is stable at the moment."

Wallander decided that Ekberg was telling the truth. He returned to the topic of the mercenaries.

"How is it you're so interested in mercenaries?"

"They stand for some of the best things in our culture, which unfortunately are disappearing."

Wallander felt an instant uneasiness at Ekberg's reply. The hardest part was that Ekberg's convictions seemed so unshakable. Wallander wondered how it could be possible. He also wondered whether more men on the Swedish Stock Exchange had tattoos like Ekberg's. It was hard to imagine that the financiers and businessmen of the future would consist of bodybuilders with vintage jukeboxes in their living rooms.

Wallander got back to the subject at hand. "How were these men who went to the Congo recruited?"

"There are certain bars in Brussels. In Paris, too. It was all handled very discreetly. It still is, for that matter. Especially after what happened in Angola in 1975."

"What was that?"

"A number of mercenaries didn't get out in time. They were captured at the end of the war. The new regime set up a court-martial. Most of them were sentenced to death and shot. It was all very ruthless. And quite unnecessary."

"Why were they sentenced to death?"

"Because they had been recruited. As if that made any difference. Soldiers are always recruited, one way or another."

"But they had nothing to do with that war? They came from outside? They took part in it just to make money?"

Ekberg ignored Wallander's remarks, as if they weren't worth commenting on.

"They were supposed to get out of the theater of combat in time, but they had lost two of their company commanders in the fighting. A plane that was supposed to pick them up landed at the wrong airstrip in the bush. There was a lot of bad luck involved. About fifteen of them were captured. The majority managed to get out. Most of them continued on to Southern Rhodesia. On a big farm outside Johannesburg there's now a monument to the men who were executed in Angola. Mercenaries from all over the world went to the unveiling."

"Were there any Swedes among the men who were executed?"

"It was mostly Brits and Germans. Their next of kin were given forty-eight hours to claim their bodies. Almost no one did."

Wallander thought about the memorial outside Johannesburg.

"In other words, there is a great sense of fellowship among mercenaries from various parts of the world?"

"Every man takes complete responsibility for himself. But yes, there is a sense of fellowship. There has to be."

"So isn't that a reason why many of them would become mercenaries? Because they're looking for fellowship."

"The money comes first. Then the adventure. Then the fellowship. In that order."

"So the truth is that mercenaries kill for money?"

Ekberg nodded. "Of course. Mercenaries aren't monsters. They're human beings."

Wallander felt his disgust rising. But he knew that Ekberg meant every word he said. It had been a long time since he had met a man with such firm convictions. There was nothing monstrous about these soldiers who would kill anyone for the right amount of money. On the contrary, it was a definition of their humanity. According to Johan Ekberg.

Wallander took out a copy of the photograph and placed it on the glass table in front of him. Then he shoved it over to Ekberg.

"I see you have movie posters on the walls. Here's a real picture. Taken in what was then called the Belgian Congo. More than thirty years ago. Before you were born. It's a picture of three mercenaries. And one of them is a Swede."

Ekberg leaned forward and picked up the photo. Wallander waited.

"Do you recognize any of those men?" he asked after a moment. He mentioned two of the names: Terry O'Banion and Simon Marchand.

Ekberg shook his head.

"Those aren't necessarily their real names. But their names as mercenaries."

"In that case, I do recognize those names," said Ekberg.

"The man in the middle is Swedish," Wallander went on. Ekberg stood up and went into an adjacent room. He came back with a magnifying glass in his hand. He studied the picture again.

"His name is Harald Berggren," said Wallander. "And he's the reason I came here."

Ekberg said nothing. He kept looking at the picture.

"Harald Berggren," Wallander said again. "He wrote a diary about that war. Do you recognize him? Do you know who he is?"

Ekberg put down the photo and the magnifying glass. "Of course I know who Harald Berggren is."

Wallander gave a start. He didn't know what kind of answer he was expecting, but it certainly wasn't that.

"Where is he now?"

"He's dead. He died seven years ago."

That was a possibility Wallander had considered. Even so, it came as a disappointment that it was so long ago. "What happened?"

"He committed suicide. Which isn't unusual for people with a great deal of courage. And who have experience fighting in combat units under difficult conditions."

"Why did he commit suicide?"

Ekberg shrugged. "I think he'd had enough."

"Enough what?"

"What is it you've had enough of when you take your own life? Life itself. The boredom. The weariness that hits you every morning when you look at your face in the mirror."

"What happened?"

"He lived in Sollentuna, north of Stockholm. One Sunday morning he stuck his pistol in his pocket and took a bus to the end of the line. Then he went out in the woods and shot himself."

"How do you know all this?"

"I just know. And that means that he couldn't have been involved with a murder in Skåne. Unless he's a ghost. Or set a time bomb for someone that just now went off."

Wallander had left the diary behind in Skåne. He thought that might have been a mistake. "Harald Berggren wrote a diary from the Congo. We found it in a safe belonging to one of the men who was murdered. A car dealer named Holger Eriksson. Does that name mean anything to you?"

Ekberg shook his head.

"Are you sure?"

"There's nothing wrong with my memory."

"Can you think of any reason why the diary would have wound up there?"

"No."

"Can you think of any reason why these two men might have known each other more than seven years ago?"

"I only met Berggren once. That was the year before he died. I was living in Stockholm at the time. He came to visit me one evening. He was very restless. He told me he was spending his time traveling around the country, working a month here and a month there, while he waited for a new war to start. He had a profession, after all."

Wallander realized that he had overlooked that possibility. Even though it was in the diary, on one of the very first pages.

"You mean the fact that he was an automobile mechanic?"

For the first time Ekberg looked surprised.

"How do you know that?"

"It was in the diary."

"A car dealer might have had use for an extra mechanic. Maybe Harald passed through Skåne and met this Eriksson."

Wallander nodded. It was a possibility.

"Was Berggren homosexual?" asked Wallander.

Ekberg laughed.

"Very," he said.

"Is that common among mercenaries?"

"Not necessarily. But it's not unusual. I presume it also occurs among cops, doesn't it?"

Wallander didn't reply.

"Does it occur among conflict-resolution consultants?" he asked instead.

Ekberg had stood up and was standing next to the jukebox. He smiled at Wallander.

"It does."

"You advertise in *Terminator*. You offer your services. But it doesn't say what those services are."

"I arrange contacts."

"What sort of contacts?"

"With various employers who might possibly be of interest."

"Combat assignments?"

"Sometimes. Bodyguards, transport protection. It varies. If I wanted to, I could supply the newspapers with amazing stories."

"But you don't?"

"I have the trust of my clients."

"I'm not part of the newspaper world."

Ekberg had sat back down in his chair.

"Terre' Blanche in South Africa," said Ekberg. "The leader of the Nazi party among the Boers. He has two Swedish bodyguards. That's just one example. But if you mention it in public I'll deny I said it, of course."

"I won't say a word," said Wallander.

He had no more questions. He still didn't know what the significance of Ekberg's answers might be.

"Can I keep the photo?" asked Ekberg. "I have a little collection."

"Keep it," said Wallander, getting to his feet. "We've got the original."

"Who has the negative?"

"I wonder that myself."

After Wallander was already out the door it struck him that there was one more question.

"Why do you do all this, anyway?"

"I get postcards from all over the world," he said. "That's all."

Wallander understood that this was the best answer he was going to get. "I don't believe it. But I might call you up, if I have any more questions."

Ekberg nodded. Then he shut the door.

When Wallander reached the street the rain was mixed with snow. It was eleven o'clock. He had nothing else to do in Gävle. He got into his car. Harald Berggren hadn't killed Holger Eriksson, or Gösta Runfeldt for that matter. What could have been a lead had dissolved into thin air.

We'll have to start all over again, Wallander thought. We'll have to go back to the beginning and cross out Harald Berggren. We'll forget about shrunken heads and diaries. Then what will we see? It must be possible to find Harald Berggren on a list of Eriksson's former employees. And we should also be able to find out if he was a homosexual.

The top layer of the investigation had yielded nothing.

They would have to dig deeper.

Wallander started the engine. Then he drove straight to Arlanda Airport. When he arrived he had some trouble finding the place to turn in the rental car. By two o'clock he was sitting on a sofa in the departure hall waiting for his plane. He leafed distractedly through an evening newspaper someone had left behind. The slushy rain had stopped just north of Uppsala.

The plane left Arlanda on time. Wallander fell asleep almost as soon as they took off. When his ears started popping during the descent to Sturup he woke up. Next to him sat a woman darning a sock. Wallander looked at her in amazement.

As he got off the plane, he remembered he'd have to call Älmhult to find out how his car was doing. He'd have to take a taxi to Ystad. But as he headed for the airport exit, he discovered Martinsson waiting for him. He knew something must have happened.

Not another one, he thought. Anything but that.

Martinsson saw him coming.

"What happened?" asked Wallander.

"You must have had your cell phone turned off," said Martinsson. "It's impossible to get hold of you."

Wallander waited. He held his breath.

"We found Gösta Runfeldt's suitcase," Martinsson said.

"Where?"

"It was practically in plain view on the road to Höör."

"Who found it?"

"A guy who stopped to take a piss. He saw the suitcase and opened it. There were papers inside with Runfeldt's name on them. He had read about the murder, so he called us right away. Nyberg is there now."

Good, thought Wallander. This is another lead.

"Then let's go there," he said.

"Don't you want to go home first?"

"No. If there's anything I don't want to do, it's that."

They walked toward Martinsson's car.

Suddenly Wallander was in a hurry.

Chapter Twenty-three

The suitcase was still lying where it had been found. Since this was right by the side of the road, many drivers had stopped out of curiosity at the sight of the two police cars and the group of people.

Nyberg was in the process of securing any tracks left at the site. One of his assistants held his crutch while he knelt down and pointed at something lying on the ground. He looked up when Wallander approached. "How was Norrland?" he asked.

"I didn't find a suitcase," replied Wallander. "But it was beautiful. And cold."

"With a little luck we'll be able to say exactly how long the suitcase has been lying here," said Nyberg. "I presume that would be an important bit of information."

The suitcase was closed. Wallander couldn't see any name tag, or any label for "Special Tours."

"Have you talked to Vanja Andersson?" asked Wallander.

"She's already been here," replied Martinsson. "She recognized the suitcase. Besides, we already opened it. Gösta Runfeldt's missing night-vision binoculars were right on top. It's definitely his bag."

Wallander thought for a moment. They were on Highway 13, south of Eneborg. Close by was the intersection where you could take the turnoff to Lödinge. Going in the opposite direction you could head south around Krageholm Lake and end up not far from Marsvinsholm. Wallander realized that they now stood almost equidistant between the two homicide scenes.

They were quite close to everything, he thought.

The suitcase lay on the east side of the road. If it had been put there by someone driving a car, then the car must have been on its way north from the Ystad area. But it could also have come from Marsvinsholm, turned off at the Sövestad intersection, and then driven north. Wallander tried to evaluate the alternatives. Nyberg was right in thinking that it would help to know how long the suitcase had been lying where they found it. "When can we remove it?" he asked.

"We can take it back to Ystad within an hour," replied Nyberg. "I'm almost done here."

Wallander nodded to Martinsson. They walked toward his car. On the drive from the airport, Wallander had explained that the trip he had just taken hadn't told them why Holger Eriksson had willed money to the church in Jämtland. On the other hand, they now knew that Harald Berggren was dead. Wallander had no doubts that Ekberg had told the truth, and that he knew what he was talking about. Berggren couldn't have been directly involved in Eriksson's death. They needed to find out whether he had worked for Eriksson, even though they couldn't count on this getting them anywhere. Certain pieces of the investigative puzzle were only valuable because they needed to be put in place before the more important pieces could be fit together properly. From now on Harald Berggren was that kind of piece in the puzzle.

They got into the car and headed back to Ystad.

"Maybe Eriksson gave unemployed mercenaries odd jobs to do?" said Martinsson. "Maybe somebody was after Harald Berggren? Someone who suddenly got it into his head to dig a pungee pit for Eriksson, for some reason or other?"

"That's a possibility, of course," said Wallander dubiously. "But how do we explain what happened to Gösta Runfeldt?"

"We can't explain it yet. Should we be concentrating on him?"

"Eriksson died first," said Wallander. "But that doesn't necessarily mean he's the first link in the chain of causality. The problem is not only that we don't have a motive, but that we're missing a real starting point."

Martinsson sat in silence for a while. They were driving through Sövestad.

"Why would his suitcase end up next to this road?" he suddenly asked. "Runfeldt was going in the opposite direction, toward Copenhagen. Marsvinsholm is in the right direction, heading for Kastrup Airport. What really happened?"

"That's what I'd like to know too," said Wallander.

"We've gone over Runfeldt's car," said Martinsson. "He had a parking place in back of the building where he lived. It was a '93 Opel. Everything seemed to be in order."

"The car keys?"

"They were in his apartment."

Wallander asked if anyone had found out whether Runfeldt had ordered a cab for the morning of his departure.

"Hansson talked to the cab company. Runfeldt ordered a taxi for five in the morning. It was supposed to take him to Malmö. The cab company later made a note that he was a no-go. The cab driver waited. He rang the bell to Runfeldt's place because he thought he might have overslept. No one responded. The driver took off. Hansson said that the person he talked to was quite precise about what happened."

"It seems to have been a well-planned assault," said Wallander.

"Which indicates there was more than one person," said Martinsson.

"Who must also have had detailed knowledge of Runfeldt's plans, and known that he was going to leave early that morning. Who would know that?"

"The list is limited. And we already have it, as a matter of fact. I think it was Ann-Britt who put it together. Anita Lagergren at the travel agency knew, and Runfeldt's children. But the daughter only knew what day he was leaving, not that it was early in the morning. Probably nobody else."

"Vanja Andersson?"

"She thought she knew. But she didn't."

Wallander shook his head slowly. "There must be someone else on that list," he said. "That's the person we're looking for."

"We're going through his client files. Altogether we've found forty or so investigative assignments over the years. In other words, not many. About four a year. But the person we're looking for might be among them."

"We have to go through them carefully," replied Wallander. "It's going to be a tedious job. But you could be right."

"I'm starting to have the feeling that this is going to take an awfully long time."

Wallander thought the same thing.

"We can always hope we're wrong, but it's not very likely."

They were approaching Ystad. It was five thirty.

"Apparently they're going to sell the flower shop," said Martinsson. "The son and daughter agreed on that. They asked Vanja Andersson if she'd like to take it over. I doubt she has the money."

"Who told you that?"

"Bo Runfeldt called. He wanted to know if he and his sister could leave Ystad after the funeral."

"When is it?"

"On Wednesday."

"Let them go," said Wallander. "We can get in touch with them again if we have to."

They turned in to the parking lot outside the station.

"I talked to a mechanic in Älmhult," said Martinsson. "Your car will be ready the middle of next week. It's going to be expensive, but I suppose you knew that. He promised to have the car delivered here to Ystad."

Hansson was sitting in Svedberg's office when they came in. Wallander briefly summarized the results of his trip. Hansson had a terrible cold. Wallander suggested that he go home.

"Chief Holgersson is sick too," said Svedberg. "I guess she's got the flu."

"Is it flu season already?" said Wallander. "That's going to give us big problems here."

"I've just got a cold," Hansson assured him. "Hopefully by tomorrow I'll feel better."

"Both of Ann-Britt's kids are sick," said Martinsson. "But I think her husband's coming home tomorrow."

Wallander asked them to let him know when the suitcase arrived, and then left the room. He was thinking of sitting down to write up the report about his trip. Maybe even put together the receipts he needed to submit for his travel expenses. But on the way to his office he changed his mind. He turned around and went back.

"Can I borrow a car?" he asked. "I'll be back in half an hour."

Several sets of car keys were offered to him. He took Martinsson's.

It was dark as he drove down to Västra Vallgatan. There were no clouds in the sky. The night would be a cold one, maybe below freezing. He parked outside the flower shop and walked down the street toward the building where Runfeldt had lived. He saw lights in the windows. He assumed that Runfeldt's children were there, going through things in the apartment. The police had released it. They could pack up and throw out whatever they liked. The last accounting of a deceased person's life. He suddenly thought about his father, and about Gertrud and his sister Kristina. He hadn't gone out to Löderup to help them go through his father's belongings. Even though there wasn't much and his help wasn't really needed, he should still have made an appearance. He couldn't quite decide whether he had repressed it out of distaste or whether he just hadn't had time.

He stopped outside the door to Runfeldt's building. The street was deserted. He wanted to imagine the course of events. He stood in front of the door and looked around. Then he crossed the street and did the same thing.

Runfeldt is on the street. The exact time is still not clear. He might have come out the door in the evening or at night. At that time he wouldn't have his suitcase with him. Something else made him leave the apartment. On the other hand, if he came out the door in the morning, he would have the suitcase. The street is deserted. He sets the suitcase down on the sidewalk. Which direction would the taxi come from? Does he wait outside the door, or across the street? Something happens. Runfeldt and his suitcase disappear. The suitcase turns up along the road to Höör. Runfeldt himself is found tied to a tree, dead, near Marsvinsholm Castle.

Wallander studied the doorways on either side of the building. Neither of them was deep enough for anyone to hide in. He looked at the streetlights. The ones that lit up Runfeldt's doorway were functioning properly.

A car, he thought. A car was waiting here, right by the door. Runfeldt comes down to the street. Someone gets out.

If Runfeldt was frightened, he would have made some sound. The nosy neighbor should have heard it. If it was a stranger, maybe Runfeldt was just surprised.

The man approaches Runfeldt. Does he knock him down? Threaten him?

Wallander thought about Vanja Andersson's reaction out in the woods. Runfeldt had grown terribly thin in the brief time since his disappearance. Wallander was convinced this was because he'd been held captive. Starved.

Runfeldt is put into the car by force, unconscious or under duress. Then he is taken away. The suitcase is found on the road to Höör, right beside the road.

Wallander's first reaction when he arrived at the place where the suitcase lay was that it had been put there to be found.

Once again the deliberate gesture.

Wallander went back to the front door. Started over. Runfeldt comes out to the street. He's about to take a trip that he's been looking forward to. He's going to Africa to look at orchids.

Wallander's thoughts were interrupted. A car passed by.

Wallander began pacing back and forth in front of the doorway. He thought about the possibility that Runfeldt had killed his wife ten years earlier. Made a hole in the ice and let her drown. He was a brutal man. He abused the woman who was the mother of his children. Outwardly he's an ordinary florist with a passion for orchids. And now he was taking a trip to Nairobi. Everyone who talked to him in the days before his departure unanimously confirmed his genuine excitement. A friendly man who was also a monster.

Wallander extended his promenade to the flower shop. He thought about the break-in. The spots of blood on the floor.

Two or three days after Runfeldt was last seen, somebody breaks in. Nothing is stolen. Not even a single flower. There's blood on the floor.

Wallander shook his head, resigned. There was something he wasn't seeing. One surface was concealing another. Gösta Runfeldt. Orchid lover and monster. Holger Eriksson. Bird watcher, poet, and car dealer. He too was cloaked in rumors about brutal behavior toward other people.

Brutality unites them, thought Wallander.

Or to be more precise: concealed brutality. It was clearer in Runfeldt's case than in Eriksson's. But there were similarities.

He went back to the doorway.

Runfeldt comes out to the street. Puts down his suitcase, if it happens in the morning. What does he do then? He waits for a taxi. But when it arrives he has already disappeared.

Wallander stopped mid-stride.

Runfeldt waits for a taxi. Could another taxi have come? A fake taxi? All Runfeldt knew was that he had ordered a cab, not which one would come. Or who the driver would be. The driver helps him with his suitcase. He gets into the car. Then they drive off toward Malmö. But they don't get any farther than Marsvinsholm.

Could it have happened like that? Could Runfeldt have been held prisoner somewhere near that part of the woods where he was found?

But the suitcase was found on the road to Höör. In a totally different direction. In Holger Eriksson's direction.

Wallander realized that he wasn't getting anywhere. He had a hard time believing the idea that a second taxi had put in an appearance. He didn't know what to think. The only thing that was perfectly clear was that whatever had happened outside Runfeldt's front door had been well planned. By someone who knew that he was about to leave for Nairobi.

Wallander drove back to the police station. He saw that Nyberg's car was badly parked outside the entrance. The suitcase had arrived.

They had spread out a plastic cloth on the conference table and placed the suitcase on top. The lid was still closed. Nyberg was having coffee with Svedberg and Hansson. Wallander saw that they were waiting for him to come back. Martinsson was talking on the phone. Wallander could tell that he was talking to one of his kids. He gave him his car keys back.

"How long was the suitcase lying out there?" asked Wallander.

Nyberg's answer surprised him. He had expected something else.

"A couple of days at most," replied Nyberg. "At any rate, not more than three."

"In other words, it was kept somewhere else for a long time," said Hansson.

"That brings up another question," said Wallander. "Why does the perpetrator wait until now to get rid of it?"

No one had an answer. Nyberg pulled on a pair of latex gloves and opened the lid. He was just about to take out the top layer of clothing when Wallander asked him to wait. He leaned over the table. What had caught his attention, he wasn't quite sure.

"Do we have a photo of this?" he asked.

"Not of the open suitcase," replied Nyberg.

"Let's get one," said Wallander. Something about the way the suitcase was packed had made him react. He just couldn't say exactly what it was.

Nyberg left the room and came back with a camera. Since his leg was injured, he instructed Svedberg to climb up on a chair and take the pictures.

Afterwards they unpacked the suitcase. Runfeldt had planned to travel to Africa with little baggage. There were no unexpected items in the suitcase. In the side pocket they found his travel documents. There was also a large sum of money in dollars. In the bottom of the suitcase they found several notebooks, literature about orchids, and a camera. They stood in silence and surveyed the various items. Wallander searched his brain intently for an explanation of what had caught his attention when the lid of the suitcase was thrown open. Nyberg had opened the toilet kit. He studied the name on a pill bottle.

"Anti-malaria pills," he said. "Runfeldt knew what he'd need in Africa."

Wallander looked at the empty suitcase. He found something wedged into the lining of the lid. Nyberg pried it loose. It was a blue plastic holder for a nametag.

"Maybe Runfeldt went to conferences," suggested Nyberg.

"In Nairobi he was going on a photo safari," said Wallander. "But of course it might be left over from some previous trip." He picked up a paper napkin from the table and held it around the pin on the back of the holder. He brought it up close to his eyes. Then he noticed a subtle fragrance. He grew pensive. He held it out to Svedberg, who was standing next to him.

"Do you know what this smells like?"

"After-shave lotion?"

Wallander shook his head.

"No," he said. "It's perfume."

They took turns sniffing it. Hansson, who had a cold, passed. They all agreed that it smelled of perfume. A woman's perfume. Wallander was even more puzzled. He also seemed to think he recognized the plastic holder.

"Who's seen this type of holder before?" he asked.

Martinsson answered. "Isn't that the kind used by the Malmöhus county government?" he said. "Everyone who works in the county hospital here has one like it."

Wallander realized that he was right. "This doesn't make sense," he said. "A plastic holder that smells of perfume is inside Runfeldt's luggage, packed for his trip to Africa."

At that instant he figured out what had puzzled him when the lid of the suitcase was opened.

"I'd like Ann-Britt to come here," he said. "Sick children or not. Maybe her amazing neighbor could help out for half an hour. The police will pay the bill."

Martinsson dialed the number. The conversation was brief. "She's on her way," he said.

"Why do you want her here?" asked Hansson.

"There's just something I want her to do with this suitcase," said Wallander. "That's all."

"Should we put everything back in?" asked Nyberg.

"That's exactly what I don't want you to do," replied Wallander. "That's why I want her to come here. To pack the suitcase."

They looked at him in surprise, but no one said a word. Hansson sniffled. Nyberg sat down on a chair and rested his injured foot. Martinsson disappeared into his own office, presumably to call home. Wallander left the conference room and went to look at the wall map of the Ystad police district. He followed the roads between Marsvinsholm, Lödinge, and Ystad.

Somewhere there is always a center, he thought. A junction between various events. A criminal returning to the scene of the crime happens only rarely. On the other hand, a perpetrator often passes the same point at least twice, sometimes more.

Höglund came rushing down the corridor. As usual, Wallander had a guilty conscience for asking her to come in. He now understood better than before the problems she had because she was so often alone with her two children. But this time he felt he had a good reason for calling her in.

"Has something happened?" she asked.

"You know that we found Runfeldt's suitcase?"

"I heard about it."

They went into the conference room.

"Everything lying here on the table was inside the suitcase," said Wallander. "I want you to put on some gloves and then pack everything up again."

"In any particular order?"

"In whatever order comes naturally to you. You've told me several times that you always pack your husband's suitcases. You're experienced, in other words."

She did as he asked. Wallander was grateful that she didn't ask any questions. They watched her. Out of long habit, she briskly selected each item and packed the suitcase. Then she took a step back.

"Should I close the lid?"

"That's not necessary."

They all stood around the table and looked at the results. It was as Wallander had suspected.

"How could you know how Runfeldt had packed his suitcase?" wondered Martinsson.

"We'll wait with any comments," Wallander interrupted him. "I saw a traffic cop sitting in the lunchroom. Go and get him."

The traffic cop, whose name was Laurin, came into the room. In the meantime they had unpacked the suitcase again. Laurin looked tired. Wallander had heard talk about a major nighttime drunk-driving campaign on the highways. Wallander asked Laurin to put on a pair of latex gloves and pack the suitcase with the contents lying on the table. Laurin didn't ask any questions either. Wallander saw that he did not do it sloppily but handled the items of clothing with care. When he was done, Wallander thanked him. He left the room.

"Completely different," said Svedberg.

"I'm not trying to prove something," said Wallander. "I don't think I can, either. But when Nyberg opened the lid of the suitcase I had a feeling that something wasn't right. It's always been my experience that men and women pack suitcases in different ways. It seemed as if this suitcase had been packed by a woman."

"Vanja Andersson?" suggested Hansson.

"No," replied Wallander. "Not her. It was Gösta Runfeldt himself who packed the suitcase. We can be quite sure of that."

Höglund was the first one to understand what he was getting at.

"So you're saying it was repacked later? By a woman?"

"I'm not saying anything for certain. I'm just trying to think out loud. The suitcase has been lying outside for only a few days. Runfeldt has been gone for a much longer time than that. Where was the suitcase all that time? It might also explain something strangely missing from the contents."

No one other than Wallander had thought about that before. But now everyone suddenly understood what he meant.

"There's no underwear in the suitcase," said Wallander. "I think it's strange that Runfeldt would pack his bag for a trip to Africa without taking along a single pair of briefs."

"It's hardly likely he would have done that," said Hansson.

"Which in turn means that someone repacked his suitcase," said

Martinsson. "For instance, a woman. And during the repacking all of Runfeldt's underwear disappeared."

Wallander could feel the tension in the room.

"There's one more thing," he said slowly. "For some reason Runfeldt's briefs have disappeared, but at the same time a foreign object wound up inside the suitcase."

He pointed at the blue plastic holder. Höglund was still wearing gloves.

"Smell it," Wallander said to her.

She did as he asked.

"A woman's discreet perfume," was her reaction.

Silence fell over the room. For the first time the whole investigation held its breath.

Nyberg was the one who finally broke the silence. "Does this mean that there's a woman mixed up in all these atrocities?"

"We have to consider it a possibility," replied Wallander. "Even if nothing directly indicates it. Apart from this suitcase."

They were all silent again. For a long time.

It was 7:30 P.M. on Sunday, the 16th of October.

She had arrived at the railway viaduct just after seven o'clock. It was cold. She kept moving her feet to stay warm. There was still some time before the man she was waiting for turned up. At least half an hour, maybe more. But she always arrived with time to spare. With a shudder she remembered those occasions in her life when she had come late. Kept people waiting. Stepped into rooms where people stared at her.

She would never again in her life arrive late. She had arranged her life around a timetable which included margins for error.

She was quite calm. The man who would soon pass under the viaduct didn't deserve to live. She couldn't feel hatred toward him. The woman who had suffered so much misfortune could do the hating. She was just standing here in the dark and waiting to do what was necessary.

The only thing she had hesitated about was whether she should postpone it. The oven was empty, but her work schedule was complicated over the next few weeks. She didn't want to risk having him die inside the oven. She had come to the decision that it would have to be done quickly. And she had no hesitations about how it should be done. The woman who had told her about her life, and who had finally given her his name, had talked about a bathtub filled with water. About how it felt to be pushed under water and almost give up breathing, bursting apart from the inside.

She had thought about Sunday school. The fires of hell that awaited the sinner. The terror was still with her. No one knew how sin was measured. And no one knew when the punishment would be dealt out. She had never been able to talk about the terror with her mother. And she had wondered about her mother's last moment alive. The police officer named Françoise Bertrand had written that everything happened very fast. She probably didn't suffer. She was probably hardly aware of what was happening to her. But how could Bertrand know that? Had she tried to omit part of the truth that was too unbearable?

A train passed overhead. She counted the cars. Then everything was quiet again.

Not with fire, she thought. But with water. With water the sinner shall perish.

She looked at her watch. Noticed that one of the laces on her running shoes was coming undone. She bent down and retied it, hard. She had strong fingers. The man she was waiting for, the one she had been tailing for the past few days, was short and overweight. He wouldn't cause her any problems. The whole thing would be over in a flash.

A man with a dog passed under the railroad viaduct on the opposite side of the street. His footsteps reverberated against the sidewalk. The situation reminded her of an old black-and-white movie. She did what was simplest: pretended to be waiting for someone. She was positive that later he wouldn't remember her. All her life she had taught herself not to be noticed, to make herself invisible. Only now did she realize that it was all in preparation for something she couldn't have known about earlier.

The man with the dog disappeared. Her car was parked on the other side of the railroad viaduct. In spite of the fact that they were right in the middle of Lund, the traffic was sparse. The man with the dog was the only one who had come past, except for a bicyclist. She was ready. Nothing would go wrong.

She saw the man she was waiting for. He came walking along the same side of the street where she was standing. In the distance she could hear a car. She doubled over, as if she had a stomachache. The man stopped by her side. He asked her if she was sick. Instead of answering, she fell to her knees. He did what she had expected. Stepped close and leaned forward. She said that she had suddenly been taken ill. Could he help her to her car? It was right nearby. He put a hand under her arm. She sagged against him. He had to strain to hold her up. Just as she had planned. His physical strength was limited. He supported her over to her car. Asked if she needed more help. But she said no. He opened the door for her. Quickly she put her hand inside where the rag lay. To prevent the ether from evaporating, she had wrapped it in a plastic bag. It took her only a few seconds to get it out. The street was still deserted. Swiftly she turned around and pressed the rag hard against his face. He fought back, but she was stronger. When he started to collapse to the ground, she held him up with one arm as she opened the back door. It was easy to shove him inside. She got into the driver's seat. A car passed by, followed closely by another bicyclist. She leaned over to the back seat and pressed the rag against his face. Soon he was unconscious. He wouldn't wake up in the time it took her to drive to the lake.

She took the road through Svaneholm and Brodda to reach the lake. She turned off near the little campground which stood empty near the shore. Shut off the headlights and got out of the car. Listened. Everything was quiet. The camping trailers were deserted. She pulled the unconscious man out onto the ground. From the trunk she took out a sack. The weights inside it clattered against some rocks. It took longer than she had counted on to get him into the sack and tie it.

He was still unconscious. She carried the sack out onto the small pier jutting into the lake. In the distance a bird fluttered past in the dark. She placed the sack at the very end of the pier. Now there was only a short wait remaining. She lit a cigarette. In the light from the glow she studied her hand. It was steady.

After about twenty minutes the man in the sack started to come to life. He began to move around.

She thought about the bathroom. The woman's story. And she remembered the cats that had been drowned when she was little. They floated away in the sack, still alive, desperately fighting to breathe and survive.

He started shouting. Now he was struggling inside the sack. She put out her cigarette on the pier.

She tried to think. But her head was empty.

She shoved the sack into the water with her foot and walked away.

Chapter Twenty-four

They stayed at the police station so long that Sunday turned into
Monday. Wallander sent Hansson home and later Nyberg too.
But the others stayed on, and they began going through the
investigative material once again.

The suitcase had forced them into a retreat. They sat in the conference room with the suitcase on the table in front of them until the
meeting broke up. Martinsson closed the lid and took it with him to his
own office.

They went over everything that had happened, going on the assumption that none of the work they had done so far could be regarded as wasted effort. In their retreat they all needed to take a fresh
look at things, stop on various details, and hope to discover something
they had missed earlier.

But they didn't come up with anything that gave them the feeling
they had made a breakthrough. The events were still murky, the connection unclear, the motive unknown. The retreat led them back to
the beginning, to the fact that two men had been killed in a gruesome
and brutal way, and that the perpetrator had to be the same person.

It was a quarter past midnight when Wallander called a halt. They
agreed to meet early in the morning to plan the next step. This would
consist primarily of determining whether anything in the investigation
should be changed as a result of finding the suitcase.

Höglund stayed for the whole meeting. Twice she left the conference room for a few minutes. Wallander assumed she was calling home
to talk to her neighbor, who was taking care of her kids. When the
meeting was over, Wallander asked her to stay for a few minutes. He
regretted this at once. He shouldn't, or couldn't, keep her there any
longer. But she merely sat back down, and they waited until the others
had left.

"I want you to do something for me," he said. "I want you to go through all of these events from a woman's point of view. Go over the investigative material and imagine that the perpetrator we're looking for is a woman, not a man. Base your work on two assumptions. First, that she was alone. Second, that she had at least one accomplice."

"You think there were at least two people involved?"

"Yes. And one of them was a woman. Of course, there might have been several people involved."

She nodded.

"As soon as possible," continued Wallander. "Preferably sometime tomorrow. I want you to give this priority. If you have other important matters that can't wait, turn them over to someone else."

"I think Hamrén from Stockholm will be here tomorrow," she said. "A couple of detectives are coming from Malmö too. I can give my other work to one of them."

Wallander had nothing more to say. They sat there a little longer.

"Do you really think it's a woman?" she asked.

"I don't know," said Wallander. "Of course it's dangerous to assign great importance to this suitcase and the scent of perfume. On the other hand, I can't ignore the fact that this whole investigation has had a tendency to elude us. There's been something funny about it right from the start. Back when we were standing out there by the ditch with Eriksson on the stakes, you said something that I've been thinking a lot about."

"That the whole thing seemed so deliberate?"

"The killer's language. What we saw smelled of war. Holger Eriksson was executed in a trap for predators."

"Maybe it *is* war," she said thoughtfully.

Wallander gave her an alert look.

"What do you mean by that?"

"I don't know. Maybe we should interpret what we see literally. Pungee pits are used to catch predators. And they're also used in war."

Wallander realized at once that what she was saying could be important. "Go on," he said.

She bit her lip. "I can't," she replied. "The woman who's taking care of my kids has to go home. I can't ask her to stay any longer. Last time I called she was pissed off. So it's not going to make any difference if I pay her extra for her time."

Wallander didn't want to cut short the discussion they had started. For a brief moment he was annoyed by her kids. Or maybe by her husband who was never home. But he regretted it at once.

"You could come over to my house," she said. "We can continue talking there."

He saw that she was pale and tired. He shouldn't pressure her. But he said yes. They drove through the deserted town in her car. The babysitter was standing in the doorway, waiting. Höglund lived in a new house on the west side of town. Wallander said hello and apologetically took the blame for her late return. They sat down in her living room. He had been there a few times before. He could see that a frequent traveler lived in the house. There were souvenirs from many countries on the walls. But it wasn't apparent that a police officer also lived there. There was a homey feeling completely missing from his own place on Mariagatan. She asked him if he'd like something to drink. He declined.

"The trap for predators and the war," began Wallander. "That's where we left off."

"Men who hunt, men who are soldiers. We also find a shrunken head and a diary written by a mercenary. We see what we see, and we interpret it."

"How do we interpret it?"

"We interpret it correctly. If the killer has a language, then we can clearly read what he writes."

Wallander suddenly thought about something that Linda happened to mention when she was trying to explain to him what an actor's work was really all about. To read between the lines, to look for the subtext.

He told Höglund about his thought. What Linda had said. She nodded.

"Maybe I'm not saying it very well," she said. "But this is approximately what I'm thinking. We've seen everything and interpreted everything, and yet it's all wrong."

"We see what the murderer wants us to see?"

"Maybe we're being duped into looking in the wrong direction."

Wallander thought for a moment. He noticed that his mind was now quite clear. His weariness was gone. They were following a trail that might prove crucial. A trail that had existed before in his consciousness, but he hadn't been able to gain control over it.

"So the deliberateness is an evasive maneuver," he said. "Is that what you mean?"

"Yes."

"Go on!"

"Maybe the truth is just the opposite."

"What does it look like?"

"I don't know. But if we think we're right, and it's all wrong, then whatever is wrong will have to end up being right in the end."

"I understand," he said. "I understand, and I agree."

"A woman would never impale a man on stakes in a pit," she said. "She would never tie a man to a tree and then strangle him with her bare hands."

Wallander didn't say anything for a long time. Höglund disappeared upstairs and then came back a few minutes later. He saw that she had put on a different pair of shoes.

"The whole time we've had a feeling that it was well planned," said Wallander. "The question now is whether it was well planned in more than one way."

"Of course I can't imagine that a woman could have done this," she said. "But I now realize that it might be true."

"Your summary will be important," said Wallander. "I think we should also talk to Mats Ekholm about this."

"Who?"

"The forensic psychologist who was here last summer."

Resigned, she shook her head.

"I guess I'm really tired," she said. "I'd forgotten his name."

Wallander stood up. It was one in the morning.

"I'll see you tomorrow," he said. "Could you call me a cab?"

"You can take my car," she said. "I'm going to need a long walk in the morning to clear my head." She gave him the keys. "My husband is coming home soon. Things will be easier."

"I think this is the first time I fully realized how hard things are for you," he said. "When Linda was little, Mona was always there. I don't think I ever once had to stay home from work while she was growing up."

She followed him out. The night was clear. It was below freezing.

"But I have no regrets," she said suddenly.

"Regrets about what?"

"About joining the force."

"You're a good cop," said Wallander. "A very good cop. In case you didn't know."

He saw that she was pleased. He nodded, got into her car, and drove off.

The next day, Monday, October 17th, Wallander woke up with a slight headache. He lay in bed and wondered if he was coming down with a cold. But he didn't have any other symptoms. He made coffee and looked for some aspirin. Through the kitchen window he saw that the wind had picked up. A cloud cover had moved in over Skåne during the night. The temperature had risen. The thermometer said it was 4° C.

By 7:15 he was at the station. He got some coffee and sat down in his office. On his desk lay a message from the officer in Göteborg he'd been working with on the matter of car smuggling from Sweden to the former–Eastern Bloc countries. He sat holding the message in his hand for a moment. Then he put it in his drawer. He pulled over a pad of paper and started looking for a pen. In one of the drawers he came across Svedberg's note. He wondered how many times he had forgotten to give it back.

Annoyed, he stood up and went out to the corridor. The door to Svedberg's office was open. He went in and put the paper on the desk, then returned to his own office, closed the door, and spent the next half-hour writing down all the questions he wanted answered as soon as possible. He had also decided to take up what he and Höglund had discussed in their late-night conversation when the investigative team met that morning.

At a quarter to eight there was a knock on the door. It was Hamrén, from the homicide department in Stockholm, who'd just arrived. They shook hands. Wallander liked him; they'd worked well together during the summer.

"Here already?" he said. "I thought you weren't coming until later in the day."

"I drove down yesterday," replied Hamrén. "I couldn't wait."

"How are things in Stockholm?"

"The same as here. Only bigger."

"I don't know where they plan to put you," said Wallander.

"In with Hansson. It's already been arranged."

"We're going to meet in about half an hour."

"I've got a lot of reading to do before then."

Hamrén left the room. Wallander absentmindedly put his hand on the phone to call his father. He gave a start. His grief was strong and instantaneous and came out of nowhere.

He no longer had a father he could call. Not today, not tomorrow. Never.

He sat motionless in his chair.

Then he leaned forward again and dialed the number. Gertrud picked up almost at once. She sounded tired and suddenly started crying when he asked her how she was doing. He had a lump in his throat too.

"I'm taking one day at a time," she said after she had calmed down.

"I'll try to come out for a while this afternoon," said Wallander. "I can't stay long. But I'll try to make it."

"There's so much I've been thinking about," she said. "About you and your father. I know so little."

"That goes for me too. But let's see if we can help each other fill in the gaps."

He hung up, knowing that it was unlikely he would make it out to Löderup that day. So why had he said that he would try? Now she would be sitting there waiting.

I live my life always disappointing people, he thought hopelessly.

Angrily he broke the pen he was holding. Tossed the pieces in the wastebasket. One missed. He kicked it away with his foot. He suddenly had the urge to flee. He wondered when he had last talked to Baiba. She hadn't called him either. Was their relationship dying a natural death? When would he have time to look for a house? Or buy a dog?

There were moments when he detested his job. This was one of those times.

He went to stand at the window. Wind and autumn clouds. Migratory birds on their way to warmer lands. He thought about Per Åkeson, who had finally decided to leave; decided there was more to life.

Once, toward the end of summer, as he and Baiba walked along the beach at Skagen, she happened to mention that it felt as if all the wealthy countries of the West shared a dream about an enormous sailboat that could take the whole continent to the island world of the Caribbean. She said that the collapse of the Eastern Bloc had opened her eyes. In the impoverished Latvia there were islands of wealth, simple joys. She had discovered great poverty even in the rich countries that she could now visit. There was a sea of dissatisfaction and emptiness. That's where the sailboat came in.

Wallander tried to imagine himself as an abandoned or maybe lost migratory bird. But the thought seemed so idiotic and meaningless that he pushed it aside.

He made a note to call Baiba that evening. He saw that it was 8:15. He went to the conference room. In addition to Hamrén, who had just arrived, there were also two detectives from Malmö, Augustsson and Hartman. Wallander had never met them before. He shook hands. Lisa Holgersson arrived and sat down. She welcomed the new arrivals. There wasn't time for anything else. She looked at Wallander and nodded.

He started with what he had decided on earlier. The conversation he had had with Höglund after the experiment with repacking the suitcase. He noticed at once that the reaction of the others in the room was marked by doubt. That's what he had expected. He shared their doubts.

"I'm not presenting this as anything but one of several possibilities. Since we know nothing, we can't ignore anything."

He nodded to Höglund.

"I've asked for a summary of the investigation from a female point of view," he said. "We've never done anything like this before. But in this instance, we have to try everything."

The discussion that followed was intense. Wallander had expected that too. Hansson, who seemed to be feeling better this morning, started things off. About halfway through the meeting Nyberg came in. He was walking without the crutch this morning.

Wallander met his glance. He had a feeling that Nyberg had something he wanted to say. He gave him an inquiring look, but Nyberg shook his head.

Wallander listened to the discussion without taking an active part in it. He noticed that Hansson expressed himself clearly and presented good arguments. It was also important at this point that they come up with all the counter-arguments they could think of.

Around nine they took a short break. Svedberg showed Wallander a picture in the paper of the newly created Protective Militia in Lödinge. Several other towns in Skåne were apparently following suit. Chief Holgersson had seen a report about it on the evening news the day before.

"We're going to end up with citizen militias all over the country before long," she said. "Imagine a situation with toy cops numbering ten times as many as us."

"It could be inevitable," said Hamrén. "Maybe it's always been true that crime pays. But the difference today is that we can prove it. If we brought in ten percent of all the money that disappears today in financial crimes, we could easily hire three thousand new officers."

The number seemed absurd to Wallander. But Hamrén stood his ground.

"The question is whether we want that kind of society," he continued. "House doctors are one thing. But house police? Police everywhere? A society that's divided up into various alarm zones? Keys and codes to visit your elderly parents?"

"We probably don't need that many new officers," said Wallander. "We need a different kind of cop."

"Maybe what we need is a different kind of society," said Martinsson. "With fewer golden-parachute agreements and a greater sense of community."

Martinsson's words had unintentionally taken on the sound of a political campaign speech. But Wallander thought he understood him. He knew that Martinsson was constantly worrying about his children. That they'd be exposed to drugs. That something would happen to them.

Wallander sat down next to Nyberg, who hadn't left the table.

"It looked like you wanted to say something."

"It's just a small detail," he said. "Do you remember that I found a press-on nail out in Marsvinsholm Woods?"

Wallander remembered.

"The one you thought had been there a long time?"

"I didn't think anything. But I didn't count that out. Now I think we can positively say that it hadn't been there very long."

Wallander nodded. He motioned Höglund over.

"Do you use press-on nails?" he asked.

"Not every day," she replied. "But I have tried them."

"Do they stick on pretty well?"

"They break off easily."

Wallander nodded.

"I thought you should know," said Nyberg.

Svedberg came into the room.

"Thanks for returning the note," he said. "But you could have tossed it."

"Rydberg used to say that it was an inexcusable sin to throw out a colleague's notes."

"Rydberg said a lot of things."

"They often proved to be true."

Wallander knew that Svedberg had never gotten along with his older colleague. What surprised him was that he still felt that way, despite the fact that Rydberg had been dead now for several years.

The meeting continued. They reassigned various tasks so that Hamrén and the two detectives from Malmö could take part in the investigation right away. At a quarter to eleven Wallander decided it was time to adjourn the meeting. A phone rang. Martinsson, sitting closest, picked it up. Wallander was hungry. Maybe he'd have time to go out to Löderup after all and say hello to Gertrud later that afternoon. Then he noticed that Martinsson had raised his hand. Everyone around the table stopped talking. Martinsson was listening intently. He glanced at Wallander, who immediately realized that something serious had happened. Not again, he thought. This can't be happening, we can't handle this.

Martinsson hung up the phone.

"They've found a body in Krageholm Lake," said Martinsson.

Wallander's first thought was that this didn't have to mean a third murder. Drowning accidents were not uncommon.

"Where?" he asked.

"There's a small campground area on the east shore. The body was right off the end of the pier."

Wallander understood that his feeling of relief was premature. Martinsson had more to tell them.

"It's a body inside a sack," he said. "A man."

It's happened again, thought Wallander. The knot in his stomach was back.

"Who was that on the phone?" asked Svedberg.

"A camper. He was calling on his cell phone. He was upset. It sounded like he was throwing up in my ear."

"Nobody would be camping now, would they?" objected Svedberg.

"There are camping trailers for rent there all year round," said Hansson. "I know where it is."

Wallander suddenly felt incapable of dealing with the situation. He wished he could run away from it all. Maybe Höglund felt the same way. She helped him out by getting to her feet.

"I guess we'd better go," she said.

"Yes," said Wallander. "We'd probably better leave right now."

Since Hansson knew where they were going, Wallander got into his car. The others followed. Hansson drove fast and recklessly. Wallander braked with his feet. The car phone rang. It was Per Åkeson wanting to talk to Wallander.

"What's this I hear?" he asked. "Did it happen again?"

"It's too early to tell. But there's a chance it has."

"Why is there a chance?"

"If it was a body floating around, it might have been a drowning accident or a suicide. A body in a sack is murder. It can't be anything else."

"God damn it to hell," said Per Åkeson.

"You might say that."

"Keep me posted. Where are you?"

"On our way to Krageholm Lake. We should be there in about twenty minutes."

Wallander hung up. It occurred to him that they were headed toward the area where they had found the suitcase.

Hansson seemed to be thinking the same thing.

"The lake is halfway between Lödinge and Marsvinsholm Woods," he said. "It's no great distance."

Wallander grabbed the phone and dialed Martinsson's number. His car was right behind them. Martinsson answered.

"What else did he say? The guy who called. What's his name?"

"I don't think I ever got his name. But he had a Skåne accent."

"A body in a sack. How did he know there was a body in the sack? Did he open it?"

"There was a foot wearing a shoe sticking out."

Even though it was a bad connection, Wallander could hear Martinsson's distress. He hung up.

They reached Sövestad and turned left. Wallander thought about the woman who was Gösta Runfeldt's client. Everywhere were reminders of the events. If there was a geographic center, then Sövestad was it.

The lake was visible through the woods. Wallander tried to prepare himself for what awaited them.

When they headed down toward the campground, which looked deserted, a man came running toward them. Wallander climbed out of the car before Hansson had even stopped.

"Down there," stammered the man. His voice was unsteady.

Wallander walked slowly down the little slope that led to the pier. Even at this distance he could make out something in the water, on one side of the pier. Martinsson came up beside him but stopped at the shore. The others waited in the background. Wallander cautiously walked out on the pier. It wobbled beneath him. The water was brown and looked cold. He shivered.

The sack was only partially visible above the water's surface. A foot was sticking out. The shoe was brown and had laces. White skin could be seen through a hole in the pants leg.

Wallander looked toward land and motioned Nyberg over. Hansson was talking to the man who had called, Martinsson was waiting farther up, Höglund stood off to one side. Wallander thought it looked like a photograph. Reality frozen, suspended. Nothing more would ever happen.

The mood was broken by Nyberg stepping onto the pier. Reality returned. Wallander squatted down. Nyberg did the same.

"A sack made of jute," said Nyberg. "They're usually strong. But this one has a hole in it. It must be old."

Wallander wished Nyberg were right. But he already knew he wasn't.

There had been no hole in the sack. It looked like the man had kicked his way through it. The fibers of the sack had been pushed out and then ripped apart.

Wallander knew what this meant.

The man had been alive when he was stuffed in the sack and thrown into the lake.

Wallander took a deep breath. He felt sick and dizzy.

Nyberg gave him an inquiring look. But he didn't say anything. He waited.

Wallander kept on taking deep breaths, one after another. Then he said what he was thinking, what he knew had to be true.

"He kicked a hole in the sack. That means he was alive when he was tossed into the lake."

"An execution?" asked Nyberg. "A war between two crime gangs?"

"We could hope for that," said Wallander. "But I don't think so."

"The same man?"

"It looks like it."

Wallander got to his feet with difficulty. His knees were stiff. He walked back to the shore. Nyberg was still standing out on the pier. The crime technicians had just arrived in their car. Wallander went over to Höglund. She was now standing next to Chief Holgersson. The others followed. Finally they were all assembled. The man who had discovered the sack was sitting on a rock with his head in his hands.

"It could be the same perpetrator," said Wallander. "If that's the case, then this time he's drowned a man in a sack."

Disgust passed like a ripple over the group.

"We have to stop this madman," said Lisa Holgersson. "What's going on in this country?"

"A pungee pit," said Wallander. "A man who's strangled while tied to a tree. And now a man who's been drowned."

"Do you still think a woman could have done something like this?" asked Hansson. His tone of voice was noticeably aggressive.

Wallander asked himself the same question in silence. What did he really think? In a matter of a few seconds all the events passed through his mind.

"I don't want to believe it. But a woman could have done this. Or at least be involved."

He looked at Hansson.

"You're asking the wrong question," he said. "It's not about what I think. It's about what's going on in this country today."

Wallander went back to the shore of the lake. A solitary swan was on its way toward the pier. It glided soundlessly across the surface of the dark water. Wallander watched it for a long time.

Then he zipped up his jacket and went back to Nyberg, who was already starting to work out on the pier.

Skåne
17 October—3 November 1994

Chapter Twenty-five

Nyberg carefully slit open the sack. Wallander went up to the pier to look at the dead man's face along with the doctor, who had just arrived.

He didn't recognize the deceased. And of course he hadn't expected to.

Wallander thought the man must be between forty and fifty years old.

He looked for less than a minute at the body that was dragged out of the sack. He simply couldn't stand any more. He felt dizzy the whole time.

Nyberg was going through the man's pockets.

"He's wearing an expensive suit," said Nyberg. "His shoes aren't cheap either."

They didn't find anything in his pockets. Someone had taken the trouble to remove his ID. On the other hand, the perpetrator must have assumed that the body would soon be discovered in Krageholm Lake. So the intention had not been to conceal it.

The body had now been pulled free. The sack was on a plastic sheet. Nyberg signaled to Wallander, who had stepped aside.

"This whole thing was carefully calculated," he said. "You'd almost think the murderer had a scale. Or knew about weight distribution and water resistance."

"What do you mean?" asked Wallander.

Nyberg pointed to several thick seams running along the inside of the sack.

"Everything was meticulously prepared. The sack has weights sewn into it that guaranteed two things. One, that the weights were light enough, along with the man's weight, so that the sack wouldn't sink to the bottom. Two, that the sack would lie with only a narrow air pocket above the water's surface. Since it was all so carefully calculated, the person who prepared the sack must have known the man's weight. At least approximately. With a margin of error of maybe four to five kilos."

Wallander forced himself to think this over, even though all thoughts of how the man had died made him feel sick.

"So the narrow air pocket guaranteed that the man would actually drown?"

"I'm no doctor," said Nyberg. "But it's probable this man was still alive when the sack was thrown into the water. So he was murdered."

The doctor, who was kneeling down to examine the body, had been listening to their conversation. He stood up and came over to them. The pier swayed under their weight.

"Of course it's too early to make any definite statements about anything," he said. "But we have to presume that he drowned."

"Not just drowned," said Wallander. "Somebody drowned him."

"The police are the ones who will have to determine whether it was an accident or a murder," said the doctor. "Whether he drowned or somebody drowned him. I can only speak about what happened to his body."

"No external marks? No contusions? Or wounds?"

"We'll need to get his clothes off to be able to answer that question. But I didn't notice anything on the parts of his body that are visible. The autopsy may turn up other results, of course."

Wallander nodded. "I'd like to know as soon as possible if you find any signs of violence."

The doctor went back to his work. Even though Wallander had met him several times before, he still couldn't remember his name.

Wallander left the pier and gathered his colleagues around him on the shore. Hansson had just finished talking to the man who had discovered the sack in the water.

"We didn't find any ID," Wallander began. We have to find out who he is. That's the most important thing right now. Until then we can't do anything. We'll start by going through the missing-persons files."

"There's a good chance he hasn't been missed yet," said Hansson. "Nils Göransson, the man who found him, claims he was here as late as yesterday afternoon. He does shift work at a machine shop in Svedala and usually takes a walk out here because he has trouble sleeping. He just started his shift right now. So he was here yesterday. He always walks out on the pier. And there wasn't any sack. So it must have been thrown into the water during the night. Or yesterday evening."

"Or this morning," said Wallander. "When did Göransson get here?"

Hansson searched his notes.

"At eight fifteen. He got off work around seven and drove over here. On the way he stopped and ate breakfast."

"So we know that much," said Wallander. "Not much time has passed. That may give us certain advantages. The difficulty is going to be to identify him."

"The sack could have been thrown into the lake somewhere else," said Nyberg.

Wallander shook his head.

"He hasn't been in the water long. And there's no current here to speak of."

Martinsson kicked at the sand restlessly, as if he were cold.

"Does it really have to be the same man?" he asked. "I think this seems different."

Wallander was as sure about the case as he could possibly be.

"No. It's the same perpetrator. We'd better assume it is, anyway. And take a look over our shoulder if we have to."

He sent them off. There was nothing more for them to do out there on the shore of Krageholm Lake.

The cars drove off. Wallander gazed out at the water. The swan was gone. He looked at the men working on the pier. At the ambulance, the police cars, the crime-scene tape. Everything about it suddenly gave him a feeling of enormous unreality. He encountered nature surrounded by plastic tape stretched out to protect crime sites. Everywhere he went there were dead people. With his eyes he could look for a swan on the water. But in the foreground lay a man who had just been pulled dead out of a sack.

He thought that his work was basically nothing more than a poorly paid test of endurance. He was being paid to endure this. The plastic tape wound through his life like a snake.

He went over to Nyberg, who was stretching his back.

"We've found a cigarette butt," he said. "That's all. At least out here on the pier. But we've already done a superficial examination of the sand. For drag marks. There aren't any. Whoever carried the sack was strong. Provided he didn't lure the man out here and then stuff him in the sack."

Wallander shook his head.

"Let's assume that the sack was carried," he said. "Carried with its contents."

"Do you think there's any reason to drag the lake?"

"I don't think so. The man was unconscious when he was brought here. There must have been a car involved. Then the sack was thrown in the water. The car drove off."

"So we'll wait on the dragging," said Nyberg.

"Tell me what you see," said Wallander.

Nyberg grimaced. "It could be the same man," he said. "The violence, the cruelty, they all look familiar. Even though he varies things."

"Do you think a woman could have done this?"

"I say the same thing you do," replied Nyberg. "I'd rather not believe that. But I can also tell you that she would have to be capable of carrying eighty kilos without difficulty. What woman can do that?"

"I don't know any," said Wallander. "But I'm sure they exist."

Nyberg went back to his work. Wallander was just about to leave the pier when he suddenly saw the solitary swan right nearby. He wished he had a piece of bread. The swan was pecking at something near the shore. Wallander took a step closer. The swan hissed and turned back toward the lake.

He went over to one of the police cars and asked to be driven to Ystad.

On the way back to town he tried to think. What he had feared most had now happened. The perpetrator was not finished. They knew nothing about him. Was he at the end or the beginning of what he had decided to do? They didn't even know whether he had motives for his premeditated acts or was just insane.

It has to be a man, thought Wallander. Anything else goes against all common sense. Women seldom commit murder. Least of all well-planned murders. Ruthless and calculated acts of violence.

It has to be a man, or maybe more than one. And we're never going to solve this case unless we find the connection between the victims. Now there are three of them. That should increase our chances. But nothing is certain. Nothing is going to be revealed all by itself.

He leaned his cheek against the car window. The landscape was brown with a tinge of gray, but the grass was still green. There was a lone tractor out in a field.

Wallander thought about the pungee pit where he had found Holger Eriksson. The tree that Gösta Runfeldt had been tied to when he was strangled. And now a man was stuffed alive into a sack and tossed into Krageholm Lake to drown.

He was suddenly sure that the only possible motive was revenge. But this went beyond all reasonable proportions. What was the perpetrator seeking revenge for? Something so horrific that it wasn't enough simply to kill. The victims also had to be conscious of what was happening to them.

There's nothing random about what's behind all this, thought Wallander. Everything has been carefully thought out and chosen.

He paused at the last thought.

The perpetrator chose. Someone was chosen. Selected from what group or for what reason?

When he reached the station he was still thinking and felt the need for some solitude before he sat down with his colleagues. He took the phone off the hook, pushed aside the phone messages lying on his desk, and put his feet up on a pile of memos from the NPB.

The hardest thing was the thought that the murderer might be a woman. He tried to remember the times he had dealt with female criminals. It hadn't happened often. He thought he could recall all the cases he had ever heard about during his years as a cop. Once, almost fifteen years back, he himself had caught a woman who had committed murder. Later the district court changed the charge to manslaughter. A middle-aged woman had killed her brother. He had persecuted and molested her ever since they were children. Finally she couldn't take it anymore and killed him with his own shotgun. She hadn't really meant to hit him. She just wanted to scare him. But she was a bad shot. She hit him right in the chest, and he died instantly. In all the other cases Wallander could remember, the women who had used violence had done so on impulse and in self-defense. It involved their own husbands, or men they had futilely tried to reject. In many cases, alcohol was part of the picture.

Never, in all his experience, had there been a woman who planned to commit a violent act. At least not according to a meticulously devised plan.

He got up and walked over to the window.

What was it that made him unable to let go of the idea that a woman was involved this time?

He had no answer to this. He didn't even know whether he believed it was a woman working alone or collaborating with a man.

There was nothing to indicate one or the other.

He was pulled away from his thoughts by Martinsson knocking on his door.

"The list is almost ready," he said.

"What list?" asked Wallander.

"The list of missing persons," replied Martinsson in surprise.

Wallander nodded. "Then let's meet," he said, motioning Martinsson ahead of him down the corridor.

When they had closed the door of the conference room behind them, he noticed that his earlier feeling of powerlessness was gone. Breaking with his normal habit, he remained standing at the head of the table. Usually he sat down. Now he felt as if he didn't have time for that.

"What have we got?" he asked.

"In Ystad no reports of anyone missing during the past few weeks," said Svedberg. "The ones we've been searching for over a longer period don't match with the man we found in Krageholm Lake. There's a couple of teenage girls, and a boy who ran away from a refugee camp. He's presumably on his way back to the Sudan."

Wallander thought of Per Åkeson.

"So we know that much," he said. "What about the other districts?"

"We've got a couple of people in Malmö," said Höglund. "But they don't match either. In one case the age might be right, but the missing person is a man from southern Italy. Our man doesn't look particularly Italian."

They went through the bulletins from the districts closest to Ystad. Wallander was aware that if necessary they might have to cover the whole country and even the rest of Scandinavia. They could only hope that the man had lived somewhere near Ystad.

"Lund took a report late last night," said Hansson. "A woman called to report that her husband hadn't come home from his evening walk. The age is about right. He's a researcher at the university."

"Check it out, of course."

"They're going to send us a photo," Hansson went on. "They'll fax it over as soon as they get it."

Wallander was still standing. Now he sat down. At that moment Per Åkeson came into the room. Wallander wished he hadn't come. It was never easy to report that they were at a standstill. The investigation was stuck with its wheels deep in the mud.

And now they had another victim.

Wallander felt uncomfortable, as if he were personally responsible for the fact that they had nothing to go on. Yet he knew they had been working as hard and as steadily as they could. The detectives gathered in that room were intelligent and dedicated.

Wallander pushed aside his annoyance at Åkeson's presence. "You're here just in time," he said instead. "I was just thinking about summarizing the state of the investigation."

"Does an investigative state even exist?" asked Åkeson.

Wallander knew he didn't mean this as some kind of nasty or critical remark. Those who didn't know Åkeson might be put off by his brusque manner. But Wallander had worked with him for so many years that he knew what he had just said was an expression of uneasiness and a willingness to help if he could.

Hamrén, who was new, regarded Åkeson with disapproval. Wallander wondered how the Stockholm prosecutors usually expressed themselves.

"There's always an investigative state," replied Wallander. "We have one this time too. But it's extremely hazy. A number of clues we were following are no longer relevant. I think we've reached a point where we have to go back to the beginning. What this new murder means, we can't yet say. It's too early for that."

"Is it the same killer?" asked Åkeson.

"I think so," said Wallander.

"Why?"

"The M.O. The brutality. The cruelty. Of course a sack isn't the same thing as sharpened bamboo stakes. But you have to admit it's a variation on a theme."

"What about the suspicion that a mercenary soldier might be behind all this?"

"That led us to the fact that Harald Berggren has been dead for seven years."

Åkeson had no more questions.

The door was cautiously pushed open. A clerk handed them a picture that had arrived by fax.

"It's from Lund," said the girl, and then she closed the door.

Everyone stood up at once and gathered around Martinsson, who stood holding the picture.

Wallander gave a low whistle. There could be no doubt. It was the man they had found in Krageholm Lake.

"Good," said Wallander in a low voice. "We just got a good jump on the murderer's lead."

They sat down again.

"Who is he?" asked Wallander.

Hansson had his papers in order.

"Eugen Blomberg, fifty-one years old. Research assistant at Lund University. His research has something to do with milk."

"Milk?" said Wallander in surprise.

"That's what it says. 'About how milk allergies are related to various intestinal diseases.'"

"Who reported him missing?"

"His wife. Kristina Blomberg. On Siriusgatan in Lund."

Wallander knew they had to make the best use of their time. He wanted to make an even bigger dent in the invisible lead.

"Then we'll go there," he said, getting to his feet. "Tell our colleagues that we've identified him. See to it that they track down the wife so I can talk to her. There's a detective in Lund named Birch. Kalle Birch. We know each other. Talk to him. I'm on my way."

"Can you really talk to her before we have a positive ID?"

"Someone else can identify him. Someone from the university. Some other milk researcher. Now we'll have to go through all the material on Eriksson and Runfeldt again. Eugen Blomberg. Is he there somewhere? We need to get through a lot of it today."

Wallander turned to Åkeson. "I guess we could say that the investigative state has changed."

Åkeson nodded without saying anything.

Wallander went to get his jacket and the keys to one of the police cars. It was quarter past two when he left Ystad. He briefly considered putting the blue emergency light on the roof of the car, but he decided against it. It wouldn't get him there any faster.

He reached Lund about 3:30. A police car met him at the entrance to town and escorted him to Siriusgatan, in a residential neighborhood east of the center of town. At the entrance to the street the police car pulled over. Another car was parked there. Wallander saw Kalle Birch get out. They had met several years back in connection with a big conference for the Southern Sweden Police District held in Tylösand, outside of Halmstad. The purpose was to improve operational cooperation in the region. Wallander had participated grudgingly; Björk, chief of police at the time, had ordered him to go. At lunch he wound up sitting next to Birch. They discovered that they shared an interest in opera. Since then they had occasionally been in contact with each other. From various sources Wallander had heard that Birch was a talented detective who sometimes suffered from deep depression. But as he came toward Wallander now, he seemed to be in a good mood. They shook hands.

"They've just filled me in on the whole thing," said Birch. "One of Blomberg's colleagues is on his way to identify the body. They'll let us know by phone."

"And the widow?"

"Not yet informed. We thought that was a little premature."

"That's going to make the interrogation more difficult," said Wallander. "She'll be shocked, of course."

"I guess we can't do much about that."

Birch pointed to a café across the street. "We can wait there," he said. "Besides, I'm hungry."

Wallander hadn't eaten lunch either. They went into the café and had sandwiches and coffee. Wallander gave Birch a summary of everything that had happened.

"It reminds me of what you were dealing with this summer," he said when Wallander stopped talking.

"Only because the murderer has killed more than one person," said Wallander. "The method seems quite different."

"What's so different about taking scalps and drowning somebody alive?"

"I might not be able to put it into words," said Wallander hesitantly. "But there's still a big difference."

Birch let the question drop. "We sure never thought about things like this when we joined the force," he said instead.

"I hardly remember anymore what I imagined," said Wallander.

"I remember an old commissioner," said Birch. "He's been dead a

long time now. Karl-Oscar Fredrick Wilhelm Sunesson. He's practically
a legend. At least here in Lund. He saw all of this coming. I remember
he used to talk to us younger detectives and warn us that everything
was going to get a lot harder. The violence would get worse and more
brutal. He also told us why. He said Sweden's prosperity was a well-
camouflaged quagmire. The decay was built in. He even took the time
to put together financial analyses and explain the connection between
various types of crime. He was also that rare sort of man who never
speaks ill of anyone. He could be critical about the politicians, and he
could use his arguments to crush suggestions for various changes in
the police force. But he never doubted that there were good, albeit
confused, intentions behind them. He used to say that good intentions
that are not clothed in reason lead to greater disasters than those
actions built on ill will or stupidity. I didn't understand much of it back
then. But I do now."

Wallander thought about Rydberg. Birch could have been talking
about him.

"That still doesn't answer the question of what we were really thinking when we decided to join the force," he said.

What Birch had in mind, Wallander never found out. The phone
rang. Birch listened without saying anything.

"They've identified him," said Birch after he hung up. "It's Eugen
Blomberg. There's absolutely no doubt about it."

"So let's go in," said Wallander.

"If you want, you can wait until we inform his wife," said Birch. "It's
usually kind of painful."

"I'll go with you," said Wallander. "It beats sitting here doing nothing. Besides, it might give me an idea what kind of relationship she had
with her husband."

They encountered a woman who was unexpectedly composed. She
seemed to understand at once the reason they were standing on her
doorstep. Wallander kept in the background as Birch told her of the
death. She sat down on the edge of a chair, as if to bear the brunt of
it with her feet, and nodded silently. Wallander assumed that she was
about the same age as her husband. But she seemed older, as if she had
aged prematurely. She was thin, her skin stretched taut across her
cheekbones. Wallander furtively studied her. He didn't think she was
going to fall apart. At least not yet.

Birch nodded to Wallander to step forward. Birch had merely said
that they had found her husband dead in Krageholm Lake. Nothing
about how it happened. That was Wallander's job.

"Krageholm Lake comes under the jurisdiction of the Ystad police," said Birch. "That's why one of my colleagues from there is with me. His name is Kurt Wallander."

Kristina Blomberg looked up. She reminded Wallander of someone, but he couldn't remember who.

"I recognize your face," she said. "I've seen you in the papers."

"That's quite possible," said Wallander, sitting down on a chair across from her. Meanwhile Birch had taken over Wallander's previous position in the background.

The house was very quiet. Tastefully furnished. But quiet. It occurred to Wallander that he didn't yet know whether there were any children in the family.

That was his first question.

"No," she replied. "We don't have any children."

"None from earlier marriages?"

Wallander immediately noticed her uncertainty. She paused before answering; it was barely noticeable but he saw it.

"No," she said. "Not that I know of."

Wallander exchanged a glance with Birch, who had also noticed her hesitation about a question that shouldn't have been difficult to answer. Wallander slowly pressed on.

"When did you last see your husband?"

"He went for a walk last night. He usually did."

"Do you know which way he went?"

She shook her head. "He was often gone for more than an hour. Where he went, I have no idea."

"Was everything normal last night?"

"Yes."

Wallander again sensed a shadow of uncertainty in her answer. He continued cautiously.

"So he didn't come back? What did you do then?"

"When it was nearly two in the morning I called the police."

"But didn't you think he might have gone to see some friends?"

"He didn't have many friends. I called them up before I contacted the police. He wasn't there."

She looked at him. Still composed. Wallander realized that he couldn't wait any longer.

"Your husband was found dead in Krageholm Lake. We have also determined that he was murdered. I regret this happened. But I have to tell you the truth."

Wallander studied her face. She's not surprised, he thought. About him being dead or that he was murdered.

"Of course it's important that we catch the person or persons who did this. Can you think of anyone it might be? Did your husband have any enemies?"

"I don't know," she replied. "I didn't know my husband very well."

Wallander paused to think before he continued. Her answer made him uneasy. "I don't know how to interpret your answer," he said.

"Is it really so difficult? I didn't know my husband very well. Once upon a time, a long time ago, I thought I did. But that was back then."

"What happened? What changed things?"

She shook her head. Wallander saw something he interpreted as bitterness come over her. He waited.

"Nothing happened," she said. "We grew apart. We live in the same house, but we have separate bedrooms. He has his own life, and I have mine."

Then she corrected herself.

"He had his own life. And I have mine."

"If I understand correctly, he was a researcher at the university?"

"Yes."

"Milk allergies? Is that right?"

"Yes."

"Do you work there too?"

"I'm a teacher."

Wallander nodded. "So you don't know whether your husband had any enemies?"

"No."

"And few friends?"

"That's right."

"And you can't imagine anyone who would want to kill him? Or why?"

Her face was strained. Wallander felt as if she were looking right through him.

"No one except me," she replied. "But I didn't kill him."

Wallander looked at her for a long time, without saying anything. Birch had stepped forward to stand next to him.

"Why would you want to kill him?" Wallander asked.

She stood up and tore off her blouse with such force that it ripped. It all happened so fast that Wallander and Birch didn't understand what was going on. Then she held out her arms. They were covered with scars.

"He did this to me," she said. "And a lot of other things that I won't even talk about."

She left the room with the torn blouse in her hand. Wallander and Birch looked at each other.

"He abused her," said Birch. "Do you think she was the one who did it?"

"No," said Wallander. "It wasn't her."

They waited in silence. After a few minutes she came back. She had put on a new shirt.

"I'm not going to grieve for him," she said. "I don't know who did it. I don't think I want to know, either. But I realize that you have to catch him."

"Yes," said Wallander. "We do. And we need all the help we can get."

She looked at him, and all of a sudden her expression was completely helpless.

"I didn't know anything about him anymore," she said. "I can't help you."

Wallander thought it was quite likely that she was telling the truth. She couldn't help them.

But that was only what she thought. She had already helped them.

When Wallander saw her arms, he lost his last shred of doubt.

He knew now that they were looking for a woman.

Chapter Twenty-six

When they left the house on Siriusgatan it was raining. They stopped next to Wallander's car. He felt restless.

"I don't think I've ever met a new widow who took the loss of her husband so lightly," said Birch with distaste in his voice.

"And yet it's something we have to bear in mind," replied Wallander.

He didn't take the trouble to explain his answer any further. Instead he tried to think ahead through the next few hours. His feeling that they were in a hurry now was intense.

"We have to go through his belongings both here and at the university. That's your job, of course. But I'd like to have someone from Ystad present too. We don't know what we're looking for, but this way we might discover something of interest more quickly."

Birch nodded. "You're not staying yourself?"

"No. I'll ask Martinsson and Svedberg to come out here. I'll tell them to leave right away."

Wallander took his cell phone out of the car, dialed the number of the Ystad police, and asked for Martinsson. He gave him a brief description of what was happening. Martinsson promised that he and Svedberg would leave at once. Wallander told him to meet Birch at the police station in Lund. He had to spell the name for Martinsson. Birch smiled.

"I would have stayed," said Wallander, "but I have to start working backwards through the investigation. I've got a hunch that the solution to Blomberg's murder is in there someplace. Even though we haven't seen it yet. The solution to all three murders. It's as if we've gone astray in a complex system of caverns."

"It would be good if we could prevent any more deaths," said Birch. "It's enough as it is."

They said goodbye. Wallander drove back toward Ystad. Rain showers came and went. When he passed Sturup Airport there was a plane coming in for a landing. As he drove he went over the investigative material again in his mind. He didn't know how many times he had done it so far. He also decided what to do when he got back to Ystad.

It was a quarter to six when he parked the car. In the lobby he stopped and asked Ebba if Höglund was in.

"She and Hansson came back an hour ago."

Wallander hurried on. He found Höglund in her office. She was on the phone. Wallander made a sign for her to wind up the call as soon as she could. He waited out in the hallway. As soon as he heard her hang up, he was back in her office.

"I thought we ought to sit down in my office," he said. "We need to do a thorough overview."

"Shall I bring anything?" She pointed at all the papers and folders strewn across her desk.

"I don't think it's necessary. If we need anything you can come back and get it later."

She followed him to his office. Wallander called the switchboard and told them to hold all calls. He didn't say for how long. What he had in mind would take as long as it took.

"You remember I asked you to go through everything that's happened and look for female characteristics," he said.

"I've done that," she replied.

"We have to go over all the material again," he went on. "I'm convinced that there's some point where we can make a breakthrough. It's just that we haven't seen it yet. We've walked right past it. We've gone back and forth, and it's been there the whole time, but we just haven't been looking in the right direction. And now I'm positive a woman must be involved."

"Why do you think that?"

He told her about his conversation with Kristina Blomberg. About how she ripped off her blouse and showed them the scars from the abuse she had been subjected to.

"You're talking about an abused woman," she said. "Not about a woman who murders people."

"It might be the same thing," said Wallander. "In any case, I have to find out if I'm right or wrong."

"Where do we start?"

"From the beginning. Like with a story. And the first thing that happened was that someone dug around in a ditch and prepared a pungee pit for Holger Eriksson in Lödinge. Imagine that it was a woman. What do you see?"

"It's not impossible, of course. Nothing was too heavy or too large."

"Why did she choose this particular M.O.?"

"So it would look like it was done by a man."

Wallander pondered her reply for a long time before he went on.

"So she wanted to throw us off the track?"

"Not necessarily. She may have wanted to demonstrate how violence comes back, like a boomerang. Or, why not both reasons?"

Wallander thought about that. Her explanation was certainly possible. "The motive," he continued. "Who wanted to kill Holger Eriksson?"

"That's not as clear as it is for Gösta Runfeldt. There at least we have various possibilities. Eriksson we still don't know enough about. So little that it seems rather odd. There doesn't seem to be any peephole into his life. As if a life could be a no trespassing zone."

He knew right away that she was saying something important.

"How do you mean?"

"Just what I said. We should know more about a man who's eighty years old and has lived his whole life in Skåne. A well-known man. We know so little that it's unnatural."

"What's the explanation?"

"I don't know."

"Are people scared to talk about him?"

"No."

"Then what is it?"

"We were searching for a mercenary," she said. "We found a man who's dead. We found out that these men often use assumed names. It struck me that the same might apply to Holger Eriksson."

"That he could have been a mercenary?"

"No, I don't think so. But he could have used an assumed name. He didn't always have to be Holger Eriksson. That might be one explanation for why we know so little about his private life. Maybe sometimes he was someone else."

Wallander recalled some of Eriksson's earliest poetry books. He had published them under a pseudonym. Later he used his real name.

"I have a hard time accepting what you're saying," said Wallander. "Mostly because I don't see any reasonable motive. Why does someone use an assumed name?"

"To do something he doesn't want to be discovered doing."

Wallander looked at her. "You mean he might have used an alias because he was homosexual? In a time when it was best to keep it secret?"

"That's one possibility."

Wallander nodded. But he was still dubious. "We've got the gift to the church in Jämtland. That must mean something. Why did he do it?

And the Polish woman who disappeared. There's something about her that makes her special. Have you thought about what it might be?"

Höglund shook her head.

"The fact that she's the only woman who appears in the investigative material on Holger Eriksson," he said.

"Copies of the investigative material on her were sent from Östersund. But I don't think anyone has started digging into it yet. Besides, she's just on the periphery. We have no proof that she and Eriksson knew each other."

Wallander was suddenly determined.

"That's right. We have to do that as soon as possible. Find out whether there's a connection."

"Who's going to do it?"

"Hansson. He reads faster than any of us. He usually goes right to the heart of the matter."

She made a note. Then they left the topic of Holger Eriksson for the moment.

"Gösta Runfeldt was a brutal man," Wallander said. "We know that for sure. On that point there's a similarity with Eriksson. Now it turns out that it applies to Eugen Blomberg too. Runfeldt abused his wife, just like Blomberg. Where does this lead us?"

"To three men with violent tendencies. And at least two of them abused women."

"It might also be true of the third, Holger Eriksson. We don't know yet."

"The Polish woman? Krista Haberman?"

"For example. It might also be true that Runfeldt killed his wife. Prepared a hole in the ice for her to fall into and drown."

They both knew that something was cooking. Wallander went back through the investigation again.

"The pungee pit," he said. "What was it?"

"Prepared, well-planned. A death trap."

"More than that. A way to kill someone slowly."

Wallander searched for a paper on his desk.

"According to the medical examiner in Lund, Eriksson may have hung there impaled on the bamboo stakes for several hours before he died."

He put down the paper in disgust.

"Gösta Runfeldt," he said then. "Emaciated, strangled, hanging tied to a tree. What does that tell us?"

"That he was held captive. He wasn't hanging in a pungee pit."

Wallander raised his hand. She didn't say a word. He was thinking, recalling the visit to Stång Lake. They found her under the ice.

"Drowning underneath the ice," he said. "I've always imagined that would be one of the most horrifying things that can happen to a person. To wind up beneath the ice and not be able to break through. Maybe even see the light through it."

"Held captive under the ice," she said.

"Precisely. That's just what I was thinking."

"You mean this perpetrator has figured out methods of killing that remind him of the event that's being avenged?"

"Something like that. It's a possibility, anyway."

"In that case, what happened to Eugen Blomberg looks more like what happened to Runfeldt's wife."

"I know," Wallander said. "Maybe we can figure that out too if we keep at it a while longer."

They went on. Talked about the suitcase. He noted once more the press-on nail that Nyberg had found out in the Marsvinsholm Woods.

Then they started on Blomberg. The pattern was repeated.

"The plan was to drown him, but not too fast. He had to be aware of what was happening to him."

Wallander leaned back in his chair and looked at her across his desk.

"Tell me what you see."

"A revenge motive is taking shape. At any rate, it runs through everything as a possible common denominator. Men who use force against women are attacked in return by a calculated male type of violence. As if they were being forced to feel their hands on their own bodies."

"That's a good way of putting it," Wallander interjected. "Go on."

"It could also be a way to hide the fact that a woman did all this. It took a long time for us to even imagine that a woman might be involved. And when we did think of it, we rejected it immediately."

"What is there to contradict the idea that a woman might be involved?"

"We still know very little. Women almost never use violence unless they're defending themselves or their children. It's not a premeditated violence, but instinctive defense reflexes. A woman normally would not dig a pungee pit. Or hold a man captive. Or throw a man in the lake inside a sack."

Wallander looked at her intently.

"Normally," he then said. "Your word."

"If a woman is involved in this, then she must be very sick indeed."

Wallander stood up and went over to the window. "There's one more thing," he said, "which could knock down this whole house of cards we're trying to construct. She isn't avenging herself. She's avenging others. Runfeldt's wife is dead. Blomberg's wife didn't do it, I'm sure of that. Eriksson has no woman. If this is revenge and if it's a woman, then she's taking revenge for *others*. And that doesn't sound likely. If it's true, I've never come across anything like it before."

"It could be more than one woman," Höglund said hesitantly.

"A number of angels of death? A group of women? A cult?"

"That doesn't sound plausible."

"No," said Wallander, "it doesn't."

He sat back down in his chair. "I'd like you to do just the opposite," he said. "Go over all the material again. And then give me all the good reasons why it isn't a woman who did this."

"Wouldn't it be better to wait until we know more about what happened to Blomberg?"

"Maybe. But I don't think we have time."

"You think it could happen again?"

Wallander wanted to give her an honest answer. He sat silently for a moment before he replied.

"There is no beginning," he said. "At least none we can see. That makes it less likely that there will be an end. It could happen again. And we don't have any idea what direction to look in."

They didn't get any further. Wallander felt impatient that neither Martinsson nor Svedberg had called. Then he remembered that he had blocked all his calls. He contacted the switchboard. Neither Martinsson nor Svedberg had been heard from. He asked for their calls to be put through, but only theirs.

"The break-ins," Höglund said suddenly. "At the flower shop and at Eriksson's house. How do they fit into the picture?"

"I don't know," he replied. "Or the blood spots on the floor. I thought I had an explanation, and now I don't know anymore."

"I've been thinking about it," she said.

Wallander noticed that she was eager. He nodded to her to continue.

"We're talking about having to distinguish what we actually see from what has happened," she began. "Holger Eriksson reported a break-in where nothing was stolen. Why did he report it at all?"

"I've thought about that too," said Wallander. "He may have just been upset that someone broke into his house."

"In that case it fits in with the pattern."

Wallander didn't understand right away what she was getting at.

"There's always the possibility that someone broke in to make him nervous. Not to steal anything."

"A first warning?" he asked. "Is that what you mean?"

"Yes."

"And the flower shop?"

"Gösta Runfeldt leaves his apartment. Or he's lured out. Or else it's early in the morning. He goes down to the street to wait for a taxi.

There he vanishes without a trace. What if he went to the shop? It only takes a few minutes. He could have left his suitcase inside the front door. Or carried it with him. It wasn't heavy."

"Why would he have walked to the shop?"

"I don't know. Maybe he forgot something."

"You mean he might have been attacked inside the shop?"

"I know it's not a great idea. But it's what I've been thinking."

"It's no worse than lots of others," said Wallander. He looked at her.

"Has anyone checked if the blood on the floor was Runfeldt's?"

"I don't think it was ever done. If not, I'm to blame."

"If we had to keep track of who was responsible for all the mistakes made during criminal investigations, there wouldn't be time for anything else," said Wallander. "I assume there aren't any samples left?"

"I can talk to Vanja Andersson."

"Do that. We can check it out. Just to be sure."

She got up and left the room. Wallander was tired. They had had a good talk. But his nervousness had increased. They were as far from a center point as they could be. The investigation still lacked a gravitational force drawing them in a specific direction.

Someone was talking loudly in an annoyed voice out in the hallway. He started thinking of Baiba, but he forced himself to concentrate on the investigation again. He imagined the dog he wanted to buy. He got up and went for coffee. Somebody asked him if he'd had time to write an opinion on whether it was proper for a local association to call itself "Friends of the Axe." He said no. Went back to his office. The rain had stopped. The cloud cover hung motionless above the water tower.

The phone rang. It was Martinsson. Wallander listened for signs in his voice that something important had happened, but he heard nothing.

"Svedberg just came back from the university. Eugen Blomberg seems to have been the type of person that blended into the woodwork. He wasn't a particularly prominent researcher when it comes to milk allergies, either. He was loosely affiliated with the children's clinic in Lund, but his achievements seem to have stopped years ago. What he was working on has been considered quite rudimentary. That's what Svedberg claims, at least. But what does he know about milk allergies?"

"Go on," said Wallander, not hiding his impatience.

"I have a hard time understanding how a man could be so utterly devoid of interests," said Martinsson. "He seems to have been completely preoccupied with his damned milk. And nothing else. Except for one thing."

Wallander waited.

"It appears he had a relationship with a woman on the side. I found some letters. The initials KA keep showing up. What's interesting about all this is that she seems to have been pregnant."

"Where'd you find that out?"

"From the letters. In the most recent letter it says that she was near the end of her pregnancy."

"When was it dated?"

"There isn't any date. But she mentions that she saw a movie on TV she liked. And if I remember correctly, it ran a few months back. Of course we'll have to check that out more exactly."

"Does she have an address?"

"It doesn't say."

"Not even whether it's in Lund?"

"No. But she's probably from somewhere in Skåne. She uses several expressions that indicate as much."

"Did you ask the widow about this?"

"That's what I wanted to talk to you about. Whether it's appropriate. Or whether I should wait."

"Ask her," said Wallander. "We can't wait. Besides, I have a strong hunch she already knows about it. We need that woman's name and address. As fast as we damn well can get it, in fact. Let me know right away when you've got something."

Afterwards Wallander sat with his hand on the telephone. A cold wave of aversion passed through him. What Martinsson had said reminded him of something.

It had to do with Svedberg. But he couldn't recall what it was.

He waited for Martinsson to call back. Hansson appeared in the doorway and said he was going to get started that evening on the investigative material from Östersund.

"There's eleven kilos of it," he said. "Just so you know."

"Did you weigh it?" Wallander asked, surprised.

"I didn't, but Jetpak did. Eleven-point-three kilos from the police station in Östersund. Want to know what it cost?"

"I'd rather not."

Hansson left. Wallander cleaned his fingernails and thought about a black Labrador sleeping next to his bed. It was twenty to eight. He still hadn't heard from Martinsson. Nyberg called and said he thought he'd call it a night.

Wallander wondered why Nyberg had let him know. So that he could be found at home? Or because he wanted to be left in peace?

Finally Martinsson called.

"She was asleep," he said. "I didn't really want to wake her. That's why it took so long."

Wallander said nothing. He knew that he wouldn't have hesitated to wake Kristina Blomberg.

"What'd she say?"

"You were right. She knew her husband had other women. This one wasn't the first. But she didn't know who she was. The initials KA didn't mean anything to her."

"Does she know where she lives?"

"She claims she doesn't. I'm inclined to believe her."

"But she must have known if he went out of town."

"I asked about that. She said no. Besides, he didn't have a car. He didn't even have a driver's license."

"That sounds like she must live in the vicinity."

"That's what I was thinking too."

"A woman with the initials KA. We have to find her. Drop everything else for the time being. Is Birch there?"

"He drove back to the station a while ago."

"Where's Svedberg?"

"He was supposed to talk to the person who apparently knew Blomberg best."

"Tell him to concentrate on finding out who the woman is with the initials KA."

"I'm not sure I can get hold of him," replied Martinsson. "He left his phone here with me."

Wallander swore.

"The widow must know who her husband's best friend was. It's important to tell Svedberg."

"I'll see what I can do."

Wallander put down the receiver, then thought better of it. But it was too late. It had suddenly come to him what he had forgotten. He looked up the phone number of the police station in Lund. He was lucky and got hold of Birch almost at once.

"I think we might have hit on something," Wallander said.

"Martinsson spoke to Ehrén, who's working with him at Siriusgatan," said Birch. "As I understand it, we're looking for an unknown woman who might have the initials KA."

"Not 'might,' they *are* her initials," said Wallander. "Karin Andersson, Katrina Alström . . . we have to find her, whatever her name is. And there's one detail I think is important."

"That she was pregnant?"

Birch was thinking fast.

"Precisely," said Wallander. "We should also contact the maternity ward in Lund. Women who have had children recently—or will soon. With the initials KA."

"I'll take care of it myself," said Birch. "This sort of thing is always a little sensitive."

Wallander said goodbye. He noticed that he had started to sweat.

Something had started moving. He went out in the hallway. It was empty. When the phone rang he gave a start. It was Höglund. She was at Runfeldt's flower shop.

"There's no blood left," she said. "Vanja Andersson scrubbed the floor herself. She thought the pool of blood was upsetting."

"What about the rag?"

"Unfortunately she threw it out. And the garbage was picked up long ago, of course."

Wallander knew that only the tiniest amount was needed to do a successful blood analysis. "Her shoes," he said. "What shoes was she wearing that day? There might be a little bit on the sole."

"I'll ask her."

Wallander waited on the phone.

"She had on a pair of clogs," said Höglund. "But they're back at her apartment."

"Go get them. Bring them here. And call Nyberg. He's at home. He can at least tell us if there's any blood on them."

During the conversation Hamrén appeared in his doorway. Wallander hadn't seen much of him since he arrived in Ystad. He also wondered what the two detectives from Malmö were working on.

"I've taken over matching the data between Eriksson and Runfeldt," said Hamrén. "Now that Martinsson's in Lund. So far there are no matches. I don't think their paths ever crossed."

"Still, it's important to do a thorough job on it," said Wallander. "Somewhere these investigations are going to merge. I'm convinced of that."

"And Blomberg?"

"He'll find a place in the pattern too. Anything else is just implausible."

"When was police work ever a matter of plausibility?" said Hamrén with a smile.

"You're right, of course. But we can hope."

Hamrén stood with his pipe in his hand.

"I'm going out for a smoke. It clears my brain."

He left. It was a little past eight. Wallander waited for Svedberg to report in. He got a cup of coffee and some cookies. The phone rang. A call that was supposed to go to the switchboard had been misrouted. At 8:30 Wallander stood in the doorway of the lunchroom and listlessly watched some TV. Beautiful pictures from the Comoro Islands. He wondered where those islands were. At quarter to nine he was back in his chair. Birch called. He reported that they had started looking for women who had given birth in recent months or would give birth the next two months. So far they hadn't found any with the initials KA. After he hung up, Wallander thought he might as well go home. They could call him on his cell phone if they wanted him. He tried to get hold of Martinsson, with no luck. Then Svedberg called. It was ten minutes past nine.

"There's nobody with the initials KA," he said. "At least not anyone known to the man who claims to have been Blomberg's best friend."

"So at least we know that," Wallander said, not hiding his disappointment.

"I'm heading home now," said Svedberg.

Wallander had hardly hung up before the phone rang again. It was Birch.

"Unfortunately," he said, "there's no one with the initials KA. And this data has to be considered reliable."

"Shit," said Wallander.

Both of them thought for a moment.

"She could have given birth somewhere else," said Birch. "It doesn't have to be in Lund."

"You're right," said Wallander. "We'll have to keep at it tomorrow." He hung up.

Now he knew what it was that had to do with Svedberg. A piece of paper that had landed on his desk by mistake. About something going on at night in the Ystad maternity ward. Had it been an attack? Something about a phony nurse?

He called Svedberg, who answered from his car.

"Where are you?" asked Wallander.

"I haven't even made it to Staffanstorp."

"Come to the station. There's something we have to check out."

"All right," said Svedberg. "I'm on my way."

It took him exactly forty-two minutes.

It was five minutes to ten when Svedberg showed up in the doorway to Wallander's office.

By that time Wallander had started to doubt his own idea.

It was all too probable that he was just imagining things.

Chapter Twenty-seven

He didn't realize what had happened until the door closed behind him. He went down the few steps to his car and got in behind the wheel. Then he said his own name out loud: Åke Davidsson.

From now on Åke Davidsson was going to be a very lonely man. He hadn't expected this to happen to him. That the woman he had been in a relationship with for so many years, even though they didn't live in the same house, would one day tell him that she wanted to call it quits. And throw him out.

He started to cry. It hurt. He didn't understand. But she had been quite firm. She told him to leave and never come back. She'd met another man who wanted to move in with her.

It was almost midnight. Monday, the 17th of October. He peered into the darkness. He knew that he shouldn't be driving after nightfall. His eyesight wasn't good enough. He could really only drive in day-light, wearing special glasses. He squinted through the windshield. With effort he could make out the contours of the road. But he couldn't stay here all night. He had to go back to Malmö.

He was upset when he started the engine and turned onto the road. He was really having a hard time seeing. Maybe it would get easier when he got to the main highway. Right now his main concern was getting out of Lödinge.

But he took a wrong turn. There were so many small side roads and they all looked alike in the dark. By 12:30 he knew he was completely lost. Just then he reached a courtyard where the road seemed to come to a dead end. He started to turn around. Suddenly he caught sight of a shadow in his headlights. Someone was coming toward the car. He felt relieved at once. There was someone out here who could tell him which way to go.

He opened the car door and got out.

Then everything went black.

It took Svedberg a quarter of an hour to find the paper Wallander wanted to see. Wallander had made himself quite clear when Svedberg went into his office just before ten.

"This might be a shot in the dark," said Wallander. "But we're looking for a woman with the initials KA who recently gave birth or will soon give birth somewhere in Skåne. We thought it was Lund, but that turned out to be wrong. Maybe it's here in Ystad instead. If I'm not mistaken, certain methods are used here that have made Ystad's maternity ward renowned even outside the country. Something strange happens there one night. And then later, a second time. So this could be a shot in the dark. But I still want to know what happened."

Svedberg found the paper with his notes. He went back to the room where Wallander was waiting impatiently.

"Ylva Brink," said Svedberg. "She's my cousin. What you'd call a distant cousin. And she's a midwife at the maternity ward. She came here to report that an unknown woman had showed up one night on her ward. It made her nervous."

"Why is that?"

"It's simply not normal for a stranger to be in the maternity ward at night."

"We need to take a good look at this," said Wallander. "When was the first time it happened?"

"The night of September 30th."

"Almost three weeks ago. And it made her nervous?"

"She came over here the following day, a Saturday. I talked with her for a while. That's when I made these notes."

"When was the second time?"

"The night of October 13th. By chance Ylva happened to be working that night too. That's when she was knocked to the ground. I was called out there in the morning."

"What happened?"

"The unknown woman showed up again. When Ylva tried to stop her, she was knocked down. Ylva said it felt like being kicked by a horse."

"She'd never seen this woman before?"

"Just that one other time."

"She was wearing a uniform?"

"Yes. But Ylva was positive she wasn't an employee."

"How could she be sure? There must be a lot of people she doesn't know who work at the hospital."

"She was positive. Unfortunately, I didn't ask her why."

Wallander thought for a moment.

"This woman had some interest in the maternity ward between September 30th and October 13th," he said. "She makes two nighttime visits and she doesn't hesitate to knock down a midwife. The question is, what was she really up to?"

"That's what Ylva wants to know too."

"She has no answer?"

"They went over the ward both times. But everything was normal."

Wallander looked at his watch. Almost quarter to eleven.

"I want you to call your cousin," he said. "Even if you have to wake her up."

Svedberg nodded. Wallander pointed at his phone. He knew that Svedberg, usually forgetful, had a good memory for phone numbers. He dialed the number. It rang and rang. No one answered.

"If she's not home, that means she's working," he said after hanging up.

Wallander quickly got to his feet.

"Even better," he said. "I haven't been back to the maternity ward since Linda was born."

"The old wing was torn down," said Svedberg. "The whole place is new."

It took them only a few minutes to drive in Svedberg's car from the police station to the emergency room of the hospital. Wallander thought of the night several years ago when he had woken up with violent pains in his chest and thought he was having a heart attack. Back then the emergency room had been in a different location. Everything at the hospital seemed to have been remodeled. They rang the bell. A guard came at once and opened the door. Wallander showed his police ID. They took the stairs to the maternity ward. The guard had called ahead to say they were on their way. A woman was waiting for them in the doorway to the ward.

"My cousin," said Svedberg. "Ylva Brink."

Wallander shook hands. He glimpsed a nurse in the background. Ylva took them to a small office.

"It's quite calm right now," she said. "But that can change at any minute."

"I'll get right to the point," said Wallander. "I know that all information is confidential regarding patients who are in the hospital. It's not my intention to challenge that rule. For now the only thing I want to know is whether between September 30th and October 13th there was a woman about to give birth here on the ward whose initials were KA. K as in Karin and A as in Andersson."

A shadow of uneasiness passed over Ylva Brink's face.

"Has something happened?"

"No," said Wallander. "I just need to identify someone. That's all."

"I can't tell you," she said. "That kind of information is confidential. Unless the woman who is giving birth has signed a release form allowing information about her presence to be given out. In my judgment that also applies to initials."

"Sooner or later someone will have to answer my question," said Wallander. "My problem is that I need to know now."

"I still can't help you."

Svedberg had been sitting in silence. Wallander saw that he was frowning.

"Is there a restroom?" he asked.

"Around the corner."

Svedberg nodded to Wallander.

"You said you needed a restroom. Better go now."

Wallander understood. He got up and left the room.

He waited in the restroom five minutes before he went back. Ylva Brink was not there. Svedberg stood leaning over several papers lying on the desk.

"What did you say?" asked Wallander.

"That she shouldn't embarrass the family," said Svedberg. "I also explained that she could spend a year in jail."

"For what?" asked Wallander in surprise.

"Obstructing the discharge of official duties."

"There isn't anything called that, is there?"

"She doesn't know that. Here are all the names. I think we'd better read fast."

They went through the list. None of the women had the initials KA. Wallander realized it was as he had feared. A dead end.

"Maybe those weren't someone's initials," said Svedberg thoughtfully. "Maybe KA means something else."

"What would that be?"

"There's a Katarina Taxell here," said Svedberg, pointing. "Maybe the letters KA are just an abbreviation of Katarina."

Wallander looked at the name. Went through the list again. There was no other name with the combination KA. No Karin, no Karolina.

"You may be right," he said doubtfully. "Write down the address."

"It's not here," he said. "Only her name. Maybe you'd better wait downstairs while I talk to Ylva one more time."

"Stick with the line that she shouldn't embarrass the family," said Wallander. "Don't mention bringing charges. That could cause us trouble later on. I want to know if Katarina Taxell is still here. I want to know if she's had any visitors. I want to know if there's anything special about her. Family relationships. But especially where she lives."

"This is going to take a while," said Svedberg. "Ylva is busy with a birth."

"I'll wait," said Wallander. "All night if I have to."

He took a biscuit from a platter and left the ward. When he reached the emergency room, an ambulance had just arrived with a drunk and bloody man. Wallander recognized him. His name was Niklasson, and he owned a junkyard outside Ystad. Normally he was sober, but occasionally he went on binges and got into fights.

Wallander nodded to the two medics, whom he knew.

"Is it bad?" asked Wallander.

"Niklasson is tough," said the older of the two. "He'll survive. They started fighting in a pub in Sandskogen."

Wallander went out to the parking lot. It was chilly. He thought that they'd also have to find out if there was any Karin or Katarina in Lund. Birch could handle that. It was 11:30. He tried the doors of Svedberg's car. They were locked. He wondered if he should go back and ask for the keys. He might have to wait a long time. But he decided against it.

He began pacing back and forth in the parking lot.

Suddenly he was back in Rome again. Ahead of him, in the distance, was his father. On his secret nightly wandering toward some unknown destination. A son tailing his own father. The Spanish Steps, then a fountain. His eyes glistened. An old man alone in Rome. Did he know he was going to die soon? That the trip to Italy had to happen now if it was ever going to happen at all?

Wallander stopped. He had a lump in his throat. When would he ever have time to work out his grief over his father? Life tossed him back and forth. He would soon be fifty. It was fall now. Night. And he was walking around behind a hospital, freezing. What he feared most was that life would become so incomprehensible that he'd no longer be able to handle it. What would be left then? Early retirement? A request for a simpler job? Would he spend fifteen years going around to schools talking about drugs and traffic accidents?

The house, he thought. And a dog. And maybe Baiba too. An outward change is necessary. I'll start with that. Later we'll see what happens with me. My work load is too heavy. I can't handle it if I have to drag around like this at the same time.

It was past midnight. He patrolled the parking lot. The ambulance had left. Everything was quiet. He knew there were a lot of things he needed to think through, but he was too tired. The only thing he could manage to do was wait. And keep moving so he wouldn't start to freeze.

At 12:30 Svedberg appeared. He was walking fast. Wallander could see that he had news.

"Katarina Taxell is from Lund," he said.

Wallander felt his excitement rise.

"Is she here?"

"She had her baby on October 15th. She's already gone home."

"Do you have the address?"

"I've got more than that. She's a single mom. And there's no father listed. And she also had no visitors while she was here."

Wallander realized that he was holding his breath. "Then it could be her," he said. "The woman Eugen Blomberg called KA."

They went back to the station. Right at the entrance Svedberg braked hard to avoid hitting a hare that had wandered into town.

They sat down in the lunchroom, which happened to be empty. A radio was playing softly somewhere. The phone rang in the room with the duty officers. Wallander had filled a cup with bitter coffee.

"She couldn't be the one who stuffed Blomberg in a sack," said Svedberg, scratching his scalp with a coffee spoon. "I have a hard time believing that a new mother would go out and kill someone."

"She's a link," said Wallander. "If what I'm thinking is true. She fits in between Blomberg and the person who seems most important right now."

"The nurse who knocked Ylva down?"

"That's the one."

Svedberg strained to follow Wallander's thoughts.

"So you think this unknown nurse shows up at Ystad's maternity ward to meet her?"

"Yes."

"But why does she come at night? Why doesn't she come during normal visiting hours? There must be certain visiting hours, aren't there? And no one writes down who visits or who has visitors, do they?"

Wallander saw that Svedberg's questions were important. He had to answer them before they could go on.

"She didn't want to be seen," he said. "That's the only conceivable explanation."

Svedberg was stubborn. "Seen by whom? Was she afraid of being recognized? Did she not want even Katarina Taxell to see her? Did she visit the hospital at night to look at a woman asleep?"

"I don't know," said Wallander. "I agree that it's strange."

"There's only one conceivable explanation," continued Svedberg. "She comes at night because she could be recognized in the daytime."

Wallander pondered this. "So you're saying that someone who works there during the day might have recognized her?"

"You can't ignore the fact that she prefers to visit the maternity ward at night, for no apparent reason. And then gets involved in a situation where it's necessary to knock down my cousin, who wasn't doing anything wrong."

"There might be an alternative explanation," said Wallander.

"What's that?"

"At night could be the only time she *can* visit the maternity ward."

Svedberg nodded thoughtfully. "That's possible, of course. But why?"

"There could be lots of reasons for it. Where she lives. Her work. Maybe she wants to make these visits in secret."

Svedberg pushed his coffee cup away. "Her visits must have been important. She went there twice."

"We can put together a timetable," said Wallander. "The first time she came was on the night of September 30th. At the hour when everyone at work is the most tired and least alert. She stays a few minutes and then disappears. Two weeks later she repeats the whole thing. The same hour. This time she's stopped by Ylva Brink, who is knocked down. The woman disappears without a trace."

"Katarina Taxell has her child several days later."

"The woman doesn't come back. On the other hand, Eugen Blomberg is murdered."

"Do you think a nurse is behind all this?"

They looked at each other without saying anything.

Wallander suddenly realized that he had forgotten to have Svedberg ask Ylva Brink about an important detail.

"Do you remember the plastic holder we found in Gösta Runfeldt's suitcase?" he asked. "The kind used by staff members at the hospital?"

Svedberg nodded. He remembered.

"Call the maternity ward," said Wallander. "Ask Ylva if she remembers whether the woman who knocked her down was wearing a name tag."

Svedberg got up to use a phone hanging on the wall. One of Ylva's colleagues answered. Svedberg waited. Wallander drank a glass of water. Then Svedberg started talking. The conversation was brief.

"She's positive she was wearing a plastic name badge," he said. "Both times."

"Could she read the name on the tag?"

"She isn't sure there was a name."

Wallander thought a moment.

"She might have lost the badge the first time," he said. "Somewhere she got hold of a hospital uniform. So she could also have gotten a new plastic holder."

"It'd be impossible to find any fingerprints at the hospital," said Svedberg. "It's always being cleaned. Besides, we don't even know if she touched anything."

"She wasn't wearing gloves, at least," said Wallander. "Ylva would have noticed that."

Svedberg tapped his forehead with the coffee spoon.

"Maybe so," he said. "If I understood Ylva correctly, the woman grabbed hold of her when she knocked her down."

"She only grabbed her clothes," said Wallander. "And we won't find anything on them."

For a moment he felt discouraged.

"We should still talk to Nyberg," he said. "Maybe she touched the bed that Katarina Taxell was lying in. We have to try. If we can find fingerprints that match with what we found in Runfeldt's suitcase, the investigation would take a big leap forward. Then we could start looking for the same fingerprints on Holger Eriksson and Eugen Blomberg."

Svedberg pushed across the piece of paper on which he had written Katarina Taxell's address. Wallander saw that she was thirty-three years old and self-employed, although it didn't say what she did. She lived in central Lund.

"Early tomorrow morning, at seven o'clock, we'll go there," he said. "Since the two of us have been working on it tonight, we might as well continue. Now I think it'd be smart for us to get a few hours sleep."

"It's strange," said Svedberg. "First we're looking for a mercenary soldier. And now we're looking for a nurse."

"Who presumably isn't a real one," Wallander interjected.

"We don't know that for sure," Svedberg pointed out. "Just because Ylva didn't recognize her doesn't mean she's not a nurse."

"You're right. We can't exclude that possibility." He got up.

"I'll drive you home," said Svedberg. "How's it going with your car?"

"I really should get a new one. But I don't know how I'm going to afford it."

One of the duty officers rushed into the room.

"I knew you were here," he said. "I think something has happened."

Wallander felt the knot in his stomach. Not again, he thought.

"There's a badly injured man lying on the shoulder of the road between Sövestad and Lödinge. A truck driver found him. We don't know whether he was run over or attacked. An ambulance is on the way out there. I thought that since it was close to Lödinge . . ."

He never finished his sentence. Svedberg and Wallander were already on their way out of the room.

They arrived just as the medics were lifting the injured man onto a stretcher. Wallander recognized the medics as the same ones he had met earlier outside the hospital.

"Ships passing in the night," said the ambulance driver.

"Was it a car accident?"

"If so, it was a hit-and-run. But it looks more like an assault of some kind."

Wallander looked around. The stretch of road was deserted.

"Who would be walking around here in the middle of the night?" he asked.

The man's face was badly injured. He wheezed faintly.

"We're going now," said the ambulance driver. "I think we've got to hurry. He might have internal injuries."

The ambulance left. They searched the site in the headlight beams of Svedberg's car. A few minutes later a night-patrol car arrived from Ystad. Svedberg and Wallander hadn't found anything. Not even any skid marks. Svedberg told the newly arrived officers what had happened. Then he and Wallander returned to Ystad. It was getting windy. Svedberg could read the outdoor temperature from inside his car. 3° Celsius.

"This is probably not related," said Wallander. "If you drop me off at the hospital, you can go home and get some sleep. At least one of us should be awake in the morning."

"Where should I pick you up?" asked Svedberg.

"At Mariagatan. Let's say six o'clock. Martinsson gets up early. Call him and tell him what happened. Ask him to talk to Nyberg about the plastic holder. Tell him we're going to Lund."

For the second time that night Wallander found himself outside the hospital's emergency entrance. When he arrived, the injured man was being treated. Wallander sat down and waited. He was tired. He couldn't stop himself from falling asleep. He woke up abruptly when someone said his name, and at first he didn't know where he was. He'd been dreaming about Rome. He was walking along dark streets and searching for his father, but he couldn't find him.

A doctor was standing in front of him. Wallander was instantly wide awake.

"He's going to make it," said the doctor. "But he was severely beaten."

"So it wasn't a car accident?"

"No. An assault. As far as we can tell, he didn't suffer any internal injuries."

"Did he have any papers on him?"

The doctor gave him an envelope. Wallander took out a wallet, which contained a driver's license, among other things. The man's name was Åke Davidsson. Wallander noticed that he was supposed to wear glasses to drive.

"Can I talk to him?"

"I think it'd be better to wait with that."

Wallander decided to ask Hansson or Höglund to follow up on it. If this was an assault case, they'd have to leave it in someone else's hands for the time being. They just didn't have time for it.

Wallander got up to leave.

"We found something in his clothing that I think might interest you," said the doctor.

He handed him a piece of paper. Wallander read the scrawled message: "A burglar neutralized by the night guards."

"What night guards?" he asked.

"It was in the papers," said the doctor. "About the citizen militia being formed. Isn't it possible they would call themselves the night guards?"

Wallander stared at the message in disbelief.

"There's something else that points to it," the doctor went on. "The paper was attached to his body. It was stapled on."

Wallander shook his head.

"This is fucking incredible," he said.

"Yes," said the doctor. "It's incredible that it's gone this far."

Wallander never liked to call a cab. He walked home through the empty town. He thought about Katarina Taxell. And Åke Davidsson, who had a message stapled to his body.

When he went into his apartment on Mariagatan, he took off only his shoes and his jacket and then stretched out on the sofa with a blanket over him. The alarm clock was set. But he still couldn't sleep. And he was starting to get a headache. He went out to the kitchen and took some aspirin. The streetlight swayed in the wind outside his window. Then he lay down again. He dozed uneasily until the clock rang. When he sat up on the sofa he felt more tired than he did lying down. He went out to the bathroom and washed his face with cold water. He changed his shirt. While he waited for the coffee to brew, he called Hansson at home. It took a long time before he answered. Wallander knew that he had woken him up.

"I'm not done with the Östersund papers," said Hansson. "I was up until two. I have about four kilos left."

"We'll talk about that later," Wallander interrupted him. "I just want you to go over to the hospital and talk to a man named Åke Davidsson. He was assaulted somewhere near Lödinge last night. By people who probably belong to some citizen militia. I want you to handle it."

"What should I do about the Östersund papers?"

"I'll let you deal with those at the same time. Svedberg and I are going to Lund. I'll tell you more later." He hung up before Hansson could ask any questions.

He didn't have the energy to answer.

At six o'clock Svedberg parked outside his door. Wallander was standing at the kitchen window with his coffee cup and saw him arrive.

"I talked to Martinsson," said Svedberg when Wallander got into the
car. "He was going to ask Nyberg to start working on the plastic
holder."

"Did Martinsson understand what we came up with?"

"I think so."

"Then let's go."

Wallander leaned back and closed his eyes. The best thing he could
do on the way to Lund was sleep.

Katarina Taxell lived in an apartment building on a square that Wallander wasn't familiar with.

"It might be best if we call Birch," said Wallander. "So there won't be
any trouble later on."

Svedberg got hold of him at home. He handed the phone to Wallander, who quickly explained what was going on. Birch said he'd be
there within twenty minutes. They sat in the car and waited. The sky
was gray. It wasn't raining, but the wind had picked up. Birch parked
his car behind them. Wallander explained in detail what had developed from their conversation with Ylva Brink. Birch listened attentively. Wallander could see that he was doubtful.

Then they went inside. Katarina Taxell lived on the third floor, in
the apartment on the left.

"I'll stay in the background," said Birch. "You can direct the conversation."

Svedberg rang the bell. The door opened almost at once. A woman
wearing a bathrobe stood in front of them. She had dark circles under
her eyes from fatigue. She reminded Wallander of Ann-Britt.

He said hello and tried to sound as friendly as possible. But when he
said he was a police officer from Ystad he saw that she reacted. They
went into the apartment, which gave the impression of being small and
cramped. Everywhere were signs that she had just had a baby. Wallander remembered how his own home had looked when Linda was a
newborn. They went into a living room with light-colored wooden
furniture. On the table lay a brochure that caught Wallander's attention. "Taxell's hair products." It gave him a feasible explanation for
what kind of work she did.

"I apologize for coming so early," he said as they sat down. "But this
can't wait."

He was in doubt about how to continue. She sat across from him
and didn't take her eyes off his face.

"You've just had a child at Ystad's maternity ward," he said.

"A boy," she replied. "He was born on the 15th. At three in the afternoon."

"Let me offer my congratulations," said Wallander. Svedberg and Birch murmured the same.

"About two weeks before that," Wallander went on, "or to be precise, on the night of September 30th, I wonder if you had a visitor, expected or not, sometime after midnight?"

She gave him a look of incomprehension. "Who would that be?"

"A nurse who you might not have seen before?"

"I knew all of the nurses who worked at night."

"This woman came back two weeks later," he continued. "And we think she was there to visit you."

"At night?"

"Yes. Sometime after 2 A.M."

"No one visited me. And besides, I was asleep."

Wallander nodded slowly. Birch was standing behind the sofa, Svedberg was sitting on a chair against the wall. All of a sudden it was quiet.

They were waiting for Wallander to go on.

And he planned to do so in a moment. But first he wanted to collect himself. He was still tired. He really should ask her why she was in the maternity ward for so long. Were there complications with her pregnancy? But he didn't ask. Something else was more important.

It hadn't escaped his notice that she wasn't telling the truth.

He was convinced that she had had a visitor. And that she knew who the woman was.

Chapter Twenty-eight

A child suddenly started crying.

Katarina Taxell got up and left the room. At the same moment Wallander decided how he was going to proceed with the interview. He was convinced she wasn't telling the truth. From the beginning he had noticed something hesitant and evasive about her. All his years as a cop had taught him how to distinguish when someone was lying. He stood up and went over to the window where Birch was standing. Svedberg followed. They huddled together, and Wallander spoke in a low voice. The whole time he kept an eye on the doorway.

"She's not telling the truth," he said.

The others didn't seem to have noticed anything. Or weren't as convinced as he was. But they made no objections.

"This may take some time," Wallander went on. "But since in my opinion she's crucial for us, I'm not going to give up. She knows who that woman is. And I'm more convinced than ever that she's important."

Birch suddenly seemed to understand the connection.

"You mean there might be a woman behind all this? The perpetrator is a woman?"

He sounded almost frightened by his own words.

"She doesn't necessarily have to be the killer," said Wallander. "But there is a woman somewhere near the center of this investigation. I'm convinced of that. If nothing else, she's blocking our view of what's behind all this. That's why we have to get to her as soon as possible. We have to find out who she is."

The child stopped crying. Svedberg and Wallander returned quickly to their places in the room. A minute went by. Katarina Taxell came back and sat down on the couch. Wallander noticed that she was very much on her guard.

"Let's return to the maternity ward in Ystad," said Wallander in a friendly voice. "You say you were asleep. And nobody visited you there at night?"

"No."

"You live here in Lund. Yet you choose to give birth in Ystad. Why?"

"I prefer the methods they practice there."

"I know about that," said Wallander. "My own daughter was born in Ystad."

She didn't react. Wallander understood that she just wanted to answer the questions. Other than that she was not going to say anything voluntarily.

"Now I have to ask you some questions of a personal nature," he went on. "Since this is not an interrogation, you can choose not to answer. But then I must warn you that we may have to take you down to the police station and arrange a formal interrogation. We came here because we're looking for information connected with several extremely brutal crimes of violence."

She still didn't react. Her gaze was fixed on his face. It felt like she was staring straight into his head. Something about her eyes made him nervous.

"Did you understand what I said?"

"I understand. I'm not stupid."

"Do you agree that I can ask you some questions of a personal nature?"

"I don't know until I hear them."

"It seems that you live alone in this apartment. You're not married?"

"No."

The reply came quickly and firmly. Hard, thought Wallander. As if she was hitting something.

"May I ask who the father of your child is?"

"I don't think I'll answer that. It's of no concern to anyone but myself. And the child."

"If the child's father has been the victim of a violent crime, I would say it has something to do with the matter."

"That would mean that you knew who the father of my child is. But you don't. So the question is unreasonable."

Wallander saw that she was right. There was nothing wrong with her mind.

"Let me ask another question. Do you know a man named Eugen Blomberg?"

"Yes."

"In what way do you know him?"

"I know him."

"Do you know that he was murdered?"

"Yes."

"How do you know that?"

"I saw it in the paper this morning."

"Is he the father of your child?"

"No."

She's a good liar, thought Wallander. But not convincing enough.

"Isn't it true that you and Eugen Blomberg had a relationship?"

"That's correct."

"And yet he isn't the father of your child?"

"No."

"How long did you have this relationship?"

"For two and a half years."

"It must have been kept secret, since he was married."

"He lied to me. I didn't find out about that until much later."

"What happened then?"

"I ended it."

"When did that happen?"

"About a year ago."

"After that you never met again?"

"That's right."

Wallander seized the moment and went on the attack.

"We've found letters at his house that you wrote to each other as recently as a few months ago."

She wouldn't budge. "We wrote letters. But we never met."

"The whole thing seems rather strange."

"He wrote letters. I answered them. He wanted us to meet again. I didn't."

"Because you had met another man?"

"Because I was pregnant."

"And you won't tell us the father's name?"

"No."

Wallander cast a glance at Svedberg, who was staring at the floor. Birch was looking out the window. Wallander knew they were both on tenterhooks.

"Who do you think might have killed Eugen Blomberg?"

Wallander sent off the question at full force. Birch moved at the window. The floor creaked under his weight. Svedberg switched to staring at his hands.

"I don't know who would have wanted to kill him."

The child started fussing again. She got up quickly and left again. Wallander looked at the others. Birch shook his head. Wallander tried to evaluate the situation. It would create big trouble to take a woman in for interrogation who had a three-day-old baby. Besides, she wasn't suspected of any crime. He made a quick decision. They huddled by the window once again.

"I'll break off here," said Wallander. "But I want surveillance on her. And I want to know everything you can possibly dig up on her. She seems to have a business that sells hair-care products. I want to know all about her parents, her friends, what she did earlier in her life. Run her through all the records you've got. I want her completely mapped."

"We'll take care of it," said Birch.

"Svedberg will stay here in Lund. We need someone who's familiar with the earlier homicides."

"Actually, I'd prefer to go home," said Svedberg. "You know I don't do well outside Ystad."

"I know," said Wallander. "Right now that can't be helped. I'll ask someone to relieve you when I get back to Ystad. But we can't have people driving back and forth unnecessarily."

Suddenly she was standing in the doorway. She was carrying the baby. Wallander smiled. They went over and looked at the boy. Svedberg, who liked kids even though he didn't have any of his own, started prattling with the baby.

All of a sudden Wallander felt that something was odd. He thought back to when Linda was a baby. When Mona had carried her around. When he had done it himself, always afraid of dropping her.

Then it came to him what it was. She wasn't holding the baby pressed against her body. It was as if the baby was something that didn't really belong to her.

He was getting angry, but he didn't show it.

"We won't bother you any longer," he said. "But we'll be in touch with you again, no doubt."

"I hope you catch the person who murdered Eugen," she said.

Wallander looked at her. Then he nodded.

"Yes, we're going to solve this. I can promise you that."

When the three men reached the street, the wind had picked up some more.

"What do you think of her?" asked Birch.

"She's not telling the truth, of course," said Wallander. "But it didn't seem like she was lying, either."

Birch gave him a quizzical look.

"How am I supposed to take that? As though she were lying and speaking the truth at the same time?"

"Something like that. What it means I don't know."

"I noticed a little detail," said Svedberg suddenly. "She said 'the person,' not 'the man.'"

Wallander nodded. He had noticed it too. She said she hoped they would catch "the person" who murdered Eugen Blomberg.

"Does that necessarily mean anything?" Birch asked skeptically.

"No," said Wallander. "But both Svedberg and I noticed it. And that might mean something in itself."

They decided that Wallander would drive back to Ystad in Svedberg's car. He promised to send someone to relieve Svedberg in Lund as soon as possible.

"This is important," he told Birch once again. "Katarina Taxell had a visit in the hospital from this woman. We have to find out who she is. The midwife she knocked down gave a good description."

"Give it to me," said Birch. "She might show up visiting her at home too."

"She was quite tall," said Wallander. "Ylva Brink herself is five-nine. She thought this woman was about five-eleven. Dark, straight, shoulder-length hair. Blue eyes, pointed nose, thin lips. She was stocky without looking fat. No prominent bust. The power of her blow shows she's strong. And we can probably assume she's in good physical shape."

"That description fits quite a few people," said Birch.

"All descriptions do," said Wallander. "Still, you know right away when you find the right person."

"Did the woman say anything? What was her voice like?"

"She didn't say a word. She just knocked her to the ground."

"Did she notice the woman's teeth?"

Wallander looked at Svedberg, who shook his head.

"Was she wearing makeup?"

"Nothing out of the ordinary."

"What did her hands look like? Was she wearing press-on nails?"

"We know for certain that she wasn't. Ylva said she would have noticed."

Birch had made some notes. He nodded.

"We'll see what we can come up with," he said. "We'll do the stakeout here very discreetly. She's going to be on her guard."

They said goodbye. Svedberg gave Wallander his car keys. On the way to Ystad Wallander tried to understand why Katarina Taxell didn't want to reveal that she had had nighttime visits twice in the time she was in the Ystad maternity ward. Who was the woman? How was she connected with Katarina Taxell and Eugen Blomberg? Where did the threads lead from there? What did the chain of events look like that led to the murder?

He was also worried that he might be on a completely wrong track, leading the investigation way off course.

Nothing caused him more torment. Ripped the sleep right out of him, gave him an upset stomach. The fact that he could be heading full-speed toward the collapse of a criminal investigation. He'd been through it all before, when investigations suddenly splintered beyond recognition. Nothing remained but to start all over from the beginning. And it would be his fault.

It was 9:30 when he parked outside the Ystad police station. Ebba stopped him in the lobby.

"It's total chaos here," she said.

"What happened?"

"Chief Holgersson wants to talk to you right away. It's about that man you and Svedberg found on the road last night."

"I'll go talk to her," said Wallander.

"Do it now," said Ebba.

He went straight to her office. The door was open. Hansson was sitting inside, looking pale. Lisa Holgersson was more upset than he had ever seen her before. She motioned him to a chair.

"I think you should hear what Hansson has to say."

Wallander took off his jacket and sat down.

"Åke Davidsson," said Hansson. "I had a long conversation with him this morning."

"How's he doing?" asked Wallander.

"It looks worse than it really is. It's still bad, but nowhere near as bad as the story he had to tell."

Afterwards he thought Hansson hadn't been exaggerating. Wallander listened first in surprise, then with growing indignation. Hansson was clear and to the point. The story still overflowed its banks. Wallander could hardly believe what he was hearing; it was something he never thought could happen. Now it *had* happened, and they'd have to live with it. Sweden was steadily changing. Usually the processes were subtle, nothing really noticeable at the time. But sometimes Wallander felt a shudder pass through the entire body of society. At least when he observed and experienced these changes as a cop.

Hansson's story about Åke Davidsson was one of these shudders, and it shook Wallander's equilibrium badly.

Åke Davidsson was a civil servant in the social-welfare office in Malmö. He was classified as partially disabled because of poor eyesight. After struggling for many years he had finally got a driver's license, with conditions that restricted its validity. Since the late 1970s, Davidsson had had a relationship with a woman in Lödinge. It had ended last night. Usually Davidsson would sleep over in Lödinge, since he wasn't allowed to drive in the dark. This time he had to try. He took a wrong turn and finally stopped to ask directions. That's when he was attacked by a night patrol consisting of volunteer guards who had organized in Lödinge. They had called him a burglar and refused to believe his explanations. His glasses vanished; maybe they were crushed. He was beaten senseless and didn't wake up until the ambulance men lifted him onto the stretcher.

That was Hansson's story about Åke Davidsson. But there was more.

"Davidsson is a peaceful man who suffers from high blood pressure in addition to his poor eyesight. I spoke with some of his colleagues in Malmö, and they were deeply distressed. One of them told me something that Davidsson himself never mentioned. Maybe because he's a modest man."

Wallander was listening.

"Davidsson is a dedicated and active member of Amnesty International," said Hansson. "The question is whether that organization ought to begin taking an interest in Sweden, starting now. If this rise of brutal night guards and the citizen militia isn't stopped."

Wallander was speechless. He felt sick and dizzy.

"These thugs have a leader," Hansson went on. "His name is Eskil Bengtsson, and he owns a trucking company in Lödinge."

"We've got to put a stop to this," said Chief Holgersson. "Even though we're up to our necks in homicide investigations. At least we have to plan what to do."

"It's quite simple," said Wallander, getting to his feet. "We just drive out and arrest Eskil Bengtsson. And we also bring in everyone who's mixed up in this citizen militia. Åke Davidsson will have to identify them, one by one."

"But his eyesight is terrible," said Chief Holgersson.

"People who don't see well often have excellent hearing," replied Wallander. "If I understand correctly, the men were talking while they were beating him."

"I wonder if this will hold up," she said doubtfully. "What kind of proof have we got?"

"It holds up for me," said Wallander. "Of course you can always order me not to leave the station."

She shook her head. "Go ahead. The sooner the better."

Wallander nodded to Hansson. They stopped out in the corridor.

"I want two patrol cars," said Wallander, poking Hansson on the shoulder with his finger for emphasis. "They should drive there with blue lights flashing and sirens going. Both when we leave Ystad and when we enter Lödinge. It wouldn't hurt to tip off the press about this either."

"We can't do that," said Hansson, worried.

"Of course we can't," said Wallander. "We're leaving in ten minutes. We can talk about your Östersund work in the car."

"I've got a kilo of papers left," said Hansson. "It's an incredible amount of research. Layer after layer. There's even a son who took over from his father as investigator."

"In the car," Wallander interrupted him. "Not here."

After Hansson left, Wallander went out to the lobby. He said something to Ebba in a low voice. She nodded and promised to do what he said.

Five minutes later they were on their way. They left Ystad with the blue lights flashing and sirens on.

"What are we going to arrest Bengtsson for?" asked Hansson.

"He's suspected of aggravated assault," replied Wallander. "Instigating violence. Davidsson must have been transported to the road, so we'll try kidnapping too. Inciting to riot."

"You're going to have Per Åkeson on your back for this."

"I'm not so sure about that," said Wallander.

"It feels like we're on our way to arrest some pretty dangerous men," said Hansson.

"You're right. We're after some dangerous people. Right now I have a hard time thinking of anything that would be more dangerous for the rule of law in this country."

They pulled up at Eskil Bengtsson's farmhouse, which lay on the road into the village. There were two trucks and a backhoe near the house. An angry dog was barking in a pen.

"Let's go get him," said Wallander.

Just as they reached the front door it was opened by a stocky man with a pot belly. Wallander glanced at Hansson, who nodded.

"Inspector Wallander of the Ystad Police," he introduced himself. "Get your jacket. You're coming with us."

"Where the hell to?"

The man's arrogance almost made Wallander lose control. Hansson noticed this and poked him in the arm.

"You're going to Ystad," said Wallander with icy calm. "And you know damn well why."

"I haven't done anything," said Bengtsson.

"Yes, you have," said Wallander. "In fact, you've done way too much. If you don't get your jacket you'll have to come along without it."

A small, thin woman appeared at the man's side.

"What's going on?" she yelled in a high-pitched, piercing voice. "What'd he do?"

"You keep out of this," said the man, shoving her back in the house.

"That does it, cuff him," said Wallander.

Hansson stared at him uncomprehendingly.

"Why?"

Wallander's patience was all used up. He turned to one of the patrol officers and took his pair of handcuffs. He told Bengtsson to stick out his hands, and snapped the cuffs on him. It happened so fast that Bengtsson didn't think to resist. At the same time there was a flash from a camera. A photographer who had just hopped out of his car had taken a picture.

"How the hell does the press know we're here?" asked Hansson.

"No idea," said Wallander. Ebba was reliable and fast. "Let's go."

The woman who had been shoved back into the house came outside again. Suddenly she jumped on Hansson and started hitting him with her fists. The photographer took more pictures. Wallander escorted Eskil Bengtsson to the car.

"You're going to catch some real shit for this," said Bengtsson.

Wallander smiled. "Maybe. But nothing compared to what you're going to get. You want to start with the names right now? The men who were with you last night?"

Bengtsson didn't say a word. Wallander pushed him hard into the back seat. Hansson had finally managed to get the furious woman off him.

"Goddamn it, she's the one who should be in the dog pen." He was so worked up he was shaking. She had scratched him deeply on one cheek.

"We're leaving now," said Wallander. "Get in the other car and drive over to the hospital. I want to know if Åke Davidsson heard any names. Or whether he saw anyone who could have been Eskil Bengtsson."

Hansson nodded and left. The photographer came over to Wallander.

"We got an anonymous tip," he said. "What's going on?"

"A number of individuals from around here attacked and severely beat an innocent man last night. They seem to be organized in some sort of citizen militia. The man was guilty of nothing but taking a wrong turn. They claimed he was a burlgar. They almost beat him to death."

"And the man in the car?"

"He's suspected of having participated," said Wallander. "We also know that he's one of the instigators of this crime. We're not going to have any citizen militia in Sweden. Here in Skåne or anywhere else in the country."

The photographer wanted to ask another question. Wallander raised his hand to stop him.

"There'll be a press conference. We're leaving now."

Wallander shouted that he wanted sirens on the way back too. Several cars full of curiosity-seekers had stopped outside the driveway of the farmhouse. Wallander squeezed into the back seat next to Eskil Bengtsson.

"Shall we start with the names?" he asked. "It'll save a lot of time. Both yours and mine."

Bengtsson didn't answer. Wallander could smell the strong odor of his sweat.

It took Wallander three hours to get Eskil Bengtsson to admit that he had taken part in the assault on Åke Davidsson. Then it went very quickly. Bengtsson told him the names of the other three men with him. Wallander ordered them all brought in at once. Åke Davidsson's car, which had been put in an abandoned shed in a field, had already been brought to the station. Just after three in the afternoon Wallander convinced Per Åkeson to keep the four men in custody. He went straight from his talk with Åkeson to the room where several reporters were waiting. Chief Holgersson had already informed them of the events of the previous night. This time Wallander was actually looking forward to meeting the press. Although he knew that the chief had already given them the background, he recounted the sequence of events for them.

"Four men have just been indicted by the prosecutor," he went on. "We have absolutely no doubt that they are guilty of assault. But what's even more serious is that there are another five or six men involved in the group, a private guard unit out in Lödinge. These are individuals who have decided to put themselves above the law. We can see what that leads to in this case, when an innocent man, with poor eyesight and high blood pressure, is almost murdered when he takes a wrong turn. The question is: Is this the way we want it to be? That you might be risking your life if you make a right or left turn? Is that how things stand? That from now on we're all thieves, rapists, and killers in one another's eyes? I can't make it any plainer. Some of the people who are lured into joining these illegal and dangerous vigilante militias probably don't understand what they're getting into. They can be excused if they resign immediately. But those who joined and were fully conscious of what they were doing, they are indefensible. These four men that we arrested today unfortunately belong to the latter group. We can only hope they receive sentences that will serve as deterrents to others."

Wallander put force into his words. The reporters immediately pounced on him with questions. There were few in attendance, and they only wanted some of the details clarified. Höglund and Hansson were standing at the back of the room. Wallander searched through the group of journalists for the man from the *Observer*, but he wasn't there.

After less than half an hour the press conference was over.

"You handled it extremely well," said Chief Holgersson.

"There was only one way to handle it," replied Wallander.

Höglund and Hansson applauded when he came over to them. Wallander was not amused. He was hungry, and he needed some air. He looked at the clock.

"Give me an hour. Let's meet at five o'clock. Is Svedberg back yet?"

"He's on his way."

"Who's relieving him?"

"Augustsson."

"Who's that?" Wallander wondered.

"One of the Malmö cops."

Wallander had forgotten his name. He nodded.

"Five o'clock," he repeated. "We've got a lot to do."

He stopped in the lobby and thanked Ebba for her help. She smiled.

Wallander walked downtown. It was windy. He sat down in the café by the bus station and had a couple of open-faced sandwiches. The worst of his hunger passed. His head was empty. He leafed back and forth through a tattered magazine. On his way back to the police station he stopped and bought a hamburger. He tossed the napkin in the trash can and started thinking about Katarina Taxell again. Eskil Bengtsson no longer existed for him. He knew they'd have another confrontation with the local citizen militia. What had happened to Åke Davidsson was only the beginning.

At ten past five they were gathered in the conference room. Wallander started by doing a run-through of everything they knew about Katarina Taxell. Instantly he noticed that everyone in the room was listening with great attention. For the first time during the present investigation he felt they were getting close to something that might be a breakthrough. This was reinforced by what Hansson had to say.

"The amount of investigative material on Krista Haberman is huge," he said. "I haven't had much time, and it's possible I may have missed something important. But I did find one thing that might be of interest."

He paged through his notes until he found the right place.

"Sometime in the mid-sixties Krista Haberman visited Skåne on three occasions. She had made contact with a birdwatcher who lived in Falsterbo. Many years later, after she was long gone, a police officer named Fredrik Nilsson traveled all the way from Östersund to talk to this man in Falsterbo. He even wrote down that he took the train the whole way. The man in Falsterbo is named Tandvall. Erik Gustav Tandvall. He states without hesitation that he did receive visits from Krista Haberman. He never says anything overt, but it seems they had a relationship. Detective Nilsson from Östersund can't find anything suspicious in all this. The relationship between Haberman and Tandvall ended long before she vanished without a trace. Tandvall certainly had nothing to do with her disappearance. So he is removed from the investigation and never shows up again."

Up to this point Hansson had been reading from his notes. Now he looked up at everyone listening around the table.

"There was something familiar about the name," he said. "Tandvall. An unusual name. I got the feeling I'd seen it before. It took me a while before I remembered where. It was in a list of men who had worked as car salesmen for Holger Eriksson."

You could have heard a pin drop in the room. The tension was high. Everyone realized that Hansson had discovered an important connection.

"The car salesman's name wasn't Erik Tandvall," he went on. "His first name was Göte, Göte Tandvall. And right before this meeting I got a confirmation that he's Erik Tandvall's son. I should probably also mention that Erik Tandvall died several years ago. I haven't been able to locate the son yet."

Hansson was done. No one said anything for a long time.

"In other words, that means there's a possibility that Holger Eriksson met Krista Haberman," Wallander said slowly. "A woman who then disappears without a trace. A woman from Svenstavik. Where there is a church that receives a donation in accordance with a stipulation in Eriksson's will."

It was silent in the room once again.

Everyone knew what it meant.

A connection was finally beginning to emerge.

Chapter Twenty-nine

Just before midnight Wallander saw that they were too tired to do any more. The meeting had been going on since five o'clock, and they had only taken short breaks to air out the conference room.

Hansson had given them the opening they needed. They had established a connection. The contours were beginning to take shape of a person who moved like a shadow among the three men who had been killed. Even though they were still cautious about stating a definite motive, they now had a strong feeling that they were skirting the edges of a number of events connected by revenge.

Wallander had called them together to make a unified advance through difficult terrain. Hansson had given them a direction. But they still had no map to follow.

There was also a feeling of doubt among the investigative team. Could this really be right? That a mysterious disappearance so many years ago, revealed through kilos of investigative materials from deceased police officers in Jämtland, might help them unmask a perpetrator who had done such things as setting up sharpened bamboo stakes in a ditch in Skåne?

It was when the door opened and Nyberg came in several minutes after six o'clock that all doubt was dispelled. Nyberg didn't even bother to take his usual place at the far end of the table. For a change he showed signs of excitement, something no one could remember ever having seen before.

"There was a cigarette butt on the pier," he said. "We were able to identify a fingerprint on it."

Wallander gave him a surprised look.

"Is that really possible? Fingerprints on a cigarette butt?"

"We were lucky," said Nyberg. "You're right that usually it's not possible. But there's one exception: if the cigarette is rolled by hand. And this one was."

Silence fell over the room. First Hansson had discovered a plausible and even likely link between a long-vanished Polish woman and Holger Eriksson. And now Nyberg said that a fingerprint had showed up both on Runfeldt's suitcase and at the site where Blomberg was found in a sack.

It almost felt like too much to handle in such a short time. A homicide investigation that had been dragging along, with hardly even any direction, was now starting to pick up speed in earnest.

After presenting his news, Nyberg sat down.

"A perpetrator who smokes," said Martinsson. "That'll be easier to find today than it was twenty years ago. Considering how few people smoke these days."

Wallander nodded thoughtfully.

"We need to find other points of intersection between these murders," he said. "With three people dead, we need at least nine combinations. Fingerprints, times, anything that can prove there's a common denominator."

He looked around the room.

"We need to put together a proper timetable," he said. "We know that the person or persons behind all of this act with gruesome cruelty. We've discovered a deliberate element in the way the victims have been killed. But we haven't succeeded in reading the killer's language, the code we discussed earlier. We have a vague feeling that the murderer is talking to us. But what is he or she trying to tell us? We don't know. The question is whether there are any more patterns to the whole thing that we haven't found yet."

"You mean something like whether the perpetrator strikes when there's a full moon?" asked Svedberg.

"Exactly. The symbolic full moon. What does it look like in this case? Does it exist? I'd like someone to put together a timetable. Is there anything there that might give us another lead?"

Martinsson promised to put together what information they had. Wallander had heard that, on his own initiative, Martinsson had obtained several computer programs developed by the FBI headquarters in Washington, D.C. He assumed that Martinsson now saw an opportunity to make use of them.

Then they started talking about whether there actually was a center. Höglund put a section of a topographic map in a slide projector. Wallander stationed himself at the edge of the slide image.

"It starts in Lödinge," he said, pointing. "A person comes from somewhere and begins surveillance of Holger Eriksson's farm. We can assume that he travels by car and that he uses the tractor path on the other side of the hill where Eriksson had his bird tower. A year earlier someone, maybe the same person, broke into his house, without stealing anything. Possibly to warn him, leave him a sign. We don't know. It doesn't have to be the same person."

Wallander pointed at Ystad.

"Gösta Runfeldt is looking forward to his trip to Nairobi, where he's going to study rare orchids. Everything is ready. His suitcase is packed, money exchanged, the tickets picked up. He has even ordered a cab for early morning on the day of his departure. But he never takes the trip. He disappears without a trace for three weeks before he turns up."

Wallander moves his finger again. "Now to Marsvinsholm Woods, west of town. A night-training orienteer finds him. Tied to a tree, strangled. Emaciated. He must have been held captive in some way during the time he was missing. So far we have two murders at two different places, with Ystad as a kind of midpoint."

His finger moved northeast.

"We find a suitcase along the road to Höör. Not far from a point where you can turn off toward Holger Eriksson's farm. The suitcase is lying in plain view at the side of the road. We think at once that it was placed there so it would be found. We can justifiably ask ourselves the question: Why that particular spot? Because the road is convenient for the perpetrator? We don't know. The question may be more important than we've realized up until now."

Wallander moved his hand again. To the southwest, to Krageholm Lake.

"Here we find Eugen Blomberg. This means we have a defined area that isn't particularly large. Thirty or forty kilometers between the outer points. Between the different sites it's no more than half an hour by car."

He sat down.

"Let's draw up some tentative and preliminary conclusions," he went on. "What does this indicate?"

"Familiarity with the local area," said Höglund. "The site in Marsvinsholm Woods was well chosen. The suitcase was placed at a spot where there are no houses from which you could see a driver stop and leave something behind."

"How do you know that?" asked Martinsson.

"Because I've personally checked it out."

Martinsson said nothing more.

"You can either be familiar with an area yourself, or you can find out about it from someone else," continued Wallander. "Which one seems likely in this case?"

They couldn't agree. Hansson thought a stranger could easily come up with the sites under discussion. Svedberg thought the opposite. The

choice of the site where they had found Runfeldt undoubtedly indicated that the perpetrator was extremely familiar with the area.

Wallander had his doubts. Earlier he had vaguely imagined a person
who was an outsider. Now he was no longer so sure.

They didn't come to any agreement. Both were possible and would
have to be considered. They couldn't find an obvious center, either.
Using rulers and compasses they ended up somewhere in the vicinity
of the place where Runfeldt's suitcase was found. But that didn't get
them any farther.

During the evening they kept returning to the suitcase. Why had it
been put there, next to the road? And why had it been repacked by
someone who was probably a woman? They also couldn't come up with
a reasonable explanation for why the underwear was missing. Hansson
had suggested that Runfeldt might be the type of person who never
wore any. No one took that seriously, of course. There had to be some
other explanation.

When it was nine o'clock they took a break to get some air. Martinsson disappeared into his office to call home, Svedberg put on his
jacket to take a short walk. Wallander went to the bathroom and
washed his face. He looked at himself in the mirror. Suddenly he had
a feeling that his appearance had changed since his father had passed
away. What the difference was, he couldn't tell. He shook his head at
himself in the mirror. Soon he would have to make time to think about
what had happened. His father had already been dead for several
weeks. He still hadn't fully grasped what had happened. It gave him a
guilty conscience in some vague way. He also thought about Baiba, the
woman he cared so much about but never called.

He often doubted that a cop could combine his job with anything
else. Which of course wasn't true at all. Martinsson had an excellent
relationship with his family. Höglund more or less had total responsibility for her two children. It was Wallander the man who couldn't
handle the combination, not the police officer.

He yawned at himself in the mirror. From the hallway he could hear
that they had started to reconvene. He decided that now they would
have to start talking about the woman who could be glimpsed in the
background. They had to try picturing her and what role she had
actually played.

That was the first thing he said when they closed the door.

"There's a woman somewhere in all of this," he said. "For the rest of
the night, as long as we can keep at it, we have to go over the background. We talk about a motive of revenge. But we're not being very
precise. Does that mean we're thinking incorrectly? That we're on the
wrong track? That there might be a completely different explanation?"

They waited in silence for him to continue. Even though they all looked sallow and tired, he could see that they were still concentrating.

He started off by backtracking. Going back to Katarina Taxell in Lund.

"She gave birth here in Ystad," he said. "On two nights she had a visitor. Even though she denies it, I'm convinced that this unknown woman did visit her. So she's lying. The question is why? Who was that woman? Why wouldn't Taxell reveal her identity? Of all the women who have turned up in this investigation, Katarina Taxell and the woman in the nurse's uniform are the first two. I also think we can assume that Eugen Blomberg is the father of the child he never got to see. I think Katarina Taxell is lying about that. When we went to see her in Lund I had a feeling that she wasn't saying one single word of truth. I don't know why. We can probably assume that she holds an important key to this whole mess."

"Why don't we just bring her in?" asked Hansson with some vehemence.

"On what grounds?" replied Wallander. "Besides, she's a new mother. We can't just treat her any old way. I don't think she would say anything more than what she's already told us if we put her in a chair in the Lund police station. We'll have to try to go around her, search in her vicinity, smoke out the truth some other way."

Hansson nodded reluctantly.

"The third woman linked to Eugen Blomberg is his widow," Wallander went on. "She gave us a lot of important information. Most significant is probably the fact that she doesn't seem to mourn him at all. He abused her. Judging by her scars, for a long time and quite severely. She also confirms, indirectly, the story about Katarina Taxell, since she says he has always had extramarital affairs."

At the moment he spoke these last words, he thought he sounded like an old-fashioned Free Church preacher. He wondered what term Höglund would have used.

"Let's say that the details surrounding Blomberg form a pattern," he said. "Which we'll come back to later."

He switched to talking about Runfeldt. He was still moving backwards, toward the event that happened first.

"Gösta Runfeldt was known to be a brutal man," he went on. "Both his son and daughter confirm it. Behind the orchid lover was concealed a whole different person. He was also a private detective. Something that we don't really have a good explanation for. Was he looking for excitement? Weren't orchids enough for him? We don't know. He seems to have been a complex personality."

He switched to Runfeldt's wife.

"I made a trip to a lake outside Älmhult without knowing for sure what I would find. I don't have any proof. But I can imagine that

Runfeldt actually killed his wife. What happened out there on the ice we'll probably never know. The main players are dead. There are no witnesses. I still have a hunch that someone outside the family knew about it. For lack of anything better, we have to consider the possibility that the death of his wife had something to do with Runfeldt's fate."

Wallander switched to the actual sequence of events.

"He's taking a trip to Africa. But he doesn't go. Something prevents him. How he disappears, we don't know. On the other hand, we can pinpoint the date quite precisely. But we have no explanation for the break-in at his flower shop. We don't know where he was held prisoner. The suitcase may, of course, provide a vague geographic clue. I also think we can venture the tentative conclusion that for some reason it was repacked by a woman. If so, the same woman smoked a hand-rolled cigarette on the pier where the sack containing Blomberg was shoved into the water."

"There could be two people," objected Höglund. "One person who smoked the cigarette and left a fingerprint on the suitcase. Someone else could have repacked it."

"You're right," said Wallander. "I'll change my statement to say that at least one person was present." He glanced at Nyberg.

"We're looking," said Nyberg. "We're going through Holger Eriksson's place. We've found lots of fingerprints. But so far none that match."

Wallander suddenly happened to think of a detail. "The name tag," he said. "The one we found in Runfeldt's suitcase. Did it have any fingerprints on it?"

Nyberg shook his head.

"It should have," said Wallander in surprise. "You use your fingers to put it on or take it off, don't you?"

No one had any logical explanation to give him.

"So far we've approached a number of women, one of whom keeps showing up," he went on. "We also have spousal abuse and possibly an undetected homicide. The question we have to ask ourselves is: Who would have known about it? Who would have had a reason to seek revenge? If the motive is revenge, that is."

"There might be one other thing," said Svedberg, scratching the back of his neck. "We have two old police investigations that were both archived. Unsolved. One in Östersund and one in Älmhult."

Wallander nodded.

"That leaves Holger Eriksson," he went on. "Yet another brutal man. After a lot of effort, or rather a lot of luck, we find a woman in his background too. A Polish woman who's been missing for almost thirty years."

He looked around the table before he concluded.

"In other words, there's a pattern," he said. "Brutal men and abused, missing, and maybe murdered women. And one step behind, a shadow that follows in the tracks of these events. A shadow that might be a woman. A woman who smokes."

Hansson dropped his pencil on the table and shook his head.

"That doesn't seem reasonable," he said. "If we imagine there's a woman involved. Who seems to have enormous physical strength and a macabre imagination when it comes to cunning methods of murder. Why would she have an interest in what happened to these women? Is she a friend of theirs? How did all these people cross paths?"

"That's not just an important question," said Wallander. "It could be crucial. How did these people come into contact with each other? Where should we start looking? Among men or among women? A car dealer, regional poet, and birdwatcher; an orchid lover, private detective, and florist; and finally an allergy researcher. Blomberg, at any rate, doesn't seem to have had any special interests. Or should we start with the women? A new mother who lies about the father of her newborn child? A woman who drowned in Stång Lake outside Älmhult ten years ago? A woman from Poland who lived in Jämtland and was interested in birds, who's been missing for almost thirty years? And finally, this woman who sneaks around in the Ystad maternity ward at night and knocks down midwives? Where are the points of connection?"

The silence lasted a long time. Everyone tried to find an answer. Wallander waited. This was an important moment. Most of all he hoped that someone would come up with an unexpected conclusion. Rydberg had told him many times that the most important task of the leader of an investigation was to stimulate his colleagues to think the unexpected. Now the question was whether he had been successful.

It was Höglund who at last broke the silence.

"There are workplaces that are dominated by women," she said. "The health-care profession is one of them."

"Patients come from all different places," Martinsson continued. "If we assume that the woman we're looking for works in an emergency room, she would have seen lots of abused women pass through. None of them knew each other. But she knew them. Their names, their patient records."

Wallander realized that together Höglund and Martinsson had said something that might fit.

"We don't know whether she really *is* a nurse," he said. "All we know is that she doesn't work in the maternity ward in Ystad."

"Why couldn't she work somewhere else in the hospital?" suggested Svedberg.

Wallander nodded slowly. Could it really be that simple? A nurse at Ystad General Hospital?

"That should be relatively easy to find out," said Hansson. "Even though patient records are confidential and aren't supposed to be touched or opened, it should be possible to find out if Gösta Runfeldt's wife was treated there for abuse. And why not Krista Haberman, for that matter?"

Wallander took a new tack. "Have Runfeldt and Eriksson ever been charged with abuse? It should be possible to search back in time. If they have, this would be a conceivable way for us to go."

"There are also other possibilities," said Höglund, as if she felt the need to question her own previous suggestions. "There are other workplaces where women are in the majority. There are crisis groups for women. The female officers in Skåne even have their own network."

"We have to investigate all the alternatives," said Wallander. "It's going to take a long time. I think we have to realize that this investigation is heading in many different directions at the same time. Especially back in time. Going through old documents is always time-consuming. But I don't see any other option."

They spent the last two hours before midnight planning various strategies to carry out simultaneously. Since Martinsson still hadn't found any new connections between the three victims in his computer searches, they had no alternative but to run searches along many different avenues at once.

Just before midnight they ran out of steam.

Hansson put the last question into words, the one they had all been waiting for the whole night.

"Is it going to happen again?"

"I don't know," said Wallander. "Unfortunately, I'm afraid it might. I have a feeling of incompleteness about what's happened so far. Don't ask me why. That's all I can say. Something as unprofessional as a feeling. Intuition, maybe."

"I have a feeling too," said Svedberg.

He said this with such force that everyone was surprised.

"Isn't it possible that what we have to look forward to is a series of murders going on indefinitely? If it's someone who's pointing a vengeful finger at men who have mistreated women, then it's never going to stop."

Wallander knew it was likely that Svedberg was right. He'd been trying to avoid the thought himself all along.

"There is that risk," he replied. "Which in turn means that we have to catch whoever did this fast."

"Reinforcements," said Nyberg, who had barely uttered a word the past two hours. "Otherwise it won't work."

"Yes," said Wallander. "I agree that we're going to need them. Especially after what we've talked about tonight. We can't manage to do much more than we're already doing."

Hamrén raised his hand to signal that he wanted to say something. He was sitting next to the two detectives from Malmö near the far end of the long table.

"I'd like to underscore that last comment," he said. "I've rarely if ever taken part in such efficient police work with so few personnel. Since I was here last summer too, I can say with certainty that it's the rule, not the exception. If you request reinforcements, no reasonable person is going to refuse you."

The two detectives from Malmö nodded their agreement.

"I'll take it up with Chief Holgersson tomorrow," said Wallander. "I'm also thinking of trying to get a few more female officers. If nothing else, it might boost morale."

The weary mood lifted for a moment. Wallander seized the opportunity and stood up. It was important to know when to end a meeting. Now it was time. They wouldn't make any more progress. They needed some sleep.

Wallander went to his office to get his jacket. He leafed through the steadily growing stack of phone messages. Instead of putting on his jacket, he sat down in his chair. Footsteps disappeared down the corridor. Soon it was quiet. He twisted the lamp down toward the desk. The rest of the room was dark.

It was 12:30. Without thinking he grabbed the phone and dialed Baiba's number in Riga. She had irregular sleep habits, just as he did. Sometimes she went to bed early, but just as often she stayed up half the night. He never knew beforehand. Now she answered almost at once. She was awake. As always he tried to hear from her tone of voice whether she was glad he had called. He never felt sure ahead of time. This time he sensed a feeling of wariness from her. He was instantly insecure. He wanted guarantees that everything was the way it should be. He asked her how she was, told her about the exhausting investigation. She asked a few questions. Then he didn't know how to continue. The silence began wandering back and forth between Ystad and Riga.

"When are you coming over?" he asked at last.

Her counter-question surprised him. Even though it shouldn't have.

"Do you really want me to come?"

"Why wouldn't I?"

"You never call. And when you do call, you say you really don't have time to talk to me. So how are you going to have any time to spend with me if I come over there?"

"That's not how it is."

"Then how is it?"

Where his reaction came from, he didn't know. Not then or later on. He tried to stop his own impulse, but he couldn't. He slammed the receiver down hard. Stared at the phone. Then he got up and left. Even before he passed the dispatch room he regretted it. But he knew Baiba so well that he knew she wouldn't answer if he called back.

He stepped out into the night air. A police car rolled past and vanished down by the water tower.

There was no wind. The night air was chilly. Clear sky. Tuesday, October 19th.

He didn't understand his own reaction. What would have happened if she had been right next to him?

He thought about the murdered men. It was as if he suddenly saw something he hadn't seen before. Part of himself was hidden in all the brutality that surrounded him. He was a part of it.

Only the degree was different. Nothing else.

He shook his head. He knew he should call Baiba early in the morning. It didn't have to be so terrible. She understood. Fatigue could make her irritable too. Then it would be his turn to be understanding.

It was one o'clock. He should go home to bed. Or ask one of the night patrols to drive him home. He started walking. The city was deserted. Somewhere a car skidded with screeching tires. Then silence. Down the hill toward the hospital.

For almost seven hours the investigative team had sat in the meeting. Nothing had really happened. And yet the evening had been eventful. *Clarity arises in the spaces in between*, Rydberg had said once when he was quite drunk. Wallander, who was at least equally drunk, had understood. He'd never forgotten it, either. They were sitting on Rydberg's balcony. Five, maybe six years back. Rydberg was not yet sick. An evening in June, right before Midsummer. They were celebrating something, Wallander had forgotten what it was.

Clarity arises in the spaces in between.

He had reached the hospital. He stopped. He hesitated, but only briefly. Then he walked around the side of the hospital and over to the emergency entrance. He rang the night bell. When a voice answered he said who he was and asked whether the midwife Ylva Brink was on duty. She was. He asked to be let in.

She met him outside the glass doors. He could see by her face that she was nervous. He smiled. Her nervousness did not diminish. Maybe his smile wasn't a real smile. Or the light was bad.

They went inside. She asked if he'd like some coffee. He shook his head.

"I'll only stay for a moment," he said. "You must be busy."

"Yes," she replied. "But I can spare a few minutes. If it can't wait until tomorrow?"

"It probably could," replied Wallander. "I stopped by because I was on my way home."

They went into the office. A nurse on her way in stopped when she saw Wallander.

"It can wait," she said and left.

Wallander leaned against the desk. Ylva Brink sat down on a chair.

"You must have wondered," he began, "about the woman who knocked you down. Who she was. Why she was here. Why she did what she did. You must have thought long and hard about it. You've given us a good description of her face. Maybe there's some detail you thought of afterwards."

"You're right, I've been thinking about it. But I've told you everything I can remember about her face."

He believed her.

"It doesn't have to be her face. She might have had a certain way of moving. Or a scar on her hand. A human being is a combination of so many different details. We think we remember with great speed. As if the memory flowed. Actually it's just the opposite. Imagine an object that can almost float, that sinks through the water extremely slowly. That's the way memory works."

She shook her head.

"It happened so fast. I don't remember anything except what I've already told you. And I've really tried."

Wallander nodded. He hadn't expected anything else.

"What did she do?" Ylva asked.

"She knocked you down. We're looking for her. We think she might have some important information for us. That's all I can tell you."

A clock on the wall showed it was 1:27. He put out his hand to say goodbye. They left the office.

Suddenly she stopped.

"There might be something else," she said hesitantly.

"What is it?"

"I didn't think about it then, when I walked toward her and she knocked me down. It wasn't until afterwards."

"What?"

"She was wearing a perfume that was special."

"In what way?"

She gave him almost an imploring look.

"I don't know. How do you describe a scent?"

"I know that's one of the hardest things to do. But give it a try."

He saw that she was really making an effort.

"No," she said. "I can't find the words. I just know that it was special. Maybe you could say that it was harsh."

"More like after-shave?"

She looked at him in surprise.

"Yes," she said. "How did you know that?"

"It was just a thought."

"Maybe I shouldn't have said anything. Since I can't express myself clearly."

"Oh no," he replied. "This could turn out to be important. We never know ahead of time."

They parted at the glass doors. Wallander took the elevator down and left the hospital. He walked fast. Now he had to get some sleep.

He thought about what she had said.

If there were any traces of perfume left on the name tag, she would be asked to smell it early the next morning.

He already knew that it would be the same.

They were looking for a woman. Her perfume was special.

He wondered if they would ever find her.

Chapter Thirty

At 7:35 A.M. she got off work. She was in a hurry, impelled by a
sudden restlessness. It was a cold, wet morning in Malmö. She
hurried toward the lot where she parked her car. Normally she
would have driven straight home and gone to bed. Now she knew that
she had to drive directly to Lund. She tossed the bag in the back and
got into the driver's seat. When she grabbed the steering wheel she
could feel that her hands were sweaty.

She had never really been able to trust Katarina Taxell. The woman
was too weak. There was always the risk that she would give in. Taxell
was the sort of person who bruised easily if you pressed her.

There had always been the worry that she might cave in. Still, she
had judged her control over Taxell to be sufficient. Now she was no
longer as convinced.

I have to get her out of there, she had thought all night long. At
least until she begins to put some distance between herself and what
happened.

It shouldn't be difficult to get her away from her apartment either.
There was nothing unusual in a woman developing psychological
problems in connection with a birth or its aftermath.

When she arrived in Lund it was raining. Her uneasiness persisted.
She parked on one of the side streets and started walking toward the
square where Katarina Taxell's building was located. Suddenly she
stopped. She took a few wary steps back, as if a predator had abruptly
appeared in front of her. She stood next to the wall of a building and
observed the front door of Taxell's building.

There was a car parked in front. There was a man, or maybe two,
sitting in it. She was instantly sure they were cops. Katarina Taxell was
being watched.

The panic came out of nowhere. Although she couldn't see it, she knew that her face was flaming red. She was having palpitations. The thoughts swirled around in her head like confused nocturnal animals in a room when a light is suddenly turned on. What had Katarina said? Why were they sitting outside her front door watching her?

Or was it only her imagination? She stood motionless and tried to think. The first thing she could be sure of was that Katarina still hadn't told them anything. Otherwise they wouldn't be watching her. They would have taken her down to the station. So it wasn't too late after all. But she probably didn't have much time. Not that she needed much. She knew what she had to do.

She lit a cigarette she had rolled during the night. According to her timetable, it was at least an hour too early. Now she broke with routine. This day was going to be special. There was no getting around it.

She stood there for several more minutes and watched the car by the front door.

Then she put out the cigarette and walked quickly away.

When Wallander woke up just after six o'clock on Wednesday morning, he was still tired. His cumulative sleep deprivation was huge. The powerlessness was like a lead sinker deep down in his consciousness. He lay motionless in bed with his eyes open. A human being is an animal who lives to endure, he thought. Right now it seems I can't handle it anymore.

He sat up on the edge of the bed. The floor was cold under his feet. He looked at his toenails. They needed cutting. His whole body needed some kind of overhaul. A month earlier he had been in Rome, storing up new energy. Now it was all used up. In less than a month it was all spent. He forced himself to stand up. He went into the bathroom. The cold water was like a slap in the face. Someday he'd have to quit doing this—using cold water to get himself going. He dried off, put on his bathrobe, and went to the kitchen. Always the same routine. The coffee water, then the window, the thermometer. It was raining. Four degrees Celsius. Autumn, and the cold already had a firm grip. Someone at the police station had predicted a long winter. That's what he feared.

When the coffee was ready, he sat down at the kitchen table. He had picked up the morning paper outside his door first. On the front page was a photo from Lödinge. He took a few sips of coffee. Already he had moved beyond the first and highest threshold of fatigue. His mornings were sometimes like a complex obstacle course. He looked at the clock. It was time for him to call Baiba.

She answered on the second ring. It was the way he'd imagined it during the night. Things were different now.

"I'm exhausted," he excused himself.

"I know," she replied. "But my question still stands."

"You mean whether I want you to come?"

"Yes."

"There's nothing I'd like more."

She believed him. Maybe she could come in a few weeks. In early November. She would start looking into the possibility that day.

They didn't need to talk long. Neither of them liked the telephone. Afterwards, when Wallander returned to his cup of coffee, he thought that this time he'd have to have a serious talk with her. About whether she would move to Sweden. About the new house he wanted to buy. Maybe he'd even tell her about the dog.

He sat there a long time. He still hadn't opened the newspaper. He didn't get dressed until almost 7:30. He had to search his closet for a long time before he found a clean shirt. It was his last one. He had to sign up to use the laundry room today. Just as he was on his way out the door, the phone rang. It was the mechanic in Älmhult. He flinched when he heard the total for the repairs, but he didn't say a word. The mechanic promised that the car would be in Ystad later that day. He had a brother who could drive it down and then take the train home. All he'd be charged for was the train ticket.

When Wallander reached the street, he saw it was raining harder than it had looked. He went back inside and called the police station. Ebba promised to send a patrol car to pick him up right away. In five minutes it pulled up in front of the door. By eight o'clock he was in his office.

He had barely managed to take off his jacket when everything suddenly seemed to start happening at once all around him.

Höglund was standing in his doorway. She was pale.

"Did you hear?"

Wallander gave a start. Had it happened again? Another man murdered?

"I just got in. What is it?"

"Martinsson's daughter was attacked."

"Terese?"

"Yes."

"What happened?"

"She was attacked outside her school. Martinsson just left. If I understood Svedberg correctly, it had something to do with the fact that Martinsson is a police officer."

Wallander gave her a baffled look. "Is it serious?"

"She was pushed and pummeled on the head. Apparently she was kicked too. She wasn't badly injured, but she's certainly had a shock."

"Who did it?"

"Other students. Older than her."

Wallander sat down in his chair. "That's outrageous! But why?"

"I don't know everything that happened. Apparently the students have been talking about the citizen militia too, saying that the police aren't doing anything. That we've given up."

"So they jump on Martinsson's daughter?"

"Right."

Wallander felt a lump in his throat. Terese was thirteen years old, and Martinsson talked about her constantly.

"Why would they attack an innocent schoolgirl?"

"Did you see the paper?" she asked.

"No, why?"

"You ought to. People are talking about Eskil Bengtsson and the others. The arrests are being viewed as scandalous. They're claiming that Åke Davidsson fought back. There's a big story about it, with pictures and placards at the newsstands that say: 'Whose side are the police on, anyway?'"

"I don't need to read that crap," said Wallander in disgust. "What's happening at the school?"

"Hansson drove over there. Martinsson took his daughter home."

"So it was some boys at the school who did this?"

"As far as I know."

"Go over there," Wallander decided quickly. "Find out everything you can. Talk to the boys. I think it's best if I stay out of it. I might fly off the handle."

"Hansson's already there. They don't need anybody else."

"I disagree," said Wallander. "I'd really like you to go over there. I'm sure Hansson can handle it himself, but I still want you to find out, in your own way, what actually happened and why. If more of us show up, it will prove we're taking this seriously. I think I'll drive over to Martinsson's house. Everything else can wait till later. The worst thing you can do in this country, like everywhere else, is to kill a policeman. The next-worst thing is to attack a policeman's child."

"I heard that other students stood around laughing," she said.

Wallander threw up his hands. He didn't want to hear any more.

He got up from his chair and grabbed his jacket.

"Eskil Bengtsson and the others are going to be released today," she said as they walked down the corridor. "But Åkeson is going to prosecute."

"What will they get?"

"People in the area are already talking about taking up a collection, in case there are fines. We can always hope for jail terms. At least for some of them."

"How's it going with Åke Davidsson?"

"He's back home in Malmö. On sick leave."

Wallander stopped and looked at her.

"What would have happened if they'd killed him? Would they have been slapped with fines then too?"

He didn't wait for an answer.

A police car drove Wallander to Martinsson's house, located in a development on the east side of town. Wallander hadn't been there many times before. The house was plain, but Martinsson and his wife had put a lot of love into their garden. He rang the doorbell. Martinsson's wife Maria opened the door. Wallander saw that she had been crying. Terese was their oldest child and only daughter. They also had two boys. One of them, Rikard, stood behind her. Wallander smiled and patted him on the head.

"How's it going?" he asked. "I just heard about it and rushed right over."

"She's sitting on her bed crying. She won't speak to anyone but her pappa."

Wallander went inside and took off his jacket and shoes. One of his socks had a hole in it. Maria asked if he wanted some coffee. He gratefully accepted. At the same moment Martinsson came down the stairs. Usually he was a cheerful man. Now Wallander saw a gray mask of bitterness. And fear too.

"I heard what happened," said Wallander. "I came right over."

They sat down in the living room.

"How's she doing?" Wallander asked.

Martinsson just shook his head. Wallander thought he was going to break into tears. It wouldn't be the first time.

"I'm quitting," said Martinsson. "I'm going to talk to the chief today."

Wallander didn't know what to say. Martinsson had good reason to be upset. He could easily imagine reacting the same way if it had been Linda who was attacked.

Even so, he had to play the devil's advocate. The last thing he wanted was for Martinsson to quit. He also realized that Martinsson would have to make up his own mind.

But it was still too soon. He could see how shocked Martinsson was.

Maria came in with coffee. Martinsson shook his head. He didn't want any.

"It's not worth it," he said, "when it starts to affect your family."

"No," said Wallander, "it's not worth it."

Martinsson didn't say any more. Nor did Wallander. Martinsson got up and went back upstairs. Wallander knew there was nothing he could do right now.

Martinsson's wife followed him to the door.

"Say hi to her from me," Wallander said.

"Are they going to come after us again?"

"No. I know that what I'm going to tell you may sound odd. As if I were trying to make light of this situation. But that's not my intention at all. It's just that we can't lose our sense of proportion and start drawing the wrong conclusions. These boys were probably only a couple of years older than Terese. They're not bad kids. They probably didn't know what they were doing. The reason behind it is that men like Eskil Bengtsson and those others out in Lödinge are starting to organize the citizen militia and incite people against the police."

"I know," she said. "I've heard that people are talking about it in this area too."

"I know it's hard to think clearly when your own child is the target of something like this. But we have to try and hold onto our common sense."

"All this violence," she said. "Where does it come from?"

"There aren't many people who are truly evil," replied Wallander. "At least I think they're quite rare. On the other hand, there are evil circumstances, which trigger all this violence. It's those circumstances we have to tackle."

"Won't it just get worse and worse?"

"Maybe," said Wallander hesitantly. "If that happens then it's because the circumstances are changing. Not because there are more evil people."

"This country has turned so cold-hearted."

"You're right. It's gotten very cold-hearted."

He shook hands with her and walked toward the waiting police car.

"How's Terese doing?" asked the officer driving.

"She's mostly upset. And her parents are, too."

"Doesn't it make you furious?"

"Yes," said Wallander. "It does."

Wallander returned to the police station. Hansson and Höglund were still at the school where Terese had been attacked. Wallander heard that Chief Holgersson was in Stockholm. For a moment it made him mad. But she had been informed about what happened. She was coming back to Ystad that afternoon. Wallander got hold of Svedberg and Hamrén. Nyberg was out at Holger Eriksson's farm searching for fingerprints. The two detectives from Malmö had gone off in different directions. Wallander sat down with Svedberg and Hamrén in the conference room. They were all upset about what had happened to Martinsson's daughter. They had a brief conversation, and then they all went back to work. They had divided up all the assignments the night before. Wallander called Nyberg on his cell phone.

"How's it going?" he asked.

"It's tough," said Nyberg. "But we think we may have found an indistinct print up in his bird tower. On the bottom of the railing. It could be it isn't Eriksson's own. We'll keep looking."

Wallander thought for a moment.

"You mean the killer might have gone up in the tower?"

"It's not totally unlikely."

"You may be right. In that case, there might be cigarette butts too."

"If there were any, we would have found them on our first pass. Now it's definitely too late."

Wallander changed the subject and told them about his nighttime talk with Ylva Brink at the hospital.

"The name tag is in a plastic bag," said Nyberg. "If she has a good nose maybe she can still recognize the scent."

"I want that tried out ASAP. You can call her yourself. Svedberg has her number."

Nyberg promised to do it. Wallander discovered that someone had put a piece of paper on his desk. It was a letter from the Patent and Registration Board reporting that no one had officially changed his name to or from Harald Berggren. Wallander put it aside. It was ten o'clock and still raining. He thought about the meeting the night before. Again he felt the uneasiness. Were they really on the right track? Or were they following a path that would lead them straight into a vacuum? He went to stand by the window. His eyes fell on the water tower. Katarina Taxell is our main lead. She has met the woman. What would someone be after in the maternity ward in the middle of the night?

He went back to his desk and put in a call to Birch in Lund. It took almost ten minutes before they managed to locate him.

"Everything's quiet outside her building," said Birch. "No visits except a woman we have a positive ID on—her mother. Katarina went out grocery-shopping once. That was when her mother was there watching her baby. There's a supermarket nearby. The only thing of interest was that she bought a lot of newspapers."

"She probably wanted to read about the murder. Do you think she knows we're in the vicinity?"

"I don't think so. She seems tense. But she never looks around. I don't think she suspects we've got her under surveillance."

"It's important that she doesn't discover it."

"We keep changing officers."

Wallander leaned over his desk and opened his notebook.

"How's it going with the profile of her? Who is she?"

"She's thirty-three years old," said Birch. "That makes an age difference of eighteen years with Blomberg."

"It's her first child," Wallander said. "She started late. Women in a hurry might not be so particular about age differences. But I don't really know much about these things."

"According to her, Blomberg isn't the child's father anyway."

"That's a lie," said Wallander, wondering how he really dared be so dead sure. "What else have you got?"

"Katarina Taxell was born in Arlöv," Birch continued. "Her father was an engineer at the sugar refinery. He died when she was little. His car was hit by a train, outside Landskrona. She has no siblings. Grew up with her mother. They moved to Lund after the father died. The mother worked part-time at the city library. Katarina Taxell got good grades in school. Went on to study at the university. Geography and foreign languages. A somewhat unusual combination. Teachers' college. She's been a teacher ever since. At the same time she has built up a small business selling hair-care products. She's supposed to be quite industrious. Of course we don't find her in any of our files. She gives the impression of being quite a normal person."

"Well, that was certainly fast work," said Wallander, impressed.

"I did what you said," replied Birch. "I put a lot of people on it."

"Obviously she doesn't know about it yet. She'd be looking over her shoulder if she did. If she found out we were profiling her."

"We'll have to see how long that lasts. The question is whether we shouldn't lean on her a little."

"I've been thinking the same thing," said Wallander.

"Should we bring her in?"

"No. But I think I'll drive over to Lund. Then you and I can start by talking with her one more time."

"What about? If you don't ask any meaningful questions she'll get suspicious."

"I'll think of something on the way there. Shall we say we'll meet outside her building at noon?"

Wallander signed out a car and drove out of Ystad. He stopped at Sturup Airport and had a sandwich. As usual he was shocked at the price. While he ate he tried to formulate some questions to ask Katarina Taxell. It wasn't good enough to show up asking the same things as last time.

He decided he'd have to start with Eugen Blomberg. He was the one who was murdered, after all. They needed all the information they could get on him. Taxell was only one of the people they were questioning.

At quarter to twelve Wallander finally managed to find a parking place in downtown Lund. When he walked through the city the rain had stopped. He had begun to plan his questions for Katarina Taxell. He saw Birch in the distance.

"I heard the news," said Birch. "About Martinsson and his daughter. It's awful."

"What isn't awful these days?" said Wallander.

"How's the girl handling it?"

"Let's just hope she can forget all about it. But Martinsson told me he's thinking about quitting the force. And I have to try and prevent that."

"If he really means it, deep down, nobody will be able to stop him."

"I don't think he'll do it. At least I think I can be sure he knows what he's doing."

"I took a rock on my head once," said Birch. "I got so mad I tore after the guy who threw it. It turned out that I'd arrested his brother once. He thought he was fully justified in throwing a rock at my head."

"A cop is always a cop," said Wallander. "At least if you believe the rock-throwers."

Birch changed the subject.

"What are you thinking of asking her about?"

"Eugen Blomberg. How they met. I have to make her think I'm asking her the same questions I ask everyone else. Routine questions, more or less."

"What do you hope to achieve?"

"I don't know. But I still think it's necessary. Something could turn up in the meantime."

They went into the building. Wallander suddenly had a premonition that something was wrong. He stopped on the stairs. Birch looked at him.

"What is it?"

"I don't know. Maybe nothing."

They continued up to the third floor. Birch rang the doorbell. They waited. He rang again. The bell echoed inside the apartment. They looked at each other. Wallander bent down and opened the letter slot. Everything was silent.

Birch rang again. Long, repetitive rings. No one came to the door.

"She's got to be home," he said. "No one reported that she went out."

"Then she went up the chimney," Wallander said. "She's not here."

They ran down the stairs. Birch tore open the door to the police car. The man at the wheel sat reading a magazine.

"Did she go out?" asked Birch.

"She's inside."

"Guess again."

"Is there a back door?" asked Wallander.

Birch relayed the question to the man behind the wheel.

"Not that I know of."

"That's no answer," said Birch, annoyed. "Either there's a back door or there isn't."

They went back inside the building. Down a half flight of stairs. The door to the basement level was locked.

"Is there a building supervisor?" Wallander asked.

"We don't have time for that," said Birch.

He examined the hinges on the door. They were rusty.

"We can try," Birch muttered to himself.

He took a running start and threw himself against the door. It was ripped off its hinges.

"You know what it means to break the regulations," he said.

Wallander noticed that there was no irony in Birch's remark. They went inside. The corridor between a row of barred storage rooms led to a door at the end. Birch opened it. They entered the lower part of a back stairway.

"So she got out the back way," he said. "And nobody even took the trouble to see if there was one."

"She might still be in the apartment," said Wallander.

Birch understood.

"Suicide?"

"I don't know. But we have to go in. And we don't have time to wait for a locksmith."

"I'm pretty good at picking locks," said Birch. "I just have to get some tools."

It took him less than five minutes. When he came back he was out of breath. In the meantime Wallander had gone back to Katarina Taxell's door and kept ringing the bell. An elderly man next door came out and asked what was going on. Wallander got mad. He took out his badge and held it right up to the man's face.

"We'd appreciate it if you'd shut your door," he said. "Now. And keep it shut until we tell you."

The man retreated. Wallander heard him putting on the safety chain.

Birch picked the lock in less than five minutes. They went in. The apartment was empty. Taxell had taken her baby with her. The back door led to a cross street. Birch shook his head.

"Somebody's going to answer for this," he said.

They went through the apartment. Wallander got the feeling that she had taken off in a big hurry. He stopped in front of a baby buggy they found in the kitchen.

"She must have been picked up by car," he said. "There's a gas station across the street. Maybe someone there saw a woman with a baby leave the building."

Birch left. Wallander went through the apartment one more time. He tried to imagine what had happened. Why does a woman leave her apartment with a newborn baby? Taking the back way meant that she wanted to leave in secret. It also meant that she knew the building was being watched.

She or someone else, Wallander thought.

Someone might have seen the stakeout from outside and then called her to arrange her escape.

He sat down on a chair in the kitchen. There was one more question he needed to answer. Were Katarina Taxell and her baby in danger? Or had their flight from the apartment been voluntary?

Someone would have noticed if she put up a struggle, he thought. So she must have left of her own volition. There was only one reason for that. She didn't want to answer questions from the police.

He stood up and went over to the window. He saw Birch talking with one of the employees at the gas station. Then the phone rang. Wallander gave a start. He went into the living room. It rang again. He picked up the receiver.

"Katarina?" asked a woman's voice.

"She's not here," he said. "Who's calling?"

"Who are you?" asked the woman. "I'm Katarina's mother."

"My name is Kurt Wallander. I'm a police officer. Nothing has happened. But Katarina isn't here. And her baby is gone too."

"That's impossible."

"It seems so. But she isn't here. Maybe you have some idea where she might have gone."

"She wouldn't have left without telling me."

Wallander made a quick decision.

"It would be good if you could come over here. I understand you don't live far away."

"It'll take me less than ten minutes," she replied. "What's happened?"

He could hear the fear in her voice.

"I'm sure there's a reasonable explanation. We can talk about it when you get here."

He heard Birch coming in the door as he hung up.

"We're in luck," said Birch. "I talked to a guy who works at the gas station. A guy who keeps his eyes peeled."

He had made some notes on a piece of paper spotted with oil.

"A red Golf stopped here this morning, sometime between nine and ten. Probably closer to ten. A woman came out the back door of the building. She was carrying a baby. They got in the car and drove off."

Wallander felt the tension rising. "Did he notice who was driving?"

"The driver never got out."

"So he doesn't know whether it was a man or woman?"

"I asked him. He gave an interesting answer. He said the car drove off as if a man was behind the wheel."

Wallander was surprised. "How did he figure that?"

"Because the car started with a roar and tore off. Women seldom drive that way."

Wallander understood. "Did he notice anything else?"

"No. But maybe he can remember more with a little help. As I said, he seemed very observant."

Wallander told him that Taxell's mother was on her way over. Then they stood in silence.

"What's happened here?" asked Birch.

"I don't know."

"Do you think she's in danger?"

"I've thought about that. I don't think so, but I could be wrong."

They went into the living room. There was a baby's sock on the floor. Wallander looked around the room. Birch followed his gaze.

"There's a solution somewhere here," said Wallander. "There's something in this apartment that will lead us to the woman we're looking for. When we find her, we'll also find Katarina Taxell. There's something here that will tell us which way to turn. We're going to find it if we have to tear up the floorboards."

Birch said nothing.

They heard the door lock click. So she had her own key. Katarina Taxell's mother walked into the room.

Chapter Thirty-one

Wallander stayed in Lund for the rest of the day. With every hour that passed his feeling grew stronger. It was through Katarina Taxell that they had the greatest chance of finding the solution to who had murdered the three men. They were searching for a woman. There was no doubt that she was deeply involved in some way. But they didn't know whether she was acting alone or what motive was driving her.

The talk with Katarina Taxell's mother had led nowhere. She started rushing hysterically around the apartment, looking for her missing daughter and grandson. Finally she became so confused that they were forced to call for assistance and make sure she came under the care of a doctor. By then Wallander was convinced that she didn't know where her daughter had gone. The few women friends she had who her mother thought might have come to get her were contacted at once. Everyone seemed equally puzzled. But Wallander didn't trust what he heard over the phone. At his request Birch followed closely in his tracks and paid visits to the people Wallander had spoken to. Katarina Taxell was still missing. Wallander was certain that the mother was quite familiar with her daughter's circle of friends. Her distress was genuine. If she could have told them where Katarina had gone, she would have.

Wallander went downstairs and across the street to the gas station. He had asked the witness, twenty-four-year-old Jonas Hader, to repeat his account of what he had seen. For Wallander it was like meeting the perfect witness. Hader seemed to look at the world around him as if his observations might at any time be transformed into crucial testimony. The red Golf had stopped outside the building at the same time as a truck carrying newspapers had left the gas station. They got hold of the driver, who in turn was positive that he had left the gas station at 9:30 sharp. Hader had noticed lots of details, including a big sticker on the rear window of the Golf. But it was too far away for him to see what the picture was or what the writing said. He insisted that the car had roared off, that it was driven in what he considered a masculine way. The only thing he hadn't seen was the driver. It was raining, the windshield wipers were going. He couldn't have seen anything even if he'd tried. On the other hand, he was convinced that Taxell was wearing a light green coat, that she had a big adidas bag, and that the child she was carrying was wrapped in a blue blanket. It had all happened very fast. She came out the door just as the car pulled to a stop. Someone inside opened the back door. She put the child inside and then put her bag in the trunk. Then she opened the back door on the street side and climbed into the car. The driver gunned the engine before Taxell had even closed the door completely. Hader couldn't catch the license-plate number, although Wallander had a feeling that he had actually tried. Hader was positive that this was the only time he had ever seen the red car stop in front of the back door.

Wallander returned to the building with a feeling that he'd had something confirmed, although he wasn't sure what it was. It seemed to be a hurried escape, but how long had it been planned? And why? In the meantime Birch had talked to the officers who had taken turns keeping the building under surveillance. Wallander specifically asked them to say whether they had seen any woman in the building's vicin-ity, anyone who had come and left, or showed up more than once. But in contrast to Jonas Hader, the officers had made few observations. They had concentrated on the front door and who had gone in and out, but it was only people who lived in the building. Wallander had insisted that they identify every person they noticed. Since fourteen families lived in the building, the whole afternoon had been filled with policemen running up and down the stairs and checking the residents. This was also how Birch found someone who might have noticed some-thing important. It was a man who lived two floors above Katarina Taxell. He was a retired musician, and according to Birch he described his life as "standing for hours at the window, staring out at the rain, and hearing in his mind music that he would never play again." He had been a bassoonist with the Helsingborg Symphony Orchestra, and—still according to Birch—seemed to be a melancholy person who lived a lonely existence. That morning he thought he saw a woman on the other side of the square. A woman on foot, who suddenly stopped, took several steps back, and then stood motionless and studied the building, before she turned around and disappeared. When Birch brought this news, Wallander immediately thought that this woman could be the one they were looking for. Someone had come up and noticed the car, which of course shouldn't have been parked right outside the door. Someone had come to visit Katarina Taxell. In the same way that she'd had a visitor in the hospital.

Wallander developed a great and energetic stubbornness. He asked Birch to contact Taxell's friends again and ask if any of them had been on their way to visit her and her newborn baby that morning. The unanimous answer was unequivocal. No one had been on their way, only to suddenly change their mind. Birch had tried to coax a description of the woman out of the retired bassoonist. But the only thing he could say with certainty was that it was a woman. It had been around eight o'clock. That information was fuzzy, though, because the three clocks in his apartment, including his wristwatch, all showed different times.

Wallander's energy on that day was inexhaustible. He had sent Birch out on various assignments. Birch didn't seem at all insulted that Wallander was giving him orders as if to a subordinate. At the same time Wallander began a methodical search of Taxell's apartment. The first thing he asked Birch was whether he could have his crime techs secure fingerprints from the apartment. They would then be compared with the ones Nyberg had found. All day long he also kept in phone contact with Ystad. On four separate occasions he talked to Nyberg. Ylva Brink had smelled the name badge, which still had a faint trace of perfume. She couldn't confirm it. It might have been the same scent she noticed on that night in the maternity ward when she was knocked down. But she wasn't positive. The whole thing was still vague.

Twice during the day he talked to Martinsson at home. Terese was still scared and depressed, of course. Martinsson was still determined to quit the force. But Wallander managed to get him to promise to wait at least until the next day before he wrote his letter of resignation. Even though Martinsson couldn't think of anything but his daughter, Wallander still gave him a detailed account of what had happened. He was sure that Martinsson was listening, although he made few comments and seemed distracted. But Wallander knew that he had to keep Martinsson in the investigation. He didn't want to risk having him make a decision he would later regret. He also talked to Chief Holgersson several times. Hansson and Höglund had taken firm action at the school where Terese was attacked. In the principal's office they interviewed the three boys who were involved, one after the other. They had been in contact with the parents and the teachers. According to Höglund, whom Wallander also managed to speak to that day, Hansson had done an excellent job when all the students had been assembled and told about what happened. The students were upset, the three boys were clearly outcasts, and she didn't think it would happen again.

Eskil Bengtsson and the other men had been released. But Per Åkeson was going to prosecute. Maybe what had happened to Martinsson's daughter would make some people reconsider. At least that was what Höglund was hoping. But Wallander had his doubts. He thought they would have to use a great deal of energy in the future to combat all the private militias.

The most important news that day came from Hamrén, who had taken over some of Hansson's assignments. Just after three in the afternoon he managed to locate Göte Tandvall. He called Wallander at once.

"He has an antique shop in Simrishamn," said Hamrén. "If I've understood correctly, he also travels around and buys antiques, which he exports to Norway and other places."

"Is that legal?"

"I don't think it's directly illegal," replied Hamrén. "It's probably a matter of the prices being higher there. Then of course it depends on what kind of antiques they are."

"I want you to pay him a visit," said Wallander. "We've got no time to lose. And we're stretched thin as it is. Go to Simrishamn. The most important thing we need to have confirmed is whether a relationship really existed between Holger Eriksson and Krista Haberman. That doesn't mean that Tandvall might not have other information that could interest us."

Three hours later Hamrén called back. He was in his car right outside Simrishamn. He had met Göte Tandvall. Wallander waited tensely.

"Tandvall was an extremely precise individual," said Hamrén. "He seemed to have a complicated sort of memory. Certain things he couldn't remember at all. On other matters he was perfectly clear."

"Krista Haberman?"

"He remembered her. I got a feeling that she must have been quite beautiful. And he was positive that Eriksson had met her. At least on a couple of occasions. Among other things he remembered one early morning out on the promontory near Falsterbo where they stood and watched returning geese. Or maybe it was cranes. On that point he was unclear."

"Is he a bird watcher too?"

"He was reluctantly dragged along by his father."

"So now we know the most important thing," said Wallander.

"It does look like it all fits together. Krista Haberman, Holger Eriksson."

Wallander felt a sudden distaste come over him. It came to him with horrifying clarity what he was now starting to believe.

"I want you to go back to Ystad," he said. "Sit down and go through all the material in the investigation that has to do with her actual disappearance. When and where was she last seen? I want you to put together a summary of that part of the investigation. The last time she was seen."

"It sounds like you have something in mind," said Hamrén.

"She disappeared," said Wallander. "She was never found. What does that indicate?"

"That she's dead."

"More than that. Don't forget that we're skirting the edges of a criminal investigation in which both men and women are subjected to the most brutal violence you could imagine."

"So you think she was murdered?"

"Hansson gave me an overview of the investigation surrounding her disappearance. The possibility of murder has been there from the start. But since nothing could be proved, it wasn't allowed to dominate other possible explanations for her disappearance. That's the correct police procedure. No hasty conclusions, all doors open until one can be closed. Maybe we're now approaching that door."

"You think Eriksson killed her?"

Wallander could hear that this idea was occurring to Hamrén for the first time.

"I don't know," said Wallander. "But from now on we can't ignore that possibility."

Hamrén promised to put together the summary. He'd call back when it was ready.

Wallander left Katarina Taxell's apartment. He had to have something to eat. He found a pizzeria close to her building. He ate much too fast and got a stomachache. Afterwards he couldn't even remember what the food had tasted like.

He was in a hurry. He had an uneasy feeling that something was going to happen soon. Since there were no indications that the series of killings was over, they were working against time. And they didn't know how much time they had. He reminded himself that Martinsson had promised to put together a timetable of everything that had happened so far. He was supposed to have done that on the day that Terese was attacked. On his way back to Taxell's apartment Wallander decided it couldn't wait. He stopped in a bus shelter and called Ystad. He was in luck. Höglund was there. She had already talked to Hamrén and knew about the positive confirmation that Krista Haberman and Holger Eriksson had met. Wallander asked her to make the timetable of events that Martinsson had promised to do.

"I have no idea whether it's important," he said. "But we know too little about how this woman moves around. Maybe a picture of the geographic center will become clear if we make a timetable."

"Now you're saying 'she,'" said Höglund.

"Yes, I am," replied Wallander. "But we don't know if she's alone. We also don't know what role she plays."

"What do you think has happened to Katarina Taxell?"

"She's run away. It happened very fast. When she discovered that the building was being watched. She's run away because she has something to hide."

"Is it really possible that she killed Blomberg?"

"Taxell is a link somewhere in the middle of the chain. If there are other links we can connect up, that is. She doesn't represent a beginning or an end. I have a hard time imagining her killing anyone. She presumably belongs to the group of women who have been victims of abuse."

Höglund sounded genuinely surprised. "Was she abused too? I didn't know that."

"She might not have been beaten up or cut with a knife," said Wallander. "But I suspect that she's been victimized in some other way."

"Psychologically?"

"Something like that."

"By Blomberg?"

"Yes."

"But she still had his child? If what you think about the father is true."

"I saw the way she held her baby, and she didn't look particularly happy. But of course there are still a lot of holes," Wallander admitted. "Police work is always a question of piecing together tentative solutions. We have to make the silence speak and the words tell us about things that have hidden meanings. We have to try to see through the events, turn them on their heads in order to set them on their feet."

"Nobody at the police academy ever talked about this. Weren't you invited to give a lecture there?"

"Never," said Wallander. "I can't talk in front of people."

"That's exactly what you can do," she replied. "You just refuse to admit it. And besides, I think you'd actually enjoy doing it."

"That's neither here nor there," Wallander concluded.

Afterwards he thought about what she had said. Was it true that he really did want to speak to the future police officers who were being trained? In the past he was always convinced that his reluctance was genuine. Now he suddenly started to doubt this.

He left the bus shelter and hurried on through the rain. It was starting to get windy. He continued to go through Taxell's apartment methodically. In a box in the back of a closet he found a large number of diaries going far back in time. She had started writing the first one when she was twelve. Wallander noticed with surprise that it had a beautiful orchid on the cover. With unabated energy she had kept on writing the diaries through her teenage years and on into adulthood. The last diary he found in the closet was from 1993. But there were no entries after September. He kept searching without finding any others. But he was certain they existed. He enlisted the help of Birch, who was now finished with running around in the building looking for witnesses.

Birch found the keys to Taxell's basement storage room. It took him an hour to go through it. There weren't any diaries there either. Wallander was now convinced that she had taken them with her. They were in the Addidas bag that Hader had seen her put in the trunk of the red Golf.

Finally only her desk was left. Earlier he had quickly gone through the drawers. Now he would do it more thoroughly. He sat down on the old chair that had dragon heads carved into the armrests. The desk was a small secretary in which the door folded down to make a desk surface. On the top shelf of the desk stood framed photographs. Katarina Taxell as a child. She was sitting on a grass mat. White garden furniture in the background. Blurry figures. Someone wearing a white hat. Katarina sitting next to a big dog. She was looking straight at the camera. A big bow in her hair with a rosette. The sun shone through the window at a slant. Another picture: Katarina with her mother and father. The engineer at the sugar refinery. He had a mustache and gave an impression of enormous self-confidence. Katarina looked a lot more like her father than her mother. Wallander took down the photo and looked on the back. No date. The picture was taken in a photo studio in Lund. The next picture. A graduation photograph. White cap, flowers around her neck. She was thin, had grown paler. The dog and the mood from the grass mat were long gone. Katarina Taxell was living in a different world. The last picture, on the end. An old photo, the contours had faded. A barren landscape near the sea. An old couple stared stiffly into the camera. Far in the distance a three-masted ship, anchored, without sails. Wallander thought the picture could be from Öland. Taken sometime at the end of the last century. Katarina's great-grandparents. There was nothing written on the back of that one either. He put the photographs back. No man, he thought. No sign of Blomberg. That might be understandable. But no other man either. The father of her child, who had to exist. Did that mean anything? Everything means something. The question was what. One by one he pulled out the small drawers in the top of the secretary. Letters, documents, bills. In one drawer old report cards. Her highest marks were in geography. She had done poorly in physics and math. The next drawer. Pictures from a photo automat. Three girls, crowded together, making faces. Another picture. The walking street in Copenhagen. The same three girls, sitting on a bench, laughing. Katarina on the far right, at the end of the bench. Another drawer full of letters. Some from as far back as 1972. A stamp with a picture of the man-of-war *Wasa*. If the secretary contains Taxell's innermost secrets, thought Wallander, then she doesn't have many. An impersonal life. No passions, no summer adventures on Greek islands. But high marks in geography. He continued going through the drawers. Nothing caught his attention. He moved on to the three large drawers underneath. Still no diaries. Not even any pocket calendars. Wallander didn't feel like sitting there digging through layer after layer of impersonal mementos. Katarina Taxell's life had left no traces. He couldn't see her. Had she even been able to see herself?

He pushed back the chair. Closed the last drawer. Nothing. He didn't know any more than he did before. He frowned. There was something that didn't add up. If her decision to leave was made suddenly, and he was convinced it was, then she wouldn't have had time to take along everything that might give away what she was trying to hide. She had the diaries within easy reach. She could rescue them if the place caught fire. But there is almost always a messy side to a person's life. Here there was nothing. He stood up and cautiously moved the desk away from the wall. Nothing was fastened to the back. He sat down in the chair again, thinking hard. There was something he had noticed. Something that only now came back to him. He sat motionless and tried to coax the image out. Not the photographs. Not the letters either. What was it then? The report cards? The rental contract? The bills from her credit card? None of those. What was left?

There's nothing else but the furniture, he thought. The secretary. Then it came to him. Something about the small drawers. He pulled one of them out again. Then the next. Compared them. Then he took them all the way out and looked inside. Nothing there either. He put the drawers back in. Pulled out the one on the top left. Then the second. That's when he discovered it. The drawers were not equally deep. He pulled out the smaller one and turned it around. There was another opening. It was a double drawer. It had a secret compartment in back. He opened the drawer. There was only one thing inside. He took it out and put it on the desk.

A timetable for SR, Swedish Railways, for the spring of 1991. The trains between Malmö and Stockholm.

He took out the other drawers, one after the other. He found another secret compartment. It was empty.

He leaned back in his chair and regarded the timetable. He couldn't understand why it would have any importance. It was even harder to understand why it had been placed inside a secret compartment. He was convinced that it couldn't have ended up there by mistake.

Birch came into the room.

"Take a look at this," said Wallander. Birch stood behind him. Wallander pointed at the timetable.

"This was in Katarina Taxell's secret hiding place."

"A timetable?"

Wallander nodded. "I don't get it," he said.

He leafed through it, page by page. Birch had pulled up a chair and sat down next to him. Wallander turned the pages. Nothing was written on it, no page had been pressed down and fell open by itself. It was only when he came to the next to the last page that he stopped. Birch saw it too. A departure time from Nässjö was underlined. Nässjö to Malmö. Departure 16:00. Arrival in Lund 18:42. Malmö 18:57.

Nässjö 16:00. Someone had drawn a line under the whole row.

Wallander looked at Birch. "Does that tell you anything?"

"Not a thing."

Wallander put down the timetable.

"Does Katarina Taxell have something to do with Nässjö?" Birch asked.

"Not as far as I know," said Wallander. "But of course it's possible. Our biggest problem right now is that everything seems to be possible. We can't separate out any details or connections that could be immediately dropped as less important."

Wallander had gotten several plastic bags from the crime techs who had gone through the apartment earlier in the day, searching for fingerprints that didn't belong to Katarina Taxell or her mother. He put the timetable in one of them.

"I'm taking this along," he said, "if you have no objections."

Birch shrugged his shoulders.

"You can't even use it anymore to tell when the trains go," he said. "It expired almost three and a half years ago."

"I rarely take the train," said Wallander.

"It can be relaxing," said Birch. "I prefer the train over flying. You get time to yourself."

Wallander thought about his most recent train trip. When he was in Älmhult. Birch was right. During the trip he had actually fallen asleep for a while.

"We're not going to get any farther right now," he said. "I think it's time for me to go back to Ystad."

"We're not going to put out an APB for Katarina Taxell and her baby?"

"Not yet."

They left the apartment. Birch locked up. Outside the rain had almost stopped. The wind was coming in gusts, and it was cold. It was already quarter to nine. They said goodbye at Wallander's car.

"What should we do about keeping her house under surveillance?" Birch asked.

Wallander thought for a moment. "Keep it going for the time being," he said. "Only don't forget the back this time."

"What do you think might happen?"

"I don't know. But people who run away can always decide to come back."

He drove out of the city. Autumn pressed in all around the car. He switched on the heat, but he was still cold.

What are we going to do now? he asked himself. Katarina Taxell is missing. After a long day in Lund I'm going back to Ystad with an old SR timetable in a plastic bag.

But in spite of everything, they had taken an important step forward that day. Holger Eriksson did know Krista Haberman. They had confirmed there was a connection between the three men who had been murdered. Involuntarily he stepped on the gas. He wanted to find out as soon as possible how things had gone for Hamrén. When he reached the exit for Sturup Airport he pulled into a bus stop and called Ystad. He got hold of Svedberg. The first thing he asked about was Terese.

"She's getting a lot of support from the school," said Svedberg. "Especially from the other students. But it's going to take time."

"And Martinsson?"

"He's depressed. He's talking about quitting the force."

"I know. I don't think that's necessary."

"Presumably you're the only one who can talk him out of it."

"I will."

He asked if anything important had happened. Svedberg was not fully informed. He had just arrived at the station himself after sitting in on a meeting with Per Åkeson about getting help in obtaining the investigative material concerning Gösta Runfeldt's dead wife in Älmhult.

Wallander asked him to call a meeting of the investigative team for ten o'clock.

"Have you seen Hamrén?" was his last question.

"He's sitting with Hansson, going over the material on Krista Haberman. That was apparently something you said was urgent."

"Ten o'clock," repeated Wallander. "If they could finish by then, I'd be grateful."

"Are they supposed to find Krista Haberman by then?" asked Svedberg.

"Not exactly. But not far from it, either."

Wallander put down the phone on the seat next to him. He sat there in the dark. He thought about Katarina Taxell's secret drawer, which contained an old timetable.

He didn't understand it. Not at all.

At ten o'clock that night they were all assembled. The only one missing was Martinsson. They began by talking about what happened that morning. Everyone knew that Martinsson had immediately decided to resign from the force.

"I'll have a talk with him," said Wallander. "I'll find out if he's really made up his mind. If he has, then of course no one is going to stop him."

Nothing more was said about it. Wallander gave a brief summary of what had happened in Lund. They tried out various explanations for why Taxell had run away and what her motive might be. They also asked themselves if it might be possible to track down the red car. How many red Golfs really existed in Sweden?

"A woman with a newborn baby can't disappear without a trace," said Wallander at last. "I think it'd be best for us to be patient. We have to keep working on what we have at hand."

He looked at Hansson and Hamrén.

"The disappearance of Krista Haberman," he said. "Something that happened twenty-seven years ago."

Hansson nodded to Hamrén.

"You wanted to know the details surrounding the disappearance itself," he said. "The last time anyone saw her was in Svenstavik on Tuesday, October 22nd, 1967. She took a walk through town. Since you've been there, you can picture it for yourself, even though the center of town has been built up since then. It wasn't unusual for her to be out walking. The last person to see her was a lumberjack who was coming from the station on his bike. It was then quarter to five in the evening. It was already dark. After that no one ever saw her again. But there are several witnesses who talked about a strange car passing through town that evening. That's all."

Wallander sat in silence.

"Did anyone mention the make of the car?" he asked at last.

Hamrén searched through the papers. He shook his head and left the room. When he came back he had another stack of papers in his hand. Finally he found what he was looking for.

"One of the witnesses, a farmer named Johansson, claimed it was a Chevrolet. A dark blue Chevrolet. He was positive about it. There was once a taxi in Svenstavik that was the same type. Except it was light blue."

Wallander nodded. "Svenstavik and Lödinge are a long way from each other," he said softly. "But if I'm not completely mistaken, Holger Eriksson was selling Chevrolets back then."

Silence fell over the conference room.

"I wonder if it's possible that Eriksson made that long trip to Svenstavik," he went on. "And that Krista Haberman went back with him."

He turned to Svedberg.

"Did Eriksson own his farm back then?"

Svedberg nodded.

Wallander looked around the room.

"Holger Eriksson was impaled in a pungee pit," he said. "If what we think is true, that the murderer takes the lives of his or her victims in a way that mirrors crimes that were committed earlier, then I think we can imagine our way to a very unpleasant conclusion."

He wished he was mistaken. But he no longer thought he was.

"I think we have to start searching Holger Eriksson's fields," he said. "I wonder whether Krista Haberman might be buried there somewhere."

It was ten minutes to eleven. Wednesday, October 19th.

Chapter Thirty-two

They went out to the farm in the early dawn.

Wallander took Nyberg, Hamrén, and Hansson along with him. They all drove separately, Wallander in his own car, finally back from Älmhult. They parked at the entrance to the empty house, which stood like a deserted and unrigged ship out there in the fog.

On that particular morning, Thursday, October 20th, the fog was thick. It had come in from the sea late in the night and now hovered motionless over the landscape of Skåne. They had agreed to meet at 6:30, but they were all late because visibility was practically nil. Wallander was the last to arrive. When he got out of his car he thought that it looked like a hunting club had gathered. The only thing missing was their shotguns. He thought with distaste about the task that awaited them. Somewhere on Eriksson's property he suspected that a murdered woman lay buried. Whatever they found, if they found anything at all, would be skeletal remains. Nothing else. Twenty-seven years was a long time.

He could also be completely wrong. His idea of what had happened to Krista Haberman might not be so clever. It wasn't implausible, either. But it was still a big leap from plausibility to fact.

Shivering, they greeted each other. Hansson had brought a surveyor's map of the farm and the adjacent fields. Wallander wondered fleetingly what the Cultural Association of Lund would say if they really did find the remains of a body. He thought gloomily that this would probably increase the number of visitors to the farm. There were few tourist attractions that could compete with a crime scene.

They spread out the map on the hood of Nyberg's car and gathered around it.

"In 1967 the fields were laid out differently," said Hansson, pointing. "It wasn't until the mid-seventies that Eriksson bought up all the fields to the south."

Wallander saw that this reduced the relevant area of land by a third. What remained was still large. He realized that they would never be able to dig up the whole area. They would have to try to find the right spot using other methods.

"The fog is making things harder for us," he said. "I thought we could try to get an overview of the terrain. It seems to me that it should be possible to eliminate certain areas. I assume that a person would choose the spot carefully for burying someone he killed."

"You'd probably pick the spot where you thought it least likely anyone would look," said Nyberg. "A study was done on it. In the U.S., of course. But it sounds reasonable."

"It's a big area," said Hansson.

"That's why we have to make it smaller right away," said Wallander. "It's like Nyberg said. He wouldn't bury her just anywhere. I imagine, for instance, that you wouldn't want a body lying in the ground right outside your front door. Unless you're completely insane. And there's nothing to indicate that Eriksson was."

"Besides, there are cobblestones there," said Hansson. "I think we can eliminate the courtyard."

They went up to the farmhouse. Wallander considered whether they should return to Ystad and come back when the fog was gone. Since there was no wind, it could last all day. He decided that in spite of everything they could spend a while trying to gain an overview.

They walked over to the large garden that lay behind the house. The soft ground was covered with fallen, rotten apples. A magpie fluttered up from a tree. They stopped and looked around. Not here either, thought Wallander. A man who commits murder in a city and has only his garden might bury the body there among the fruit trees and berry bushes. But not a man who lives out in the country.

He told the others what he was thinking. No one had any objections.

They started walking out to the fields. The fog was still thick. Hares popped up against all the whiteness and then vanished. They headed first toward the northern border of the property.

"A dog wouldn't be able to find anything, I guess?" asked Hamrén.

"Not after twenty-seven years," replied Nyberg.

The mud was sticking to their boots. They tried to balance their way along the narrow ridges of plowed grass that formed the boundary of Eriksson's property. A rusty harrow stood mired in the earth. It wasn't just their task that bothered Wallander. The fog and the damp gray earth also oppressed him. He was fond of the landscape of Skåne where he was born and raised, but he could do without the fall. At least on days like this.

They reached a pond that lay in a hollow. Hansson pointed on the map to where they were. They looked at the pond. It was about a hundred meters in circumference.

"This one is full of water year round," said Nyberg. "At the middle it's probably between two and three meters deep."

"It's a possibility, of course," said Wallander. "To sink a body with weights."

"Or a sack," said Hansson. "Like what happened to Blomberg."

Wallander nodded. There was the mirror image again. But he still wasn't sure. He said as much.

"A body can float to the surface. Would Eriksson choose to sink a corpse in a pond when he has thousands of square meters of land to dig a grave in? I have a hard time believing that."

"Who actually worked all this land?" asked Hansson. "Surely not him. He didn't have it leased out. But land has to be worked. Otherwise the weeds take over. And this land is well tended."

Hansson had grown up on a farm outside of Ystad and knew what he was talking about.

"That's an important question," said Wallander. "We have to find out."

"It might also give us the answer to another question," said Hamrén. "Whether any changes have occurred on the land. A mound that suddenly appeared. If you dig in one place, a mound appears somewhere else. I'm not thinking about a grave. But a ditch, for example. Or something else."

"We're talking about events that occurred almost thirty years ago," said Nyberg. "Who would remember that far back?"

"It happens," said Wallander. "But of course we'll have to look into it. So who worked Holger Eriksson's land?"

"Thirty years is a long time," said Hansson. "There could have been more than one person."

"Then we'll talk to all of them," replied Wallander. "If we can find them. If they're still alive."

They moved on. Wallander suddenly remembered that he had seen several old aerial photos of the farm inside the house. He asked Hansson to call the Cultural Association in Lund and ask someone to bring the keys out.

"It's unlikely anyone would be there at quarter after seven in the morning."

"Call up Höglund," said Wallander. "Ask her to contact the lawyer who handled Eriksson's will. He might still have a set of keys."

"Lawyers might be morning people," said Hansson doubtfully and dialed the number.

"I want to see those aerial shots," said Wallander. "ASAP."

They kept walking. Hansson talked to Höglund. The field now sloped downward. The fog was still just as thick. In the distance they heard a tractor. The sound of the engine died away. Hansson's phone rang. Höglund had spoken to the lawyer. He had turned in his keys. She'd tried to get hold of someone in Lund who could help them but hadn't found anyone yet. She promised to get back to them. Wallander thought about the two women he had met the week before. With distaste he remembered the snobbish, aristocratic woman.

It took them almost twenty minutes to reach the next boundary marker. Hansson pointed to the map. They were now at the southwest corner. The property stretched another five hundred meters south. But Eriksson hadn't bought this section until 1976. They walked east, now approaching the ditch and the hill with the bird tower. Wallander felt his uneasiness growing. He thought he could sense the same silent reaction from the others.

It was turning into an image of his life, he thought. My life as a cop during the last part of the twentieth century in Sweden. An early morning, dawn. Fall, fog, a damp chill. Four men slogging around in the mud. They approach an incomprehensible predator trap where a man was impaled on exotic bamboo stakes. At the same time they're searching for a possible burial site for a Polish woman who disappeared twenty-seven years ago.

I'm going to end up trudging around in this mud until I collapse. Other places in the fog people are huddled around their kitchen tables, organizing various militias. Anyone who takes a wrong turn in the fog runs the risk of being beaten to death.

He noticed that he was walking along carrying on a conversation in his mind with Rydberg. Without words, but still quite vivid. Rydberg was sitting on his balcony toward the end of his illness. The balcony hovered before Wallander's eyes like an airship in the fog. But Rydberg didn't answer. He just listened with his wry smile. His face was already heavily marked by illness.

All of a sudden they were there. Wallander came last. The ditch lay off to the side. Then they reached the pungee pit. A torn remnant of police tape had gotten caught under one of the collapsed planks. We didn't clean up this crime scene very well, thought Wallander. The bamboo stakes were gone. He wondered where they were stored. In the basement of the police station? At forensics in Linköping? The bird tower was on their right. It was barely visible in the fog.

Wallander noticed an idea trying to take shape in his mind. He took a few steps to the side and nearly slipped on the mud. Nyberg stood staring into the ditch. Hamrén and Hansson were discussing a detail on the map in low voices.

Someone keeps an eye on Holger Eriksson and his farm, thought

Wallander. Someone who knows what happened to Krista Haberman. A woman, missing for twenty-seven years, declared dead. A woman who is buried somewhere in a field. Eriksson's time is being measured out. Another grave with sharpened stakes is prepared. Another grave in the mud.

He went over to Hamrén and Hansson. Nyberg had disappeared in the fog. He told them what he'd just been thinking. He would repeat it for Nyberg later.

"If the perpetrator is as well-informed as we think, then he also knew where Krista Haberman was buried. On several occasions we've talked about the murderer having a language. He or she is trying to tell us something. We've only had partial success in breaking the code. Eriksson was killed with what can be described as deliberate brutality. His body was guaranteed to be found. It's also possible that this place was chosen for another reason. A challenge to us to keep searching. Right here. And if we do, we'll also find Krista Haberman."

Nyberg reappeared out of the fog. Wallander repeated what he'd said. Everyone realized he could be right. They made their way over the ditch and went up to the tower. The woods below were shrouded in fog.

"Too many roots," said Nyberg. "I don't think it's that grove of trees."

They turned around and continued eastward until they were back where they had started. It was close to eight o'clock. The fog was just as thick. Höglund had called to say the keys were on the way. Everyone was cold and wet. Wallander didn't want to keep them there unnecessarily. Hansson would spend the next few hours trying to find out who had worked the land.

"An unexpected change twenty-seven years ago," Wallander emphasized. "That's what we want to know about. But don't mention that we think there's a body buried here. Then there'll be an invasion."

Hansson nodded. He understood.

"We'll go over this again sometime when there's no fog," Wallander went on. "But I think it's good that we already have this overview."

They all left but Wallander, who stayed behind until he was alone. He got in his car and turned on the heat. It wasn't working. The repairs had cost an incredible amount of money. But apparently that didn't cover the heating system. He wondered when he'd have time and money to trade it in for another car. When was this one going to fall apart again?

He waited, thinking about the women. Krista Haberman, Eva Runfeldt, and Katarina Taxell. Plus the fourth one who didn't have a name. What was the common point of contact? He had a feeling it was so close that he should be able to see it. He was looking at it without seeing it.

He went back over his thoughts. Abused, maybe murdered women. A vast stretch of time arched like a vault over the whole thing.

As he sat in his car he realized that there was one other possible conclusion. They hadn't seen everything. The events they were trying to understand were part of something bigger. It was important for them to find the connection between the women, but they also had to consider the possibility that the connection was coincidental. Someone was making choices. But what were the choices based on? Circumstances? Coincidences, maybe available opportunities? Holger Eriksson lived alone on a farm. Didn't socialize, watched birds at night. He was someone it was possible to get near. Gösta Runfeldt was leaving on an orchid safari. He was going to be gone for two weeks. That also provided an opportunity. He also lived alone. Eugen Blomberg regularly took solitary walks in the evening.

Wallander shook his head at his own thoughts. He couldn't make any progress. Was he thinking in the right direction or not? He didn't know.

It was cold in the car. He got out to move around. The keys should be arriving soon. He walked across the courtyard, remembering the first time he had come here. The flock of crows down by the ditch. He looked at his hands. He was no longer tan. The memory of the sun over Villa Borghese was definitely gone. Like his father.

He stared into the fog. Let his gaze wander over the courtyard. The house was well taken care of. Once a man named Holger Eriksson sat here and wrote poems about birds. The lonely flight of the common snipe. The middle spotted woodpecker, which had disappeared from Sweden. One day he got into a dark blue Chevrolet and made the long drive to Jämtland. Was he driven by passion? Or something else? Krista Haberman was a beautiful woman. In the stacks of investigative material from Östersund there was a photograph of her. Did she go with him willingly? She must have.

They drive toward Skåne. Then she disappears. Holger Eriksson lives alone. He digs a grave. She's gone. The investigation never catches up with him. Until now. When Hansson finds the name Tandvall and they see a previously undiscovered connection.

Wallander noticed that he was standing and looking at the deserted dog pen. At first he wasn't aware of what he was thinking. The image of Krista Haberman slowly slipped away. He frowned. Why wasn't there a dog? No one had asked that question before. He hadn't either. When had the dog disappeared? Did that have any significance at all? These were questions he wanted to have answered.

A car braked outside the house. A moment later a boy who couldn't be more than twenty came into the courtyard. He walked over to Wallander.

"Are you the cop that needs the key?"

"Yes, I am."

The boy regarded him doubtfully.

"How can I be sure? You could be anybody."

Wallander felt annoyed. At the same time he realized that the boy's doubts could have a certain basis. He had mud all over his pants legs. He took out his ID. The boy nodded and gave him the set of keys.

"I'll see to it that they get back to Lund," said Wallander.

The boy nodded. He was in a hurry. Wallander heard the car roar off as he looked through the keys for the one to the front door. He thought fleetingly about what Jonas Hader had said about the red Golf outside Katarina Taxell's building.

Don't women gun their engines? he thought. Mona drives faster than I do. Baiba always stomps on the gas pedal. But maybe they don't gun their engines.

He opened the door and went inside. Turned on the light in the big entryway. It smelled musty. He sat down on a bench and pulled off his muddy boots. When he went into the main room he noticed to his surprise that the poem about the middle spotted woodpecker was still lying on the desk. The night of September 21st. Tomorrow it would be a month since then. Were they really any closer to a solution? They had two more murders to solve. A woman who had disappeared. Another woman who might be buried out in Eriksson's fields.

He stood motionless in the silence. The fog outside the windows was still dense. He felt uneasy. The objects in the room were watching him. He walked over to the wall where the two aerial photographs hung in their frames. He searched his pockets for his glasses. That morning he had remembered to bring them along. He put them on and leaned forward. One of the photos was black-and-white, the other a faded color shot. The black-and-white picture was from 1949. Taken two years before Holger Eriksson bought this farm. The color photo was from 1965. Wallander opened a curtain to let in more light. Suddenly he saw a lone deer walking around and grazing among the trees in the garden. He stood quite still. The deer raised its head and looked at him. Then it calmly went on grazing. Wallander stayed where he was. He had a feeling that he would never forget that deer. How long he stood there and watched it, he didn't know. A sound that he himself didn't notice caught the deer's attention. It took off running and vanished. Wallander kept on looking out the window. The deer was gone. He went back to the two photographs that had been taken by the same company, Air Photo, at an interval of sixteen years. The plane carrying the camera had come in from due south. All the details were clear. In 1965 Eriksson hadn't yet built his tower. But the hill was there. So was the ditch. Wallander squinted his eyes. He couldn't make out a footbridge. He followed the contours of the fields. The picture was taken early in the spring. The fields had been plowed, but nothing was growing yet. The pond was quite clear in the photo. A grove of trees stood next to a narrow tractor path separating two of the fields. He frowned. He couldn't remember those trees. This morning he wouldn't have seen them because of the fog. But he didn't remember them from his previous visits either. The trees looked tall. He ought to have noticed them standing alone out in the fields. He switched over to studying the house, which stood in the middle of the picture. Between 1949 and 1965 the house had acquired its new roof. An outbuilding that might have been used as a pigsty had been torn down. The approach road was wider. But otherwise everything was much the same. He took off his glasses and looked out the window. The deer was still gone. He sat down in a leather armchair. Silence surrounded him.

A Chevrolet goes to Svenstavik. A woman comes back to Skåne. Then she vanishes. Twenty-seven years later the man dies who might have gone to Svenstavik to get her.

He sat there in silence for half an hour. He backtracked again in his mind. He thought about the fact that right now they were looking for no less than three different women. Krista Haberman, Katarina Taxell, and one without a name. But one who drove around in a red Golf. Who smoked hand-rolled cigarettes and might wear press-on nails.

He wondered whether it could be true that they were really looking for two women. Whether two of them could be one and the same. Whether Krista Haberman, in spite of everything, was still alive. If so, she would be 65 years old. The woman who knocked down Ylva Brink was a lot younger.

It didn't add up. Most of it didn't.

He looked at his watch. Quarter to nine. He stood up and left the house. The fog was still just as thick. He thought about the deserted dog pen. Then he locked up and drove away.

At ten o'clock Wallander succeeded in gathering everyone involved on the investigative team for a meeting. The only one missing was Martinsson. He had promised to come sometime in the afternoon. In the morning he would be at Terese's school. Höglund could tell them that he had called her late the night before. She thought he sounded drunk, which almost never happened. Wallander felt vaguely jealous. Why had Martinsson called her and not him? In spite of everything, it was the two of them who had worked together all these years.

"He still seems determined to quit," she said. "But I got the feeling that he also wished I would talk him out of it."

"I'll talk to him," said Wallander.

They closed the door to the conference room. Per Åkeson and Chief Holgersson were the last ones to arrive. Wallander had a feeling that they had just completed their own meeting.

Lisa Holgersson took the floor as soon as the room was quiet.

"The whole country is talking about the citizen militia," she said. "From now on Lödinge is a town that everyone in Sweden knows about. We've had a request for Kurt to participate in a discussion program on TV tonight. From Göteborg."

"Not on your life," replied Wallander, horrified. "What would I say?"

"I've already turned them down on your behalf," she replied with a smile. "But I'm thinking of asking for a favor in return later on."

Wallander realized at once that she was referring to the lectures at the Police Academy.

"The debate is inflamed and vigorous," she went on. "We can only hope that something good comes out of it, now that this feeling of insecurity regarding the rights of individuals is actually being discussed."

"In the best-case scenario it might also force the upper echelons of the police administration in this country to be a little more self-critical," said Hansson. "The police themselves aren't without blame for the way things have developed."

"What are you getting at?" asked Wallander, curious. Hansson rarely participated in discussions about the police force.

"I'm thinking about all the scandals in which the police have been actively involved," said Hansson. "Maybe they've always existed. But not as often as they do now."

"That's something we should neither exaggerate nor ignore," said Per Åkeson. "The big problem is the gradual shifting of what the police and the courts see as a crime. What would have brought a conviction yesterday is suddenly considered a trifle today, and the police shouldn't even bother to investigate. I think that's offensive to the national sense of justice, which has always been strong in this country."

"They're probably related," said Wallander. "I have strong doubts that a discussion of the citizen militia will have any effect on the development. Even though I'd like to believe otherwise."

"I'm thinking of prosecuting as much as I can," said Åkeson when Wallander fell silent. "The assault was vicious. That's something I can emphasize. There were four men involved. I think I can convict at least three of them. The fourth one is less certain. I think I should also tell you that the Chief Prosecutor wants to be kept informed. I consider that quite surprising. But it indicates that at least some of the higher-ups are taking this seriously."

"Åke Davidsson sounds intelligent and articulate in an interview in *Arbetet*," said Svedberg. "And by the way, he's not going to have any permanent injuries."

"Then there's Terese and her father," said Wallander. "And the boys at the school."

"Is Martinsson thinking of resigning?" asked Åkeson. "I heard a rumor about it."

"That was his first reaction," replied Wallander. "Which seems both reasonable and natural. But I'm not sure he's really going to go through with it."

"He's a good cop," said Hansson. "Doesn't he know that?"

"Yes," said Wallander. "The question is whether that's enough. Other things can come up when something like this happens. Especially our unreasonable workload."

"I know," said Chief Holgersson. "And it's just going to get worse."

Wallander remembered that he still hadn't done what he had promised Nyberg; talk to Holgersson about his workload. He made a note of it on his pad.

"We'll have to take up this discussion later," he said.

"I just wanted to inform you," said Holgersson. "That's all, except that former Chief Björk called to wish you luck. He was sorry to hear about what happened to Martinsson's daughter."

"He knew enough to resign in time," said Svedberg. "What did we give him as a going-away present? A fly rod? If he was still working here, he'd never have time to use it."

"He probably has enough on his hands now too," objected Holgersson.

"Björk was a good man," said Wallander. "But I think we'd better move on."

They started with Höglund's timetable. Next to his notepad Wallander had placed the plastic bag with the schedule for SR that he had found in Katarina Taxell's desk.

As usual, Höglund had done a thorough job. All the times that had anything to do with the various events were mapped out and listed in relationship to each other. While Wallander listened, he thought that this was an assignment he himself never could have done particularly well. In all probability he would have been sloppy. All cops are different, he thought. It's only when we can work with something that challenges our strong sides that we're of any real use.

"I don't really see any pattern emerging," said Höglund as she neared the end of her presentation. "The medical examiners in Lund have succeeded in establishing the time of Eriksson's death as late on the evening of September 21st. How they actually managed to do this, I can't tell you. But they're quite certain. Gösta Runfeldt's death also occurred at night. The times correspond without it being possible to draw any logical conclusions. And there's no correspondence in terms of the days of the week. If we add the two visits to the Ystad maternity ward and the murder of Eugen Blomberg, there might be a fragment of a pattern."

She broke off and looked around the table. Neither Wallander nor anyone else seemed to understand what she meant.

"It's almost pure mathematics," she said. "But it seems as if our perpetrator is active according to a pattern that is so irregular that it's interesting. On September 21st Holger Eriksson dies. On the night of September 30th, Katarina Taxell has a visitor in the Ystad maternity ward. On October 11th Gösta Runfeldt dies. On the night of October 12th the woman is back at the maternity ward and knocks down Svedberg's cousin. Finally, on October 17th Eugen Blomberg dies. To this we can also add the day when Gösta Runfeldt probably disappeared. The pattern I see is that there is no regularity whatsoever. Which might be surprising. Since everything else seems to be minutely planned and prepared. A perpetrator who takes the time to sew weights into a sack and carefully balance them to the victim's body weight. So we can choose to see it as having no intervals that can tell us anything. Or we can decide that the irregularity was caused by something else. And then we have to ask: By what?"

Wallander noticed that he wasn't quite following her.

"One more time," he said. "Slowly."

She repeated what she had said. This time Wallander understood what she meant.

"Maybe we can just say that it doesn't have to be a coincidence," she concluded. "I won't try to stretch it farther than that. There might be a regularity that's repeated. But there doesn't have to be."

Wallander now started to see the picture more clearly.

"Let's assume that in spite of everything there is a pattern," he said. "Then what's your interpretation? What are the outside forces that affect a perpetrator's timetable?"

"There could be various explanations. The perpetrator doesn't live in Skåne, but makes regular visits here. He or she has a job that follows a certain rhythm. Or something else I haven't been able to think of."

"So you think these dates could be days off that were saved and used later? If we could follow them for another month, would it be clearer?"

"That's possible. The perpetrator has a job that follows a rotating schedule. In other words, the days off don't always occur on Saturdays and Sundays."

"That might turn out to be important," said Wallander hesitantly. "But I have a hard time believing it."

"Otherwise I couldn't manage to read much from the times," she said. "The person is always slipping away."

"The things we *can't* figure out also tell us something," said Wallander, holding up the plastic bag. "Now that we're talking about timetables. I found this in a secret compartment in Katarina Taxell's desk. If she was trying to hide her most important possession from the world, then this has to be it. A timetable for SR's intercity trains. Spring of 1991. With a line drawn under a train departure: Nässjö 16:00. It goes every day."

He pushed the plastic bag over to Nyberg.

"Fingerprints," he said.

Then he switched to talking about Krista Haberman. He presented his ideas. Told them about the morning visit in the fog. There was no mistaking the somber mood in the room.

"So I think we have to start digging," he concluded his summary. "When the fog lifts and Hansson has had a chance to find out who worked the land. And whether any dramatic changes took place after 1967."

For a long time there was complete silence. Everyone was evaluating what Wallander had just said. Finally it was Åkeson who spoke.

"This sounds both incredible and at the same time highly plausible," he said. "I assume that we have to take this possibility seriously."

"It would be good if this didn't get out," said Chief Holgersson. "There's nothing people like better than having old, unsolved missing-person cases come up again."

They had made a decision.

Wallander now wanted to end the meeting as quickly as possible because everyone had a lot of work waiting.

"Katarina Taxell," he said. "She has disappeared. Left her home in a red Golf. With an unknown driver. Her departure has to be regarded as sudden. Birch in Lund is probably waiting for us to say something. Her mother wants us to put out an APB on her. Which we can hardly refuse her since she's the next of kin. But I think we should wait, at least a few more days."

"Why?" asked Åkeson.

"I have a suspicion that she'll make contact," said Wallander. "Not with us, of course. But with her mother. Katarina Taxell knows she'll be worried. She'll call to reassure her. Unfortunately she probably won't say where she is. Or who she's with."

Wallander now turned to face Åkeson. "I want someone to stay with Taxell's mother. To record the conversation. Sooner or later it'll come."

"If it hasn't happened already," said Hansson, getting to his feet. "Give me Birch's phone number."

He got it from Höglund and quickly left the room.

"I guess there's nothing more right now," said Wallander. "Let's say that we'll meet again at five o'clock. If nothing else happens before then."

When Wallander got to his own office, the phone was ringing. It was Martinsson. He wondered if Wallander could meet him at two o'clock at his house. Wallander promised to be there. He left the station. He ate lunch at the Hotel Continental. He didn't really think he could afford it, but he was hungry and didn't have much time. He sat alone at a window table. Nodded to people passing by, surprised and hurt that no one stopped to offer condolences at the death of his father. It was in the papers. News of a death travels fast, and Ystad was a small town. He ate halibut and drank a light beer. The waitress was young and blushed every time he looked at her. He wondered sympathetically how she was going to stand her job.

At two o'clock he rang Martinsson's doorbell. He opened the door himself. They sat in the kitchen. The house was quiet. Martinsson was home alone. Wallander asked about Terese. She had gone back to school. Martinsson looked pale and dejected. Wallander had never seen him so depressed.

"What should I do?" asked Martinsson.

"What does your wife say? What does Terese say?"

"That I should keep working, of course. They're not the ones who want me to quit. I'm the one."

Wallander waited. But Martinsson didn't say anything.

"Remember a few years back?" Wallander began. "When I shot a man to death in the fog near Kåseberga? And ran over another one on the Öland Bridge? I was gone almost a year. All of you even thought I had quit. Then there was that case with the two lawyers named Torstensson. And suddenly everything changed. I was about to sign my letter of resignation, and instead I went back on duty."

Martinsson nodded. He remembered.

"Now, after the fact, I'm glad that I did what I did. The only advice I can give you is that you shouldn't do anything rash. Wait to make up your mind. Work one day at a time. Decide later. I'm not asking you to forget. I'm asking you to be patient. Everyone misses you. Everyone knows that you're a good cop. Everyone notices when you're not there."

Martinsson threw out his arms.

"I'm not that important. Sure, I know a few things. But you can't tell me that I'm in any way irreplaceable."

"You *are* irreplaceable," said Wallander. "That's what I'm trying to tell you."

Wallander had expected the conversation to take a long time. Martinsson sat in silence for a few minutes. Then he got up and left the kitchen. When he came back he had his jacket on.

"Shall we go?" he asked.

"Yes," said Wallander. "We've got a lot of work to do."

In the car on the way to the station, Wallander gave him a brief summary of the events of the past few days. Martinsson listened without making any comments.

When they entered the lobby, Ebba stopped them. Since she didn't take the time to welcome Martinsson back, Wallander knew at once that something had happened.

"Ann-Britt is trying to get hold of you two," she said. "It's important."

"What's happened?"

"Someone named Katarina Taxell called her mother."

Wallander looked at Martinsson. So he was right.

But it happened faster than he had expected.

Chapter Thirty-three

They weren't too late.

Birch had managed to get there in time with a tape recorder. In just over an hour the tape from Lund was in Ystad. They gathered in Wallander's office where Svedberg had set up a tape recorder.

They listened tensely to Katarina Taxell's conversation with her mother. The conversation was brief. That was the first thing that occurred to Wallander. Taxell didn't want to talk any longer than necessary.

They listened to it once, then a second time. Svedberg handed Wallander a pair of earphones so he could listen to the two voices more closely.

"Mamma? It's me."

"Dear God. Where on earth are you? What happened?"

"Nothing happened. We're fine."

"Where on earth are you?"

"With a good friend."

"Who?"

"A good friend. I just wanted to call and tell you everything's fine."

"What happened? Why did you disappear?"

"I'll explain some other time."

"Who are you staying with?"

"You don't know her."

"Don't hang up. What's your phone number?"

"I'm going now. I just wanted to call so you wouldn't worry."

Her mother tried to say something else, but Katarina hung up.

They listened to the tape at least twenty times. Svedberg wrote down what was said on a piece of paper.

"It's the eleventh line that interests us," said Wallander. " 'You don't know her.' What does she mean by that?"

"Just what she says," said Höglund.

"That's not what I'm getting at," Wallander clarified. " 'You don't know her.' That could mean two things. That her mother has never met her. Or that her mother doesn't understand what she means to Katarina."

"The first one is the most plausible," said Höglund.

"I hope you're wrong," replied Wallander. "That would make it much easier for us to identify her."

While they talked Nyberg had put on the earphones and listened. The sounds seeping out told them that he was listening with the volume turned up high.

"There's something audible in the background," said Nyberg. "A banging noise."

Wallander put on the earphones. Nyberg was right. There was a steady dull pounding somewhere in the background. The others took turns listening. No one could say for sure what it was.

"Where is she?" asked Wallander. "She's arrived somewhere. She's staying with the woman who came to pick her up. And somewhere in the background something is banging."

"Could it be near a construction site?" suggested Martinsson.

That was the first thing he had said since he decided to come back to work.

"That's a possibility," said Wallander.

They listened again. It was definitely a banging sound. Wallander made a decision.

"Send the tape to Linköping," he said. "Ask them to do an analysis. If we can identify the sound, it might help us."

"How many construction sites are there in Skåne alone?" said Hamrén.

"It could be something else," said Wallander. "Something that might give us an idea where she is."

Nyberg left with the tape. They stayed in Wallander's office, leaning against the walls and desk.

"Three things are important from now on," said Wallander. "We have to concentrate. For the time being we'll have to put aside certain aspects of the investigation. We have to keep mapping out Katarina Taxell's life. Who is she? Who was she? Her friends? Her movements in life? That's the first thing. The second thing is related, namely: Who is she staying with?"

He paused briefly before he went on.

"We'll wait until Hansson comes back from Lödinge. But I think our third task will be to start digging at Eriksson's place."

No one had any objections. The meeting broke up. Wallander had to go to Lund, and he was thinking of taking Höglund with him. It was already late afternoon.

"Do you have a babysitter?" he asked when they were alone in the office.

"Yes," she said. "Right now my neighbor needs the money, thank God."

"How can you afford it on a police salary?" asked Wallander.

"I can't," she said. "But my husband makes a good living. That's what saves us. We're one of the lucky families today."

Wallander called Birch and said they were on their way.

He let Höglund drive. He no longer trusted his own car, in spite of the expensive repairs.

The landscape slowly vanished in the twilight. A cold wind blew across the fields.

"We'll start at the home of Katarina Taxell's mother," he said. "Later we'll go back to her apartment."

"What do you think you might find? You've already gone over the apartment. And you're usually thorough."

"Maybe nothing new. But maybe a connection between two details that I didn't see before."

She drove fast.

"Do you usually rev the engine when you start?" asked Wallander suddenly.

She gave him a quick look. "Sometimes. Why do you ask?"

"Because I wonder if it was a woman driving the red Golf that picked up Katarina Taxell."

"Don't we know that for sure?"

"No," said Wallander firmly. "We hardly know anything for sure."

He looked out the window. They were just passing Marsvinsholm Castle.

"There's something else we don't know with certainty," he said after a while. "But I'm becoming more and more convinced of it."

"What's that?"

"She was alone. There's no man anywhere near her. There's no one at all. We're not looking for a woman who might give us a possible lead. There's no background to her. There's nothing behind her. There's just her. No one else."

"So she's the one who committed the murders? Dug the pungee pit? Strangled Runfeldt after holding him captive? Tossed Blomberg in the lake, alive in a sack?"

Wallander replied by asking another question.

"Do you remember, early on in the investigation, when we talked about the perpetrator's language? That he or she wanted to tell us something? About the deliberateness of the M.O.?"

She remembered.

"It strikes me now that from the start we saw things correctly. But we were thinking *wrong*."

"That a woman was behaving like a man?"

"Maybe not exactly the behavior. But she committed deeds that made us think of brutal men."

"So we were supposed to think about the victims? Because they were brutal?"

"Exactly. Not about the perpetrator. We read the wrong message into what we saw."

"But here's where it gets difficult," she said. "Believing that a woman could really be capable of this. I'm not talking about physical strength. I'm just as strong as my husband, for example. He has a lot of trouble beating me at arm wrestling."

Wallander looked at her in surprise. She noticed and laughed.

"People amuse themselves in different ways."

Wallander nodded.

"I remember having a finger-pulling match with my mother when I was little," he said. "I think I was the winner."

"Maybe she let you win."

They turned off toward Sturup.

"I don't know what motivation this woman has for her actions," said Wallander. "But if we find her, I think we'll be dealing with someone the likes of whom we've never encountered before."

"A female monster?"

"Maybe. But that's not certain either."

The car phone interrupted their conversation. Wallander answered. It was Birch. He gave them directions for getting to the home of Katarina Taxell's mother.

"What's her first name?" asked Wallander.

"Hedwig. Hedwig Taxell."

Birch promised to warn her they were coming. Wallander figured they should be there in about half an hour.

The twilight wrapped around them.

Birch was standing on the steps to receive them. Hedwig Taxell lived in an end row house on the outskirts of Lund. Wallander guessed that the house had been built in the early sixties. Flat roofs, square boxes facing onto small courtyards. He recalled having read that the roofs sometimes caved in during heavy snowfalls. Birch had been waiting for them as they searched for the right address.

"They almost started talking before I got the machine set up," he said.

"We haven't exactly been overwhelmed with good luck," replied Wallander. "What's your impression of Hedwig Taxell?"

"She's worried about her daughter and grandson. But she seems more composed than before."

"Do you think she'll help us? Or is she protecting her daughter?"

"I think she simply wants to know where she is."

He let them into the living room. Without being able to define it, Wallander had a feeling that the room was somehow similar to Katarina Taxell's apartment. Hedwig Taxell came in and said hello. As usual, Birch stayed in the background. Wallander studied her. She was pale. Her eyes flitted restlessly. Wallander wasn't surprised. He had heard that in her voice on the tape. She was nervous and tense, close to the breaking point. That's why he had brought Höglund along. She had a great ability to reassure nervous people. Mrs. Taxell didn't seem to be on her guard. He had a feeling that she was glad not to be alone. They sat down. Wallander had prepared his first questions.

"Mrs. Taxell, we need your help. Can you answer some questions about Katarina for us?"

"How is she supposed to know anything about those horrible murders? She just had a baby, you know."

"We don't think she's involved in any way," said Wallander in a friendly voice. "But we have to look for information from many different sources."

"What's she supposed to know?"

"That's what I'm hoping to find out."

"Can you go searching for her instead? I don't understand what's happened."

"I'm absolutely sure she's in no danger," said Wallander, but he wasn't entirely successful in hiding his doubt.

"She's never behaved like this before."

"So you have no idea where she is, Mrs. Taxell?"

"My name is Hedwig."

"You have no idea where she is?"

"No. This is unbelievable."

"Does Katarina have a lot of friends?"

"No, she doesn't. But the ones she has are close friends. I don't understand where she could be."

"Maybe there's someone she didn't see very often? Someone she had gotten to know recently?"

"Who would that be?"

"Or maybe someone she met earlier? Someone she had started seeing again recently?"

"I would have known about it. We have a good relationship. Much better than most mothers and daughters."

"I'm not implying that you had any secrets from each other," said Wallander patiently. "But it's rare that someone knows everything about another person. Do you know, for instance, who the father of her child is?"

Wallander hadn't meant to throw the question in her face like that. She flinched.

"I've tried to get her to talk about it," she said. "But she refuses."

"So you don't know who he is? You can't even guess?"

"I didn't even know she was seeing anyone."

"You knew she had a relationship with Eugen Blomberg?"

"I knew about it. I didn't like him."

"Why not? Was it because he was already married?"

"I didn't know that until I saw the obituary in the paper. It was a shock."

"Why didn't you like him?"

"I don't know. He was unpleasant."

"Did you know that he had abused Katarina?"

Her horror was completely genuine. For a moment Wallander felt sorry for her. Her world was threatening to collapse. She would now be forced to realize that there was a lot she didn't know about her daughter. That the intimacy she thought existed was hardly more than a shell. Or at least very limited.

"Did he hit her?"

"Worse than that. He abused her in many different ways."

She looked at him in disbelief. She saw that he was telling the truth. She couldn't defend herself.

"I also think it's possible that Eugen Blomberg is the father of her child. Even though they weren't seeing each other anymore."

She shook her head slowly and said nothing. Wallander was afraid she might fall apart again. He looked at Höglund. She nodded. He took this to mean that he should go on. Birch stood motionless in the background.

"Her friends," said Wallander. "We need to meet them. Talk to them."

"I've already told you who they are. And you've already talked to them."

She rattled off three names. Birch nodded in the background.

"There aren't any others?"

"No."

"Does she belong to any clubs?"

"No."

"Has she taken any trips abroad?"

"We usually go somewhere once a year. Usually when the schools have vacation in February. To Madeira. Morocco. Tunisia."

"Does she have any hobbies?"

"She reads a lot. Likes to listen to music. Her hair products business takes up most of her time. She works hard."

"Nothing else?"

"Sometimes she plays badminton."

"Who with? One of the three girlfriends?"

"With a teacher. I think her name is Carlman. But I've never met her."

Wallander didn't know if this was important. At least it was a new name.

"Do they work at the same school?"

"Not anymore. In the past. A few years ago."

"You don't remember her first name?"

"I've never met her."

"Where did they usually play?"

"At Victoria Stadium. It's within walking distance of her apartment."

Birch discreetly left his place and went into the entryway. Wallander knew that he was now starting to trace the woman named Carlman.

It took him less than five minutes.

Birch signaled to Wallander, who stood up and went over to the entryway. In the meantime Höglund tried to clarify what Mrs. Taxell really knew about her daughter's relationship with Eugen Blomberg.

"That was easy," said Birch. "Annika Carlman. She's the one who reserved and paid for the court. I have her address. It's not far from here. Lund is still a small town."

"Let's go there," said Wallander.

He went back into the room.

"Annika Carlman," he said. "She lives on Bankgatan."

"I've never heard her first name before," said Mrs. Taxell.

"We'll leave you two alone for a while," Wallander went on. "We need to talk to her right away."

They drove away from the house in Birch's car. It took less than ten minutes to get there. It was 6:30. Annika Carlman lived in a turn of the century apartment building. Birch picked up the security phone. A man's voice answered. Birch identified himself. The door opened. A door on the second floor stood open. A man stood there waiting for them. He introduced himself.

"I'm Annika's husband," he said. "What's happened?"

"Nothing," said Birch. "We just need to ask a few questions."

He invited them in. The apartment was big and lavish. Somewhere in another room they could hear music and children's voices. A moment later Annika Carlman came in. She was tall and wore workout clothes.

"These police officers want to talk to you. But nothing seems to have happened."

"We need to ask some questions about Katarina Taxell," said Wallander.

They sat down in a room where the walls were lined with books. Wallander wondered whether Annika Carlman's husband was also a teacher.

He got right to the point.

"How well do you know Katarina Taxell?"

"We played badminton. But we didn't socialize."

"But you do know she just had a baby?"

"We haven't played badminton for five months for precisely that reason."

"Were you going to start up again?"

"We'd agreed she would give me a call."

Wallander mentioned the names of Katarina's three girlfriends.

"I don't know them. We just played badminton."

"When did you start playing?"

"About five years ago. We were teachers at the same school."

"Is it really possible to play badminton regularly with someone for five years without getting to know her?"

"It's totally possible."

Wallander pondered how to continue. Annika Carlman gave clear, concise answers. And yet he could feel that they were moving away from something.

"You never saw her together with anyone else?"

"Man or woman?"

"Let's start with a man."

"No."

"Not even when you were working together?"

"She kept pretty much to herself. There was one teacher who seemed interested in her. She acted very cold. You might almost say hostile. But she was good with the students. She was smart. A stubborn and smart teacher."

"Did you ever see her with a woman?"

Wallander had given up hope in the value of that question before he even asked it. But he had resigned himself too soon.

"Yes, as a matter of fact," she replied. "About three years ago."

"Who was it?"

"I don't know her name. But I know what she does. It was a very peculiar situation."

"What does she do?"

"What she's doing now, I don't know. But back then she was a waitress in a dining car."

Wallander frowned.

"You ran into Katarina Taxell on a train?"

"I just happened to catch sight of her in town with another woman. I was walking on the other side of the street. We didn't even say hello to each other. A few days later I took the train to Stockholm. I went into the café car somewhere after Alvesta. When I was paying the bill I recognized the woman working there. It was the same woman I had seen with Katarina."

"You say you don't know what her name is?"

"No."

"But you mentioned this to Katarina later on?"

"Actually, I didn't. I guess I forgot all about it. Is it important?"

Wallander suddenly thought about the timetable he had found in Taxell's desk.

"Maybe. What day was it? Which train?"

"How would I remember that?" she said in surprise. "It was three years ago."

"Do you happen to have an old calendar? We'd like you to try and remember."

Her husband, who had been sitting quietly and listening, stood up.

"I'll get the calendar," he said. "Was it 1991 or 1992?"

She thought for a moment.

"1991. In February or March."

Several minutes passed as they waited tensely. The music from somewhere in the apartment had been replaced by sounds from a TV. The husband came back and handed her an old black calendar. She leafed through a few months. Then she found the right place.

"I went to Stockholm on February 19th, 1991. On a train that left at 7:12 A.M. Three days later I came back. I went to see my sister."

"You didn't see this woman on your return trip?"

"I've never seen her again."

"But you're positive it was the same woman? The one you saw on the street here in Lund? With Katarina?"

"Yes."

Wallander regarded her thoughtfully.

"There's nothing else you think might be important for us?"

She shook her head.

"I realize now that I don't really know anything about Katarina. But she's a good badminton player."

"How would you describe her as a person?"

"That's hard. Maybe that describes her right there. A hard-to-describe person. She's temperamental. She can be depressed. But that time I saw her on the street with the waitress she was laughing."

"Are you sure about that?"

"Yes."

"There's nothing else you think might be important?"

Wallander saw that she was making an effort to be helpful.

"I think she misses her father," she said after a moment.

"Why do you think that?"

"That's hard to say. It's more a feeling I got. The way she acted toward men who were old enough to be her father."

"How did she act?"

"She'd stop behaving naturally, as if unsure of herself."

For a moment Wallander pondered what she had said. He thought about Katarina's father, who had died when she was still young. He also wondered if what Annika Carlman had said could explain the relationship Katarina had had with Eugen Blomberg.

He looked at her again. "Anything else?"

"No."

Wallander nodded to Birch and stood up.

"Then we won't bother you any more," he said.

"I'm curious, of course," she said. "Why are the police asking questions if nothing has happened?"

"A lot has happened," said Wallander. "But not to Katarina. I'm afraid that's all the answer I can give you."

They left the apartment and stood in the stairwell.

"We've got to get hold of this waitress," said Wallander. "Except for a photograph when she was young and visiting Copenhagen, no one has described Katarina Taxell as someone who laughs."

"SR must have lists of employees," said Birch. "But I wonder if we're going to find out anything more tonight. It was three years ago, after all."

"We have to try," said Wallander. "Of course I can't ask you to do it. We can handle it from Ystad."

"You have enough to do," replied Birch. "I'll take care of it."

Wallander could tell that Birch was sincere. It was no sacrifice.

They drove back to Hedwig Taxell's row house. Birch dropped Wallander off and continued on to the police station to start looking for the train waitress. Wallander wondered whether it was an impossible task.

Just as he rang the doorbell, his phone buzzed. It was Martinsson. Wallander could hear from his voice that he was managing to pull himself out of his depression. It was clearly going faster than Wallander had dared hope.

"How are things?" asked Martinsson. "Are you still in Lund?"

"Right now we're trying to trace a train waitress," replied Wallander.

Martinsson was wise enough not to ask any further questions.

"A lot's been going on here," Martinsson went on. "To start with, Svedberg managed to get hold of the person who printed Holger Eriksson's poetry books. He was evidently a very old man. But his mind was sharp. And he didn't mind telling us what he thought of Eriksson. Apparently he always had a hard time getting paid for his printing work."

"Did he have anything to say that we didn't already know?"

"Eriksson seems to have made constant, regular trips to Poland ever since the war. He took advantage of the misery there to buy women. Afterwards, when he came home, he would boast about his conquests. That old printer really told us what he thought."

Wallander remembered what Sven Tyrén had told him during one of their first conversations. Now it had been confirmed. So Krista Haberman wasn't the only Polish woman in Eriksson's life.

"Svedberg wondered if it would be worth the trouble to contact the Polish police," said Martinsson.

"Maybe," replied Wallander. "But for the time being, I think we'll wait on that."

"There's more," said Martinsson. "I'll let you talk to Hansson now."

There was a scraping sound in the receiver. Then Wallander heard Hansson's voice.

"I think I have a clear picture of who worked Holger Eriksson's land," he began. "It all seems to be distinguished by one thing."

"What?"

"An unsolved crime. If I can believe my source, Eriksson had an incredible ability to make enemies. You'd think it was his life's greatest passion. To constantly make new enemies."

"The fields," said Wallander impatiently.

He could hear how Hansson's voice changed when he replied. He sounded more serious.

"The ditch," said Hansson. "Where we found Eriksson hanging on the stakes."

"What about it?"

"It was dug some years back. It wasn't there to start with. Nobody really understood why Eriksson needed to put it in. It wasn't necessary for drainage. The mud was shoveled out and made the hill taller. Where the tower is."

"A ditch isn't what I had in mind," said Wallander. "It doesn't seem believable that it could have anything to do with a possible grave."

"That was my first thought too," said Hansson. "But then something else came out that made me change my mind."

Wallander held his breath.

"The ditch was dug in '67. The farmer I talked to was sure about that. It was dug in the late fall of 1967."

Wallander immediately understood the import of what Hansson was saying.

"So that means the ditch was dug about the same time that Krista Haberman disappeared," said Wallander.

"My farmer was even more specific. He was positive the ditch was dug at the end of October. He remembered it because of a wedding held in Lödinge on the last day of October that year. If we take into account the date that Krista Haberman was last seen alive, then the times match exactly. A car trip from Svenstavik. He kills her. Buries her. A ditch appears. A ditch that wasn't really necessary."

"Good," said Wallander. "This means something."

"If she's there, then I know where we should start searching," Hansson went on. "The farmer claimed that they started digging the ditch to the southeast of the hill. Eriksson had rented a backhoe. The first few days he did the digging himself. He let others finish it."

"Then that's where we'll start digging," said Wallander, noticing how the uneasiness inside him was growing. Most of all he wished he was wrong. But now he was sure that Krista Haberman was buried somewhere near the area Hansson had pinpointed.

"We'll start tomorrow," Wallander went on. "I want you to make all the preparations."

"It's going to be impossible to keep this secret," said Hansson.

"We have to try, at least," Wallander said. "I want you to talk to Chief Holgersson about it. Per Åkeson. And the others."

"There's one thing that puzzles me," said Hansson hesitantly. "If we do find her, what does it really prove? That Holger Eriksson killed her? We can assume so, even if we can never prove a dead man's guilt. Not in this case. But what will it really mean for the homicide investigation we're doing right now?"

It was a reasonable question.

"Most of all it'll tell us that we're on the right track," said Wallander. "That the motive connecting these murders is revenge. Or hatred."

"And you still think it's a woman behind this?"

"Yes," replied Wallander. "Now more than ever."

When the conversation was over, Wallander remained standing outside in the autumn night. The sky was clear, without a cloud. A faint breeze blew against his face.

He thought that now they were slowly approaching something. The center he had spent exactly one month searching for.

But he still didn't know what they would find there.

The woman he tried to visualize kept slipping away.

At the same time he sensed that in some way he might be able to understand her.

He knocked on the door and went in.

Cautiously she opened the door to where they were sleeping. The child lay on his back in the crib she had bought that day. Katarina Taxell was curled up in a fetal position on the edge of the bed. She stood quite still and looked at them. *It was as if she were looking at herself. Or maybe it was her sister lying in the crib.*

Suddenly she could no longer see clearly. She was completely surrounded by blood. It's not just a child who is born in blood. Life itself had its source in the blood that ran out when the skin was cut. Blood that had its own memories of the arteries it had once flowed through. She could see it clearly. Her mother screaming and the man who stood leaning over her as she lay on a table with her legs spread. Even though it was forty years ago, time came rushing toward her from the past. All her life she had tried to escape. But she couldn't. The memories always caught up with her.

But now she knew that she no longer needed to fear these memories. Now that her mother was dead, and she was free to do what she wanted. What she had to do. To keep all those memories at bay.

The feeling of dizziness passed as quickly as it had come. Cautiously she approached the bed and looked at the sleeping child. It wasn't her sister. This child already had a face. Her sister hadn't lived long enough to have anything. This was Katarina's newborn baby. Not her mother's. Katarina's child, who would never have to be tormented, never be haunted by memories.

She felt quite calm again. The remembered images were gone. They no longer came rushing toward her behind her back.

What she was doing was right. She was preventing people from being tormented in the same way she had been. She had forced those men, who had committed violent acts unpunished by society, to take the heaviest of all roads. At least she imagined that was true. That a man whose life was taken by a woman would never be able to understand what had really happened to him.

It was quiet. That was the most important thing. It was the right thing for her to go and get the woman and child. Speak calmly, listen, and tell her that everything that had happened was for the best. Eugen Blomberg had drowned. What it said in the papers about a sack was all rumor and exaggeration. Eugen Blomberg was gone. Whether he had stumbled or tripped and then drowned, nobody was to blame. Fate had decided. And fate was just. That's what she had repeated over and over again, and it seemed as if Katarina was now starting to understand.

She was right to go and get her. Even though it meant that yesterday she had to tell the women who were supposed to come that they would have to skip their meeting this week. She didn't like interrupting her timetable. That created disorder and made it hard for her to sleep. But it was necessary. It wasn't possible to plan everything. Even though she didn't like to admit it.

As long as Katarina and her child stayed with her, she would live at the house in Vollsjö. From the apartment in Ystad she had brought along only the essentials: her uniforms and the small box in which she kept her slips of paper and the book of names. Now that Katarina and her child were asleep, she didn't have to wait any longer. She dumped the slips of paper onto the top of the baking oven, shuffled them, and then began picking them up.

The ninth slip she unfolded had the black cross on it. She opened the ledger and slowly scanned the list. Stopped at number 9. Read the name. Tore Grundén. She stood motionless and stared straight ahead. His picture slowly materialized. First as a vague shadow, a few barely visible contours. Then a face, an identity. Now she remembered him. Who he was. What he had done.

It was more than ten years ago. She was working at the hospital in Malmö back then. An evening right before Christmas. She was working in the emergency room. The woman in the ambulance was dead on arrival. She had died in a car accident. Her husband had come with her. He was upset, and yet composed. She was immediately suspicious. She had seen it so many times before. Since the woman was dead, there was nothing they could do. But she had taken one of the cops aside and asked him what happened. It was a tragic accident. Her husband had backed out of the garage without noticing that she was standing behind the car. He had run over her, and her head was crushed under one of the back tires of the heavily loaded car. It was an accident that shouldn't have happened. In a moment when she wasn't being observed, she had pulled the sheet away and looked at the dead woman. Even though she wasn't a doctor, she thought she could tell from the woman's body that she had been run over more than once. Later she started investigating. The woman who now lay dead on the stretcher had been admitted to the hospital several times before. Once she had fallen from a ladder. Another time she hit her head hard on a cement floor when she tripped in the basement.

She wrote an anonymous letter to the police and said it was murder. She talked to the doctors who examined the body. But nothing happened. The man was given a fine, or maybe a suspended sentence, for what came to be regarded as gross negligence. Nothing else happened. And the woman had been murdered.

Now everything would be made right again. Everything except the life of the dead woman. She couldn't bring her back.

She started planning how it would all take place.

But something bothered her. The men who were watching Katarina's house. They had come to stop her. They were trying to get to her through Katarina. Maybe they had started to suspect that a woman was behind what had happened. She was counting on that. First they would think it was a man. Then they would begin to have doubts. Finally everything would rotate on its own axis and turn into the opposite.

Of course they would never find her. Never.

She looked at the baking oven. Thought about Tore Grundén. That he lived in Hässleholm and worked in Malmö.

Suddenly she realized how it would happen. It was almost embarrassingly easy.

She could do it on the job.

During work hours. With pay.

Chapter Thirty-four

They started digging early in the morning on Friday, October 21st. The light was still quite dim. Wallander and Hansson had marked off the first quadrant with crime-scene tape. The police, wearing their overalls and rubber boots, knew what they were looking for. Their apprehension was mixed with the cool morning air. Wallander felt as though he were in a cemetery. Somewhere in the earth they might come upon the remains of a dead body. He had told Hansson to take charge of the digging. Wallander himself had to work with Birch to track down as soon as possible the waitress who had once made Katarina Taxell laugh on a street in Lund.

For half an hour, Wallander stayed out in the mud where the officers had started digging. Then he walked up the path toward the farm where his car was waiting. He called Birch and caught him at home in Lund. The night before, all Birch had managed to find out was that in Malmö they might be able to find the name of the waitress they were looking for. Birch was having coffee when Wallander called. They decided to meet outside the Malmö train station.

This is the fourth woman involved in the investigation, Wallander thought, which has now been going on for exactly one month. Before there was Krista Haberman. Then Eva Runfeldt and Katarina Taxell. The unknown waitress was the fourth woman. He asked himself if there was another woman, a fifth one. Was she the one they were looking for? Or had they reached their goal if they succeeded in finding the train waitress? Was she the one who made the nighttime visits to Ystad's maternity ward? Without being able to explain why, he doubted that the waitress was the woman they were really searching for. Maybe she could give them a lead. He couldn't hope for much more than that.

He drove through the gray fall countryside in his old car. Wondered absentmindedly how the winter would be. When had they had snow for Christmas in the past few years? It was so long ago he couldn't even remember.

When he reached the Malmö station, he found a parking place right next to the main entrance. He was briefly tempted to try to get a cup of coffee before Birch arrived. But he dropped the idea. Time was tight.

He found Birch on the other side of the canal, on his way across the bridge. He must have parked up by the square. They shook hands. Birch was wearing a knit cap that was much too small. He was unshaven and looked like he hadn't had enough sleep.

"Have you started digging?" he asked.

"Seven o'clock," replied Wallander.

"Are you going to find her?"

"Hard to tell. It's possible."

Birch nodded gloomily. He pointed at the station.

"We're supposed to meet a man named Karl-Henrik Bergstrand," he said. "Normally he doesn't get to work this early. He promised to come extra-early today to meet with us."

They went into the administrative offices of Swedish Railways and were met by Bergstrand. He was in his early thirties. Wallander assumed that he represented SR's new, youthful image. They shook hands and introduced themselves.

"Your request is unusual," said Bergstrand and laughed. "But we'll see if we can help you."

He invited them into his spacious office. Wallander found his self-confidence extraordinary. When Wallander himself was thirty, he was still insecure about almost everything.

Bergstrand sat down behind the big desk. Wallander looked at the furniture in the room. Maybe that explained why SR's ticket prices were so high.

"We're looking for an employee in a dining car," Birch began. "All we know is that it's a woman."

"An overwhelming majority of the people working in 'Train Service' are women," replied Bergstrand. "It would have been significantly easier to find a man."

Wallander raised his hand.

"What's it really called? 'Traffic Restaurants' or 'Train Service'?"

"Both names are fine."

Wallander was satisfied. He looked at Birch.

"We don't know her name," he said. "All we know is what she looks like."

Bergstrand gave him a surprised look.

"Do you really have to try to find someone you know so little about?"

"We have to," Wallander interjected.

"We know which train she worked on," said Birch.

He gave Bergstrand the information they had gotten from Annika Carlman. Bergstrand shook his head.

"This was three years ago," he said.

"We know that," said Wallander. "But I assume that SR has personnel records?"

"That's really not something I can answer," said Bergstrand. "SR is divided into many enterprises. The Traffic Restaurants are a subsidiary. They have their own personnel administration. They're the ones who can answer your questions. Not us. But we cooperate, of course, when necessary."

Wallander was starting to get both impatient and annoyed. "Let's get one thing clear," he interrupted. "We're not looking for this waitress just for the fun of it. We want to find her because she may have important information relating to a complicated homicide investigation. So we don't care who answers our questions. But we're anxious to get it done as fast as possible."

His words had an effect. Bergstrand seemed to understand. Birch gave Wallander a look of encouragement as he went on.

"I assume you can get hold of this person who can answer our questions," he said. "And we'll sit here and wait."

"Is it about the murders in the Ystad area?" asked Bergstrand with interest.

"Exactly. And this waitress might know something that's important."

"Is she a suspect?"

"No," replied Wallander. "She's not a suspect. No shadow will be cast on either the train or the sandwiches."

Bergstrand got up and left the room.

"He seemed a little arrogant," said Birch. "It was good what you said to him."

"It'd be even better if he could give us an answer," said Wallander. "As soon as possible."

While they waited for Bergstrand, Wallander called Hansson in Lödinge. The reply was negative. They were digging toward the middle of the first quadrant. They still hadn't found anything.

"Unfortunately it's already leaked out," said Hansson. "We've had a number of curious spectators up at the farm."

"Keep them at a distance," said Wallander. "I guess that's all we can do."

"Nyberg wants to talk to you. It's about that tape recording of Katarina Taxell and her mother."

"Were they able to identify the noise in the background?"

"If I understood Nyberg correctly, the results were negative. But it's better if you talk to him yourself."

"They really couldn't say anything at all?"

"They thought someone near the phone was pounding on the floor or the wall. But what good does that do us?"

Wallander realized that he had started to hope too soon.

"It couldn't very well be Katarina Taxell's newborn baby," continued Hansson.

"Apparently we have access to an expert who can filter out frequencies or something like that. Maybe he can figure out whether the phone call came from far away. Or whether it was close to Lund. But obviously it's a complicated process. Nyberg said it would take at least a couple of days."

"We'll have to settle for that," said Wallander.

At that moment Bergstrand came back into the office. Wallander quickly ended his conversation with Hansson.

"It'll take a while," Bergstrand said. "First, because we have to get hold of a personnel list that's three years old. Second, the company has undergone a lot of changes since then. But I've explained that it's important. They're getting right on it."

"We'll wait," said Wallander.

Bergstrand didn't seem overly enthusiastic about having two police officers sitting in his office, but he didn't say anything.

"Coffee's one of SR's specialties, isn't it?" Birch asked. "Can we get some outside the café car?"

Bergstrand left the room.

"I don't think he's used to getting the coffee himself," said Birch gleefully.

Wallander didn't reply.

Bergstrand returned with a tray. Then he excused himself, saying that he had an urgent meeting. They stayed where they were. Wallander drank the coffee and felt his impatience growing. He thought about Hansson. Thought about whether he should leave Birch to wait alone for the waitress to be identified. He decided to stay half an hour. No more.

"I've been trying to get caught up on everything that's happened," said Birch suddenly. "I admit I've never been involved in anything like this before. Could it really be a woman behind it?"

"We can't ignore what we know," replied Wallander.

At the same time the feeling that kept plaguing him returned. The fear that he was steering the whole investigation into terrain that consisted of nothing but pitfalls. At any moment the trap door could open under their feet.

Birch sat in silence.

"We haven't had many female serial killers in this country," he said then.

"If any," said Wallander. "Besides, we don't know if she's committed the murders. Our clues will either lead us to her alone or to someone else who exists in her background."

"And you think she regularly serves coffee on trains between Stockholm and Malmö?"

Birch's doubt was unmistakable.

"No," replied Wallander. "I don't think she serves coffee. The waitress is probably just the fourth step along the way."

Birch stopped asking questions. Wallander looked at the clock and wondered if he should call Hansson again. The half hour was almost up. Bergstrand was still busy with his meeting. Birch was reading a brochure touting SR's excellence.

Another half-hour passed. Wallander's patience was starting to run out.

Bergstrand came back.

"It looks like we're going to solve it," he said encouragingly. "But it'll take a little while longer."

"How long?"

Wallander didn't hide his irritation. He realized it probably wasn't justified, but he couldn't help it.

"Maybe half an hour. They're driving the files out here. It takes time."

Wallander nodded mutely.

They continued to wait. Birch put down his brochure and dozed off. Wallander went over to the window and looked out at Malmö. To the right he caught a glimpse of the hydrofoil terminal. He thought about the times he had stood there waiting for Baiba. How many times? Twice. It felt like more than that. He sat down again and called Hansson. They still hadn't found anything. The digging was going to take time. Hansson also said it had started to rain. Wallander gloomily realized the scope of the depressing work.

The whole thing is going to hell, he thought suddenly. I've steered the whole investigation right into perdition.

Birch started snoring. Wallander kept on checking his watch.

Bergstrand came back. Birch woke up with a start. Bergstrand had a piece of paper in his hand.

"Margareta Nystedt," he said. "That's probably the person you're looking for. She was the only one handling the serving that day for the departure in question."

Wallander jumped up from his chair. "Where is she now?"

"I don't actually know. She stopped working for us about a year ago."

"Damn," said Wallander.

"But we have her address," Bergstrand went on. "She might not have moved just because she stopped working for Traffic Restaurants."

Wallander grabbed the piece of paper. It was an address in Malmö.

"Carl Gustaf's Road," said Wallander. "Where's that?"

"Near Pildamm Park," replied Bergstrand.

Wallander saw that there was a phone number, but he decided not to call it. He would go there himself.

"Thanks for your help," he said to Bergstrand. "I assume that this information is correct? That she was the one on duty that day?"

"SR is known for its reliability," said Bergstrand. "That also means that we keep good track of our employees. Both in the administration and in the subsidiaries."

Wallander didn't understand the connection, but he didn't have time to ask. "Then let's go," he said to Birch.

They left the station. Birch left his car behind and went with Wallander. It took them less than ten minutes to find the address. It was a five-story apartment building. Margareta Nystedt lived on the fifth floor. They took the elevator. Wallander rang the bell before Birch was even out of the elevator. Waited. Rang again. No one opened the door. He swore to himself. Then he made a quick decision. He rang the bell next door. The door opened almost at once. An elderly man gave Wallander a stern look. His shirt was unbuttoned over his paunch. He was holding a partially filled-out betting form. Wallander thought it had something to do with harness racing. He took out his ID.

"We're looking for Margareta Nystedt," he said.

"What has she done?" asked the man. "She's a very friendly young woman. Her husband too."

"We just need some information," said Wallander. "She's not home. No one came to the door. Do you happen to know where we could find her?"

"She works on the hydrofoil," replied the man. "She's a waitress."

Wallander looked at Birch.

"Thanks for your help," said Wallander. "Good luck with the horses."

Ten minutes later they braked in front of the hydrofoil terminal.

"I don't think we can park here," said Birch.

"To hell with it," said Wallander.

He felt like he was running, and everything would fall apart if he stopped.

It took them only a few minutes to find out that Margareta Nystedt was working that morning on *Springaren*. It had just left Copenhagen and was expected to dock in half an hour. Wallander used the time to move his car. Birch sat on a bench in the departure hall and read a tattered newspaper. The terminal manager came over and said they could wait in the staff room. He wondered whether they wanted him to contact the boat.

"How much time does she have?" asked Wallander.

"She's really supposed to go back to Copenhagen on the next trip."

"That won't be possible."

The man was helpful. He promised to see to it that Margareta Nystedt could stay ashore. Wallander assured him that she wasn't suspected of any crime.

Wallander went out into the wind when the boat pulled up to the dock. The passengers struggled against the wind. Wallander was surprised that so many people were traveling across the Sound on a weekday. He waited impatiently. The last passenger was a man on crutches. Right afterwards a woman wearing a waitress uniform came out onto the deck. The man who had received Wallander stood at her side and pointed. The woman named Margareta Nystedt walked down the gangplank. She was blonde, with her hair cropped very short, and she was younger than Wallander had expected. She stopped in front of him and crossed her arms. She was cold.

"Are you the one who wants to talk to me?" she asked.

"Margareta Nystedt?"

"That's me."

"Let's go inside. We don't have to stand out here freezing."

"I don't have much time."

"More than you think. You're not going back on the next trip."

She stopped mid-stride.

"Why not? Who decided that?"

"I have to talk to you. But you have nothing to worry about."

He suddenly had a feeling that she was scared. For a brief moment he started to think he was mistaken. That she was the one they were waiting for. That he already had the fifth woman at his side, without having met the fourth.

Then he realized just as quickly that he was wrong. Margareta Nystedt was young and slender. She would never have been able to handle the physical demands. And something about her whole presence told him she wasn't the murderer.

They went into the terminal building where Birch was waiting. The staff had their own waiting room. They sat down on a worn plastic sofa ensemble. The room was empty. Birch introduced himself. She shook hands with him. Her hand was fragile. Like a bird's foot, Wallander thought to himself.

He studied her face. He judged her to be twenty-seven or twenty-eight years old. Her dress was short. She had nice legs. She was wearing harsh makeup. He got the impression that she had painted over something on her face that she didn't like. She was nervous.

"I'm sorry we had to contact you like this," said Wallander. "But sometimes there are things that can't wait."

"Like my boat, for instance," she replied. Her voice had a strangely hard sound to it. Wallander hadn't expected that. He didn't really know what he was expecting.

"It's not a problem. I've talked to your supervisor about it."

"What have I done?"

Wallander looked at her thoughtfully. She had no idea why he and Birch were there. There was no doubt about that.

The trap door of his doubt creaked and groaned under his feet.

She repeated her question. What had she done?

Wallander glanced at Birch, who was surreptitiously looking at her legs.

"Katarina Taxell," said Wallander. "You know her?"

"I know who she is. Whether I know her is a different story."

"How did you meet her? What have you had to do with her?"

She suddenly gave a start on the black plastic sofa. "Has something happened to her?"

"No. Answer my questions."

"Answer mine! I only have one. Why are you asking me about her?"

Wallander saw that he had been too impatient. He had moved too fast. Her aggressiveness was actually understandable.

"Nothing has happened to Katarina. And she's not suspected of committing any crime. You aren't either. But we need to get some information about her. That's all I can tell you. After you've answered my questions, I'll leave and you can go back to work."

She gave him a searching look. He noticed that she was starting to believe him.

"About three years ago you spent time with her. Back then you were working as a waitress in the train dining cars. You were employed by what's known as the Traffic Restaurants."

She seemed surprised that he knew about her past. Wallander had the impression that she was on her guard, which in turn made him sharpen his attention. "Is that true?"

"Of course it's true. Why should I deny it?"

"And you knew Katarina Taxell?"

"Yes."

"How did you meet her?"

"We worked together."

Wallander gave her a surprised look before he continued.

"Isn't she a teacher?"

"She was taking a break. That's when she worked on the train."

Wallander looked at Birch, who shook his head. He hadn't heard about this either.

"When was this?"

"The spring of 1991. I can't be any more specific than that."

"And you worked together?"

"Not always. But often."

"And you also spent time together when you were off?"

"Sometimes. But we weren't close friends. We had fun. That's all."

"When did you last see her?"

"We drifted apart when she stopped waitressing. It wasn't a close friendship."

Wallander saw that she was telling the truth. Her wariness was also gone.

"Did Katarina have a steady boyfriend during that time?"

"I actually don't know," she replied.

"If you worked together and also spent time together, wouldn't you have known that?"

"She never mentioned anyone."

"And you never saw her with any men?"

"Never."

"Did she have any girlfriends she spent time with?"

Margareta Nystedt thought for a moment. Then she gave Wallander three names. The same names Wallander already knew about.

"No one else?"

"Not as far as I know."

"Have you ever heard the name Eugen Blomberg before?"

She thought about it.

"Wasn't he the guy who was murdered?"

"That's right. Can you remember Katarina ever talking about him?"

She suddenly gave him a serious look.

"Was she the one who did it?"

Wallander pounced on her question.

"Do you think she could have killed anyone?"

"No. Katarina was a very peace-loving person."

Wallander was uncertain how to continue.

"You went back and forth between Malmö and Stockholm," he said. "I'm sure you had a lot to do. But you still must have talked to each other. Are you positive she never mentioned any other girlfriend? It's important."

He could see that she was making an effort.

"No," she said. "I can't remember anyone."

At that moment Wallander noticed her hesitate for a split second. She saw that he had noticed.

"Maybe," she said. "But I'm having a hard time remembering."

"What?"

"It must have been right before she quit. I'd been sick for a week with the flu."

"What happened then?"

"When I came back she was different."

Wallander was on tenterhooks now. Birch had also noticed that something was up.

"Different in what way?"

"I don't know how to explain it. She could switch between gloom and exhilaration. It felt like she had changed."

"Try to describe the change. This could be crucial."

"Usually when we didn't have anything to do we would sit in the little kitchen in the restaurant car. We talked and leafed through the magazines. But when I came back we didn't do that anymore."

"What happened instead?"

"She left."

Wallander waited for her to go on. But she didn't.

"She left the dining car? She couldn't very well have left the train. What did she say she was going to do?"

"She didn't say anything."

"But you must have asked her. She was different? She didn't sit and talk anymore?"

"Maybe I asked. I don't remember. But she didn't say anything. She just left."

"Did this always happen?"

"No. Right before she quit she was different. She seemed completely closed off."

"Do you think she was meeting someone on the train? A passenger who was on board each time? It sounds strange."

"I don't know whether she met anyone."

Wallander had no more questions. He looked at Birch, who had nothing more to add either.

The hydrofoil was just about to leave the harbor.

"You can have a break now," said Wallander. "I want you to contact me if you think of anything else."

He wrote his name and phone number on a piece of paper and handed it to her.

"That's all I can remember," she said.

She stood up and left.

"Who would meet Katarina on a train?" Birch asked. "A passenger who travels nonstop back and forth between Malmö and Stockholm? Besides, they can't be serving all the time on the same train. That doesn't sound logical."

Wallander was only half-listening to what Birch said. An idea had occurred to him that he didn't want to lose. It couldn't be a passenger. So it had to be someone else who was on the train for the same reason she was. Someone who worked there.

Wallander looked at Birch.

"Who works on a train?" he asked.

"I assume there's an engine driver."

"Who else?"

"Conductors. One or more. I think they're called trainmasters."

Wallander nodded. He thought about what Höglund had discovered. The faint glimmer of a pattern. A person who had irregular but recurring days off. Like people who work on a train.

There was also the train timetable in the secret compartment.

He stood up.

"I think we'll go back and see Bergstrand," said Wallander.

"Are you looking for more waitresses?"

Wallander didn't reply. He was already on his way out of the terminal building.

Karl-Henrik Bergstrand did not look at all happy to see Wallander and Birch again. Wallander moved fast, practically shoving him through the door to his office.

"The same time period," he said. "Spring of '91. There was a woman named Katarina Taxell working for you. Or the company that sells coffee. I want you to get out all the documents on conductors or trainmasters and engine drivers who worked the shifts when Katarina Taxell was working. I'm especially interested in a week during the spring of 1991 when Margareta Nystedt called in sick. Do you understand what I'm saying?"

"You can't be serious," said Bergstrand. "It's an impossible job to piece together all that information. It'll take months."

"Let's say you have a couple of hours," replied Wallander in a friendly voice. "If necessary, I'll ask the national police commissioner to call up his colleague, the general manager of SR. And I'll ask him to complain about the slow response of an employee in Malmö named Karl-Henrik Bergstrand."

Bergstrand understood. He also seemed to accept the challenge.

"So let's do the impossible," he said. "But it's going to take hours."

"If you work as fast as you can, then you can have as long as you need," replied Wallander.

"You can spend the night in one of the railroad's dormitory rooms at the locomotive station," said Bergstrand. "Or at the Hotel Prize, which we have an agreement with."

"No thanks," said Wallander. "When you have the information I've asked for, send it to me by fax at the police station in Ystad."

"Let me just point out that it's not conductors *or* trainmasters," said Bergstrand. "They're called trainmasters. Nothing else. They function as the commanders-in-chief on the train. Our system is actually based on military ranks."

Wallander nodded.

When they came out of the railroad station it was almost eleven o'clock.

"So you think there's someone else who worked for SR back then?" Birch asked.

"There has to be. There's no other reasonable explanation."

Birch put on his knit cap. "That means we wait."

"You in Lund and me in Ystad. Keep the recorder on at Hedwig Taxell's apartment. Katarina might call again."

They parted outside the station building. Wallander got in his car and drove through the city. He wondered whether he had now reached the innermost Chinese box. What would he find? An empty space? He didn't know. He felt terribly uneasy.

He turned into a gas station right before the last roundabout to the road to Ystad. He filled up the car and went inside to pay. When he came out he heard the phone he had put on the passenger seat ringing. He yanked open the door and grabbed the phone. It was Hansson.

"Where are you?" asked Hansson.

"On my way to Ystad."

"I think you'd better come out here."

Wallander gave a start. He almost dropped the phone.

"Did you find her?"

"I think so."

Wallander didn't say anything.

He drove straight to Lödinge.

The wind had picked up and shifted direction until it was blowing due north.

Chapter Thirty-five

They had found a thighbone. That was all.

It took several more hours before they found any more skeletal remains. There was a cold, blustery wind blowing that day, a wind that cut right through their clothes and magnified the dreariness and repugnance of the situation.

The femur lay on a plastic sheet. Wallander thought that it had really gone quite fast. They had dug up an area no larger than twenty square meters, and were surprisingly close to the surface, for that matter, when a spade had struck the bone.

A doctor came and examined it, shivering. Naturally he couldn't say anything except that it was human. But Wallander didn't need any additional confirmation. In his mind there was no doubt that it was part of Krista Haberman's remains. They had to keep digging. Maybe they would find the rest of her skeleton, and maybe then they could determine how she had been killed. Had Holger Eriksson strangled her? Had he shot her? What had actually happened so long ago?

Wallander felt tired and melancholy on that endless afternoon. It didn't help any that he had been right. It was as though he were looking right into a terrible story he would rather not deal with. The whole time he was waiting tensely for what Karl-Henrik Bergstrand would come up with. After he spent a couple of hours out in the mud along with Hansson and the other policemen doing the excavation, he returned to the station. By then he had also informed Hansson about what had happened in Malmö, about the meeting with Margareta Nystedt and the discovery that Katarina Taxell had worked, for a brief period, as a waitress on the train between Malmö and Stockholm. Sometime during one of these trips she had met an unknown person who had a great effect on her. They didn't know exactly what happened. The unknown person she met had somehow taken on crucial importance for her. Wallander didn't even know whether it was a man or a woman. He was only sure that when they finally found out, they would have taken an enormous stride toward the center of the investigation, which had eluded them for so long.

When he got to the police station he gathered all the colleagues he could find and repeated what he had told Hansson half an hour earlier. Now all they had to do was wait for the paper to start creeping out of the fax machine.

While they were sitting in the conference room, Hansson called to say they had also found a shinbone. The discomfort around the table was palpable. Wallander thought that they were all sitting there waiting for the skull to appear in the mud.

It was a long afternoon. The first fall storm was building over Skåne. Leaves whirled across the parking lot outside the station. They stayed in the conference room even though there was nothing for them to discuss as a group. Besides, all of them had many other assignments waiting on their desks. Wallander thought that what they needed most right now was to gather their strength. If they managed to break through and open up the investigation with the help of the information coming from Malmö, they could count on having to get a lot of work done in a very short time. That's why they were slumped in their chairs around the conference table, resting.

Sometime that afternoon Birch called and said that Hedwig Taxell had never heard of Margareta Nystedt. She also couldn't understand how she could have forgotten that her daughter Katarina had worked as a waitress on the train for a while. Birch stressed that he thought she was telling the truth. Martinsson kept leaving the room to call home. Then Wallander would talk in a low voice with Höglund, who thought everything was already going much better for Terese. Martinsson hadn't mentioned wanting to quit the force again. Even that topic had to be postponed for the time being, thought Wallander. Investigating serious crimes means putting the rest of your life on hold.

At four in the afternoon Hansson called and said they had found a middle finger. Soon after he called again and said the skull had been uncovered. That's when Wallander asked him if he wanted to be relieved, but he said he might as well stay.

They didn't need any more of them catching a cold.

An icy ripple of revulsion passed through the conference room when Wallander announced that he assumed the skull that had just been found was Krista Haberman's. Svedberg quickly put down the half-eaten sandwich he had in his hand.

Wallander had been through this before.

A skeleton meant nothing until the skull appeared. Only then was it possible to imagine the person who had once existed.

In this mood of weary anticipation, when the members of the investigative team sat around the table like small isolated islands, spurts of conversations would erupt from time to time. Various details were mentioned. Someone would ask a question. An answer was given, something was clarified, and then it would be silent again.

Svedberg suddenly started talking about Svenstavik.

"Holger Eriksson must have been a strange man. First he entices a Polish woman to come with him down to Skåne. God knows what he promised her. Marriage? Wealth? The chance to be a car-dealer baroness? Then he kills her almost at once. That happened nearly thirty years ago. But when he himself feels death approaching, he buys a letter of indulgence by donating money to the church up there in Jämtland."

"I've read his poems," said Martinsson. "At least some of them. You can't deny that he occasionally shows some sensitivity."

"For animals," said Höglund. "For birds. But not for human beings."

Wallander remembered the abandoned dog pen. He wondered how long it had been empty. Hamrén grabbed a phone and got hold of Sven Tyrén in his tanker truck. Then they got the answer. Eriksson's last dog was discovered dead in the pen one morning. It happened a few weeks before Eriksson himself had fallen into the pungee pit. Tyrén had heard it from his wife, who in turn had heard it from the rural letter-carrier. What the dog died of he didn't know. But it was pretty old. Wallander silently thought that someone must have killed the dog so it wouldn't bark. And that person was the one they were looking for.

They had succeeded in coming up with another explanation. But they still lacked an overall framework. Nothing had been fully clarified yet.

At 4:30 Wallander called Malmö. Karl-Henrik Bergstrand came to the phone. They were still working on it, he said. They would soon be able to fax over all the names and other information Wallander had requested.

The waiting continued. A reporter called and asked what they were digging for at Eriksson's farm. Wallander cited technical investigative reasons for not being able to tell him. But he wasn't negative. He expressed himself in his friendliest manner. Chief Holgersson sat with them during large parts of the long wait. She also drove out to Lödinge with Per Åkeson. But in contrast to their former chief, Björk, she didn't say much. The two of them were quite different. Björk would have taken the opportunity to complain about the latest memo from the National Police Board. In some way he would manage to connect it with the investigation that was under way. Lisa Holgersson was different. Wallander absentmindedly decided that they were both good in their own ways.

Hamrén was playing tic-tac-toe, Svedberg was searching for any remaining hairs on his scalp, and Höglund was sitting with her eyes closed. Now and then Wallander would get up and take a walk down the corridor. He was very tired. He wondered if it meant anything that Katarina Taxell hadn't been heard from. Should they start a search for her after all? He was dubious. He was afraid they would scare off the woman who had come to get her. He heard the phone ringing in the conference room, and hurried back to stand in the doorway. Svedberg had picked it up. Wallander mimed the word "Malmö?" with his mouth. Svedberg shook his head. It was Hansson again.

"A rib this time," said Svedberg when he hung up. "You think he has to call here every time they find another bone?"

Wallander sat down at the table. The phone rang again. Svedberg picked it up. He listened briefly and then handed it to Wallander.

"You'll have it in a few minutes on your fax," said Bergstrand. "I think we've found all the information you wanted."

"Then you've done a good job," said Wallander. "If we need any explanation or additional information I'll call you back."

"I'm sure you will," said Bergstrand. "I get the impression you aren't the type to give up."

They all gathered around the fax machine. After a few minutes the paper started coming out. Wallander saw instantly that there were many more names than he had imagined. When the transmission was done he tore it off and made copies for everyone. Back in the conference room they studied the pages in silence. Wallander counted thirty-two names. And seventeen of the trainmasters were women. He didn't recognize any of the names. The lists of hours of service and the various combinations seemed endless. He searched for a long time before he found the week when Margareta Nystedt's name wasn't included. No fewer than eleven female trainmasters had been on duty on the days that Katarina Taxell was working as a waitress. He also wasn't sure that he had really understood all the abbreviations and codes for the various people and their shifts.

For a moment Wallander felt his powerlessness return. Then he forced it aside and tapped his pen on the table.

"There are a lot of people listed here," he said. "If I'm not completely mistaken, we have to concentrate on the eleven female trainmasters. There are also fourteen men. But I want us to start with the women. Does anyone recognize any of the names?"

They bent their heads over the pages. No one could remember any of the names from other parts of the investigation. Wallander missed

Hansson's presence. He was the one with the best memory. He asked one of the detectives from Malmö to make a copy and see to it that someone drove it out to Hansson.

"Then let's get started," he said when the detective left the room. "Eleven women. We have to look at every one of them. Hopefully somewhere we'll find a point of connection with this investigation. We'll divide them up. And we'll start now. It's going to be a long night."

They divided up the names and left the conference room. The brief moment of powerlessness that Wallander had felt was gone. He knew the hunt was on. The waiting was finally over.

Many hours later, when it was almost eleven, Wallander started to despair again. By that time they had gotten no further than eliminating two of the names from the list. One of the women had died in a car accident long before they found Eriksson's body. The other had wound up on the list by mistake: She had already transferred to an administrative job in Malmö. It was Bergstrand who discovered the mistake and called Wallander at once.

They were searching for points of intersection but found none. Höglund came into Wallander's office.

"What should I do with this one?" she asked, shaking a paper she had in her hand.

"What about her?"

"Anneli Olsson, thirty-nine years old, married, four children. Lives in Ängelholm. Husband a pastor in the Free Church. She previously worked managing the cold buffet at a hotel in Ängelholm. Then she was retrained, but I can't figure out why. If I understood correctly, she's deeply religious. She works on trains, takes care of her family, and spends the little free time she has on handicrafts and various efforts for the mission. What should I do with her? Call her in for an interview? Ask her if she killed three men in the past month? If she knows where Katarina Taxell and her newborn baby are?"

"Put her aside," said Wallander. "That's a step in the right direction too."

Hansson had come back from Lödinge at eight o'clock when the rain and wind made it impossible to keep working. He also reported that in the future he'd need more people digging. Then he immediately started working on profiling the eight remaining women. Wallander tried in vain to send him home, at least to change out of his wet clothes. But Hansson refused. Wallander sensed that he wanted to shake off as soon as possible the unpleasant experience of standing out in the mud digging for Krista Haberman's remains.

At just after eleven, Wallander was on the phone trying to track down a relative of a female trainmaster named Wedin. She had moved no fewer than five times in the past year. She had gone through a messy divorce and was on the sick list large parts of the time. He was just dialing information when Martinsson showed up in the doorway. Wallander quickly hung up. He could see by Martinsson's face that something had happened.

"I think I've found her," he said softly. "Yvonne Ander. Forty-seven years old."

"Why do you think she's the one?"

"We can start with the fact that she actually lives here in Ystad. She has an address on Liregatan."

"What else have you got?"

"She seems strange in many ways. Elusive. Like this whole investigation. But she has a background that ought to interest us. She has worked both as an assistant nurse and an ambulance attendant."

Wallander looked at him for a moment in silence. Then he got up quickly.

"Get the others," he said. "Now, right away."

In a few minutes they were gathered in the conference room.

"Martinsson may have found her," said Wallander. "And she lives here in Ystad."

Martinsson went over everything he had managed to find out about Yvonne Ander.

"First of all, she's forty-seven years old," he began. "Born in Stockholm. She seems to have come to Skåne fifteen years ago. The first few years she lived in Malmö. Then she moved here to Ystad. She's worked for Swedish Railways for the past ten years. But before that, when she was younger, she studied to be an assistant nurse and worked for many years in health care. Why she suddenly took up something else I can't say, of course. She has also worked as an ambulance assistant. Then you can also see that for long periods she doesn't seem to have worked at all."

"What was she doing then?" asked Wallander.

"There are big gaps."

"Is she married?"

"She's single."

"Divorced?"

"I don't know. There are no children in the picture. I don't think she's ever been married. But her railway employment matches with Katarina Taxell's."

Martinsson had been reading from his notebook. Now he dropped it on the table.

"There's one more thing. Which was what I first reacted to. She's active in SR's Recreational Association division in Malmö. I think a lot of people are. But what surprised me was that she was involved in weight training."

It got very quiet in the room.

"In other words, she's presumably strong," Martinsson went on. "And isn't it a woman with great physical strength we're looking for?"

Wallander made a quick evaluation of the situation. Could she be the one? Then he decided.

"We'll put all the other names aside for the time being. Now we'll all work on Yvonne Ander. Take it from the beginning one more time. Slowly."

Martinsson repeated what he had said. They came up with new questions. Many of the answers were missing. Wallander looked at his watch. Quarter to twelve.

"I think we should talk to her tonight."

"If she's not working," said Höglund. "If you look at the lists, she has the night train occasionally. Which seems strange. Otherwise it looks like the trainmasters either work days or nights. Never both. Or am I wrong?"

"Either she's home or she's not," said Wallander.

"What are we actually going to talk to her about?"

The question came from Hamrén. It was legitimate.

"I think it's possible that Katarina Taxell might be there," said Wallander. "If nothing else, we can use it as an excuse. Her mother is worried. We can start with that. We have no evidence against her. We don't have a thing. But I also want to get some fingerprints."

"So we're not sending a whole team," said Svedberg.

Wallander nodded at Höglund.

"I thought the two of us should visit her. We can have another car follow as backup. In case something happens."

"Like what?" asked Martinsson.

"I don't know."

"Isn't that a little irresponsible?" Svedberg wondered. "We do suspect she's involved in homicide."

"Of course we'll be armed," said Wallander.

They were interrupted by a man from the dispatch center knocking on the door.

"There's a message from a doctor in Lund," he said. "He did a preliminary evaluation of the skeletal remains you found. He thinks they're from a woman. And they've been in the ground a long time."

"So we know that," said Wallander. "If nothing else, we're on our way to solving a twenty-seven-year-old missing-persons case."

The officer left the room. Wallander went back to what they were talking about. "I don't think anything's going to happen," he repeated.

"How are we going to explain it if Taxell isn't there? After all, we're thinking of knocking on her door in the middle of the night."

"We'll ask for Katarina," Wallander said. "We're looking for her. That's all."

"What happens if she's not home?"

Wallander didn't have to think it over.

"Then we go in. And the backup car will watch in case she's on her way home. We'll have our phones turned on. In the meantime I'd like to ask the rest of you to wait here. I know it's late. But it can't be helped."

No one had any objections.

They left the police station just after midnight. The wind was now at gale force. Wallander and Höglund drove in her car. Martinsson and Svedberg were in the backup car. Liregatan was right in the middle of Ystad. They parked a block away. The city was almost deserted. They met only one other car, one of the police night patrols. Wallander wondered briefly if the new bicycle commando team being planned would be able to handle patrol duty when it was blowing as hard as it was now.

Yvonne Ander lived in an old restored half-timbered building. Her door faced the street. There were three apartments, and hers was in the middle. They crossed the street and observed the façade. Apart from a window on the far left with a light on, the whole building was dark.

"Either she's asleep or she's not home," said Wallander. "But we have to assume she's in there."

It was twenty minutes past midnight. The wind was blowing hard.

"Is she the one?" asked Höglund.

Wallander was freezing and out of sorts. Was it because they were now hunting a woman?

"Yes," he replied, "I think she is."

They crossed the street. To their left was the car with Martinsson and Svedberg in it. The headlights were turned off. Höglund rang the doorbell. Wallander pressed his ear to it and could hear the bell ringing inside the apartment. They waited tensely. He nodded to her to ring again. Still nothing. A third time with the same result.

"Is she asleep?" asked Höglund.

"No," said Wallander, "I don't think she's home."

He tried the door. It was locked. He took a step into the street and waved at the car. Martinsson came walking up. He was the best at opening locked doors without using force. He had a flashlight and a bundle of lock-picking tools with him. Wallander held the light while Martinsson worked. It took him more than ten minutes. Finally he got the lock to open. He took the flashlight and went back to the car.

Wallander looked around. The street was deserted. He and Höglund went inside. They stood listening in the silence. The entryway didn't seem to have a window. Wallander turned on a lamp. To the left was a living room with a low ceiling, to the right a kitchen. Straight ahead a narrow staircase led to the upper floor. It creaked under their feet. There were three bedrooms on the top floor, all empty. There was no one in the apartment.

He tried to take stock of the situation. It was almost one o'clock. Could they count on the woman who lived there coming back during the night? He thought it was highly unlikely. Especially since she had Taxell and her newborn baby with her. Would she move them around at night?

Wallander walked up to a glass door in one of the bedrooms and discovered a balcony outside. Big flowerpots filled almost the entire space. But there were no flowers in them, just dirt.

The image of the balcony and the empty flowerpots filled him with sudden dismay. He quickly left the room.

They returned to the entryway.

"Get Martinsson," he said. "And ask Svedberg to drive back to the station. They have to keep looking. I think Yvonne Ander has another residence besides this apartment. Maybe a house."

"Shouldn't we have some surveillance on the street?"

"She won't come back tonight. But you're right, we should have a car outside. Ask Svedberg to take care of it."

Höglund was just about to leave when he held her back. Then he looked around. He went into the kitchen and lit the lamp over the drainboard. There were two dirty cups there. He wrapped them in a handkerchief and handed them to her.

"Prints," he said. "Give them to Svedberg. And he has to give them to Nyberg. This could be our crucial break."

He went back upstairs. Heard Höglund lock the front door. He stood still in the dark. Then he did something that surprised even him. He went in the bathroom, picked up a hand towel, and sniffed it. He smelled the faint scent of a special perfume.

But the smell suddenly reminded him of something else.

He tried to capture the mental image. The memory of a scent. He sniffed the towel again, but he couldn't pin it down. Even though he knew he was close.

He had smelled that scent somewhere else too. On another occasion. He just couldn't remember where or when. But it had been quite recently.

He jumped when he heard the door downstairs open. Then Martinsson and Höglund showed up on the stairs.

"Now we have to start looking," said Wallander. "We're searching not only for something to connect her to the murders, but for something that indicates she has another residence. I want to know where it is."

"Why should she?" asked Martinsson.

They were almost whispering the whole time, as if the person they were looking for was in the vicinity after all and could hear them.

"Katarina Taxell," said Wallander. "Her baby. And we've believed all along that Gösta Runfeldt was held captive for three weeks. I have a strong hunch that it wasn't here, in the middle of Ystad."

Martinsson and Höglund stayed upstairs. Wallander went downstairs. He closed the curtains in the living room and turned on some lamps. Then he stood in the middle of the room and turned slowly as he observed the room. The woman who lived here had beautiful furniture. And she smoked. He saw an ashtray on a little table next to a leather sofa. There were no cigarette butts in it, but there were faint traces of ashes. Paintings and photographs hung on the walls. Still lifes, vases of flowers. Not very well done. Down in the lower right corner of one was a signature: *Anna Ander '58*. A relative. He thought that Ander was an unusual surname. It also occurred in the history of Swedish crime, although he couldn't recall the context. He looked at one of the framed photographs. A Scanian farm. The picture was taken from above at an angle. Wallander guessed that the photographer had been standing on a roof or a tall ladder. He walked around the room. Tried to feel her presence. He wondered why it was so difficult. Everything gave an impression of abandonment, he thought. A prim, pedantic abandonment. She isn't here very often. She spends her time somewhere else.

He went over to her little desk next to the wall. Through the gap in the curtain he glimpsed a small yard. The window was drafty. The cold wind was noticeable in the room. He pulled out the chair and sat down. Tried the biggest drawer. It was unlocked. A car passed by outside. Wallander saw the headlights catch a window and disappear. Then only the wind remained.

In the drawer were stacks of bundled letters. He found his glasses and took out the top bundle. The sender was A. Ander. This time with an address in Spain. He took out the letter and quickly scanned it. Anna Ander was her mother. That was clear at once. She was describing a trip. On the last page she wrote that she was on her way to Africa. The letter was dated April 1993. He put back the letter on the top of the bundle. The floorboards upstairs were creaking. He stuck one hand inside the drawer. Nothing. He started to go through the other drawers. Even paper can feel abandoned, he thought. He found nothing to make him take notice. It was too empty to be natural. Now he was convinced that she lived somewhere else. He kept going through the drawers.

The floor upstairs creaked.

It was 1:30 in the morning.

She was driving through the night and feeling very tired. Katarina was worried. She had been listening to her for hours. She often wondered about the weakness of these women. They let themselves be tortured, abused, murdered. If they survived, they then sat night after night moaning about it. She didn't understand them. Now that she was driving through the night she thought she actually felt contempt for them. Because they didn't fight back.

It was one o'clock. Normally she would have been asleep by now. She had to go to work early the next day. Besides, she had planned to sleep at Vollsjö. Finally she dared to leave Katarina alone with her baby. She had convinced her to stay where she was. Just a few more days, maybe a week. Tomorrow night they would call her mother again. Katarina would call. She would sit next to her. She didn't think Katarina would say anything she wasn't supposed to. But she wanted to be there anyway.

It was ten minutes past one when she drove into Ystad.

Instinctively she sensed the danger when she turned down Liregatan. The parked car with its headlights off. She couldn't turn around. She had to keep going. There were two men in it. She thought she saw a light in her apartment too. Furious, she stomped hard on the gas pedal. The car leaped ahead. She braked just as suddenly after she turned the corner. So they had found her. The ones who were watching Katarina's house. Now they were in her apartment. She felt dizzy. But it wasn't fear. She had nothing there that could lead them to Vollsjö. Nothing that told them who she was. Nothing but her name.

She sat motionless. The wind tore at the car. She had turned off the engine and headlights. She would have to return to Vollsjö. Now she realized why she had come here—to see if the men who were following her had gotten into her apartment. She was still way ahead of them. They would never catch up with her. She would keep unfolding her slips of paper as long as there was a single name left in the ledger.

She started the car, and decided to drive by her building one more time.

The car was still parked there. She stopped twenty meters behind it without shutting off the engine. Even though it was far away and the angle difficult, she could see that the curtains in her house were drawn. Whoever was inside had turned on the light. Now they were searching. But they wouldn't find anything.

She drove off, forcing herself to do so nonchalantly, without gunning the engine as she usually did.

When she got back to Vollsjö, Katarina and her baby were asleep. Nothing would happen. Everything would continue according to plan.

Wallander had returned to the bundle of letters when he heard quick steps on the stairs. He got up from his chair. It was Martinsson. Right behind him came Höglund.

"I think you'd better take a look at this," said Martinsson. He was pale, his voice shaky.

He placed a worn notebook with a black cover on the desk. It was open. Wallander leaned over and put on his glasses. There was a column of names. In the margin they each had a number. He frowned.

"Go forward a few pages," said Martinsson.

Wallander did as he said. The column of names was repeated. Since there were arrows, strikethroughs, and changes, he got the feeling it was a draft for something or other.

"A couple more pages," said Martinsson.

Wallander could hear he was shaken.

The column of names appeared again. This time the changes and deletions were fewer.

Then he saw it.

He recognized the first name. Gösta Runfeldt. Then he found the others, Holger Eriksson and Eugen Blomberg. At the end of the rows there were dates written in.

The dates of their deaths.

Wallander looked up at Martinsson and Höglund. Both of them were pale.

There was no longer any doubt. They had come to the right place.

"There are more than forty names here," said Wallander. "You think she intends to kill them all?"

"At least we know who might be next," said Höglund. She pointed to a name.

Tore Grundén. In front of his name was a red exclamation point. But there was no death date in the margin.

"In the back there's a loose sheet of paper," said Höglund.

Wallander carefully took it out. There were meticulously written notes on it. Wallander had a fleeting thought that the handwriting reminded him of his ex-wife Mona's. The letters were rounded, the lines even and regular. Without strikethroughs and changes. But what was written there was hard to interpret. There were numbers, the name Hässleholm, a date, something that could be a time from a timetable: 07:50. Tomorrow's date. Saturday, October 22nd.

"What the hell does this mean?" Wallander asked. "Is Tore Grundén getting off the train in Hässleholm at 07:50?"

"Maybe he's getting *on* a train," said Höglund.

Wallander understood. He didn't hesitate.

"Call up Birch in Lund. He's got the phone number of a guy named Karl-Henrik Bergstrand in Malmö. Wake him up and get the answer to this question. Is Yvonne Ander working on the train that stops in or leaves from Hässleholm at 07:50 tomorrow morning?"

Martinsson pulled out his phone. Wallander stared at the open notebook.

"Where is she?" asked Höglund. "Right now? We know where she'll probably be tomorrow morning."

Wallander looked at her. In the background he saw the paintings and photographs. Suddenly he knew. He should have realized it at once. He went over to the wall and unhooked the framed picture of the farm. Turned it over. *Hansgården in Vollsjö, 1965,* someone had written in ink.

"That's where she lives. And that's where she probably is right now."

"What should we do?" she asked.

"We'll go out there and bring her in."

Martinsson had gotten hold of Birch. They waited. The conversation was brief.

"He'll chase down Bergstrand for us," said Martinsson.

Wallander stood with the notebook in his hand.

"Let's go, then. We'll pick up the others on the way."

"Do we know where Hansgården is?" she asked.

"We can find it in our real-estate register," said Martinsson. "It won't take me ten minutes."

They were now in a real hurry. At five past two they were back at the police station. They gathered up their weary colleagues. Martinsson looked up Hansgården on his computer. It took longer than he thought. He didn't find it until almost three. They looked on the map. Hansgården was on the outskirts of Malmö.

"Should we be armed?" asked Svedberg.

"Yes," said Wallander. "But don't forget that Katarina Taxell and her baby are there too."

Nyberg came into the conference room. His hair was standing on end and his eyes were bloodshot.

"We found what we were looking for on one of the cups," he said. "The fingerprint matches. From the suitcase and the cigarette butt. Since it isn't a thumbprint I can't say whether it's the same one we found on the bottom of the bird tower. The funny thing is, that print seems to have been put there later. As if she had been there a second time. If she's the one. But it's probably a match. Who is she?"

"Yvonne Ander," said Wallander. "And now we're going to bring her in. If only Bergstrand had called."

"Do we really have to wait for him?" asked Martinsson.

"Half an hour, tops," said Wallander.

They waited. Martinsson left the room to check that the apartment on Liregatan was still under surveillance.

Twenty-two minutes passed before Bergstrand called.

"Yvonne Ander is working on the northbound train from Malmö tomorrow morning," he said.

"So, we know that much," Wallander said simply.

It was a quarter to four when they left Ystad. The storm had reached its peak.

The final thing Wallander did was make two last phone calls. First to Lisa Holgersson, then to Per Åkeson.

Neither of them had any objections.

They were to arrest her as soon as humanly possible.

Chapter Thirty-six

At just after five o'clock they were gathered at the property called Hansgården. The wind was a hard, gusty gale. They were all freezing. They had surrounded the house in a shadow-like maneuver. After a brief discussion they decided that Wallander and Höglund should go in. The others had taken up positions where they each had close contact with at least one colleague.

They had left the cars out of sight of the farmhouse and approached the last stretch on foot. Wallander instantly spotted the red Golf parked in front of the house. During the ride up to Vollsjö he was worried that she might have already taken off. But her car was there. She was still home. The house was dark and quiet. No movement could be seen. Wallander couldn't see any watchdogs either.

It all went very fast. They took up their positions. Wallander asked Höglund to announce over the walkie-talkie that they would wait a few more minutes before they went in.

Wait for what? She didn't understand why. Wallander hadn't explained it either. Maybe it was because he had to prepare himself. Complete an internal transmission that wasn't yet ready. Or did he need to create a free zone for himself for a few minutes so that he could think through everything that had happened? He stood there freezing, and everything seemed unreal. They had been pursuing a strange, elusive shadow for a month. Now they were close to their goal, at a point where the pounce would conclude the hunt. It was as if he had to free himself from the feeling of unreality that surrounded everything that had happened. Especially in relation to the woman in the house, whom they now had to catch. For all this he needed breathing space. That's why he said they would wait.

He stood along with Höglund in a windbreak next to a dilapidated barn. The front door was about twenty-five meters away. Time passed. Soon it would be dawn. They couldn't wait any longer.

Wallander had approved the use of weapons. But he wanted everything to proceed calmly. Especially since Katarina Taxell was inside with her newborn baby.

Nothing must go wrong. The most important thing was for them to stay calm.

"Now we go," he said. "Pass it on."

She spoke softly into the walkie-talkie. Received a series of acknowledgments from the others. She took out her pistol. Wallander shook his head.

"Keep it in your pocket," he said. "But remember which one."

The house was still quiet. No movement. They approached, Wallander in the lead, Höglund behind him to one side. The wind was blowing hard and gusting the whole time. Wallander took another quick look at his watch. Nineteen minutes past five. Yvonne Ander should be up by now if she was going to make it to work with the early morning train. They stopped outside the door. Wallander took a deep breath. Knocked on the door and took a step back. He had his hand on the pistol in his right-hand jacket pocket. Nothing happened. He took a step forward and knocked again. He tried the latch. The door was locked. He knocked again. Suddenly he felt uneasy. He pounded on the door. Still no reaction. Something was wrong.

"We'll have to break in," he said. "Tell the others. Who has the crowbar? Why didn't we bring it along?"

Höglund spoke with a firm voice into the walkie-talkie. She turned her back to the wind. Wallander kept an eye on the windows next to the door. Svedberg came running up with the crowbar. Wallander asked him to return to his position at once. Then he stuck in the crowbar and started prying. He put all his strength into it. The door sprang open at the lock. There was a light on in the entryway. Without planning it he drew his pistol. Höglund quickly followed his lead. Wallander crouched and went in. She stood to one side behind him and covered him with her pistol. Everything was quiet.

"Police!" yelled Wallander. "We're looking for Yvonne Ander."

Nothing happened. He yelled again. Cautiously he moved toward the room straight ahead of him. She followed at his flank. The sense of unreality returned. He stepped quickly into a large, open room. With his pistol he swept over the room. It was completely empty. He let his arm drop. Höglund was on the other side of the door. Lamps were lit. A strangely shaped baking oven stood against one wall.

Suddenly a door opened across the room. Wallander gave a start and raised his weapon again, and Höglund went down on one knee. Katarina Taxell came through the door. She was dressed in a nightgown. She looked scared.

Wallander lowered his pistol, and Höglund did too.

At that moment Wallander knew that Yvonne Ander wasn't in the house.

"What's happening?" asked Taxell.

Wallander went quickly up to her.

"Where's Yvonne Ander?"

"She's not here."

"Where is she?"

"I assume she's on her way to work."

Wallander was now in a big hurry.

"Who came and picked her up?"

"She always drives herself."

"But her car is still parked outside the house."

"She has two cars."

So simple, thought Wallander. There wasn't just the red Golf.

"Are you feeling all right?" he asked then. "And your baby?"

"Why shouldn't I feel all right?"

Wallander took a quick look around the room. Then he asked Höglund to call in the others. They didn't have much time and had to get going.

"Get Nyberg out here," he said. "The house has to be gone over from the rafters to the cellar."

The freezing police officers gathered in the big white room.

"She's gone," said Wallander. "She's on her way to Hässleholm. At least there's no reason to believe otherwise. She's supposed to start her shift there. A passenger named Tore Grundén will be getting on there too. He's the next one on her hit list."

"Is she really going to kill him on the train?" asked Martinsson incredulously.

"We don't know. But we don't want any more murders. We have to catch her."

"We'll have to warn our colleagues in Hässleholm," said Hansson.

"We'll do that on the way," said Wallander. "I think Hansson and Martinsson should come with me. The rest of you start on the house. And talk to Katarina Taxell."

He nodded at her. She was standing next to the wall. The light was gray. She almost blended in with the wall, dissolved, faded. Could a person become so pale that she was no longer visible?

They took off. Hansson drove. Martinsson was just about to call Hässleholm when Wallander told him to wait.

"I think it's best we do this ourselves," he said. "If there's chaos, we don't know what will happen. She could be dangerous. I understand that now. Dangerous for us too."

"Of course she is," said Hansson in surprise. "She's killed three people. Impaled them on stakes, strangled them, drowned them. If a person like that isn't dangerous then I don't know who is."

"We don't even know what Grundén looks like," said Martinsson. "Are we going to page him on the PA system at the station? And she'll probably be in uniform."

"Maybe," said Wallander. "We'll see when we get there. Put on the blue light. We've got no time to lose."

Hansson drove fast. Still, time was tight. When they had about twenty minutes left Wallander knew they wouldn't make it.

They had a blowout. Hansson swore and braked. When they saw that the left rear tire had to be changed, Martinsson wanted to call their colleagues in Hässleholm again. If nothing else, they could send a car for them. But Wallander said no. He had made up his mind. They would make it.

They changed the tire at lightning speed while the wind tore at their clothes. Then they were on the road again. Hansson drove very fast. Time was running out and Wallander tried to decide what they should do. He had a hard time imagining that Yvonne Ander would kill Tore Grundén in plain sight of the passengers waiting for trains. It didn't fit with her previous M.O. He decided that for the time being they'd have to forget about Grundén. They would look for her, a woman in uniform, and they would grab her as discreetly as possible.

They reached Hässleholm and Hansson nervously started heading the wrong direction, even though he claimed he knew the way. Now Wallander was irritated too, and when they reached the station they had almost started screaming at each other. They hopped out of the car with the blue light flashing and ran toward the platform. We look like we're about to rob the ticket office, thought Wallander, or at least try to make a train that's just leaving. The clock showed that they had exactly three minutes left. 07:47. The loudspeakers announced the train. But Wallander couldn't hear if it was just arriving or was already there.

He told Martinsson and Hansson that now they had to calm down. They should walk out on the platform, a little apart from each other, but stay in contact at all times. When they found her they should grab her from both sides and ask her to come with them. Wallander sensed that this was the critical moment. They couldn't be sure how she would react. They should be prepared, not with pistols, but with their hands. He emphasized that several times. Yvonne Ander didn't use weapons. They should be prepared, but they had to take her without firing a shot.

They went outside. The wind was still blowing hard. The train hadn't arrived at the station yet. The passengers were huddled in whatever shelter from the wind they could find. The station was crowded. They went out on the platform, Wallander first, Hansson right behind him, and Martinsson out by the track. Wallander instantly spotted a male trainmaster standing smoking a cigarette. He felt the tension making him sweat. He couldn't see Yvonne Ander. No women in uniform. Quickly he scanned the crowd for a man who might be Tore Grundén. But it was useless, of course. The man had no face. He was just a name in a macabre notebook.

He exchanged glances with Hansson and Martinsson. He looked back toward the station to see if she was coming from that direction. At the same time the train entered the station. He knew that something was going very wrong. He refused to believe that she intended to kill Grundén on the platform. But he couldn't be entirely sure. Far too often he'd seen calculating individuals suddenly lose control and start acting impulsively and contrary to their usual habits. The passengers started picking up their suitcases. The train was slowing to a stop. The trainmaster had thrown away his cigarette. Wallander no longer had any choice. He had to talk to him. Ask whether Yvonne Ander was already on the train. Or whether something had happened with her work schedule.

The train came to a halt, brakes shrieking. Wallander had to push his way through the passengers who were in a hurry to board the train and get out of the wind. Suddenly Wallander noticed a lone man standing farther down the platform. He was just picking up his bag. Right next to him stood a woman. She was wearing a long overcoat that was being whipped by the wind. A train was on the way in from the other direction. Wallander was never sure whether he consciously understood the situation. But he still reacted as though everything was perfectly clear. He shoved aside the passengers who were standing in his way. Hansson and Martinsson were somewhere behind him, without knowing exactly where they were headed. Wallander saw the woman abruptly grab the man from behind. She seemed to be very strong. She almost lifted him off the ground. Wallander sensed more than understood that she intended to throw him in front of the train on the other track. Since he couldn't reach them in time, he yelled. Despite the roar of the locomotive she heard him. The brief instant of hesitation was enough. She looked at Wallander. At the same time Martinsson and Hansson appeared at his side. They rushed toward the woman, who had now released the man. The long coat had blown up, and Wallander caught a glimpse of her uniform underneath. Suddenly she raised her hand and did something that made both Hansson and Martinsson freeze in their tracks for a moment. She ripped off her hair. It was caught at once by the wind and vanished down the platform. Under the wig her hair was short. They started running again.

Tore Grundén still didn't seem to understand what had almost happened to him.

"Yvonne Ander!" shouted Wallander. "Police!"

Martinsson was now almost upon her. Wallander saw him stretch out his arms to grab her. Then everything happened very fast. She jabbed with her right fist, hard and accurate. The blow struck Martinsson on the left cheek. He dropped to the platform without a sound. Behind Wallander someone was shouting. A passenger had seen what was going on. Hansson stopped in his tracks when he saw what happened to Martinsson. He made an attempt to draw his pistol, but it was already too late. She grabbed his jacket and kneed him hard in the groin. For a brief moment she leaned over him as he buckled forward. Then she started running down the platform. She tore off the long coat and tossed it. It fluttered and then blew away on a gust of wind. Wallander stopped beside Martinsson and Hansson to see how they were. Martinsson was out cold. Hansson was moaning and white in the face. When Wallander looked up she was gone. He took off down the platform running. He caught sight of her just before she vanished across the tracks. He knew his chance of catching up with her was small. Besides, he didn't know how badly Martinsson was hurt. He turned back and saw that Tore Grundén was gone. Several railway workers came running up. No one understood in the confusion what had actually happened, of course.

Afterwards Wallander would recall the next few hours as a never-ending chaos. He tried to handle a lot of things at once. On the platform, no one understood what he was talking about. Train passengers kept swarming around him too. In the midst of the improbable confusion Hansson began to recover. But Martinsson was still unconscious. Wallander raged at the ambulance that took so long to arrive, and not until some bewildered Hässleholm police appeared on the platform did he start to make some sense of the situation.

Martinsson had been truly knocked out, but his breathing was steady. By the time the ambulance attendants carried him off, Hansson had managed to get to his feet again, and he went with them to the hospital. Wallander explained to the police officers that they had been trying to arrest a female trainmaster, but she had escaped. By that time the train had left. Wallander wondered whether Tore Grundén had boarded it. Did he have any idea how close to death he had come? Wallander realized that no one had any idea what he was talking about. Only his police ID and seeming authority made them believe that he was a cop and not a madman.

Aside from Martinsson's health, the only thing that interested him was where Yvonne Ander had gone. He called Höglund during the confused minutes on the platform and told her what had happened. She promised to see to it that they were prepared if she came back to Vollsjö. The apartment in Ystad was also put under surveillance immediately, but Wallander didn't think she'd show up there. Now she knew she wasn't just being watched. They were hot on her heels, and they wouldn't give up until they caught her. Where could she go? On an aimless flight? He couldn't ignore that possibility, but it didn't seem likely. She was always planning. She was a person who sought premeditated escape routes. Wallander called Höglund back. He told her to talk to Katarina Taxell. They should ask her one question. Did Yvonne Ander have any other hideout? Everything else could wait for the time being.

"I think she always has an escape hatch," said Wallander. "She may have mentioned an address, a location, without Katarina thinking of it as a hideout."

"So maybe she'll decide on Taxell's apartment in Lund?"

Wallander saw that she might be right.

"Call up Birch. Ask him to check it out."

"She has keys to it," said Höglund. "Katarina told me so."

Wallander was escorted to the hospital by a police car. Hansson was feeling bad and lay on a stretcher. His scrotum had swollen up and he had to be kept for observation. Martinsson was still unconscious. A doctor diagnosed a severe concussion.

"The man who hit him must have been extremely strong," said the doctor.

"You're right," said Wallander, "except that the man was a woman."

He left the hospital. Where had she gone? Something was nagging at Wallander's subconscious. Something that could give him the answer to where she was or at least where she might be headed.

Then he remembered what it was. He stood quite still outside the hospital. Nyberg had been absolutely clear on that point. *The fingerprints in the tower must have been put there later.* It was a possibility, even though it wasn't very great. Yvonne Ander might be a person similar to himself. In tense situations she sought out solitude. A place where she could take stock, make a decision. All her actions gave the impression of detailed planning and precise timetables. Now her ordered life had come crashing down around her.

He decided it was worth a try.

The site was blocked off, of course. But Hansson had said that the work wouldn't be resumed until they got the extra help they had requested. Wallander also assumed that the surveillance was being done by patrol cars. And she could also reach the spot by the same route she had used before.

Wallander said goodbye to the police who had helped him. They still didn't quite understand what had happened at the train station. Wallander promised to inform them later that day. It was only a routine arrest of a suspect who had slipped out of their hands. But no damage was done. The officers who had been admitted to the hospital would soon be on their feet again.

Wallander got into his car and called Höglund for the third time. He didn't tell her what it was about, just that he wanted her to meet him at the turnoff to Holger Eriksson's farm.

It was past ten when Wallander arrived in Lödinge. Höglund was standing by her car waiting for him. They drove the last stretch up to the farmhouse in Wallander's car. He stopped a hundred meters from the house. Until now he had said nothing. Now she gave him a questioning look.

"I might be wrong," he said. "But there's a chance she might come back here. To the bird tower. She's been here before." He reminded her of what Nyberg said about the fingerprints.

"What would Yvonne Ander be doing here?" she asked.

"I don't know. But she's on the run. She needs to make some kind of decision. Besides, she's been here before."

They got out of the car. The wind was sharp.

"We found the hospital uniform," she said. "And a plastic bag with briefs in it. We can probably assume that Gösta Runfeldt was held captive at Vollsjö."

They were approaching the house.

"What do we do if she's up in the tower?"

"We take her. I'll go around the other side of the hill. If she comes here, that's where she'll park her car. Then you walk down the path. This time we'll have our guns drawn."

"I don't think she'll come," said Höglund.

Wallander didn't reply. He knew there was a good chance she was right.

They found some shelter inside the courtyard. The crime-scene tape down by the ditch where they had dug for Krista Haberman had been torn away by the wind. The tower was empty. It stood out sharply in the autumn light.

"Let's wait a while anyway," Wallander said. "If she comes it'll be soon."

"There's a district alarm out for her," she said.

"If we don't find her, she'll soon be hunted all over the country."

They stood silent for a moment. The wind tore at their clothes.

"What is it that drives her?" she asked.

"She's probably the only one who can answer that question. But shouldn't we assume that she was abused too?"

Höglund didn't reply.

"I think she's a lonely person," said Wallander. "And she thinks the purpose of her life is a call to kill on behalf of others."

"Once I thought we were out after a mercenary," she said. "And now we're waiting for a female trainmaster to pop up in an abandoned bird tower."

"That mercenary angle might not have been so far-fetched," Wallander said thoughtfully. "Other than the fact that she's a woman and doesn't get paid for it. As far as we know. Still, there's something that reminds me of what we mistakenly started out with."

"Katarina Taxell said that she had met her through a group of women who used to meet in Vollsjö. But their first meeting was held on a train. You were right about that. Apparently she asked about a bruise Taxell had on her temple. She had seen through her evasions. It was Eugen Blomberg who had abused her. I never found out exactly how it all happened. But she confirmed that Yvonne Ander had previously worked in a hospital and also as an ambulance attendant. She saw plenty of abused women. Later she got in contact with them. Invited them over to Vollsjö. You might call it an extremely informal crisis group. She found out which men had abused the women. And then something happened. Katarina also acknowledged that of course it was Yvonne Ander who visited her at the hospital. On the last occasion she gave Ander the father's name. Eugen Blomberg."

"That signed his death warrant," said Wallander. "I also think she's been preparing this for a long time. Something happened that triggered it all. And neither you nor I know what it was."

"Does she know it herself?"

"We have to assume she does. If she isn't completely insane."

They waited. The wind came and went in strong gusts. A police car drove up to the entrance of the courtyard. Wallander asked them not to come back until further notice. He gave no explanation, but he was firm.

They kept on waiting. Neither of them had anything to say.

At quarter to eleven Wallander cautiously put a hand on her shoulder.

"There she is," he whispered.

Höglund looked. A person had appeared up by the hill. It had to be Yvonne Ander. She stood there and looked around. Then she began to climb the stairs to the tower.

"It takes me twenty minutes to go around," Wallander said. "Then you start to walk down the path. I'll be on the back side if she tries to escape."

"What happens if she attacks me? Then I'll have to shoot."

"I'll make sure that doesn't happen. I'll be there."

He ran to the car and drove as fast as he could to the tractor path that led to the back side of the hill. He didn't dare drive all the way, so he ran. The run made him out of breath. It took longer than he thought. A car was parked by the tractor path. Also a Golf, but a black one. The phone rang in Wallander's jacket pocket. He stopped in his tracks. It might be Höglund. He answered and kept walking along the tractor path.

It was Svedberg.

"Where are you? What the hell is going on?"

"We're at Holger Eriksson's farm. I can't go into it right now. It would be good if you could come out here with someone. Hamrén, for instance. I can't talk right now."

"I called because I have a message," said Svedberg. "Hansson called from Hässleholm. Both he and Martinsson are feeling better. Martinsson is conscious again, anyway. But Hansson wondered if you had picked up his pistol."

Wallander froze.

"His pistol?"

"He said it was lost."

"I don't have it."

"It couldn't still be lying on the train platform, could it?"

At that instant Wallander knew. He could see the events play out clearly before him. Yvonne Ander grabbed hold of Hansson's jacket and then kneed him hard in the groin. Then she quickly bent over him. That's when she took the pistol.

"Shit!" Wallander yelled.

Before Svedberg could answer he had hung up and stuffed the phone back in his pocket. He had put Höglund in mortal danger. The woman up in the tower was armed.

Wallander ran. His heart pounded like a hammer in his chest. He saw by his watch that she must already be on her way down the path. He stopped and dialed her cell-phone number. No contact. She must have left her phone in the car.

He started running again. His only chance was to get there first. Höglund didn't know that Yvonne Ander was armed.

His terror made him run even faster. He had reached the back side of the hill. She must be almost to the ditch now. Walk slowly, he tried to tell her in his mind. Trip and fall, slip, anything. Don't hurry. Walk slowly. He had pulled out his gun and was stumbling up the hill on the back side of the bird tower. When he reached the top he saw Höglund at the ditch. She had her pistol in her hand. The woman in the tower still hadn't seen her. He shouted.

"Ann-Britt, she's got a gun! Get out of there!"

He aimed his pistol at the woman standing with her back to him up there in the tower.

At the same moment a shot rang out. He saw Höglund jerk and fall backwards into the mud. Wallander felt like someone had thrust a sword right through him. He stared at the motionless body in the mud and sensed only that the woman in the tower had quickly turned around. Then he dived to the side and fired toward the tower. The third shot hit home. She lurched and dropped Hansson's gun.

Wallander rushed down into the mud. He stumbled into the ditch and scrambled up the other side. When he saw Höglund on her back in the mud he thought she was dead. She had been killed by Hansson's pistol and it was all his fault.

For a split second he saw no way out but to shoot himself. Right where he stood, a few meters from her.

Then he saw her moving feebly. He fell to his knees by her side. The whole front of her jacket was bloody. She was deathly pale and stared at him with fear in her eyes.

"It'll be all right," he said. "It'll be all right."

"She was armed," she mumbled. "Why didn't we know that?"

Wallander could feel the tears running down his face. He called for an ambulance.

Later he would remember that while he waited, he had steadily murmured a confused prayer to a god he didn't really believe in. In a haze he was aware that Svedberg and Hamrén had arrived. Ann-Britt was carried away on a stretcher. Wallander was sitting in the mud. They couldn't get him to stand up. A photographer who had raced after the ambulance when it drove off from Ystad took a picture of Wallander as he sat there. Dirty, forlorn, hopeless. The photographer managed to take that one picture before Svedberg, in a rage, chased him off. Under pressure from Chief Holgersson the photo was never published.

Meanwhile, Svedberg and Hamrén brought Yvonne Ander down from the tower. Wallander had hit her high on the thigh. She was bleeding profusely, but her life was not in danger. She too was taken away in an ambulance. Svedberg and Hamrén finally managed to get Wallander up from the mud and helped him up to the farmhouse.

The first report came in from the Ystad hospital.

Ann-Britt Höglund had been shot in the abdomen. The wound was severe, and her condition was critical.

Wallander rode with Svedberg to get his own car. For a while Svedberg was unsure about letting Wallander drive alone to Ystad. But Wallander said there was no danger. He drove straight to the hospital and then sat in the corridor waiting for news of Ann-Britt's condition. He still hadn't had time to get cleaned up. He didn't leave the hospital until many hours later, when the doctors assured him that her condition had stabilized.

All of a sudden he was gone. No one had noticed him leave. Svedberg began to worry, but he thought he knew Wallander well enough: He just wanted to be alone.

Wallander left the hospital right before midnight. The wind was still blowing hard, and it was going to be a cold night. He got into his car and drove out to the cemetery where his father lay buried. He found his way to the grave in the dark and stood there, completely empty inside, still caked with mud.

Around one o'clock he got home and called Baiba in Riga. They talked for a long time. Then he finally undressed and took a hot bath.

Afterwards he dressed and returned to the hospital. Just after three in the morning he went into the room where Yvonne Ander lay, under intensive guard. She was asleep when he cautiously entered the room. He stood for a long time looking at her face. Then he left without saying a word.

After an hour he was back. At dawn Lisa Holgersson came to the hospital and said they had gotten hold of Höglund's husband, who was in Dubai. He would arrive at Kastrup Airport later that day.

No one knew if Wallander was listening to anything anyone said to him. He sat motionless on a chair, or stood at a window staring into the gale. When a nurse wanted to give him a cup of coffee he burst into tears and locked himself in the bathroom. But most of the time he sat unmoving on his chair and stared at his hands.

At about the same time Höglund's husband landed at Kastrup, a doctor gave them the news they had all been waiting for. She was going to make it, and she probably wouldn't have any permanent injuries. She was lucky. But her recovery would take time and the convalescence would be long.

Wallander was standing as he listened to the doctor, as if he were receiving a sentence in court. Afterwards he walked out of the hospital and disappeared somewhere in the wind.

On Monday, October 24th, Yvonne Ander was indicted for murder. She was still in the hospital. So far she hadn't spoken a single word, not even to the attorney appointed for her. Wallander had tried to question her that afternoon. She just stared at him. Just as he was about to leave, he turned in the doorway and told her that Ann-Britt Höglund was going to recover. He thought he saw a reaction from her; she looked relieved, maybe even glad.

Martinsson was put on the sick list for his concussion. Hansson went back on duty, even though he had a hard time both walking and sitting for several weeks.

Their primary focus during this period was to complete the laborious task of figuring out exactly what had happened. One thing they never managed to find conclusive evidence for was whether the skeleton they had dug up in Holger Eriksson's field in its entirety, with the mysterious exception of a shinbone that was never found, was really the remains of Krista Haberman or not. There was nothing to disprove it, but no hard evidence either.

And yet they knew. A crack in the skull also provided the proof of how Eriksson had killed her more than twenty-five years before. Everything else began to be cleared up, although slowly. There was another question mark they hadn't erased yet. Had Gösta Runfeldt killed his wife? Or was it an accident? The only one who might give them the answer was Yvonne Ander, and she still wasn't talking. They explored her life and came out with a story that only partially told them who she was and why she might have acted as she did.

One afternoon, as they were sitting in a long meeting, Wallander abruptly concluded it by saying something he had been thinking for a long time.

"Yvonne Ander is the first person I've ever met who is both intelligent and insane."

He didn't explain any further. No one doubted that he really believed it.

Every day during this period Wallander also went to visit Ann-Britt at the hospital. He couldn't get over his guilt. Nothing anyone said made any difference. He recognized that the responsibility for what had happened was his alone. It was something he would have to live with.

Yvonne Ander kept silent. One evening Wallander was sitting in his office late, reading through the extensive collection of letters she had exchanged with her mother.

The next day he visited her in jail.

That day, she finally started to talk.

It was November 3rd, 1994.

On that morning frost lay over the countryside around Ystad.

Skåne

4—5 December 1994

Epilogue

On the afternoon of December 4th, Kurt Wallander spoke with Yvonne Ander for the last time. He didn't know it would be the last, although they didn't make an appointment to meet again.

They had come to a provisional end point. There was nothing more to add. Nothing to ask about, no reply to give. And after that the long and complex investigation began to slip out of his consciousness for the first time. Although more than a month had passed since they captured her, the investigation had continued to dominate his life. In all his years as a criminal detective, he had never had such an intense need to understand. Criminal acts were always just the surface. Often this surface was tangled up with its own undergrowth. The surface and the subsoil were directly connected. But sometimes, once the surface of a crime had been cracked, chasms opened that no one could have imagined. This was the case with Yvonne Ander. Wallander punched through the surface and immediately looked down into a bottomless pit. He then decided to tie a symbolic rope around his waist and start to climb down. He didn't know where it would lead, for her or for himself.

The first step had been to get her to break her silence. He was successful when for the second time he read the letters she had exchanged all her adult life with her mother and then assiduously saved. Wallander intuitively sensed that it was here he could start to break through her aloofness. And he was right. That was November 3rd, more than a month earlier. He was still depressed that Ann-Britt had been shot. He knew by then that she would survive and even regain full health, with no injuries except a scar on the left side of her abdomen. But the guilt weighed so heavily on him that it threatened to suffocate him. His best support during that period was his daughter Linda. She came down to Ystad, even though she really didn't have time, and took care of him. But she also pressured him, forcing him to admit that circumstances were to blame, not him. With her help he managed to crawl through the first terrible weeks of November. Aside from the sheer effort of functioning, he spent all of his time on Yvonne Ander. She was the one who had shot and could have killed Ann-Britt if fortune had willed it so. In the beginning he had attacks of hostility and felt like hitting her. Later it became more important to try and understand who she really was. He finally managed to break through her silence and get her to start talking. He knotted the rope around himself and started down into the pit.

What was it he found down there? For a long time he was unsure whether she was insane or not, whether all she said about herself was confused dreams and sick, deformed fantasies. He also didn't trust his own judgment during this time, and he could hardly disguise his distrust of her. But somehow he sensed that she was telling him the truth. He realized that Yvonne Ander was that rare type of person who couldn't lie.

He had read the correspondence from her mother. In the last bundle he opened there was an odd letter from a police officer in Africa named Françoise Bertrand. At first he had no luck deciphering the contents of the letter. It accompanied a stack of unfinished letters from her mother, letters that had never been sent. They were all from the same African country, written the year before. Françoise Bertrand had sent her letter to Yvonne Ander in August 1993. It took him several hours one night to puzzle out the answer. Then he understood. Yvonne Ander's mother Anna had been murdered by mistake in a meaningless happenstance, and the police had covered up the whole thing. Politics were clearly behind the killing, although Wallander felt incapable of fully understanding what it involved. But Françoise Bertrand had in all confidence written the letter, relating what had really happened. Without any help from Yvonne Ander at this point, he discussed with Chief Holgersson what had happened to the mother. The chief listened and then contacted the national criminal police. The matter was thus removed from Wallander's purview. But he read through all the letters one more time.

Wallander had met with Yvonne Ander in jail. She slowly came to understand that he was a man who wasn't hunting her. He was different from the others, the other men who populated the world. He was introverted, seemed to sleep very little, and was also tormented by worry. For the first time in her life Yvonne Ander discovered that she could actually trust a man. She told him this at one of their last meetings.

She never asked him straight out, but she still believed she knew the answer. He had probably never struck a woman. If he had, it happened only once. No more, never again.

The descent began on November 3rd. The same day, Ann-Britt underwent the last of the three operations the surgeons had to perform. Everything went well, and her convalescence could finally begin. During this entire month Wallander set up a routine. After his talks with Ander he would drive straight to the hospital. He seldom stayed long. He told her about Yvonne Ander. Ann-Britt became the discussion partner he needed in order to understand how to penetrate further into the depths he had begun to plumb.

His first question to Ander was about the events in Africa. Who was Françoise Bertrand? What actually happened?

A pale light was falling through the window into the room they were in. They sat facing each other at a table. In the distance a radio could be heard, and someone drilling into a wall. The first sentences she uttered he didn't catch. It was like a powerful roar when her silence finally broke. He just listened to her voice, which he had never heard before, only tried to imagine.

Then he started to listen to what she was saying. He seldom took notes during their meetings, and he used no tape recorder.

"Somewhere there's a man who killed my mother. Who's looking for him?"

"Not me," he had replied. "But if you tell me what happened, and if a Swedish citizen has been killed overseas, we will have to react, of course."

He didn't mention the conversation he had had a few days before with Chief Holgersson. About the fact that the mother's death was already being investigated.

"Nobody knows who killed my mother," she went on. "Random fate selected her as a victim. Whoever who killed her didn't even know her. He thought he was justified. He believed he could kill anybody he wanted to. Even an innocent woman who spent her retirement taking all the trips she never had the time or the money to take before."

He could hear her bitter rage. She made no attempt to conceal it.

"Why was she staying with the nuns?" he asked.

Suddenly she looked up from the table, straight into his eyes.

"Who gave you the right to read my letters?"

"No one. But they belong to you, a person who has committed several heinous murders. Otherwise I never would have read them."

She turned away again.

"The nuns," repeated Wallander. "Why was she staying with them?"

"She didn't have much money. She stayed wherever it was cheap. She never imagined it would be the death of her."

"This happened more than a year ago. How did you react when the letter arrived?"

"There was no reason for me to wait any longer. How could I justify doing nothing? When no one else seemed to care."

"Care about what?"

She didn't reply. He waited. Then he changed the question.

"Wait to do what?"

She answered without looking at him.

"To kill them."

"Who?"

"The ones who went free in spite of all they had done."

It was then that he realized he had figured it out correctly. It was when she received Françoise Bertrand's letter that some force locked inside her had been released. She had gone around harboring thoughts of revenge. But she could still control herself. Then the dam broke. She decided to take the law into her own hands.

Later Wallander thought there really wasn't much difference from what had happened in Lödinge. She had been her own citizen militia. She had placed herself outside the law and dispensed her own justice.

"Is that how it was?" he asked. "You wanted to dispense justice? You wanted to punish those who should have wound up before a court but never did?"

"Who's looking for the man who killed my mother?" she countered. "Who?"

She fell silent again. Wallander thought back to how it all began. Some months after the letter came from Africa she broke into Holger Eriksson's house. That was the first step. When he asked her point blank if it was true, she didn't even act surprised. She took it for granted that he knew.

"I heard about Krista Haberman," she said. "That it was the car dealer who killed her."

"Who did you hear it from?"

"A Polish woman in the hospital in Malmö. That was many years ago."

"You were working at the hospital then?"

"I worked there several different times. I often talked to women who had been abused. She had a friend who used to know Krista Haberman."

"Why did you break into Eriksson's house?"

"I wanted to prove to myself that it was possible. Besides, I was looking for signs that Krista Haberman had been there."

"Why did you dig the pit? Why the stakes? Why the sawed-through footbridge? Did the woman who knew Krista Haberman suspect that the body was buried near that ditch?"

She didn't answer that one. But Wallander understood anyway. Despite the fact that the investigation had always been hard to grasp, Wallander and his colleagues had been on the right track without knowing it. Yvonne Ander had mimicked the men's brutality in her methods of killing them.

During the five or six meetings Wallander had with Yvonne Ander, he methodically went through the three murders, clearing up details and piecing together the connections that had previously been so vague. He continued to talk to her without a tape recorder. After the meetings he would sit in his car and make notes from memory. Then he would have them typed up. A copy went to Per Åkeson, who was preparing the indictment, which could never lead to anything but a conviction on three counts. The whole time, Wallander knew he was just scraping the surface. The real descent hadn't even started yet. The upper strata, the burden of proof, would send her to prison. But he wouldn't find the actual truth he was after until later, when he reached the deepest depths of the pit. If then.

She had to undergo a psychiatric evaluation, of course. Wallander knew it was unavoidable. He insisted that it be postponed. Right now the most important thing was that he be able to talk to her in peace. No one objected to this. Wallander had an argument no one could ignore. Everyone understood that she would probably clam up again if she was upset.

She was ready to talk to him and him alone.

They went farther, slowly, step by step, day by day. Outside the jail the fall was deepening and drawing them toward winter. Wallander never did find out why Holger Eriksson drove up to get Krista Haberman in Svenstavik and then almost immediately killed her. Presumably it was because she had denied him something he was used to getting. Maybe an argument turned violent.

He moved on to Gösta Runfeldt. She was convinced that Runfeldt had murdered his wife. Drowned her in Stång Lake. And even if he hadn't done it, he still deserved his fate. He had abused her so severely that she actually wanted nothing more than to die. Höglund was right when she sensed that Runfeldt had been attacked in the flower shop. Ander had found out that he would be leaving for Nairobi and lured him to the shop with the story that she had to buy flowers for a reception early the next morning. Then she knocked him to the ground. The blood on the floor was indeed his. The smashed window was a diversion to trick the police into believing it was a break-in.

Then came a description of what for Wallander was the most terrifying element. Until that point he had tried to understand her without letting his emotional reactions take over. But then he couldn't go any further. She recounted in utter calm how she had undressed Gösta Runfeldt, tied him up, and forced him into the old baking oven. When he could no longer control his bodily functions she took away his underwear and laid him on a plastic sheet.

Later she led him out into the woods. By that time he was quite powerless. She tied him to the tree and strangled him. It was at that moment that she turned into a monster in Wallander's eyes. It didn't matter if she was a man or a woman. She became a monster, and he was glad they had stopped her before she killed Tore Grundén or anyone else on the macabre list she had made.

The list was also her only mistake—she hadn't destroyed the notebook in which she drew up her plans before she copied them into her main book, the ledger she kept in Vollsjö. Wallander never asked her why. Even she admitted it was a mistake. That was the only one of her actions she couldn't understand.

Later Wallander pondered whether it might mean she actually wanted to leave a clue, that deep inside she wanted to be discovered and stopped.

He wavered. Sometimes he thought it was true, sometimes he didn't. He never reached absolute clarity on that point.

She didn't have much to say about Eugen Blomberg. She described how she mixed up the slips of paper, one of which had a cross. She let chance decide who would be next, just as chance had killed her mother.

This was one of the times he interrupted her story. Normally he let her speak freely, inserting questions when she couldn't decide how to go on. But now he stopped her.

"So you did the same thing as the men who killed your mother," he said. "You let chance select your victim. Chance ruled."

"It's not comparable," she replied. "All those men whose names I had written down deserved their death. I gave them time with my slips of paper. I prolonged their lives."

He pursued it no further, since he realized that in an obscure way she was right. Reluctantly he admitted to himself that she had her own peculiar and impenetrable sort of truth.

When he read through the transcripts of the notes he made from memory, he also thought that what he had in his hands was certainly a confession. But it was also an extremely incomplete account.

Did he ever succeed with what he intended? Afterwards, Wallander was always quite taciturn when he spoke of Yvonne Ander. He always referred to the printed notes. They didn't include everything, of course. The secretary who typed them up complained to her colleagues that they were often extremely hard to read.

As it turned out, what became Yvonne Ander's last will and testament was her story of a life full of terrifying experiences in her childhood. Wallander was almost the same age as Ander, and he thought time after time that the era he was living in was concerned with one single decisive question: What are we actually doing with our children? She had told him how her mother was constantly abused by her stepfather, who had replaced the biological father who had disappeared and then faded in her memory like a blurry, soulless photograph. The worst thing was that the stepfather had forced her mother to have an abortion. She had never had the chance to have the sister her mother was carrying. She couldn't have known if it really was a sister—maybe it was a brother—but to her it was a sister, brutally ripped from her mother's womb against her will, in her apartment one night in the early fifties. She remembered that night as a bloody hell. When she was telling Wallander about it, she raised her eyes from the table and looked straight into his. Her mother had lain on a sheet on the extended kitchen table, the abortionist was drunk, the stepfather locked in the cellar, probably drunk too. That night she was robbed of her sister and for all time learned to view the future as darkness, with threatening men lurking around every corner, violence lurking behind every friendly smile, every word.

She had barricaded her memories in a secret interior room. She had been educated, become a nurse, and she had always harbored the vague notion that it was her duty someday to avenge the sister she never had, and the mother who wasn't allowed to give birth to her. She had collected the stories from abused women, she had tracked down the dead women in muddy fields and Småland lakes, she had entered names in a ledger, played with her slips of paper.

And then her mother had been murdered.

She described it almost poetically to Wallander. *Like a silent tidal wave*, she said. *No more than that. I knew that it was time. I let a year pass. I planned, completed the timetable that had kept me alive all those years. Then I dug in a ditch at night.*

Precisely those words. *Then I dug in a ditch at night.* Maybe those words best summed up Wallander's experience of the many conversations with Yvonne Ander in jail that fall.

He thought it was a picture of the time he was living in.

What ditch was *he* digging?

One question was never answered: why she suddenly, sometime in the mid-eighties, changed professions and became a trainmaster. Wallander had understood that the train timetable was the liturgy she lived by, her handbook of structure. But he never saw any real reason to delve deeper. The trains remained her private world. Maybe the only one; maybe the last one.

Did she feel any guilt? Per Åkeson asked him about that many times. Lisa Holgersson asked less often, his colleagues almost never. The only person besides Åkeson who really insisted on knowing was Ann-Britt Höglund. Wallander told her the truth: He didn't know.

"Yvonne Ander reminds me of a coiled spring," he told her. "I can't express it any better than that. I can't say whether guilt is part of it, or whether it's gone."

On December 4th it was over. Wallander had nothing more to ask, and Yvonne Ander had nothing more to say. The confession was prepared. Wallander had reached the end of the long descent. Now he could pull on the invisible rope and return to the surface. The psychiatric examination could begin, the defense attorney who got wind of the attention surrounding the case could sharpen his pencils, and only Wallander had any idea how it would turn out.

He knew Yvonne Ander would fall silent again, with the determined will of someone who has nothing more to say.

Just before he left, he asked her about two more things he still didn't know the answer to. The first was a detail that no longer had any significance, more a manifestation of his own curiosity.

"When Katarina Taxell called her mother from the house in Vollsjö, there was something making a banging noise," he said. "We never could figure out where that sound was coming from."

She gave him a baffled look. Then her serious face broke open in a smile, which was the only one Wallander saw in all his talks with her.

"A farmer's tractor had broken down in the field next to us. He was hitting it with a big hammer to get something loose from the undercarriage. Could you really hear that on the phone?"

Wallander nodded. He was already thinking of his last question.

"I think we actually met once," he said. "On a train."

She nodded.

"South of Älmhult? I asked you when we would get to Malmö."

"I recognized you. From the newspapers. From last summer."

"Did you already know then that we'd catch you?"

"Why should I?"

"A policeman from Ystad who gets on a train in Älmhult. What's he doing there? Unless he's following the trail of what happened to Gösta Runfeldt's wife?"

She shook her head. "I never thought about that. I should have."

Wallander had nothing more to ask. He had found out everything he wanted to know. He stood up, muttered goodbye, and left.

That afternoon Wallander visited the hospital as usual. Ann-Britt was asleep when he arrived. She was under observation after her last operation. Wallander received the confirmation he was looking for from a friendly doctor. Everything had gone fine. In six months she could return to work.

Wallander left the hospital just after five. It was already dark, one or two degrees below freezing, no wind. He drove out to the cemetery and went to his father's grave. Withered flowers had frozen solid to the ground. It was still less than three months since they had come back from Rome. The trip was vivid in his mind as he stood by the grave. He wondered what his father had actually been thinking when he took his nighttime promenade to the Spanish Steps, to the fountains, with a gleam in his eyes.

It was as if Yvonne Ander and his father could have stood on either side of a river and waved to each other, even though they had nothing in common. Or did they? Wallander wondered what he himself had in common with her. He had no answer for that, of course.

That night, out by the grave in the dark cemetery, the investigation came to an end too. There would still be papers he would have to read over and sign. There was nothing left to investigate. The case was clear-cut, finished. The psychiatric examination would declare that she was in full possession of her faculties. If they could get anything out of her, that is. Then she would be convicted and hidden away at Hinseberg. The investigation of the circumstances surrounding her mother's death in Africa would also continue. But that had nothing to do with his own work.

The night of December 4th he slept very poorly. The next day he decided to look at a house just north of town. He was also going to visit a kennel in Sjöbo where they had a litter of black Labrador puppies for sale. The next day he had to go to Stockholm and speak about his view of police work to some classes at the Police Academy. Why he suddenly acquiesced when Chief Holgersson asked him again, he didn't know. And now that he lay awake wondering what the hell he was going to say, he didn't understand how she had managed to talk him into it.

On that restless night, he thought mostly about Baiba. Several times he got up and stood at the kitchen window, staring at the streetlight swaying on its wire.

Right after he came back from Rome, at the end of September, they had decided that she would come to Ystad, and soon—no later than November. Then they would have a serious discussion about whether she should move to Sweden from Riga. But all of a sudden she couldn't come, the trip was postponed, first once, then a second time. Each time there were reasons, even excellent reasons, for why she couldn't come—not yet, not just yet. Wallander believed her, of course. But a feeling of uncertainty arose. Was it still there, invisible, between them? A rift he hadn't seen? If so, why hadn't he seen it? Because he didn't want to?

Now she was really going to come. They were supposed to meet in Stockholm on December 8th. He would go straight from the Police Academy to Arlanda to meet her. Linda would join them in the evening and they would all head south to Skåne the following day. How long she would stay, he didn't know. This time they would have a serious discussion about the future, not just about the next time they could meet.

The night turned into a long, drawn-out vigil. The weather had turned warmer. The meteorologists were predicting snow. Wallander wandered like a lost soul between his bed and the kitchen window. Now and then he sat down at the kitchen table and made a few notes, in a futile attempt to find a starting point for the lecture he was going to give in Stockholm. At the same time he couldn't stop thinking about Yvonne Ander and her story. She was constantly on his mind, and occasionally she even blocked out thoughts of Baiba.

The person he thought very little about was his father. He was already far away. Wallander had discovered that at times he had difficulty recalling all the details of his lined face. Then he had to reach for a photograph and look at it so that the memory wouldn't completely slip away. In November he sometimes went out to visit Gertrud in the evening. The house in Löderup seemed empty. The studio was cold and forbidding. Gertrud always gave the impression of being composed—but lonely. It seemed to him that she had accepted the fact that an old man had died, and it was preferable to a slow withering-away from a disease that was gradually erasing his consciousness.

Maybe he slept for a few hours toward dawn. Maybe he was awake the whole time. By seven o'clock, at any rate, he was already dressed.

At 7:30 he drove his car, which sputtered suspiciously, over to the police station. It was particularly quiet that morning. Martinsson had a cold; Svedberg had reluctantly gone to Malmö on an assignment. The hallway was deserted. He sat down in his office and read through the transcript of his notes, written from memory, of his last conversation with Yvonne Ander. On his desk there was also a transcript of an interview Hansson had carried out with Tore Grundén, the man she had decided to push in front of the train at the Hässleholm station. His background contained the same ingredients as all the other names in her macabre death ledger. A bank teller, Tore Grundén had once even served time for abusing a woman. When Wallander read through Hansson's papers, he noted that Hansson had made it emphatically clear to Grundén that he had been close to being torn to bits by the oncoming train.

Wallander had noticed that there was a tacit understanding among his colleagues about what Yvonne Ander had done. That this understanding existed at all surprised him. She had shot Höglund. She had attacked and killed men. Normally a group of policemen would definitely not be in support of a woman like Yvonne Ander. It was even possible to ask whether the police force had a friendly attitude toward women at all. Unless they were cops who had the special stamina that both Ann-Britt Höglund and Lisa Holgersson possessed.

He scribbled his signature and pushed the papers aside. It was quarter to nine.

The house he was going to see was due north of the city. The day before, he had picked up the keys from the realtor. It was a two-story brick house enthroned in the middle of a big old garden. The house had lots of nooks and crannies. From the upper floor there was a view of the sea. He unlocked the door and went in. The previous owner had removed all the furniture. The rooms were empty. He walked around in the silence, opened the terrace door to the garden, and tried to imagine himself living there.

To his surprise, it was easier than he thought. Apparently he wasn't as attached to Mariagatan as he had feared. He asked himself whether Baiba might be happy there. She had talked about her own longing to get away from Riga—out to the country, but not too far away, not too isolated.

It didn't take him long to make up his mind that morning. He would buy the house if Baiba liked it. The price was also low enough that he could manage to get the necessary loans.

Just after ten he left the house. He went straight to the realtor and promised to give a definite answer within the week.

After looking at the house, he went on to look for a dog. The kennel was located along the road to Höör, right outside of Sjöbo. Dogs barked from various cages when he turned into the courtyard. The owner was a young woman who, much to his surprise, spoke with a strong Göteborg accent.

"I'd like to look at a black Labrador," said Wallander.

She showed them to him. The puppies were still too small to leave their mother.

"Do you have children?" she asked.

"Unfortunately none that still live at home," he replied. "Do you have to have children to buy a puppy?"

"Not at all. But this breed of dog is better with children than almost any other type."

Wallander explained his situation. That he might buy a house outside of Ystad. If he decided to do that, he also wanted to have a dog. One depended on the other. But first he had to have the house.

"I'll hold one of the pups for you. Take your time. But not too long.

I always have buyers for Labradors. The day always comes when I have to sell them."

Wallander promised to let her know within the week, just as he had promised the realtor. He was shocked at the price she mentioned. Could a puppy really cost that much? But he said nothing. He already knew that he would buy the dog if the house purchase went through.

He left the kennel at noon. When he came out onto the main road, he suddenly didn't know where he was going. Was he on his way anywhere at all? He wasn't going to see Yvonne Ander. For the time being they had no more to say to each other. They would meet again, but not now. The provisional end point would hold for the moment. Maybe Per Åkeson would ask him to expand on some of the details. He doubted it. The indictment was already more than adequately substantiated.

The truth was that he had nowhere to go. On that particular day, December 5th, no one really needed him.

Without being fully aware of it himself, he headed toward Vollsjö and stopped outside Hansgården. It was unclear what would happen to the house. Yvonne Ander owned it and would presumably continue to do so during all the years she would spend in prison. She had no close relatives, only her deceased mother. Whether she even had any friends was questionable. Katarina Taxell had been dependent on her, had received her support, just like the other women. But friends? Wallander shuddered at the thought. Yvonne Ander didn't have a single person who was close to her. She stepped out of a vacuum and she killed people.

Wallander got out of his car. The house emanated desolation. When he walked around it, he noticed a window stood slightly open. That wasn't good. Someone could easily break in. Yvonne Ander's house could become the target of attacks by trophy hunters. Wallander found a wooden bench and put it under the window. He climbed inside and looked around. There were no signs of a break-in. The window had just been left open out of carelessness. He walked through the rooms. Looked at the baking oven with distaste. There was the invisible boundary. Beyond it he would never be able to understand her.

He thought again that now the investigation was over. They had drawn a final line through the macabre list, interpreted the murderer's language, and finally found the solution.

That's why he felt superfluous. He was no longer needed. When he returned from Stockholm he would go back to the investigation of car smuggling to the former Eastern Bloc.

Not until then would he truly feel real to himself again.

A phone rang in the silence. Only on the second ring did he realize that it was ringing in his jacket pocket. He took it out. It was Per Åkeson.

"Am I interrupting anything?" he asked. "Where are you?"

Wallander didn't want to tell him where he was.

"I'm sitting in my car," he said. "But I'm parked."

"I assume you haven't heard the news," said Åkeson. "There's not going to be a trial."

Wallander didn't understand. The thought had never occurred to him, although it should have. He should have been prepared.

"Yvonne Ander committed suicide," said Åkeson. "Sometime last night. She was found dead early this morning."

Wallander held his breath. There was still something resisting, threatening to burst.

"She seems to have had access to pills. She shouldn't have had them. At least not so many that she could take her own life. Spiteful people are, of course, going to ask whether you were the one who gave them to her."

Wallander could hear that this was not a veiled question, but he answered it anyway.

"I didn't help her."

"The whole thing had a feeling of serenity about it. Everything was in perfect order. She seems to have made up her mind and carried it out. Died in her sleep. It's easy to understand her, of course."

"Is it?" asked Wallander.

"She left a letter. With your name on it. I have it here on the desk in front of me."

Wallander nodded mutely into the phone.

"I'm on my way," he said. "I'll be there in half an hour."

He stood where he was, with the silent phone in his hand. Tried to figure out what he was really feeling. Emptiness, maybe a vague hint of injustice. Anything else? He couldn't come to any clarity.

He checked that the window was closed properly and then left the house through the front door, which had a safety lock on it.

It was a clear December day. Winter was already lurking somewhere nearby.

Wallander went to Ystad to pick up the letter.

He went into Per Åkeson's office. The letter was lying in the middle of the desk.

He took it with him and went down to the harbor. He walked out to the Sea Rescue Service's red shed and sat down on the bench.

The letter was quite brief.

Somewhere in Africa there is a man who killed my mother. Who is looking for him?

That was all. She had elegant handwriting.

Who is looking for him?

She had signed the letter with her full name. In the upper right-hand corner she had written the date and time.

December 5, 1994. 02:44.

The next-to-last entry in her timetable, he thought.

She wouldn't write the last one herself.

The doctor would do that, when he put down what he believed to be the time of death.

Then there would be nothing more.

The timetable would be closed, her life concluded.

Her departure was formulated as a question or accusation. Or maybe both.

Who is looking for him?

He didn't sit on the bench for long because it was cold. He slowly tore the letter into strips and tossed them into the water. He remembered that once, several years ago, he had torn up a letter that he decided not to send to Baiba. He had tossed that one into the water too.

There was still a great difference. He would see Baiba again, and very soon.

He stood and watched the pieces of paper float away over the water. Then he left the harbor and went up to the hospital to visit Ann-Britt.

Something was over at last.

The autumn in Skåne was moving toward winter.